KYRIE WANG

HEALER'S BLADE

ENEMY'S KEEPER BOOK ONE

For my daughter, Ariane

A Note to My Readers

Enemy's Keeper is a **no-magic historical fantasy** series in which the last Vikings, now rebels and mercenaries, discover gunpowder in a world that's almost 11th-century Europe, but not quite.

I've blended in elements from other times and places, including:

- The first hand grenades

- Celtic tribes thriving beyond their historical timeframe

- Advanced shipbuilding (vessels with hulls and hammocks, ahead of their time)

Historical purists may find these liberties challenging, but readers seeking heart-pounding adventure, wholesome romance, and boldly reimagined worlds will find much to love. Welcome to the journey!

Newsletter Subscriber Bonuses

Receive a free ebook of *The Thief's Keeper* (*An Enemy's Keeper Prequel*) when you <u>subscribe to my newsletter!</u> **KyrieWang.com/EK**

Bonus: **A free medieval fantasy coloring book and a graphic novel, The First Dance (An Illustrated Epilogue of The Thief's Keeper)**

***

Once a month, I send a newsletter with book giveaways, raffle prizes, new character art, historical tidbits, and more!

N
W
E
S
York
HUMBER
Barton-Upon Humber
Ravenser's Point
Brocklesby
The North Sea
Myton
WITHAM
Norwich
England of Enemy's Keeper, 1075 AD

CHARACTERS

	LOYAL TO KING WILLIAM	REBELS
BISHOP	HIS EXCELLENCY, GEOFFREY DE MONTBRAY	
EARL		LORD RALPH DE GAEL
BARON	LORD SEVILLE	LORD YEATON
KNIGHT	JACQUES VERDUN	RANSLEY BOLTAN EDWARD BOLTAN TOBY BOLTAN
SQUIRE	MATTHEW MARCOTTE	
FOOT SOLDIER/ MERCENARY	AELFRIC NORMAN ROCHEFORT	AXLAN CILEBI
ORPHAN	EVELYN MARCOTTE MARIE MARCOTTE	ZELRIN EMMA

UNDETERMINED ALLEGIANCE
ALIWYN
KATO
MIRIAM (DECEASED)

VASFIANS
REIYA
NAMANTI
ABITHI
DOMILO

CHARACTERS LIST

Loyal to King William

Aelfric – Aliwyn's childhood sweetheart. An English foot soldier serving the Marcotte family and Lord Seville.

Matthew Marcotte – Norman squire. Aelfric's close friend.

Evelyn Marcotte – Matthew's older cousin.

Marie Marcotte – Matthew's younger cousin.

Norman Rochefort – Former Norman knight. Dismissed due to drunken behavior.

Lord Seville – Norman baron training Matthew for knighthood.

Geoffrey de Montbray ("His Excellency") – High-ranking Norman bishop tasked with crushing the rebellion.

Sir Jacques Verdun – Norman knight serving under Bishop Geoffrey de Montbray.

Rebels

Tobias (Toby) Boltan – Young rebel leader with many secrets.

Ransley Boltan – Toby's father; mastermind behind the murder of the Marcotte family.

Edward Boltan – Toby's uncle.

Emma – A girl Toby rescued from the streets.

Zelrin – A teenage boy Toby rescued from the streets.

Lord Ralph de Gael – One of the three earls leading the Revolt of the Earls; resides in Norwich.

Lord Yeaton – English baron who lives in Brocklesby's manor.

Axlan – Former English aristocrat whose land was confiscated by the Normans.

Cilebi – Danish mercenary.

Undetermined Allegiance

Aliwyn – Healer's apprentice living in a watermill.

Miriam – Former healer of Brocklesby and the mentor of Aliwyn and Aelfric.

Kato – English peasant who sells ale for Norman Rochefort. Unwanted by the Vasfian tribes.

Vasfians

Reiya – Chief of the Mehi tribe.

Abithi – Reiya's mother.

CHAPTER 1

AD 1075, nine years after the Norman conquest of England
September 25

ALIWYN'S DESCENT INTO OUTLAWRY began the afternoon she welcomed a murdered knight's daughter.

She had been rinsing her fishing spear in a stream behind her watermill. Water trickled around her bare feet as she stood on smooth stones, and her chickens ruffled their feathers in hollow dirt baths nearby. A linen sheet she'd hung out to dry dripped in the sun's golden rays.

All was tranquil until the door of her mill creaked open on the other side. And shut again.

Aliwyn straightened, scowling as she wiped a wet hand on her apron. Ever since her mentor Miriam had died, she'd padlocked her door shut whenever she stepped out. No one had the key except her close friend, Aelfric, but he wasn't expected back until Christmas.

Had a thief just broken in?

Aliwyn gripped her fishing spear. Biting her lower lip, she stepped onto the muddy bank of the stream. Stories of theft had abounded since the latest rebellion against King William had begun, but the manorial village she belonged to had remained peaceful. The new lord of her manor had promised to send guards to her mill, but he never did. Aliwyn had lived by herself for months.

Whoever had opened her door made no other sound. Birds warbled from the woods nearby, and water roared from deep within the gorge behind her. No one traversed the bridges crossing the ravine to her lord's castle, and the noisy peasants who came to grind grain had all left. Aliwyn's pulse quickened as she gazed at the distant rooftops of their homes. The throng earlier that day had made her feel suffocated, and she had taken refuge inside all morning. Now she wished a few had stayed so she wouldn't have to investigate her door alone.

The calmness persisted. Maybe she was imagining things. Aliwyn curled her cold toes over the rocks and longed for the stockings hanging by the hearth inside. She untied the knot holding up her ragged dress and stepped out of the stream that powered her mill's waterwheel. Her shadow stretched over fallen yellow leaves as she tiptoed along the building's stone walls. Holding her breath, she peered around the corner.

The grassy clearing before her home was empty. The rolling hills in the distance revealed no one, but the padlock hanging from her watermill's door latch was gone, and the door was still shut. Someone had removed her lock and entered her home.

Tendrils of dread crept up her spine.

How many bandits had just broken in? They might be armed with swords and daggers. She had better fetch the manor's bailiff across the bridge.

Aliwyn spun around to leave and kicked a hen who had followed her. She yelped, and the hen screeched and scampered over the rustling leaves.

The watermill's door cracked open.

"Aliwyn," came Aelfric's husky voice.

"Oh, it's you!" Her shoulders slumped with relief, but she scowled at his nasty trick. "Why did you sneak—"

"Shhh! Come quick."

Aliwyn blinked. Switching the spear to her less sweaty hand, she strode across the clearing.

Aelfric came out in a flash, grabbed her arm, and pulled her inside. The door closed again, quietly. Aliwyn's eyes widened in the dimness—only one of his eyes was visible, and the other was wrapped in bandages. "What happened to—"

Aelfric placed one hand over her mouth. "I'll tell you. Please calm down."

His hand smelled of metal and dirt, and Aliwyn swallowed. He chopped firewood daily in the manor he served; maybe flying splinters had injured his eyelid. Aelfric glanced around the mill, unoccupied save for the two of them, and continued. "I'm sorry for scaring you, but I wanted to get inside. Fast."

His chest was heaving, though his hand remained still and warm against her cheeks. They had rarely stood this close face-to-face. Aliwyn's heart fluttered, but the tension clouding his dark eye set a different mood. She twitched as he let go. He wore a woolen black tunic she didn't recognize, but now wasn't the time to ask where it had come from. His tall frame shifted toward a wheelbarrow laden with turnips by the door. It hadn't been there before.

"Marie," Aelfric said, "you can come out now."

Turnips fell from the wheelbarrow, revealing a moving blanket underneath. One corner flew up, and a girl about eight years old pushed to her elbows. Wavy brown hair fell to her shoulders, and dirt streaked her face.

"Marie, this is Aliwyn. Someone I trust." Aelfric took the child's hand and helped her step out. She came up to his elbow in height. The girl glanced at Aliwyn, who still gripped the fishing spear, and buried her face into Aelfric's tunic.

Aliwyn gawked. With a shaking hand, she slapped her spear against the door frame. She lifted a wooden plank and barred the door shut.

Aelfric hugged the girl's shoulders. "Don't be scared, Marie. We made it." He turned to Aliwyn and continued. "This is Marie Marcotte, Master Marcotte's youngest child. She needs a place to stay."

The Marcottes were a prosperous family of two Norman knight brothers, their wives, and their children. Aelfric served one brother as a foot soldier and sent home his income to help Miriam pay for medicinal herbs and honey. Miriam had been a healer, and most of her patients couldn't afford to pay for their remedies.

Ragged and thin, the child Aelfric had brought home didn't look like the daughter of a wealthy family.

Aliwyn stared at her. "What happened to her parents?"

"English rebels attacked Master Marcotte and his brother. Only two Marcotte girls and a few servants survived, including me. We've been hiding in churches."

Aliwyn stepped back, her stomach twisting. Other peasants had chattered about distant battles for months, but the English rebellion against their Norman conquerors had affected no one she knew. Until now.

"I'm so sorry," she said. "And your eye...do you want me to look at it?"

"No. It doesn't bother me anymore. I lost it weeks ago."

She gasped. "You lost it? What happened?"

"Forget about my eye. The Marcottes have been dead for weeks, and that's why I'm here."

Heat rose to her face, followed by a surge of tears. She wanted to pull off his bandage and see how badly he'd been scarred, but Aelfric's frown warned her this wasn't the time.

"Their murder was staged to look like an accident, a shipwreck," he said. "I tried to keep you out of this, Ali. I tried to get help for the Marcottes elsewhere. But this rebellion won't end. The roads are full of bandits. Bridges torn down. Ports burned."

He looked older, with a sunken eye and his black hair unusually wild. His solemn gaze told of horrors unspoken, and Aliwyn wrung her hands. She couldn't offer comfort when she couldn't pretend to understand. For years she had submitted to the Norman king in exchange for peace, and she hoped his army would restore order again.

"It's safe here, Aelfie. You're always welcome." She walked into his chest and embraced him. "Welcome home."

He was bonier than she remembered, and his arms hung by his sides. Where was the warm hug he gave whenever he came home? Her heart sank. Beside him, the girl he'd brought back watched them with her lips pinched. Poor thing, she probably missed her loved ones.

Aliwyn released Aelfric and extended her hand. "It's nice to meet you, Marie. You're also welcome here."

Marie gazed back with a blank face and slid behind Aelfric's back. Aliwyn sighed. The girl's dark brown hair and brown eyes matched Aelfric's description of his best friend, Matthew Marcotte, who was Marie's cousin.

"Aelfie, what about Matthew? Did he…" she was afraid to finish.

"Matthew was training away with Lord Seville, so he wasn't on the ship. He's still alive, but the rebels just caught him. He's being held hostage. I must get him out."

"You?" She shook her head. "Why you? You just came back."

"I can't stay. I'm here to drop Marie off for safekeeping—if you're willing to watch her. The rebels have started scouring the churches for the last Marcotte children."

Aliwyn swallowed several times. She eyed the hilt of Aelfric's sword hanging from his belt and wanted to squeeze him and never let go. Five years ago, she had opposed his decision to enlist as a foot soldier out of fear he'd get hurt. Now, he'd already lost an eye. What would he lose next?

"What about all the king's men? His barons, knights?" she asked. "They're not doing anything for Matthew?"

Aelfric scratched the inner corner of his eyebrow. "His Grace is out of the country. He appointed his bishops to control the rebellion."

"Oh, for goodness' sake," Aliwyn muttered. Bishops were busy enough managing their dioceses, and since when did they march to battle?

"Ali, I can't…it's hard for me to explain what's been happening away from here. The rebels are perfect citizens by day, but they go torching the fields at night to destroy the Normans' food supply. Then they vanish. The Norman knights are busy hunting them down. Matthew is only one of their squires, and he's not a priority."

Aliwyn crossed her arms and gazed at her feet. In the last nine years, repeated rebellions had attempted to overthrow King William, a Norman duke who had seized the English throne. With each uprising came theft, kidnappings, and murders as criminals took advantage of the civil unrest. Peasants of each manor had to take justice into their own hands. The neighboring manors could be hours away by foot, and the rebel army attacked messengers who sped away for help.

Marie left Aelfric's side and wandered toward a shelf of carved farm miniatures and clamshells on display. Aelfric had fashioned the miniatures for Aliwyn when she was young, and the iridescent clamshells had been his special gift. Without asking for permission, Marie picked up the animal toys and plopped down to play on the dirt floor. Aliwyn scowled, but she had other things to worry about.

"Did you ask Lord Yeaton for help?" she asked. "He's loyal to the Normans."

"I tried. He wasn't home. And his bailiff refused to see me." He ran his hand over his face.

Aliwyn paced the floor. She had never met Lord Yeaton, the lord of her manor who had just risen to power in mid-summer. She paid his taxes but had yet to receive the benefits of his protection.

"I don't want you to go," she said. "How can you possibly save Matthew by yourself?"

"I'm not by myself. I've spoken to one of the Vasfian chiefs. Her tribe will help me."

"The Vasfians?" She tensed all over. "You're going to work with the Vasfians?"

The Vasfians were tribal pagans who lived independently of Norman rule and inhabited the hillforts between the manors. They had fed King William's army that fateful day when he'd slain the king of England. Maybe they'd won his favor years ago, but it wouldn't last. King William was too greedy, and Aliwyn waited for him to crush those pagans the way he'd conquered her own people.

"You can't work with Vasfians," she said. "They have countless rituals we don't understand. You could insult one of their gods without knowing it, and they'd kill you."

"But we've lived on their territory for years, and they've never hurt us." Aelfric widened his stance. "You must've heard that Reiya is now chief. She wants the rebels dead for trespassing and offers to help me rescue Matthew. I don't have another group to help me."

He pulled out a slender whistle that hung beneath his tunic. It was a Vasfian whistle that the tribal warriors blew to communicate. Aliwyn gritted her teeth. Aelfric had become one of them. The Vasfians were hot-tempered, superstitious redheads who were quick to kill. If only her mill hadn't been built on their territory! Then Aelfric wouldn't have traded with the Vasfians for five years and grown so bold around them. But the river ran through their territory, leaving her manor's lord no choice but to negotiate with the pagans and place the mill there.

"They kill their own children." Aliwyn strode to Aelfric's side. "Even Miriam had noticed how they bury their little boys. It must be some child sacrifice—"

"Enough," Aelfric said with a flash of his teeth. "I've told you for years to stop repeating false rumors. We've seen nothing of the sort. You just don't like the way they look."

Aliwyn clenched her fists. No, she didn't like how the Vasfians looked, and neither did her villagers. Red hair sprouted from the scalps of crafty traitors, and despite years of living on Vasfian territory, Aliwyn's mouth still soured upon seeing their freckled faces. The freckles resembled the rash that had struck her birth family seven years ago and killed her only sister. The agony of seeing that darling toddler die still haunted her; she had three brothers but never another sister.

Aliwyn glanced at Marie, who sat surrounded by the wooden toys, and her vision blurred. Aelfric's expression soon softened. He knew about Aliwyn's sister but never accepted her dread of the freckled redheads.

"I'm not here for you to approve my decisions," he said. "I brought Marie here so you can take care of her."

Aliwyn's nostrils flared, but she held her tongue. It pained her to argue with him, and if Miriam had been present, she would've ended the quarrel long ago.

The silence spoke louder than words. Aelfric looked around the spacious mill, and Aliwyn followed his gaze. Three empty stools huddled underneath their dining table, and a pair of battered shoes rested in the corner. A familiar apron hung on the kitchen wall over the stone slab where Aliwyn prepared vegetables and fish. No one greeted them from the guardrail of the mill's second floor.

The sorrow on Aelfric's face washed away Aliwyn's anger. Miriam had died after his last visit. She had accepted Aliwyn and Aelfric as apprentices after the prior rebellion had left them both orphaned. Aelfric remained her apprentice in the manor records and returned to the mill for two months a year. He had always greeted Miriam with a kiss and a hug.

When he looked back at Aliwyn with a tearful eye, she trembled with chills.

"I'm sorry I wasn't here when Miriam passed," he said.

"You...you know? Who told you?"

"Reiya. She told me on my way here. If you can't care for Marie alone, I'll ask the Vasfians to watch her."

"Oh no. Don't do that to this little girl. I'll keep her."

"Thank you." He rubbed the bandage over his eye. "I have to go. Reiya and her tribe will protect our mill like they always have. Farewell, Ali."

He walked past Marie, who hummed to herself as she rolled Aliwyn's precious toys in a muddied area. Aelfric extended his hand, and she bid him goodbye.

Aliwyn struggled to swallow a still-racing heart. Beams of sunlight filtered through the vent holes on either side of the triangular thatched roof, and Aelfric passed through them and into the shadows. He was a soldier with responsibilities, and when he talked like this, nothing she said could stop him.

"Who exactly killed the Marcottes?" She approached him as he lifted the plank barring the door.

"An Englishman named Ransley Boltan and his household. They wear black surcoats with a golden griffin, but you won't see them."

He hesitated before pulling out the padlock he'd removed from the outside. Setting it on a barrel nearby, he said, "Keep Marie hidden, and the next time the bailiff comes to collect eggs, tell him Ransley Boltan's son has been riding to Myton. Something is happening there."

Aliwyn registered none of it. "When are you coming back?"

"Within a week. If I don't, then..."

"You'll be back within a week, Aelfie." She gave a trembling smile. "And I'll be here waiting for you."

He didn't look at her, as if lost in another world. Opening the door, he slipped out, and the garlic bulbs drying beside the frame trembled. The door shut with a hollow thud. The home suddenly felt upside down. Both the joy and heartache of seeing Aelfric settled as an icy lump in Aliwyn's throat. He had left the mill within a year of arriving in Brocklesby to earn money and send it back to Miriam and Aliwyn. If only he had stayed. If only he weren't a soldier bound to protect the foreign king's reign during yet another revolt. Staring at her feet, Aliwyn suppressed a sob.

Aelfric's footfalls echoed outside. He was running back, and she swung the door open as he skidded to a stop.

She looked at him up and down. "Did you forget something?"

He threw his arms around her shoulders, and she gasped.

"This," he whispered in her ear. Aliwyn grinned. She closed her eyes and wrapped her arms around him. They rocked side-to-side. When she had been younger, he'd pick her up and spin her in a circle. This was the Aelfric she knew and loved.

His chest vibrated against her cheek as he spoke. "I'm sorry I wasn't here for you and Miriam all these years, and that I must go again."

"Don't be sorry. You had to work."

His tunic and cloak were warm with the smell of fresh hay and wood smoke. She loved that smell, loved the sound of his beating heart. She could have stayed there all day, but Aelfric pulled back and put his hands on her shoulders. "Pray for us, will you? That you and Marie will stay safe, and that I'll get Matthew out."

"I will." She could hardly speak.

"And when I come back, take me to where Miriam is buried. We'll spend time together. You, me, and her."

His face flushed, and Aliwyn managed a nod as his image grew hazy between blinks.

Aelfric smiled and stroked her shoulder with his thumbs. "Thank you for all you've done for me. I know you'll make something delicious out of those turnips."

He backed away, still smiling. The afternoon sun gleamed on the golden clovers she had embroidered along the neckline of his brown cloak, one for each of his birthdays. Under this same sun, they'd once walked to the lord's land to plow the wheat fields. His face would beam as he told her the silliest stories and made her laugh.

Aliwyn yearned to turn back time. Her chin quivered as Aelfric turned and ran along the outskirts of the forest, stretching into the grassy hills beyond. He had trained for years under the Norman knight he served. It was his duty to defend Norman authority. She couldn't fight, but she could help him care for Marie.

Redheads appeared at the edge of the woods, and Aliwyn held her breath. One of them had to be Reiya. Aelfric ran to meet them as the only one wearing black amongst the Vasfians in their fur vests and red-and-green checkered tunics. They marched into the forest and disappeared. Aelfric must be desperate to save his friend, Matthew, but she had never met this Norman squire. Was he worth all this trouble?

Her numbed feet stepped back into the mill. Marie was on the floor, flicking a toy horse onto a stack of wooden miniatures and seashells to knock them down, and Aliwyn pressed her lips together. She had never been so rough with her toys, and she tiptoed to the girl's side, intending to scold her. Marie flicked a second horse onto the stack and sent everything tumbling down. When she sat back with a giggle, Aliwyn bit back her words. The toys had been collecting dust for years. She might as well let this lonely child enjoy them.

But Aelfric had said that two Marcotte girls survived. Where was the other one?

"Marie, you have a sister, don't you? I heard her name is Evelyn."

The girl lowered her eyes. "Yea, I have an older sister. But Evie jumped off the ferry coming here and ran. Aelfric was mad, but the ferryman wouldn't turn back for her. So I'm here by myself."

Aliwyn retrieved her stockings and shoes from behind the glowing hearth. "Why did she jump off?"

"Evie wanted to help Aelfric save Matthew. Our papa taught her how to fight so she thinks she can do it." Marie crossed her arms. "My sister's really brave, and a bit stupid. I miss her…"

Evelyn and Marie's father did well in teaching his Norman daughter how to fight in this foreign land. Aliwyn wished she knew how to fight, too. She sat on a stool, pulled on her stockings, and wrapped them with linens to garter them in place.

"Evelyn will come back soon, Marie. Until then, I'll take care of you." Aliwyn put on her shoes and waited until Marie looked up. "Do you want a hot foot soak? I have clean stockings for you to change into. And I'll make you some egg pottage."

Marie smiled. "Oh, yes. Please."

The girl spoke perfect English. Many Norman children born since the conquest did because the servants who tended to them, like Aelfric, were English. It warmed Aliwyn inside to have this child for company.

She stepped outside again to fetch fresh eggs. Padlocking the door behind her, she turned to find Clover the brown hen trotting nearby.

Aliwyn picked her up and smoothed her feathers. "I'm so sorry for kicking you, dear. That was very careless of me."

Leaves rustled underfoot as she carried the chicken toward the coop, and her legs grew heavier with every step. Aelfric could be sitting by the hearth right now, comfortable and safe and in her company, and the rebellion could rage on elsewhere.

"Here, chick chick chick," Aliwyn called. Her chickens came scampering to her side and followed her toward their coop.

The golden sunlight warmed her face. Crickets chirped near and far, and her footsteps lifted the earthly scent of leaves and autumn rain. Across the ravine, Lord Yeaton's manor house and courtyard stood beside his manorial farms. Sheep roamed the sloping fields, and smoke drifted from the peasant cabins scattered between vast strips of farmland. At around thirty households, Brocklesby was one of the largest settlements for leagues, and a gatehouse on either side of the bridge guarded its access in case of attacks.

If outlaws came looting, Aliwyn could dart across the stone bridge and into the protected courtyard without stopping. That was her hope, anyway. She clutched Clover to her chest and prayed that day would never come. Better focus on making the egg stew she had promised her little guest.

Stepping into the dusty chicken coop, Aliwyn released Clover. The hen trotted toward a ladder leaning against the back wall and flapped onto the second rung. Aliwyn rummaged through the nesting boxes, but her shaking hands couldn't grasp any eggs.

She should've pleaded for Aelfric to stay with her and the child. She should've continued their argument about the Vasfians until the fact that she loved him burst out of her mouth. Aelfric wasn't just her best friend; he was the man she wanted to marry. At eighteen and twenty years old, they were both older than most villagers who married, but she had lacked the courage to confess her love.

Aliwyn leaned against the nesting boxes and wiped her hands on her apron. The next time Aelfric returned, she would tell him she loved him. Chills sprinkled down her scalp as she gathered her resolve.

But tonight, her beloved was gone again. Aliwyn was hiding a Norman girl the rebels wanted dead, and her lord of the manor didn't know. What had she just gotten herself into?

CHAPTER 2

SOMEONE BANGING ON THE watermill's door jolted Aliwyn awake. She struggled to open her eyes. The rapping on the wood echoed like thunder within the stone walls.

"Marie?" Aliwyn croaked as she sat up.

No answer. Next to her, Marie's straw mattress was empty in the ember's glow, and Aliwyn's stomach clenched. Fists continued to pound on the door downstairs. She was on the second-story loft, which only partially covered the floor below and granted her a view of the entryway. Aliwyn pushed to her bare feet and ran for the staircase, but what felt like a small boulder barreled into her chest. She gasped. It was Marie, who had been running up the stairs simultaneously. The girl grimaced from the collision and rubbed her nose.

"Is it Aelfric?" Aliwyn cried with a burst of hope. It had been four days since he had left. She began to hurry down the steps again in her ragged dress, but Marie grabbed her arm.

"It's not Aelfric," she murmured. "I looked through the cracks in the door. Th-they're soldiers with black surcoats."

Lord Yeaton's men didn't wear black surcoats. Were they Ransley Boltan's soldiers?

Aliwyn pushed Marie away. "Go hide, now!"

Where were those rotten Vasfians who were supposed to guard her mill? Aelfric should never have trusted them.

As Marie scurried into the shadows, Aliwyn gripped the dagger hanging from her waist. Downstairs, the banging continued. The plank of wood bolting the door shut jumped within its supporting brackets. Muffled shouting echoed from the other side, and it wasn't friendly. What did they want?

Aliwyn darted down the steps and crept along the closest wall. Her shadow trailed before her in the dim hearth's glow, and torchlight shined through the slit below the door. Above the deafening banging, a booming voice demanded a key. But what key? Her mind scrambled for a plan. The room she stood in was built of stone, and the wooden water wheel and its gears were in an adjacent chamber. If the men tossed torches on the mill's thatched roof, would Lord Yeaton have time to rush over and save his manor's watermill?

Regardless, the soldiers might break the door's hinges and crash in at any moment. She had to make sure Marie escaped.

Aliwyn raced back upstairs and found the girl squeezed in a crevice formed by a stack of crates and the wall. The child stared back from the shadows, her eyes wide with panic and her cheek pressed against the wall.

Days ago, Aliwyn had taught her how to escape in case something like today ever happened. Aliwyn fell to her knees beside a loose stone in the watermill's wall and pulled it out in jerks.

"Marie," she said, "remember this little hole I told you about? You need to slip out."

The displaced stone revealed a small opening leading to her chicken coop. Her hens clucked from within the darkness, but no soldier shouted from behind the mill. The girl still had time to run out the back, but Marie whimpered from her hiding place and didn't move. Aliwyn struggled to keep her voice calm.

"Don't be scared, sweetheart." She got up and took the girl's arm. "You know what to do. There's a ladder in the coop. Climb down and run for the woods. Don't look back."

"Come with me," Marie sobbed.

"I won't fit." Aliwyn drew the child out of the crevice and hugged her. "You've been lovely, Marie. Go and be brave."

Her arms shook as she let go. Marie turned to the gaping black hole of the mill's wall and took one step.

Downstairs, scuffling noises came from the kitchen. Both Aliwyn and Marie froze.

"I told you this would be easier," said a man's voice.

Pins sank into Aliwyn's scalp. How did that man get in? She pulled Marie toward the escape hole and squeezed the girl's hand, pleading with her eyes for the child to hurry. Marie's chin trembled, but she fell on her hands and knees and extended a leg toward the gaping blackness.

More scuffling noises and grunting sounded from downstairs. Aliwyn crept to the second-floor railing and peered between the wooden planks. The kitchen wall had a rubbish hole she always sealed with a wooden block. Bushes hid its location from the outside, but a soldier with a black surcoat had discovered it. He had pushed the block aside and was crawling onto a stone slab used for gutting fish. Pushing to his feet, he stepped into the mill and looked left and right. Fish scales and apple peels clung to his conical helmet.

"Hello!" he called out. "Anyone here?"

Aliwyn's mouth hung open. She tried to withdraw from the rail but smacked the back of her head against a wooden plank.

The soldier looked up, straight at where Aliwyn's face protruded overhead. She froze, and so did he. The whites of his wide eyes gleamed in the hearth's glow.

Aliwyn's pulse roared in her ears. More grunting and shouting echoed outside the rubbish hole, signaling that other men were about to enter.

The soldier downstairs kept his stare on Aliwyn. "You must be the watermill's keeper?"

He was probably a few years older and thinly built. The black sleeveless surcoat covering his other clothes featured a large golden griffin.

Aliwyn stared at the griffin, that ugly symbol of the Boltan's household. Aelfric had told her she wouldn't meet these vicious rebels who had slaughtered the Marcottes for being loyal to the king, but now they were in her mill.

When the soldier approached her staircase to ascend, Aliwyn jerked back her head and scrambled to her feet. Behind her, Marie lay on her belly with two feet in the escape hole and tears drenching her face. She didn't move.

Aliwyn tensed her jaw; this was no time to raise her voice. Squeezing her dagger handle, she stomped down the steps.

Get out already, Marie! She jumped before the foot of the stairs, squaring her shoulders.

The intruder took a step back. A sword handle peeked from the side of his dark cape, but he didn't reach for it.

"Does Miriam still live here?" he asked.

Aliwyn glared at the man. How did he know her mentor's name? Something stopped her from pulling out her dagger, but her chest seized when another man's pointy helmet burst through the hole. He grunted as he pulled himself through.

The first soldier grinned at his companion before turning to Aliwyn again. "My name is Toby. We're wondering if—"

"Bloody nails! Stop wasting time!" The second soldier hoisted himself into the room with heavy panting. He was older and bulkier than Toby.

Standing up, he turned to Aliwyn with a snarl. "Where is the key? For that bridge crossing the gorge?"

This man could only be talking about the stone bridge leading to the baron's manor house. A stone gatehouse guarded the bridge's entrance, and Aliwyn had never locked its double doors. Chills skittered down her back when a third soldier crawled through her rubbish hole.

"But the bridge isn't locked," she sputtered.

"Yes, it is!" the second soldier shouted. "Are you mocking me?"

His voice echoed within the stone walls as he pulled out his sword. Its iron blade swept upward in a half-circle, and Aliwyn stumbled back against the step. She yanked out her dagger and pointed it at his face, but the man advanced on her.

"Produce the key! And how dare you not open the door!"

A hand appeared from behind the man and pulled back his arm. It was Toby, the first soldier who had entered. "Ed, let her talk."

Aliwyn glanced at Toby, but she shouldn't have. A pair of brawny arms wrapped around her chest from behind and pulled her back. She slammed against the man who had grabbed her and stiffened when a blade's edge pressed against her throat.

"Struggle and you'll die," came a menacing voice in her ear. It was the third man who had entered.

He had a massive chest, and his arm pinned down both of hers at the stomach level.

"We'll let you go." Toby stepped forward, his voice soft but hurried. "Just unlock the Brocklesby Bridge and let us pass. My men seek shelter with Lord Yeaton. It's urgent."

Aliwyn squirmed but couldn't break free. Was Marie outside yet? Edward, the second soldier who had entered, marched to her door and threw off the plank barring it shut. It bounced on the floor with a thunk, and the watermill's door creaked open. Soldiers flooded into the room. The amber light from their torches cast long shadows onto the ground.

Toby continued to speak, but she didn't register his words as she stared at the golden griffin embroidered onto his surcoat. These rebels wanted to see Lord Yeaton? All this time, her lord of the manor had been on the rebels' side. He had fooled everyone, including Aelfric. None of Yeaton's soldiers would be coming to her aid. What a wretched traitor!

Something touched her shoulder, and Aliwyn jolted.

"Did you hear me?" Toby tapped her again, a scowl shadowing his face. "Come with us and unlock the bridge's gates."

"I didn't even know the gates were locked!" she cried.

The knife prodded into her neck, and her breath hitched.

"Stop!"

At Toby's order, the man withdrew his blade. Aliwyn gasped for air. Her right hand grasped her dagger's handle, but she couldn't fight all these men.

"What do you mean, you didn't know?" Toby asked. "The bridge is locked from your side. Who else would lock it?"

"Scour this place!" Edward shouted. "Report every key you find!"

Men stomped for the perimeters of the room. They tore down herbs and dried fish hanging on the walls as they searched for a key she didn't have. Baskets fell over. Crab apples and turnips thudded and rolled across the floor. Torches were everywhere, and it would only be a matter of time before they pounded upstairs and found the displaced stone with a suspicious hole. Either that, or Marie was still face-down on the second floor.

Aliwyn needed to get everyone out of her mill.

"Wait, I remember now," she declared. "The key is outside, by the bridge."

The soldiers hesitated, and Edward narrowed his eyes. "There is no key by the bridge."

"Yes, there is," Aliwyn lied. "I can show you."

"She's making fools out of us," Edward said, turning to his men. "Keep searching!"

Aliwyn struggled to break free when men bypassed her and began tearing up the stairs.

"You're wasting your time here!" she shouted. "The key is outside!"

Toby held up a fist, and all the soldiers halted. "She may be telling the truth. Take her to the Brocklesby Bridge."

Aliwyn's chest heaved. Even she wouldn't have believed the key was by the bridge. And how did he know Aliwyn's mentor, Miriam? She was afraid to know. When Toby turned back to her, she averted her eyes. At his command, another soldier wrenched the dagger from her hand.

They pushed her outside with two soldiers locking her bent arms behind her and a frigid night wind slicing through her clothes. In the clearing stood the soldiers' many horse-drawn, covered wagons. Aliwyn turned the corner toward the back of her mill with her heart drumming in her ears. Overhead, barren tree branches stretched like black skeletons against the flickering torchlight. When one of the two men grabbed the back of her neck, she straightened but kept quiet.

There had to be a way out of this. She'd break loose and dash for the woods when the soldiers let their guards down.

A bird call echoed in the distance, but no bird was calling at this hour. It was a Vasfian whistle mimicking a bird's tweeting, and Aelfric had worn such a whistle around his neck. None of the soldiers seemed to react, but Aliwyn almost tripped.

Was Aelfric back with a band of redheads? He had to be—he wouldn't leave her like this. Aliwyn quivered, her hands pinned behind her and clawing at her back. But if Aelfric had returned, why didn't he and the Vasfians attack?

The men forced her to walk parallel to the river powering the watermill. The stream flowed toward the ravine, where it would plummet as a narrow waterfall.

Behind the mill and several arm lengths from the waterfall, two bridges passed over the ravine. One was a decrepit rope bridge unfit for crossing, while the other was a broad stone bridge with heavy wooden doors barring its entrance—the Brocklesby Bridge.

The wind scattered Aliwyn's hair as she and the soldiers stopped before the stone bridge's gates. Heavy chains wrapped countless times around the twin doors' handles, and a large padlock fastened the two ends of the chains. Someone *else* had locked the bridge. Heat flushed her face. Which dirty numbskull had done this?

"Where are the keys?" came Edward's voice from behind.

"I had locked it," she stammered—another lie. "But someone else added those chains. I can't do anything about it."

She was buying time, and Aliwyn writhed and shivered.

"You simply refuse to let us pass!" Edward growled.

"Wait," Toby said. "She made me realize something. What if the Vasfian tribe secured the gates after dark? Then they herded us right into this dead end."

The soldiers behind her grumbled among themselves.

With her arms and neck immobilized, Aliwyn's teeth chattered as Toby stepped into her field of view. The awful reek of fish from the rubbish hole wafted from his body. His face anxious in the torchlight, he reached for the lock and scrutinized it. Then he peered down into the deep gorge, where rocky rapids roared beneath the two long bridges.

"This is not a lock I can pick," he said. "Maybe we can pry one of the chain's links, or we can reroute—"

"Regardless, we're not leaving witnesses." Edward's voice boomed behind Aliwyn.

Footsteps stomped toward her. Edward was coming, and she caught a flash of metal—the blade of a sword.

Toby lunged to his left. "Edward!"

At his shout, she squeezed her eyes shut. Her knees buckled, but the man gripping her pulled her back upright. The strike to kill her didn't come. Footsteps scuffled around her, and Aliwyn opened her eyes again, her body racked with chills.

She wasn't hurt, and Toby had shoved Edward backward. The older man regained his balance with his sword in hand and his teeth bared. A loud exchange and more shoving between the two soldiers followed. One of the two men holding her let go and stepped forth, probably to intervene, and Aliwyn saw her chance. She stomped on the other man's foot.

He flinched with a surprised grunt. His grip loosened, and Aliwyn spun around and kneed the spot armor didn't protect well—the groin. If the man howled, she didn't hear it. She twirled around and bolted for the woods, the night air coursing through her lungs and sparks flying before her vision. Voices shouted after her, and pounding footsteps followed.

Aliwyn had reached a row of tall bushes when torches appeared as golden dots further ahead, along the edge of the woods behind her home. Firelight illuminated the red hair of a line of warriors as they rose forth from the shadows, each aiming a crossbow. Aliwyn's heart gave a great leap. Somewhere in the darkness, a Vasfian woman barked the command to fire. The whipping sound of released crossbows echoed across the clearing. Silvery arrow tips flew toward her and the soldiers behind.

Her hope lurched into terror at the barrage of arrows, darkening as they soared into the moonless night like a monstrous cloud.

Aliwyn ducked into the prickly bushes and covered her head with her arms. Behind her, men screamed and scattered. Arrows clanged off helmets and thwacked into the rustling leaves, and the neighs of panicked horses pierced the air. With branches whipping her face, she pressed deeper into the tangled undergrowth.

Dear Lord, was Marie outside right now, or was she still face-down in the mill? Aliwyn had to find her.

But the arrows kept falling, and another whizzed past her face when she dared to rise above the bushes. The acrid scent of blood wafted to her nose.

Aliwyn prayed for the girl's safety. Time passed, and enough sunlight paled the sky to outline her dirty fingernails.

Arrows no longer fell like before. Aliwyn released her stiff muscles and pushed to her hands and knees. Her eyes rounded on the back of a doomed soldier as he twitched on the ground with an arrow protruding from his neck.

A Vasfian woman stomped by and clubbed him on the temple. His limbs gave a final jolt. The redheaded warrior left as swiftly as she had come with a shield around one arm and her club swinging for the next enemy.

Aliwyn's head spun. Behind the fleeing rebels and the Vasfians pursuing them, her mill with its wooden wheel glistened in the pale morning light. She scrambled to her feet and bolted for the front of her mill, weaving between the men strewn on the ground. Other soldiers shoved past her and shouted about crossing a rope bridge, but no one grabbed her again.

Aliwyn turned the corner to the grassy clearing. A donkey and cart had parked in the shadows beside the mill. Who had driven it there?

There wasn't time to wonder. Two Vasfians guarded the door of her mill, one holding a crossbow and the other a club. Aliwyn ignored them and dashed through the doorway of her home. She spun around, slammed the door shut, and barred it with the plank. The thump of the door echoed through the mill. Her fingers ran over the knotted wood of the door as her arms slid down to her sides. Behind her, the hearth flickered as though nothing had happened.

Something was wrong. If Aelfric had arrived, he would've rushed to see her and wrapped her in his arms. If he wasn't here, then who was? She didn't recognize the cart and donkey outside.

"Marie?" she whispered.

No answer. Aliwyn shook with cold sweat as she turned and searched the railing above. The wooden planks cast wavering shadows on the walls and thatched roof, and nothing else moved. She had better check upstairs. Maybe the girl had dashed into the woods after all.

She picked up her dagger by the door and sheathed it. Her panting seared her throat as she stepped around scattered and broken pottery. Agonized cries from outside drifted into her home, interspersed with the voices of

Vasfians shouting in their language. The redheads had never hurt her, but they were ruthless with those they defeated. They would strike down all the scamps who had infiltrated her mill and threatened her.

Maybe she should've been relieved, but images of the dead and dying rebels outside flooded Aliwyn's mind and made her shudder. She had obeyed Norman rule since they had invaded to avoid witnessing bloodshed again. What had been the use?

Aliwyn wiped her eyes and looked around her mill one more time. No one appeared. She had lifted one foot for the staircase when creaking sounded from above.

Aliwyn looked up. The shadowy figure of a man stood at the top of the stairs. She shrieked and yanked out her dagger.

CHAPTER 3

"THAT'S ALIWYN!" A GIRL'S voice rang out from upstairs.

The man at the top of the steps scowled down at her with his sword gripped in one hand. His haircut was unmistakably Norman—left to grow in the front and on top of his head but shaved behind his ears. A black cape draped over his gray tunic, and he appeared formidably tall even from this distance. The leather straps cross-gartering his stockings seemed thick and expensive. Marie ran to his side with her tousled hair bouncing, and he held out his arm to stop her from going downstairs.

"Marie, I told you to stay hidden."

"Marie!" Aliwyn cried with a smile. She sheathed her dagger.

"That's Aliwyn, and she saved me!" The child threw aside the man's arm and darted past him.

She hurried down the stairs and into Aliwyn's arms. Aliwyn hugged her with the tightness released from her chest. Marie was safe and sound, thank Heaven. She closed her eyes and cherished the child's warmth.

"Thank you, Ali," Marie sniffled into Aliwyn's dress. "But I wasn't brave."

"You're not hurt. That's the most important."

Aliwyn held onto the crying child and tried not to shake as memories of all she had experienced flashed in her mind. None of it felt real.

Upstairs, the man cleared his throat.

"I'm Matthew Marcotte." He sounded grim and tired. "I understand Aelfric hid my cousin Marie here."

Matthew Marcotte. Aliwyn released the child and looked up. Here was the squire Aelfric said he had to rescue. Matthew was two years older and had been away training for knighthood when his family died. So much for being Aelfric's best friend; he didn't look friendly at all.

"Where's Aelfric?" she asked.

Matthew looked away. "I'll tell you later. Your mother, Miriam, is she home?"

Aliwyn frowned. Miriam was her mentor, not her mother, but it wasn't time to discuss details. "Miriam passed away months ago, in the spring."

The young man raised his eyebrows. "Aelfric didn't…he never told me that."

"He only found out when he dropped off Marie four days ago. I guess he didn't tell you yet."

"No, he…" Matthew sighed. "It was chaos. We had no time to talk."

"Where is he?"

A grimace flashed across Matthew's face. "I'll tell you soon. But right now, I need your help with an injured Vasfian. He's outside."

Aliwyn's throat tightened. No, she needed to know where Aelfric was *now*. Before she could respond, another person darted from the opened door of her storage room. Aliwyn nearly pulled out her dagger again, but the newcomer was a young woman about her age with her brown hair tied back into a ponytail. Her face and tunic were filthy, but her features were delicate and her eyes a bright blue.

"Please," she said, "my friend is in the cart, and he's hurt. I know we're barging in, but—"

"This door should be wide enough for the cart to enter." Matthew slid his sword back into its sheath and marched down the steps toward Aliwyn.

He strode past and removed the wooden bar from the door without glancing at her. Aliwyn frowned at his every movement. So rude. He hadn't even thanked her for protecting his cousin. Shafts of morning light broke into the room when Matthew opened the door, and a swirl of brisk air carried inside the moaning of wounded men. Aliwyn locked her arms around her torso.

Miriam had trained her to be a healer, but it made no sense for her to help the enemy.

"Perfect timing," said a man's voice. "I didn't know if I should knock or kick my way in."

Before the opened door stood a balding man with a plump face and sagging eyes. He stank of old ale and sweat, and Aliwyn wrinkled her nose.

Matthew didn't flinch. "Norman, have the Vasfians secured the area?"

Norman, the newcomer, wore a lopsided grin. "Absolutely. But you must come see this—we've got one of Ransley Boltan's sons."

Capturing a Boltan heir was certainly a victory, but Aliwyn bristled as she peered from behind Matthew's broad shoulders. It was as though she didn't exist. Where was Aelfric?

Matthew glanced behind at where Aliwyn, Marie, and the other woman stood. "Evelyn, you stay here with Marie."

Norman's grin revealed several missing teeth. "The Vasfians nailed them rebels good. Nothing to worry about."

Matthew stepped out, his right hand always around the hilt of his sword. As he left, Aliwyn was confronted with the sight of the bodies outside the mill, stretching into the distance one after another. They covered the ground where she let her chickens run free. She staggered backward. The rays of dawn brightened the sky, and redheaded Vasfian warriors dragged the bodies away by their feet. Aliwyn couldn't watch, and she spun to the side.

"I never got to introduce myself," said a soft voice beside her. "My name is Evelyn. I'm Matthew's cousin and Marie's sister. Thanks for taking care of Marie."

Aliwyn looked up at the speaker, Evelyn Marcotte. Aelfric had spoken highly of her before—too highly. Aliwyn always had a smoldering worry that Aelfric was in love with Evelyn, even if he was only her father's servant during times of peace. Aliwyn locked gazes with the woman's round eyes, framed by feathery dark lashes, and swallowed the sourness flooding her mouth. This lady Marcotte must've been stunning back home, bedecked in sweeping robes and shimmering headdresses.

Marie hugged her sister around the waist, and Aliwyn scowled at the fraying hem of her stained dress. Even with the little she had, Aliwyn had shared her clean stockings with Marie, and Aliwyn's dirty feet remained bare.

"You're welcome," she muttered. "You...the cart—"

"Yes, it's right outside. My friend is resting on it." Evelyn nudged Marie's arms off her and stepped toward the exit.

"Where's Aelfric?"

Evelyn's expression fell with sorrow, and she brushed aside her dark bangs. "Oh...you must not have heard—"

"No, I've heard nothing." Aliwyn clenched her jaw. "Aelfric told me to hide your sister because Matthew needed help. Days passed without a word, and then Ransley Boltan's soldiers showed up and almost killed—"

Aliwyn let out a shuddering breath. Her instincts warned her she was about to hear terrible news.

Evelyn shuffled her feet. "Ransley Boltan's men captured Matthew because he was the last male descendant of my family. Aelfric and I went to rescue Matthew from the Boltans' stronghold, but..." She hesitated before whispering, "When Matthew comes back, can we sit down and talk together?"

Aliwyn's eyes stung with tears. She knew.

A man's cry of pain pierced through the background of the voices in the clearing, and Aliwyn tensed. Evelyn looked toward the source of the cry, but the corner of the watermill hid it from view.

"Leave me here! Go! Go!"

It sounded like the first soldier who had entered her home, Toby. He seemed desperate, and his words became overwhelmed by what sounded like cheering from a crowd. Why were these noises difficult to endure? Aliwyn scowled in the cry's direction, and Marie scampered toward the donkey cart.

Evelyn hurried after her sister. "Marie! Don't run off like that!"

"Why? Didn't Norman just say we won? And poor donkey. He was so scared he wouldn't walk in the mill."

The child reached out to pet the donkey's head. Evelyn's expression relaxed when a young man with carrot-red hair sat up in the cart.

"Oh, he's awake now. May I introduce you?"

Aliwyn stared at the redhead rubbing his eyes in the cart. Why a Norman lady would call a Vasfian man her friend, she couldn't guess.

But before she could speak, another cry of pain rang out from around the corner of the mill. Aliwyn winced; now she was certain that it was Toby. Had he not protected her from Edward, she'd be dead, and hearing him scream made her hair stand on end. Many voices soon shouted from the same direction as one garbled roar. What was still happening around her home?

Aliwyn felt drawn toward the cries. She pointed at her door. "You can go inside, Evelyn. Take what you need for your friend."

She didn't wait for the other woman's reaction. Aliwyn rushed toward the commotion, careful not to stomp on the arrowheads underfoot. She tensed at the blood gleaming over blades of grass. Never had so much violence erupted around her mill, and what were the Vasfians doing to Toby?

THE VOICES BEHIND HER mill became distinct as she grew closer. Matthew was among the ones yelling. A crowd of Vasfians, both men and women, stood against the pale sky like a wall of rabbit's fur vests and checkered tunics. They had gathered before the entrance to the narrow plank bridge, which was so decrepit that no one crossed it anymore. Yet, it must've been the only escape route for the Boltans' soldiers during the ambush.

Two Vasfian men on the crowd's edge turned as she approached, staring at her from underneath their bushy red eyebrows. Their crossbows were loaded and held across their chests. Aliwyn shifted between them and examined their freckled faces with her heart tapping in her throat. Miriam had forced her to learn Vasfian for trading purposes. Aliwyn recognized Reiya and her mother from her bartering experiences, but they weren't in this group.

"What's that idiot saying?"

Aliwyn jumped when a hand landed on her shoulder. It was a Vasfian man who had asked the question.

"What—what idiot?" she asked, facing the speaker.

"You speak their language?" Matthew appeared at the front of the group, pushing through the crowd to approach Aliwyn. "Then ask them why they stopped shooting!"

"Shooting what?"

"That! This—" Matthew turned around and flung his arm toward the bridge.

Aliwyn stepped past the other warriors to see what Matthew had gestured at. One of the four ropes suspending the rope bridge had been cut, leaving the structure twisted and hanging by the remaining three cords. She walked closer to the edge of the ravine and looked down.

A lone figure hung upside-down from the middle of the bridge, and Aliwyn stiffened. Somehow, Toby's foot had become lodged between the planks of the bridge, and he dangled over the ravine with his dark brown cape flapping behind his head.

When Toby's gaze met hers, she inhaled sharply. His helmet was gone, and the wind tousled his blond hair. He clenched one ungloved hand against his stomach. Blood flowed down his leg from the foot that was caught, soaking the cross-gartered stockings that covered his shins. The wide-eyed terror on his face, upside down, made her throat swell.

"That is Ransley Boltan's son." Matthew crossed his arms. "The Vasfian warriors were shooting at his men, but they've suddenly stopped."

It made sense now, why Toby had been screaming for his men to abandon him. He was the son of a heinous murderer, and Aliwyn's mouth hung open.

"Tell the Vasfians to shoot him!" Matthew shouted. He shuffled his feet and lowered his voice. "Please. Just ask."

Aliwyn teetered away from the ravine. She spoke to a Vasfian man nearby and translated his response for Matthew.

"They say they've already shot his hand to make him drop his sword. And it's better that he...that he hangs from the bridge to die, because he'll suffer more—"

Before she could finish, Matthew stooped, grabbed two fist-sized rocks, and hurled one after another at Toby. Ransley Boltan's son tried to protect himself, but one stone struck his forearm while the other smashed into his forehead. He cried out, his head thrown back and his body swaying on the bridge. Aliwyn's chest clenched.

"That's a great idea!" Matthew's deep voice rang out in the open. "You deserve this! For killing my father, my uncle, my entire family!"

When Matthew bent down for another stone, Aliwyn lunged and grabbed his arms with both hands. Matthew glowered at her. His snarl was so menacing that she almost let go.

"Don't you understand?" he yelled. "Because of him, Aelfric is dead!"

Aliwyn's hands slipped off Matthew's arm. Hadn't she suspected all along that Aelfric was dead? But her last bastion of hope hadn't crumbled until now.

"Are you sure?" she whispered. Such a useless question.

"Yes." Matthew's frown faded. "We buried his body in a shallow grave. It was all that we could do."

Aliwyn couldn't breathe. She stared back without seeing Matthew. Just a shallow grave. The image of her sweetheart, with his black hair and dark eyes forever closed, surfaced in her mind. She wanted to ask how he had died and where he was buried, but no words came. Aliwyn's legs melted beneath her.

Matthew dropped the rock he was holding. As Aliwyn fell, he gripped her arms and guided her to the ground. His deep brown eyes gazed into hers. Her eyes blurred until she saw nothing. Shaking her head, she wanted to talk but only tasted the salty tears streaming down her face.

She never got to tell Aelfric that she loved him.

"I'm sorry, Aliwyn," Matthew said. "He fought for us until the end. I owe my life to him."

He released her but remained kneeling with his gaze on the rocks. Aliwyn sat in a daze. Matthew stood and departed without throwing another stone, and other feet came and went. Someone wrapped something warm around her. Hands tried to lift her, but she wouldn't budge. Miriam had hired Aliwyn and Aelfric as apprentices five years ago. He used to play the recorder while she sang and slapped her knees to the rhythm. One winter, he had sent her flying downhill on a sled he'd nailed together. Aelfie had been her only friend since she arrived in Brocklesby and the best friend she could've asked for.

But he would never come back.

She fell asleep on the ground. The Brocklesby chapel bells rang to mark mid-morning, but she curled into a tighter ball and slept again. Finally, someone grabbed her by the shoulders and hoisted her up to sit as if she were a sack of wheat.

"Why is it always me that has to fix things like this?" came a low, raspy voice. Stale ale crept up her nostrils, and Aliwyn's eyes blinked open to crooked teeth. She gasped and flailed her arms.

"Ha, I know I'm scary!" It was Norman, the one who had come to the watermill's door earlier. "But at least I got you up."

Aliwyn scowled at his wrinkled face as he stood. Someone had covered her with a rabbit's fur cape, and she wrapped it back around her shoulders.

"Look." Norman tapped his foot. "I know it's been goin' bad for you, but you're alive and well, so act like it."

She looked around her. How long had she been lying close to the cliff's edge? The Vasfians and even Matthew had retreated. The morning sky was bright yellow and pink, and the peasant cabins across the bridge fell under the shadows of the looming manor house that resembled a castle. Toby still hung from the bridge over the ravine, motionless like a butchered animal against the colorful sky. Aliwyn averted her eyes and shuddered.

During the last revolt, the Normans had caught the wealthier rebels and ransomed them back to their households for an easy profit. Toby wore a suit of padded armor and had led an army with horses and carts; he had to be rich. The Norman army should arrive soon to assess the situation and capture Toby alive.

But Aelfric was still dead. The truth crushed her once more, but she kept her posture straight and wiped strands of hair from her cheeks. The Vasfians and Matthew and all those other strangers had to be close by, even if she couldn't see them. She wanted to mourn alone.

"Where did everyone go?" she asked.

Norman scratched his bald spot. "Looking for some live captives to question. See, Boltan's son dangling there refuses to talk, so we're trying to find some talkers."

"Talk about what?"

"Ehh...we found some strange things in his wagons. Seen nothing like 'em before, and we don't know what they are."

A shrill scream rang out from behind Aliwyn. She looked up in alarm—it sounded like Marie, but how could it be? Norman's expression became grave, and he walked away.

The screams came again, shorter and now mixed with whimpering. It was a child. Aliwyn couldn't turn her head around enough to see. She pressed her hands on the uneven ground, forcing her stiff legs to stand.

To her amazement, the same child's voice screamed, "Toby! Help me!"

Chapter 4

Matthew approached them with one hand gripping the throat of a girl about nine years old. His other hand held her arms behind her back. She wore an oversized black surcoat with the golden griffin emblem worn by all of Boltans' soldiers.

Although he hung out of sight, Toby cried, "Matthew! She knows nothing!"

The child squirmed, whining and shaking her messy black curls about her face. Aliwyn gaped at Matthew as he marched past. His hold was almost strong enough to lift the girl off the ground with each stride. A threatening glare darkened his face.

"Good! You're talking!" His voice boomed over the child's whimpers. "So, tell me—where did your father go?" He stopped an arm's length short of the cliff's edge.

Aliwyn tiptoed to Matthew's side.

Norman followed her and muttered, "Who's going to give a rat's tail about this runt?"

From where she stood, Aliwyn looked down over the edge. Toby bent his neck and stared back with his eyes wide. His face was flushed and swollen from hanging upside down, and blood smattered his hair to his forehead.

"Matthew, I know you're going to kill me, but let her go! She's only a child!"

"That doesn't answer my question!" Matthew shouted. "Where did your father go? She's dead if you don't tell me!"

Aliwyn's throat throbbed as the child gasped and tried to breathe. When she reached for Matthew's arm to stop him, Norman gripped her by one shoulder and pulled her several steps backward.

"Let me ask a question!" the balding man interjected. "Your wagons be loaded with tiny pellets that reek like my farts! What is that muck?"

"They...those pellets, they're used to start fires." Toby's voice shook. "My father was in a separate procession. He told me to meet him at Myton. Please, let her go."

"Myton?" Matthew demanded. "Myton is a riverside hamlet. Where is he sailing from there?"

"I...don't know."

"Stop lying! How can you be Ransley Boltan's son and not know?"

"My father and Uncle Edward are the ones leading the—"

Matthew tightened his grip and shoved the girl forward, forcing her closer to the edge.

"No!" Toby reached forward but winced. The suspension bridge swayed with a groan of its overstretched ropes.

Aliwyn had been standing with her legs as stiff as wood, but when the girl's tearful eyes rolled back to look at her, something within her snapped. She charged with all her might, ready to tackle Matthew to the ground.

Before she reached him, the child stomped on Matthew's foot. The man jolted, and the girl bit the hand holding the dagger. Matthew yelped. He tried to withdraw his hand, but this only pulled on the skin clenched between her teeth. Without a sound, she wriggled free from his grasp and bolted.

Matthew pulled out his sword and chased the escapee.

"Stop! Matthew!" Aliwyn tore after him, but he was too fast.

Norman also ran for the child, but he followed from the side and forced the child to scurry along the cliff's edge. Matthew soon caught up to her from behind. Aliwyn screamed when he swung his sword and struck her on the side.

"Emma!" Toby cried.

The girl fell over the cliff. Aliwyn changed course and stopped running short of the edge herself. A faint shriek echoed from below, but it was swallowed by the roar of the waters that frothed over black boulders. Panting, Aliwyn searched for the girl along the course of the rapids, but she had vanished. Fury ignited in Aliwyn's chest and coursed through her like liquid fire.

Matthew stood where he was when the girl had fallen, his bitten and bloody hand holding the sword in midair as he stared over the edge. He didn't notice Aliwyn charging toward him. She shoved him away from the cliff, and he dropped his sword when he stumbled to regain balance.

"You monster!" Aliwyn shouted. "You're no better than the Boltans!"

The perpetual frown had vanished from his face. "I—I hit her with the flat side of my sword. I wanted to knock her down, to make her stop running."

"You killed a child!"

"That was an accident. Look at my blade. There's no blood."

Matthew's sword lay by his feet. No blood stained the blade's surface, and none was visible on the rocks beneath it. A quick survey around where the child had been struck revealed no blood anywhere. He seemed to tell the truth, but what kind of demon would attack a little girl? What if he attacked Aliwyn next?

"I don't want you here!" she cried. "Leave and take everyone with you!"

Matthew glanced at his bitten hand. He rolled back his shoulders and crossed his arms. "Marie went back to sleep in your mill, and everyone's exhausted."

The sunlight revealed two bags under his eyes, and Aliwyn hesitated as she panted through her dry mouth. Marie must be reeling from the previous night's chaos, poor thing. Aliwyn could avoid Matthew until the child recovered. The image of her sunny garden beside a sparkling lake beckoned from the fog in her mind. It was a fair walk away, and she'd find solace there until everyone left her mill.

"You can all rest until the bells strike the afternoon hour," Aliwyn said. "Then go to Little Limber, just downstream. You can take shelter at their church."

Matthew cocked his head. "I was going to take you with me."

"Me!" She scoffed. "What makes you think I'll leave with you?"

When he opened his mouth again to speak, Aliwyn stomped away from the gorge. What a pompous numbskull. Why on earth had Aelfric sacrificed himself for this man?

"No more throwing rocks out here!" she called back at Matthew.

She hurried for the narrow dirt path along the ravine's edge. Was there a chance she'd find Emma just downstream, clinging onto a piece of driftwood?

"Where are you going?" Matthew yelled after her.

"Finding that little girl!"

"You'll get yourself killed! The Boltans are still nearby!"

Aliwyn clutched her hands with what felt like a rock thudding within her chest, and she stumbled to a stop. The torrents gushed below her and drowned out the sound of her shaking breaths. Matthew may be right, but reason didn't soothe the angst inside. Another innocent child had been lost in the strife. But why in the world had Emma been traveling with the Boltans?

Downstream, a soldier's helmet flashed along the rocky shoreline. Scattered arrow tips glinted from between the boulders, and Aliwyn's face crumpled. She had been trained to heal people, not fight them. Heading downstream now was indeed dangerous. She finally turned back for her mill, whispering an almost incoherent prayer that the child would be saved. Devastation nonetheless pierced her heart.

Matthew stood by the ravine's edge, scowling in the direction of the water's flow, and Aliwyn eyed the sword he once again carried at his waist. She ducked her head and kept walking.

Pining for time alone, she meandered around the sharpest rocks in her path. Norman had disappeared. Instead, three Vasfian warriors stood watching her near the entrance to the bridge. Crossbows hung from their sides, and each of them carried a bundle of tree branches in their arms. She didn't ask what they were doing with the wood bundles, but it had to be another superstitious ritual, probably involving the rebel hanging upside down.

The way Toby Boltan had screamed for the little girl he couldn't save made her shake, and she didn't want to see bloodshed outside her home again. She approached the three male warriors who stood in a circle by the gorge.

"The Englishman on the bridge is under Norman governance," she said. "They will decide whether he lives or dies."

Three pairs of green eyes turned to her. "We don't need a reminder, peasant girl."

The warriors sat down with their tree branches. Aliwyn met their frowns and clenched her hands. With all the bodies washed downstream, the nearby manors should've raised the alarm. Maybe the Norman authorities were already on their way to capture Toby. He wouldn't be hanging there for long.

The redheads sat and tied their sticks in pairs. Bathed in the morning sun, the fur of their brown vests undulated with the wind. They didn't reach for their crossbows, and Matthew didn't return to throw another rock, either.

Things had calmed down, and a trickling relief soothed Aliwyn's body. She turned to walk for her garden, which was beyond the rolling hills where she had last seen Aelfric. Someone bumped into her shoulder, but she kept walking.

"Oh, sorry," said a male voice.

Aliwyn glanced back. It was the young redhead she had seen sitting up in the donkey cart. He grinned and opened his mouth as though to say something else, but she kept moving. She caught sight of him limping before she turned away, and her gait slowed. Why was he limping? Maybe she had hurt him by colliding with him. She paused when she reached the stone wall of her watermill and looked back.

The man had stopped beside the rabbit fur cape she'd left on the ground, close to the ravine's edge. He bent to retrieve it and stood again, pushing against his thigh to straighten himself. His frame was less muscular than that of the other Vasfian men standing nearby. He turned around and met Aliwyn's stare.

"Do you still want to borrow it?" He held up the fur cape in question.

So he had been the one who had covered her while she'd slept on the ground. Aliwyn remained silent but couldn't turn away from his earnest smile and warm eyes. He was about her age and had the Vasfian hair color, but he had no freckles on his face. Aliwyn squinted in confusion. As he hobbled toward her, what looked like an orange tin fell from his side and tumbled onto the ground.

Aliwyn remembered how he'd had difficulty bending down. "Wait, I'll get it for you."

She approached him, picked up the tin, and returned it to him.

He smiled and tossed the fur cape over one shoulder. "Thanks. My name is Kato, by the way."

The young man spoke with no Vasfian accent. He extended his gloved hand, and Aliwyn blinked. When was the last time she had shaken anyone's hand? Much to Aelfric and Miriam's dismay, she hadn't tried to socialize since moving to Brocklesby. Memories of the carnage and famine from the previous rebellion still made her jittery around crowds and adult strangers. Even people who seemed normal on the surface could degenerate into backstabbing murderers and thieves within a matter of weeks, so why befriend them?

But Kato's hand remained extended before her, and it would be rude to walk away. He wore a gray tunic and stockings, the attire of an English peasant and not the garish colors of the Vasfians. Aliwyn hesitantly accepted his hand. He had a firm grip.

"You must be Aliwyn?" he asked. "I hope you don't mind, but your chickens were getting rowdy, so I let them out earlier. They went pecking 'round the waterwheel."

"Oh...thank you."

A voice nearby spoke in the Vasfian language.

"If you have no other business with Ransley Boltan's son, then leave."

Both Aliwyn and Kato turned to the warrior who had spoken. He was one of the three men who had been sitting in a circle by the cliff, tying pairs of sticks together with dried straw. His comrades continued their strange task without looking up.

"I just have to ask Toby about the poison," Kato said in Vasfian.

Aliwyn knitted her brows. "Poison?"

"Yea. Toby's father poisoned me about four days ago, mostly 'cause he hates redheads. I had some antidote in that orange tin, but I've eaten it all and I still have nosebleeds—"

"It's arsenic," Norman cut in. "I knew it was all along."

Aliwyn almost jumped when the older man appeared behind her. Despite his brawny appearance, he had approached them without a sound.

"With all your vomitin' blood and your breath smellin' like garlic, there's nothin' else it could be," Norman said, taking a sip from his costrel.

"What?" Kato covered his mouth with one hand. "I smell like garlic?"

Aliwyn couldn't resist a grin. He smelled fine, but before she could reassure him, Norman put his hand behind the redhead's shoulder and guided him toward the watermill.

"It's not only arsenic but also sweet clover," Toby called after them. "The antidote is mugwort, meadow—"

"Shut your trap!" Norman shouted back. "As if you care!"

Aliwyn flinched at the harshness in Norman's voice. The rebel hanging upside down sure was bold, butting into their conversation like that.

"But that sounds right, if the poison was indeed arsenic and sweet clover," she said. "Let him continue."

"Mugwort, meadowsweet, and lovage. Boil in wine or mix with honey," Toby finished.

"I could've told you that. Been poisoned twice with arsenic myself." Norman spat on the ground.

Aliwyn pinched her fingers. Since when did rebels know the antidote for arsenic by heart? But she didn't want to speak to Toby with Kato and Norman staring at her. She still wanted to get away from everyone, but it would be cruel to leave Kato without treatment.

"I'll get the herbs for you, Kato." She stepped past the other two.

The confidence in her voice made her twitch with guilt. Kato and Norman didn't know what kind of blundering healer she was. The last time she had prepared medicine, she'd confused two ingredients, and her patient had vomited all night.

Kato followed her. "You're sure Toby told you the right recipe? Maybe I shouldn't have asked him...it was his father who poisoned me."

"Yes, his formula sounds correct. It's like the one my mentor taught me. You may need several doses until your nosebleeds stop."

"And you have all the ingredients?" Kato asked. "You must run an apothecary!"

"Heh, she used to, with a nice older lady," Norman said. "But Miriam didn't just mix herbs, she also fixed wounds. A full healer she was. She saved my life years ago, but then she died, and this girl didn't take over. Am I right?"

Aliwyn kept walking, her fists clenched. Why couldn't this noisy loudmouth mind his own business? Of course she had tried to carry on her mentor's legacy. But within days of Miriam's death, Aliwyn's shaking hands had dropped a searing iron rod on a patient whose wound needed cautery. She had been too vigorous in debriding a boy's thigh injury, and he had cried and bled for hours in the arms of his distraught parents.

The final blow had come when she froze during a difficult delivery. Both the mother and unborn baby had almost died, and nobody sought Aliwyn for medical care afterward. Months had passed. Her former patients, their families, and the rest of Brocklesby must all resent her. Aliwyn was too ashamed to look the other villagers in the eyes.

Steeling herself under Norman's stare, she said through her teeth, "You must leave by this afternoon." But she turned to see Kato's bewildered expression, and her voice faltered. "I—it's because I don't have food to feed you all."

"How about some respect?" Norman chuckled. "I may not look like it, but I used to be one of Lord Seville's knights—Sir Norman Rochefort! Matthew's father was my friend."

Why should she care? Aliwyn hurried toward the end of the mill's side wall. Around the corner, light footsteps rustled the leaves, and Marie bounced before her.

"Ali, did I hear you're worried about food?" Grease coated her grinning mouth. "Well, don't worry. The forest people gave us meat!"

"Whoa! What kind of meat?" Kato's eyebrows shot up.

"Boar! I just ate a trotter and we're boiling more!"

Aliwyn's shoulders slumped. That slimy Matthew Marcotte. Marie wasn't sleeping at all, and meat was saved for celebratory feasts, not to be consumed when Aelfric was dead and nothing deserved celebration. She took a steadying breath. Thankfully, these strangers won't be staying for long.

Kato and Norman walked ahead toward the front of her home, but Aliwyn approached her watermill's entrance while reciting the dosages of the antidote's ingredients. At least the Vasfians had cleared all the dead soldiers away. Evelyn stood in the grassy clearing and stirred a wide clay pot that simmered over a low fire. The fragrance of meat and turnips bubbling inside made Aliwyn's mouth water, but she didn't enjoy it.

Evelyn asked Marie to fetch bowls. When the child skipped into the watermill, Evelyn turned to Kato with a smile. "I'm glad you finally have an appetite."

She flashed a row of straight teeth, a rare sight. Kato walked toward her, and they embraced with sunlight glimmering over their red and chestnut brown hair. Aliwyn stared. A Vasfian hugging a wealthy Norman lady? How had the two of them become this close?

Norman broke into a hacking cough by the pot. The couple raised their heads, and the joy drained from Evelyn's face. She almost fell backward as she released Kato.

CHAPTER 5

MATTHEW STOOD AT THE clearing's edge with a sullen gaze, his hand resting on the handle of his sword.

"What are you doing, Evelyn?"

Evelyn turned back to the clay pot and stirred it, her brows furrowing with the rising heat.

Matthew marched toward her. "I only let Kato stay with us because he speaks Vasfian. But we don't need him anymore. He must go home with Norman."

Evelyn stabbed the stir stick into the pot and glared at her cousin. "I won't let you send him away. I care about him, and he's been a great translator."

"We're not staying with the Vasfians anymore, so why keep a translator? And anyway, that Vasfian chief...what's her name—Reiya, she speaks English."

"You are so superficial, Matthew."

"Superficial? I'm being realistic. He's a wretched redhead *and* a street rat! He can't provide for you!"

"Kato was selling ale for Norman when—"

"You call that a job?" Matthew threw up his arms.

His thunderous voice reverberated from the surrounding trees. Aliwyn stood before her door with goosebumps kling her neck. Heaviness filled her heart as Kato stared at the ground. He was a street rat? Why didn't the Vasfian tribes want him?

Back by the hearth, Norman gave Kato a nudge on the shoulder and told him to go inside.

Evelyn walked up to her cousin and shook out her tattered sleeves. "Look at us, Matthew. Marie and I have been wearing anything the church could give us. How are we different from beggars now?"

Matthew bared his teeth. "Once His Excellency settles the rebellion, I'll inherit my father's land. The land that's rightfully mine!"

"Then *we* can provide for Kato."

"Flying Krakens! That's not how it works! You're a woman, and—"

"Matthew, after my parents died, Kato helped us find food and shelter on the streets. Marie and I would probably be dead without him. Why doesn't that matter to you?"

"It matters, but he's still a street—"

"You trained at Sir Devereux and Lord Seville's manor, and for seven years you didn't come back to visit our family." Evelyn narrowed her eyes. "Why start caring now?"

Matthew's mouth fell open. "You know...you know I didn't come back because of my parents."

Silence. He ducked his head, his chest heaving. But he looked up again with a toothy snarl and muttered something in French.

Evelyn also responded in French, and their voices escalated. Aliwyn shook her head and pulled open her door. She couldn't get rid of Matthew and his family drama fast enough.

"Kato, come inside. I'll prepare the antidote."

Kato and Norman approached her, and the redhead gave a shaky smile. "I really appreciate it, Aliwyn."

"Hmm." Norman rubbed his neck. "Maybe I can calm things down out here."

He strolled back into the clearing, and Aliwyn slipped into her mill. Kato followed her inside and she shut the door after them.

The scent of lard from her rushlights and the sunshine beaming through the vent holes steadied her nerves. Everything inside her home remained comforting and familiar, even if it was a mess. She blinked to adjust to the dimness. Marie sat at the dining table, her arms crossed and her knees locked together. She sniveled as the sound of her older relatives arguing echoed in the room.

Aliwyn walked to Marie's side and rubbed the girl's shoulders.

"Marie, sweetheart," she said. "The fighting outside isn't your fault. Please don't feel bad."

Kato pulled up a stool beside them. "Listen to Aliwyn, Marie. She's right."

The girl looked up, and Aliwyn stroked her hair. "I need to make something for Kato. You can play with my toys if you'd like."

"Or how about some thumb-wrestling?" Kato scooted forward.

As he took over comforting the child, Aliwyn walked toward her kitchen where a medicinal chest stood beneath Miriam's apron on the wall. Kato seemed to be a kind person, but she remained fidgety at the sight of a redhead sitting at her table. She focused on reciting the antidote formula again and opened the chest filled with herb satchels.

Picking up a mortar and pestle, she mixed honey with dried meadowsweet flower. Its fragrance was heady in her nostrils. She sprinkled flakes of lovage and mugwort into the mortar, and her heart settled at the rhythmic movements of the pestle in her hand.

Aliwyn scraped the finished antidote into a clay jar. With a serving stick in hand, she carried the jar back to the main room.

Kato and Marie looked up from a match of thumb-wrestling, and Aliwyn smiled. In one brief moment, Kato had brought cheer back to the girl's face. But as she stood there, Marie's bright laughter stirred an iciness beneath her breastbone.

After today, she might never see Marie again. The least she could do was to prepare more antidote for Kato, enough for several days in case this dose wasn't enough. His presence was special to this child.

Aliwyn placed the jar she had prepared on the table and handed Kato the serving stick. "Here's the antidote, but I want to make you more. I'll harvest fresh herbs from my garden."

"Really?" Kato looked up, and his smile faded. "I...forgot to tell you, I don't have any money to pay you."

"Don't pay me. All my herbs are going to waste anyway. I hardly made any medicine this summer."

Marie turned with questioning eyes. "Why?"

Because after Miriam's death, Aliwyn had lost the trust of the villagers. She had spent years memorizing remedies only to freeze when faced with distressed patients on her own. Now, the ailing turned to the priest or the bailiff's wife instead.

Aliwyn looked away. "I don't want to talk about it."

Thankfully, her guests did not press her for answers. She hurried back to her kitchen and took the empty mortar and pestle. Outside, in her sunny garden, she would clear her head and prepare more antidote from fresh ingredients.

Back in the main room, Kato smacked his lips. "Heifers, is this medicine? It's delicious! I can eat it every day!"

She turned to him and grinned. "It's the honey."

"Oh, can I try?" Marie reached for the jar, but Kato laughed and jerked it out of her reach.

Aliwyn stepped out of her mill. The bright sunshine made her squint. Having a sister like Marie would've been wonderful, but she wasn't there to stay. Aliwyn's shoulders sagged, but when Kato and Marie's laughter rang through the door, a tender warmth kindled within and lifted her sorrow. Kato's arrival had given her a chance to practice medicine again for the first time in months.

With a lingering smile, Aliwyn turned around. Visiting her garden now served a purpose beyond serving herself.

NORMAN AND EVELYN HAD left the grassy clearing. The clay pot stood on the grass with undercooked trotters protruding from the top, and the fire had died. To the far right, Matthew sat on a pile of firewood with his elbows on his knees. He stared at the chickens scratching and pecking nearby, and browned leaves drifted overhead. A hen's occasional cluck broke the silence.

Aliwyn bristled when his surly gaze lifted to hers. What was he doing there, just waiting for her to come out?

"Don't you have a knight you're supposed to serve?" she asked.

"My tutor is Lord Seville, but he's too far away." The bags under Matthew's eyes seemed to have gotten darker. "He probably doesn't know I had been captured, but other knights should be on their way."

What a pleasure it would be, having arrogant knights on horseback frightening her chickens. Their horses were notorious for dropping manure everywhere.

"Make sure they remove the rebel from the bridge," she said. "I don't speak French."

Matthew arched one eyebrow. "Why do you care?"

A prickling sensation crept up her neck, but she didn't know why. "I don't want a body hanging behind my mill."

"I'll let the Norman leaders decide what to do with him. They must negotiate with the redheads, too."

Aliwyn played with a tear on her sleeve. Matthew told her nothing new, and talking to him was a miserable waste of time. Her garden was waiting. Finally, she was off to somewhere tranquil, with sunny hills ahead of her.

She'd only taken a few steps when Matthew called out, "Hey! Where are you going?"

Oh, what a meddling fiend. She gritted her teeth and ran.

Matthew's boots pounded after her. "Wait! Stay with the others!"

It was no use trying to outrun him. He was over a head taller and faster. Aliwyn tried to pass the Boltans' wagons parked at the outskirts of the clearing, but Matthew latched onto her arm. Jerking away, she whirled around and pulled out her dagger. She pointed the blade at his nose.

"Don't touch me!" she yelled. "I'm getting more antidote for Kato!"

Matthew froze. He stepped back, glancing at her dagger, and grief washed over his face. "Kato's been getting better even without it. He threw it up, all the poison."

"He should still take medicine with him, just in case." Aliwyn's dagger flashed in the sun. "Leave me alone. You've caused me enough trouble."

"If you want to be alone, go lock yourself in your chicken coop. You can't wander. I don't know what bizarre ritual the redheads are up to, and they're everywhere now."

She should've locked Aelfric in her chicken coop a week ago and made Matthew save himself. "The Vasfians have never hurt me, but you've just attacked a child!"

Matthew winced as though she had slapped him. Aliwyn took that moment to spin around and weave in between the thick tree trunks.

His voice bellowed after her. "You—I can't believe you're Aelfric's sister! You've got no common sense!"

Aliwyn skidded to a stop. Her breaths rasped in her throat, and she turned around with her eyes wide.

"Who said that? That I'm Aelfric's *sister*?"

"Aelfric did." Matthew crossed his arms. "What? He said you became his adopted sibling after you two started living in Brocklesby. Evelyn told me the same. And Miriam's your adoptive mum, correct?"

His words pounded into her consciousness until a deep ache began at her temples.

"I loved Miriam like my mum," she stuttered, "but I was her apprentice, and so was Aelfric. That's how we're recorded in the village census. I'm not his sister!"

Matthew blinked. "Of course you're his sister. Adopted sister still counts as a sister."

The two of them stood panting, and Aliwyn stared at the fallen leaves behind Matthew. She and Aelfric were not siblings, not even adopted ones. Aliwyn had dreamed one day of marrying Aelfric, but he had left home at fifteen and told everyone she'd become his sister. Siblings couldn't marry. Why would he lie to the Marcottes? There could only be one reason—he must've desired some pretty woman in the Marcotte manor, like Evelyn. Aliwyn's chest trembled, caught between a sob and bitter laughter.

Matthew narrowed his eyes. "What's so funny?"

"Get out of my sight, Matthew Marcotte! This is my home and I can do whatever I want!"

Aliwyn sheathed her dagger and hurried down the path she'd been following. Sharp rocks dug into her feet, but she pressed on, wiping her wet face until it stung. Over the past few years, Aelfric had stopped holding her hand and dancing with her. He'd often spoken of how content he was serving in Sir Marcotte's manor. And who else was there, if not other women eager for his attention? The warning signs had been there, but she'd ignored them, blaming it on his exhaustion from travel and work, always hoping he would return to the sweetness he'd shown when they'd first arrived in Brocklesby. Then, she'd been sure, he would ask for permission to court her...

Now, she had never been so furious with him. But what was the use?

At least Matthew's rustling footsteps no longer followed her.

The forest sloped upward as she neared a lake, which fed the river driving the mill's waterwheel. The lake flooded her garden every spring, leaving behind fertile ground.

Aliwyn trudged uphill until the yellowing leaves of her thorn apple trees rose into view. Song thrushes chirruped from the nearby forest, and the sight of her sunbathed garden cooled her nerves like a breath of fresh mint.

Aliwyn shoved Aelfric out of her mind. The last sugar snap peas she plucked off the vine burst in her mouth with refreshing sweetness. She pulled out a pair of tweezers and used them to pluck leaves off the thorn apple tree, careful to avoid the spikey apples that dangled overhead. Aliwyn then gathered the rest of the plants she needed. She pounded each herb into a paste with her mortar and pestle and collected it in a spare jar from her belt pouch. Although she usually did this in her kitchen, she needed the fresh air today.

Her arms ached as she filled a third jar of antidote for Kato, and she hummed songs Miriam had taught her. A long time passed. Memories of the poor girl who fell into the water still made her eyes blur, and Aliwyn continued to pray for her. In the distance, the Brocklesby chapel bells rang to mark noontime.

"Hey! Have you been left behind?" a woman shouted. She spoke English with a Vasfian accent.

Aliwyn looked up. A Vasfian woman, probably a few years older than Aliwyn, approached the garden. Her braid bounced over one shoulder, and a brown fur vest added warmth to her blood-red tunic. As she drew closer, Aliwyn recognized her as Reiya, the new Vasfian chief. They knew each other from the occasional Sunday Aliwyn had followed Aelfric to trade with the redheads.

The woman stopped beside Aliwyn, still smiling, and made a circular gesture around her forehead before bringing her palm over her chest.

Aliwyn stood but shuffled a step back. The Vasfian's gesture was both a greeting and a sign of reverence to their god, Lenus.

"This is my garden," Aliwyn muttered. "I wasn't left behind."

Her scalp crawled with invisible insects as she eyed the freckles covering the Vasfian's face and hands. From what Aliwyn had heard one Sunday, Reiya had become chief because her mother was injured.

"I know you live here," said the redhead, "but all the people at your watermill just disappeared. Were you supposed to go with them?"

Had the others just left without saying goodbye? Aliwyn straightened her stiff back and struggled to keep a blank face. Although she had wanted to be alone, she felt strangely betrayed. She had told Matthew she was collecting herbs for Kato.

"W-why did they leave?" she asked.

"An army wearing blue and yellow tunics approached the border of my territory, and I let them enter because I have a treaty with them. Then the army left, and I noticed your friends were gone."

Aliwyn wiped a twitchy hand on her dress. "What do you mean, *gone*? Did that army do something to them?"

"I didn't see them interact." The Vasfian woman shrugged. "They were Bishop Geoffrey's soldiers, though. I assumed your friends wanted to follow them."

Aliwyn hung her head as she clenched her mortar. Bishop Geoffrey was a man of high ranking within the church. Maybe he'd heard of the Marcottes' plight and had taken Matthew, Evelyn, and Marie somewhere for shelter. Or maybe that obnoxious Matthew Marcotte had gone away after all.

So be it. On impulse, she dumped out her mortar of smashed flowers. Evelyn seemed to care a great deal for Kato; she would find the antidote for him elsewhere.

"You've become skin and bones since Miriam died," Reiya said with a sigh. "Follow me. My people are having a celebratory feast, and you can eat with us."

"Celebrating...what?" Aliwyn muttered. The fact she was unscathed, while Aelfric was dead?

Reiya put a hand on her hip, and her full lips parted with a smile. "I achieved great victory last night. I ordered the bridges locked, and my warriors herded the rebels right into our trap. The mighty Lenus has delivered to us the men who once dumped feces into his sacred hot springs." She extended an upturned hand. "You're invited to our celebration."

Aliwyn gritted her teeth. So, Reiya admitted to locking the Brocklesby Bridge without telling her and inadvertently sending the Boltans to pound on the mill's door. Aliwyn and Marie could've died that night. Reiya should be apologizing instead of holding her head high.

When the chief turned to leave, Aliwyn frowned after her sturdy frame. "No thanks for the food. I have enough stores at home."

Reiya paused. She turned around with a deepening scowl. "Do you not realize this is an invitation to begin our partnership?"

"Partnership?" Aliwyn scoffed.

"Why are you laughing?" Reiya's green eyes flashed. "I'm not my mother, and you're not Miriam, but we must continue the alliance they've begun."

Aliwyn curled her toes. "I'm not ready. Aelfric just died. Please, just leave me alone."

She darted past Reiya, afraid the chief would pursue her for her rudeness. Reiya didn't.

Aliwyn ran for home. Being abandoned by her guests, whether or not she wanted them, chilled her like a sinister night mist. They had rejected her act of goodwill for Kato and departed even when she hadn't made a mistake. Aliwyn struggled to calm herself. The mill was hers again to live in, was it not? And the bishop's knights should've removed the doomed man from the bridge. She should be relieved. It was time to clean up her home, heat herself a lavender foot soak, and try to live life normally once more.

As Aliwyn neared her watermill, a different thought began to trouble her. The rebel Lord Yeaton and his bailiff had not shown their faces since the attack last night. What were they doing now?

HER HOME APPEARED IN the distance, flanked by the forest on the left and the river on the right. No one stood in the clearing, and the only movement was the trickling rotation of the waterwheel. The Vasfians had probably moved the Boltans' covered wagons, which had all vanished.

The gates to the broad stone bridge, peeking from behind and to the side of the mill, stood wide open to reveal a path leading to the manor ramparts. Matthew and the others must've crossed over with ease. Aliwyn held her chin high and kept walking.

Her guests were gone, but they had forgotten to close the door to her mill. She sighed and walked past the clay pot Evelyn had used to boil trotters. The food was finished, but no one had bothered to rinse the pot. A new stench of horses wafted around Aliwyn. Covering her nose, she walked around the crumbly piles of manure and almost stepped on the shards of clay scattered in the grass.

They were the bowls Marie had probably carried outside for their meal. All shattered.

Who had smashed them? The gaping door of her mill confronted her again, and chills crawled up Aliwyn's back. She had assumed that Matthew, Evelyn, and the others had left peacefully with Bishop Geoffrey's men, but maybe she was wrong. Maybe Matthew had clashed with the bishop's troops while she had been working in the garden.

Aliwyn rushed into her mill and called for Marie, Matthew, and Kato. No answer.

Light from the doorway revealed overturned baskets and stools, and many muddy boots had trampled the straw strewn on her floor. Smoked eels once hanging from twine overhead had disappeared. Even the chest with her linen hair coverings and dresses was gone. The storage room door to the left was open, and the sled—Aelfric's gift to her—had been dragged out.

No blood and no bodies littered the floor; all evidence pointed to a robbery. She had trusted her guests to keep intruders out, but they hadn't. Who were the looters, and where were her chickens? Scattered feathers stirred by her feet. Her hens, her faithful companions, were nowhere in sight.

Aliwyn grabbed the rope attached to Aelfric's sled with a fleeting wish that it was his hand. She darted out of the watermill to search for her chickens.

CHAPTER 6

ALIWYN DASHED ALONG THE stone wall with the sled banging at her heels. Up ahead, the rocky clearing behind her mill was empty except for the golden oak tree and the rack for drying laundry. She slowed to a halt.

"Here, chick chick," she began, but she shook with sobs and couldn't continue.

"Aliwyn?" a voice called from the bridge.

Oh, no. Toby Boltan was still there, hanging beyond the edge of the ravine and out of sight. Why had the Normans not pulled him onto land?

He was conscious, but he wouldn't be for long. Blood was pooling in the wrong half of his body, and no one could live like this. What a horrid way to die. Aliwyn hugged herself as though caught in a rainstorm.

He likely knew what had happened to her home, but her stomach flipped at the thought of talking to him. Nothing brought back the haunting memories of last night like his presence.

"How come you didn't leave with Matthew and the others?" continued the disembodied voice.

Shouldn't he be scared out of his wits? Aliwyn didn't want to answer, but the need to know what had happened to her mill unsettled her, and it felt strange to speak to someone she couldn't see. She tiptoed to the edge and peered down.

The rebel remained motionless where he hung from the plank bridge. He had gathered up his brown cape and wrapped it around his body. His bloody face made Aliwyn jolt, and she shuffled back from the edge.

"I was in my garden since this morning," she stammered. "What happened here?"

Toby coughed and cleared his throat. "When His Excellency's knights came, they ransacked your mill and sent dogs after your chickens. But maybe some of your chickens ran and hid. I hope you find them."

'His Excellency' referred to one of the Norman bishops tasked with crushing the rebellion in the king's absence. And if his knights had just stormed her mill to feed themselves, there was nothing 'excellent' about him. Aliwyn looked back at her home. Maybe a few chickens survived, but she feared she'd sob again if she opened her mouth to call them. She scrutinized the surrounding bushes for any sign of her chickens.

Nothing.

This was too much. She needed help. Maybe someone within the manor walls would pity her and lend a hand. Aliwyn sucked all the water from her costrel and fingered her dagger with a shaking hand. Her head lowered, she trudged toward the stone bridge.

She had just stepped through the bridge's gate when Toby called out, "The doors on the other end are locked."

Aliwyn squinted ahead of her in the afternoon sun. The doors a stone's throw away were shut. She sprinted to the other end and stumbled over the weeds growing between the stone blocks. Pounding on the closed gates, she shouted for someone to open the double doors. There was no answer.

Gnashing her teeth, Aliwyn turned around and pulled at her hair. Toby spoke from the adjacent bridge. "The bishop's knights crossed this bridge and ordered it closed." He inhaled in short gasps. "Closed until the rebellion is over."

She wasn't surprised. After all, the killing and screaming had happened from her side of the gorge. The other peasants needed protection, but being cut off from her village rattled her.

"Where's my lord?" her voice broke.

"I think he escaped last night. He left me here, too."

Water from the gorge below roared in Aliwyn's ears. She pressed her forehead against the cold stone pillar of the bridge and glared at the thick wooden logs forming the manor's fortifications. The wooden church tower peaked above the ramparts, and smoke wafted from the peasants' homes as they enjoyed their side of quiet security.

The lord of her manor had been a rebel all along, but one who paid taxes and acted like the perfect English subject under the conqueror's rule. Lord Yeaton's double life had fooled everyone, but he was a coward. When Toby and the other knights under his authority had failed in combat, he turned tail and ran. The Norman bishop's knights arrived one step behind. When was this rebellion ever going to end?

Indignation burned within Aliwyn. Human beings were a flaming mess and terrible to each other. Forget asking for anyone's help; she didn't want it. She squared her shoulders and marched back toward her mill.

There was no peace like living alone, in her watermill, until kingdom come.

Aliwyn reached the clearing behind her mill and trampled several rows of sticks. The Vasfians had probably left them there. She ignored them, walked to the barrels of rainwater behind her mill, and took the ladle for a drink. The presence of a rebel hanging just a few steps away made her skin crawl.

Without warning, the young man called from the bridge, "Here chick, chick, chick! Here chick, chick, chick!"

Aliwyn spat out her first sip of water.

"What are you doing?" She threw down the ladle.

Toby continued to shout, and her hair stood on end. This doomed man was calling cheerfully for her chickens. It was so inappropriate that she cringed and covered her ears. She wanted him to shut up, but his voice and call sounded almost identical to Aelfric's. Would Aelfie reappear next to tell her this was all a bad dream? She rubbed her temples and chased away that unbearable fantasy.

Toby's voice broke, and he coughed with an agony that made chills sweep down her scalp. She couldn't save him, and she didn't want to see or hear him deteriorate further. Desperate to distance herself, she darted toward the front of the mill. A startled brown hen squawked in the bushes nearby.

"Clover!" Aliwyn cried. Panting with excitement, she knelt and held out her arms for her hen. "Here, Clover! Chick, chick, chick..."

The animal stepped back into view among the bare branches, and Aliwyn's outstretched fingers trembled with disbelief. It had to be a coincidence. Surely many people called back their chickens the same way, even in the wealthy Boltan household. Clover strutted forward with gleeful clucks, and Aliwyn gathered the hen in her arms. The soft feathers warmed her chin, and she blinked back tears of joy.

As she carried Clover back to the chicken coop, Toby asked, "Did you find one?"

The kindness in his voice appalled her. It made no sense that Ransley Boltan's son would want to help or be happy that one of her chickens lived. And he had asked for Miriam when he'd first crawled into her mill. Aliwyn still didn't know why, yet she was afraid to ask.

Billowing gray clouds gathered overhead, but the day remained warm. She found three more chickens by calling for them. Each time she carried a bird past the bridge, she avoided looking in Toby's direction. She couldn't bear to interact with a person who would soon die. Thankfully, he hung below the level of the ground, and she couldn't see him unless she approached the edge.

Retrieving Aelfric's sled, Aliwyn placed it inside the mill close to the entrance. She cleaned up the clearing outside her home and entered the coop to fetch chicken feed. The sack just inside the coop's door was untouched. So those plundering, 'excellent' Norman knights hadn't bothered to steal the insect-infested grain intended for chickens. What rotten rascals. But if the bishop's army was full of Normans like Matthew, it was no surprise that they would rob helpless peasants.

As her hens pecked away at the wheat and barley, Aliwyn sat behind her mill beside the water barrels. She rummaged through her belt pouch and pulled out strips of smoked fish and shelled walnuts. Each rush of salty and fatty pleasure reminded her that Toby was hanging upside down without nourishment.

With the Brocklesby Bridge locked, no sympathetic villager would arrive to throw him a rope, and Vasfians must be prowling nearby to ensure no one would try. Perhaps worse than his physical agony was the devastation of dying alone.

A creeping guilt made her stuff her food into her pockets. When she turned back to the barrel for another drink, he called out, "Aliwyn, may I ask you something?"

She was already gulping down the water from the ladle. A lump formed in her throat, and she plunged the ladle back into the barrel.

"Why should...why should I talk to you?" She tried to sound tough, but her words came out like a whimper.

"I was wondering if—" He coughed twice before continuing. "If anyone found any signs of that child. The one who fell into the water. Her name is Emma."

"I...I didn't look."

Guilt surged within Aliwyn, even if it would've been dangerous for her to search earlier that day. The Boltans must've abandoned the area by now, especially since Norman troops had passed by.

"I don't think anyone went to look." She gazed at her feet. "Matthew said he never slashed her. I'll go look now."

As she turned to leave, Toby called after her. "Wait, do you have someone to go with you?"

"No. And I'm not asking the Vasfians for help."

Toby coughed again. He couldn't seem to control it, and Aliwyn scowled at the water pouch hanging from her belt. When Toby spoke again, his voice was broken and hoarse, and she resisted the urge to fill up her costrel and toss it to him. Hadn't she gotten herself into enough trouble already?

"Be very careful," he croaked. "I think my men are long gone, but there's an ongoing fight for the land you live on."

Toby's words sank like claws into her heart. Lord Yeaton had never given the impression that a fight smoldered over his territory. His father-in-law was a Norman, and when he'd died, Lord Yeaton had simply inherited the territory of Brocklesby.

"There's a leper colony just downstream," she said. "I'll ask them. Maybe they found Emma."

"Oh…I've heard about those lepers," Toby said. "Whatever you do, stay calm around them. And if you do find Emma, you should both seek shelter at a church. Don't come back here."

"Of course I'm coming back here. This is my home, and I need to take care of my chickens."

Toby fell silent other than his laborious breathing, and Aliwyn's heart pulsed in her ears. She had already spoken longer than she ever intended to with Ransley Boltan's son, and in their brief exchanges, he had expressed more concern about her welfare than anyone in her village. Who was this man, really? What had his life been like before the rebellion?

"It was only a suggestion," Toby suppressed a cough. "You don't have to listen."

The person dangling upside down should be Edward or the man who had pressed a knife to her throat, not Toby. She crossed her arms over her stomach and turned to leave, but the young man called again.

"Aliwyn, before you go, please take my recorder."

"Your recorder?"

Toby tossed a small object toward her feet. It landed amongst the rocks and bounced out of sight, and Aliwyn clenched her jaw.

"Emma made me play it for her every day," he said.

Aliwyn glanced in the direction of his voice with her chest squeezing. Maybe Emma was Toby's little sister. Aliwyn would've done everything to help her sister, too, even if it meant befriending a stranger while hanging upside down. There should be no harm done if she took his instrument. She searched the ground and found what looked like a short stick amongst clumps of grass.

Picking it up, she stroked the smooth wood with her fingers. It was light and only the length of her hand, etched with delicate vine carvings that spiraled around the fingering holes. Her eyes rounded. It was identical to the recorder Miriam had carved for Aelfric, but Aelfric's had been made with darker wood. This must be a coincidence. Aelfric and Toby might own nearly identical recorders, but this meant nothing.

Aliwyn twirled the instrument between her fingers. Who was she trying to fool? She needed to know how Toby knew Miriam.

"If you don't want it," Toby said softly, "you can throw it away."

Aliwyn shook her head. She walked to the ravine's edge and dared to study his inverted face. The sight stole her breath. Dangling upside down had made his darkening bruises bulge. Scrapes crisscrossed his forehead and dried blood crusted his lips. His right hand, the one that had been shot, was bloodied almost beyond recognition, and he couldn't stop shivering. He could hardly keep his swollen eyes open, but he struggled to bend his neck to look up at her. An agitated restlessness shook her from within.

"How come you know Miriam?" she asked.

"My arm was broken once, and I was sent here to recover. Miriam took care of me for many months."

"What?" Aliwyn almost dropped the recorder. "Then how come she's never talked about you?"

"I don't know. But is Miriam still living around here?" He spoke as if he knew his time was up. "Are you Miriam's assistant? Or a relative? Was Aelfric an assistant, too? Maybe you were gone the time that I stayed—"

"No!" she shouted. "You're lying!"

"I'm not lying."

Aliwyn wrung her hands. Miriam used to rise with the rooster's crow to prepare breakfast and would sing for her apprentices at bedtime. She had skipped meals so the two hungry teenagers had food. She couldn't have done such things for Toby, couldn't have. Aliwyn backed away from the cliff's edge until the man was out of sight.

"Aliwyn," Toby called after her. "Miriam took care of many patients over the years. I needed extra help, so I stayed longer. She taught me how to speak Vasfian." He paused. Several coughs later, he continued. "I didn't see her. Does she still live here?"

"No. She passed months ago."

He inhaled sharply as he hung out of sight, and Aliwyn wiped her eyes. Her mentor had rushed out in snowstorms to assist in childbirths and stayed overnight with the families of the dying. Her patients treasured her, and Aliwyn couldn't compare.

She tugged at a tear on her tunic and changed the subject. "When the bishop's knights came by, did they try to get you off the bridge?"

Toby didn't answer. His breathing was ragged, more than before, and Aliwyn forced herself to approach the ledge again to look at this battered face. Good Heavens. His eyes were wet. He was weeping upside down. They were both quiet for a moment, and a dull ache started at the back of Aliwyn's skull.

She could deny it if she wanted to, but Toby wasn't lying. He had known Miriam from before.

"I'm sorry," he whispered.

Aliwyn widened her stance. The last thing she wanted was to collapse in a heap again.

"Did the Norman knights try to get you off the bridge?" she repeated.

"No. They were in a rush to catch my father and uncle. The Vasfians convinced them to…to let their clan deal with me. They'll burn the bridge, and me with it."

Aliwyn took a step back. Burning to death was beyond painful, and burning the bridge would be the last step. The Vasfians would ensure that he suffered before that final act; maybe they had left to gather their torture equipment.

If Toby's misery was supposed to avenge Aelfric's death, where was her satisfaction? Aliwyn couldn't swallow the lump in her throat. Wealthy rebels were usually exiled or fined, but the same Norman knights who had raided her mill had left Toby to die under Vasfian jurisdiction. He was an English citizen who deserved an inquest and last rites, not to face an end under the pagans. Her eyes strayed over the length of the locked stone bridge until the truth struck her.

The Normans had left Toby there because he was English. They wouldn't have done that to one of their own.

She paced the edge of the gorge and could almost see Miriam appearing from around the corner of her mill. If what Toby had said about his relationship with her was true, Miriam would've thrown a rope to pull Toby off the bridge. She would've negotiated with the Vasfians to direct their time elsewhere and brought Toby to a church sanctuary, where any criminal would be granted sanctuary for forty days.

But Aliwyn had no relationship with the Vasfians, and she couldn't negotiate anything. The consequences of her indifference over the years towered over her like a cold shadow.

She looked left and right. The Vasfians were nowhere to be seen, and she could ease Toby's suffering. She placed his recorder in her pocket. Back by her barrels of water, she took out the largest handkerchief she had, soaked it, and returned to the cliff's edge. With a trembling smile, she squatted and showed Toby the dripping cloth.

"You can drink some water from this," she said, tossing it to him.

Toby caught the handkerchief with a swing of his left arm. He brought the cloth to his lips, his eyebrows raised, and the memory of him pushing away the vicious soldier last night flashed in her mind. Aliwyn hugged her knee, her eyes blurring. At least he sucked the cloth dry and didn't cough again.

He was remarkably calm. What could he be thinking?

"If you see Emma again, please take care of her." Toby's quiet voice drew her from her thoughts.

"You...you want me to care for her?"

"You have a kind heart. I wish we could've met under different circumstances."

But under different circumstances, how would this knight have noticed her? Aliwyn was just another scrawny peasant and one who smelled like fish.

"I'm going to find Emma now," she whispered.

She stared at his bloody ankle, strangled between two wooden planks and a tangle of ropes, and hoped he'd wiggle free. He'd plummet into the water to his freedom. Maybe he was waiting for the sunset to escape.

Her heart gave a leap, but a sinking weight soon pressed over her shoulders. Had she become a rebel supporter by wishing such a thing? She had better leave. Aliwyn was about to turn away when Toby's eyes widened on her. He dropped her handkerchief, and it fluttered into the wind.

"What is it?" she stepped toward him.

Toby remained frozen, and she looked around. She nearly screamed. To her left, a line of armed Vasfian warriors advanced along the edge of the cliff. Hostility darkened their faces, and they aimed their crossbows at her. She stumbled backward.

"You're not supposed to enter this area!" It was Reiya's livid voice. "This is now forbidden ground!"

"What?" Aliwyn searched for the Vasfian woman who had spoken. "Why is this forbidden ground?"

"This row of branches." Reiya stepped forward and pointed to the line of the stick bundles with her crossbow. "No one is to go beyond this line until this man is dead. You've just defiled our sacrifice to Lenus!"

"How was I supposed to know what those sticks meant?" Aliwyn shouted.

"Were you planning to rescue him?"

"N-no!"

"Then why were you talking to him?"

Aliwyn couldn't answer, and a row of freckled faces glared at her under the bright afternoon sky. No wonder Toby had fallen silent. Asking him a question and demonstrating that they were on speaking terms had been a mistake. There were so many arrows pointed at her, and Aliwyn's head spun with panic. She backed closer to the ravine's edge.

"It's all right." Toby's firm voice came from behind. "Just leave."

His words forced her back to her senses. From the corner of her eye, she glanced at Toby one more time.

"You'll be fine," he said.

His words made her stomach drop. Aliwyn turned to her right, stumbling over her feet as she darted for the entrance of her chicken coop.

From behind, the Vasfians argued about where on Toby's body they should aim their arrows. Aliwyn glanced behind to see Vasfian warriors dumping piles upon piles of firewood on the ground. Her chin quivered with the release of rising sobs. Someone had to be punished for Ransley Boltan's massacres and trespasses, but it didn't feel right to heap so much hatred upon one person. And that person happened to be Toby.

Please, please. Have his padded armor withstand those arrows.

She clapped her hands over her ears, not wanting to hear any projectiles about to be fired.

CHAPTER 7

HEAVY RAIN STARTED THAT afternoon. The mill's straw roof rustled in the downpour, and water dripped inside from a hole in the roof. Each droplet plopped into a bucket, rippling the surface of the water in the hearth's glow. Aliwyn reorganized her belongings and swept the unpaved floor, the broom's brushing sound adding rhythm to the rain's pattering.

When dirt piled up along both walls, she stopped and stared at the shadows cast over her dining table. The stillness was thick in her ears.

Marie's sudden departure had left her hollow, and Aliwyn ached over Emma, another child she couldn't forget. The Vasfians had forbidden her from exiting the mill to look for the girl. They had yelled at her for emerging to feed her hens, but she had done it anyway.

Aliwyn had last looked at Toby on her way out of the chicken coop. He had appeared asleep with his eyes closed, his blond hair blowing in the wind and his arms dangling. The Vasfians had shot him in the lower stomach and left him to die upside down. Maybe he'd already died. The thought of his body swaying from the wooden planks washed her in waves of grief. No other living thing mistreated its own kind the way humans did. She kept Toby's recorder in her front tunic pocket, but she didn't know what to do with it.

Footsteps came and went as the Vasfians changed shifts. She sipped watered-down pottage, and time trickled on.

Until someone knocked on her door.

Aliwyn shot to her feet with a flash of annoyance. Fear seeped in as she slammed her bowl on the dining table. Vasfians? Rebels? She grabbed the spear beside her. What more did they want?

The knocking came again. "Aliwyn! It's Matthew Marcotte!"

She tensed with a growl in her throat. When Matthew continued to knock, she adjusted the grip on her spear and tiptoed to the side of the door. If she just ignored him, would he go away?

"Aliwyn!" Matthew shouted. "I'm here to fetch you. Open the door!"

Why would he want to fetch her? Aliwyn scowled at the plank barring the entryway, and Matthew broke into a sneezing fit on the other side. He cursed in French and his boots squelched as he paced. It sounded like he was soaked. Aliwyn chewed on her lip. When the squelching footsteps wouldn't leave, she set aside her spear, removed the plank, and cracked open the door.

"Bloody Kraken! Let me in!" Matthew cried.

He pushed his way into the mill along with a blast of chilling wind. The sudden entrance of a huge man with a pointy helmet made her chest seize, and Aliwyn grabbed her spear again. Matthew swung the door shut behind him with an echoing slam. His loud breathing filled the room, and he struggled to pull a wet shoulder bag over his head. Aliwyn clenched her weapon and traced the movements of his head with her spear tip.

He straightened and tilted backward upon seeing the pointy metal. "What took you so long to open the door?"

"Why do you want to fetch me?"

Matthew lowered his shoulder bag to the floor. He frowned at her, his two dark eyes separated by the metal nose prong of his helmet.

"Is it not obvious? You're alone in this watermill and surrounded by bloodthirsty Vasfians. It's too dangerous for you to stay."

"No, it's not," she said. "I've lived here for years."

Water sprayed from his cropped brown hair as he pulled off his helmet, and the muscles of his jaws bulged.

"Maybe you don't know what is happening," he said. "Several earls are trying to overthrow His Grace. They've hired some English folks like the Boltan household to do their dirty work. Now His Grace is eliminating the rebels, and it's gotten dangerous in your area. Gather your belongings and we'll leave tomorrow, all right?"

"No, it's not all right. I don't want to leave with you."

Matthew shifted his weight, his nostrils flaring. Aliwyn kept a steely gaze despite shuddering. He was over a head taller and could drag her wherever he wanted. Letting him in had been a mistake.

"Edward Boltan is still roaming the forest with his soldiers." His voice boomed in her ears. "What if he comes back? The Brocklesby Bridge is locked, and that dastard Yeaton fled. No lord protects you now!"

"I already know the Brocklesby Bridge is closed, but I'm not leaving. This is my home. I don't belong anywhere else."

"You think the rebels care that it's your home? They'll come and burn it. And kill you!"

Aliwyn flinched as his shout echoed in her watermill. She eyed her spear tip, but the thought of thrusting it toward Matthew's body made her stomach lurch. All those years spent spearing eels hadn't prepared her for fighting a person.

Matthew had stopped yelling. Aliwyn scrutinized his every move, but he only licked his lips and looked beyond her with orange firelight gleaming on his wet face. Maybe this mill with its hearth and staircase was exactly the way his best friend had described it. Matthew's frown changed into a tired squint. When he scratched his inner eyebrow, Aliwyn's heart twinged. Aelfric used to make the same gesture when something distressed him.

"It's raining," she said. "The rebels can't start any fires. And if you're coming to get me because of Aelfric, then don't bother."

"Why?" His voice had grown quiet. "Aelfric was my best friend."

"I've already told you. I'm not his sister. Not even his adopted sister. Miriam took us in as apprentices at the same time."

He wasn't listening. His eyes wandered up and down her body with a look of judgment, and she stiffened. He must be scorning her for wearing a drab tunic and trousers instead of a dress and head covering like a proper peasant woman. The Normans had carried off the chest with her clothes. All she could do was wrap her feet in linen and wear Aelfric's tunics from his boyhood, which had been stored in a cache behind Miriam's apron.

Matthew rolled his eyes away. "You can't stay here even if it's safe. What are you going to eat next week? The revolt is making food scarce, and even His Excellency's men tried to steal from this place."

His mouth twisted to one side, and Aliwyn glowered at him. Was he one of the Normans who had raided her mill? Matthew squatted to pull open the shoulder bag he'd tossed down, and Aliwyn saw the answer. She recognized the bag and its frayed drawstrings; it was hers. The smoked eels and turnips inside were also *hers*. She dug her big toes into the dirt. The nerve of him to bring back stolen items without an apology. She wanted to demand which Norman knight had ordered the looting, but she dared not ask. Those senseless Norman soldiers. To them, English peasants were not people, they were a commodity.

Matthew unwrapped a speckled egg and turned it as though inspecting it for cracks. Aliwyn held her breath. The sound of Toby's voice calling back her chickens echoed in her mind.

Who was worse—English rebels or a hoard of hungry Normans?

"Is Toby still out there?" she whispered.

"Yes. Why wouldn't he be?"

"Be-because I want to know if the Vasfians removed his body. They shot him. I think he's...dead."

"Well, good." Matthew pulled out a loaf of bread and tore it with his teeth. "Or maybe not good. He didn't suffer long enough—"

Aliwyn darted past him and began tearing up the stairs.

"Hey, come back!" Matthew stood, his mouth full. "I brought food for you!"

She gripped the rail. "Does it make you feel better?"

"What are you talking about?"

"With Toby dead, does that change anything?"

"That dastard deserved every—" Matthew coughed into his elbow. He marched to the watermill's exit and opened the door with a gust of frigid air. A moment later, he slammed the door shut again, pulled off his helmet, and tossed it down with a thump. He shed his black cape and dropped it on the floor close to the hearth. His boots, belt, rattling chain mail, padded jacket, and outer tunic all came off in a scattered and wet mess.

Aliwyn stepped onto the second floor with sweat chilling her hairline. He had decided to stay. A *Norman soldier*, to be exact, and it was just him and her. Alone. What if he became violent and treated her the way he'd treated Emma?

Now in his beige inner tunic, Matthew walked to her clay pot of leftover pottage and picked up the ladle. Aliwyn squirmed. This was her home, but he was acting as though everything was his.

Matthew froze with the ladle in hand. He looked up and found Aliwyn standing upstairs.

"I couldn't stop the knight from robbing you," he said, his brows drawn.

He hung his head and sunk the ladle back into her watery pottage without taking a sip. Aliwyn shrunk back from the railing and out of his sight. No words came to mind when Matthew's coughing and sneezing echoed from the floor below. She stared at the dry blankets folded on the three straw mattresses at her feet, and her shoulders sagged. Matthew was a squire. He had no authority to stop any knights from doing anything, but it appeared as though he'd tried.

Still, Aliwyn hesitated to go downstairs and offer him a change of clothes or a dry blanket. She sat on a mattress and laid her spear at her feet. Scenes from Matthew's rage by the Brocklesby Ravine resurfaced in her mind.

From what Aelfric had told her, Matthew had avoided his parents and lived strictly with his tutor, Lord Seville, for seven years. Matthew's father had been so desperate to remain in contact with his only child that he arranged for Aelfric to serve both the Seville and Marcotte households in an alternating fashion. That way, Aelfric could interact with Matthew and report his progress to his parents. Aliwyn would never know why Aelfric had befriended this brash squire.

Matthew coughed intermittently, and she finally peered over the rail. Why was he coughing so much? He sat against the stairwell's support pillar, arms folded and legs stretched out. Water from the roof continued to fall into a half-filled bucket close to his stockings, which had holes at the tip of both big toes. Aliwyn grinned. Despite all that pompous armor, Matthew had no one to patch up all the holes underneath. She couldn't imagine him mending stockings the way she had always done for Aelfric.

A long time passed. Matthew stopped coughing, and the stillness settled her nerves. She gathered up a dry blanket and a set of Aelfric's clothes—folded into her patched pillow coverings and not stolen—and tiptoed down the stairs. The scent of damp wool and rusty metal now permeated the mill's first floor.

Matthew had placed the bag of salvaged food on her table. Beside the bag were four eggs, each partially wrapped in its own handkerchief. Scowling, she approached and inspected the eggs. None of them were cracked. Who knew this brute was capable of some thought?

Matthew seemed to be asleep. Firelight cast wavering shadows over his chiseled features, and his wet bangs were pushed to one side. The hand Emma had bitten was swollen with a semi-circle of red teeth marks. He seemed less intimidating now, but Aliwyn trembled as she finished her bowl of pottage. His hair was shaved along the ears—that unsightly haircut of Norman men—and his presence brought back ghastly memories of the previous rebellion.

She wrung out Matthew's clothes and hung them over the railing to dry alongside the clothes she had worn earlier. When he slept on, she emptied the pot into two bowls. She took the bucket of rainwater and poured it into the cooking vessel to rinse it.

The sound of splashing water made Matthew yelp with a flailing of his arms.

Aliwyn shrieked. The bucket flew from her hands and bounced with a thunk. She backed into the opposite wall with her heart thudding. Matthew searched the mill with wide eyes, and his panting filled the silence. When his stare met hers, he slumped back against the wall with his forehead wrinkled in misery. Aliwyn dared to breathe again.

"You had a nightmare?" she asked.

Matthew's dull gaze seemed to settle on his holey big toes. "Did you eventually go searching for that girl? The girl that I..."

Sympathy flickered within her. He wasn't good at hiding his emotions, and it was jarring to see a Norman soldier express sorrow.

"I wanted to look for her, but the Vasfians outside were working on some sort of ritual," Aliwyn said. "They wouldn't let me leave my mill."

"Then it's too late," he muttered.

"Why are you so sure? I'm going to search around here for a few days."

His frown came back in a flash. "You're supposed to leave with me tomorrow. Why are you so bent on staying here?"

"Why are you so bent on getting me out?"

"I already told you my reasons. But obviously...you despise me."

"Well, I..." There was no denying it. He would still be outside, shouting at a door, if it weren't for the downpour that guilted her into letting him in. Her face grew warm. If Aelfric knew how she was treating his best friend, he'd be so disappointed.

With shaking hands, Aliwyn picked up the blanket and clothes she had placed on a barrel.

"Take this. You can get changed."

Without thinking, she tossed everything at his face. The tunic and stockings fell on the ground. Matthew tried to catch the blanket with his bitten right hand, but he winced when the cloth landed on his wound.

As he picked up the fallen clothes, Aliwyn walked upstairs with wobbly legs. More sneezing echoed from downstairs as she sat on her mattress and stared at the wall. She could try to be a better host. Offer him some food. Offer to dress the bite wound on his hand. Aliwyn pulled back the edge of her mattress to look for a corked jar with pine sap.

"I'm done changing," Matthew called out. "Come down."

Aliwyn shuffled to the staircase again with her pulse racing. Matthew looked up at her with his hands on his hips. He was the same height as Aelfric but bulkier, and Aelfric's clothes stuck to his body like a second layer of skin. His chest and abdomen were a solid sheet of muscle. She swallowed; she was going to ignore that.

The scorn was gone from Matthew's face, and he looked tired.

"I don't know why you're so afraid to leave," he said. "I'll take you to the Saint Peter's church where Norman, Evelyn, and Marie are staying, and then I'll go away. That's right, I'll go *away*. I suppose you'd like that."

"Where will you go?"

"I'm going to Myton to rejoin Sir Jacques Verdun. He's the knight who found me at your mill and accepted me as his squire. We'll track down Ransley and Edward Boltan."

She squeezed the jar by her side. Jacques Verdun was therefore the knight who had ordered the looting of her mill, and Matthew had to return to him.

"Great," she mumbled. "Good luck."

"Are you coming with me or not?"

"I haven't decided." The thought of abandoning her home and her chickens made her chest flutter with panic. Matthew crossed his arms with a darkening scowl, and she changed the subject. "I'll dress your hand. It's festering."

"Fine, but don't bandage it, or else I can't hold my sword properly."

She walked to one of the three stools around her dining table and sat. Matthew took the seat across from her and set his right hand on the table. Aliwyn inverted the jar, and pine sap drizzled onto the raw bite marks. Above them, rain washed over her roof in rhythmic waves.

Matthew sniffed and rubbed his nose. "So, uh...do you have any extended family around here?"

She spread the sap over his wound with her ring finger. "My uncles and aunts escaped to Scotland six years ago when His Grace burned Northern England. I never saw them again. And my father and brothers died."

Matthew inhaled through his teeth. "I—I'm sorry to hear that."

"I guess you and Aelfric didn't talk about these things."

Matthew squinted at the hearth with two frown lines forming between his brows, and Aliwyn regretted answering with the cold facts. He was too young to have been one of the Norman soldiers who had crushed the revolt. It wasn't his fault, and it appeared Aelfric had deftly avoided talking about the massacre, the burnt farm fields, and the subsequent famine that still haunted the mind of every English peasant.

Aliwyn corked the jar of sap and sat back, but Matthew kept his gaze on the glowing embers. His brown eyes darted in the firelight as though he were chased by mirages he couldn't escape. Aliwyn's shoulders grew heavy, but she couldn't take back her words.

"Matthew," she said softly. "Tell me about your childhood. What was it like to move to England as a boy?"

He flinched. "It was fine. I just didn't know a word of English."

"But your English is very good now." Aliwyn managed a smile. "Most Norman soldiers can't speak as well as you."

"Oh...I practiced with Aelfric."

She thought so, and Aelfric had probably become fluent in French thanks to Matthew. The two boys had grown up with a remarkable friendship—one that had been severed by the strife between the Normans and the English. She ducked her head.

"Matthew," she struggled to talk. "I don't hold it against you for being Norman. I want there to be peace, and so I hope His Grace will stop the rebellion. Aelfric wanted the same thing, I'm sure, and I also support your efforts..."

She felt his eyes turn back to her.

"Does that mean you're coming with me?" he asked.

"If I go, when can I come back here?"

"I don't know. It could take a long time for His Grace to stop the revolt."

Aliwyn gripped the edge of her stool, a stool she had sat on for years. She put the corked jar in her pocket and stood again. Backing toward the stairwell, she held Matthew's gaze.

"I can't leave," she said. "This is my home, and all my chickens are here. I can't leave knowing that I might never come back. I'm...I'll make some tea for your cough."

Matthew shook his head. This time, he looked hurt.

"How are you going to last the winter?" he challenged as she walked up the stairs. "You have almost no food left."

"I'll find a way."

"Find what way? Food won't fall from the sky!"

The thought of being stuffed into a church sanctuary with filthy strangers made her want to scream. She had been through that before, shortly after a clergyman had picked her off the street of her ravaged village. The churches and monasteries surrounding York had been so packed with starving children that many died from dysentery and strange fevers. People beat each other over bread and trampled infants to seize blankets and clothing. And Aliwyn, barely in her teens, had to bite and kick others to survive.

Aliwyn saw people differently after that; either they would hurt her, or she would hurt them. Attending festivals and other noisy, crowded events still made her faint with palpitations.

She wished she could've moved on the way Aelfric had.

"What if you come with me and *try* living at the church?" Matthew asked. "You can bring one chicken with you."

Aliwyn paced the second floor. She appreciated his attempt to compromise more than she could express. But the longer he tried to reason with her, the more desperate she was to hide inside a home she thought she'd never leave.

"I've lived in a church before," she stammered. "It's crowded and disgusting and dark—"

"What are you talking about? The Saint Peter's is huge. It's almost empty, and it has big windows with plenty of light."

Aliwyn blinked at the shadows flickering on her roof. Of course, Matthew didn't know what she had lived through.

"Matthew?" she called out. "Can I tell you tomorrow if I'll come?"

He didn't answer.

With time, her empty stomach churned. Drinking watered-down pottage wasn't sustaining her, and Aliwyn halted her pacing and looked over the rail again. Matthew was curled on his side by the hearth. Even then, the blanket she had given him was too small to cover him completely and his feet stuck out. She stiffened when she saw a puddle collecting close to where he lay. No bucket stood to catch drops from the leaking roof.

Aliwyn hurried downstairs, replaced the bucket, and dried the puddle with rags. Matthew coughed intermittently in his sleep, the kind of agonizing cough that threatened to become something worse. Aliwyn knelt beside him and hovered her hand over his forehead. The heat rising from his head made her catch her breath; he had a fever.

Sick, alone, and stuck in a rainstorm, Matthew had returned for a single peasant the rest of her manor had deemed as good as dead.

Aliwyn studied his dark brows and eyelashes. All the reasons he'd given for her to leave her mill were logical. Too logical, even insensitive. But how else did she expect a Norman squire to think? When her stomach growled again, Aliwyn pressed her hand over the ache of her belly. She quelled her angst enough to look over her remaining food stores objectively.

The truth was harsh. There were only enough stores for a week, and considering what strange dishes the Vasfians ate, she wouldn't beg them for food.

Aliwyn's throat pulsed as she eyed the broken pottery and chicken feathers she had swept into a dark corner. Matthew had been right in saying the rebels could return at any time. She needed to seek shelter until the conflict settled down. Which hen was she going to take, and which others would she perhaps never see again?

Aliwyn unfurled another blanket and covered Matthew's exposed feet. His legs twitched, and she crawled into his field of view to check on him. He squinted at her, his eyes bloodshot. Aliwyn folded her legs beneath her and smiled.

"Sorry to wake you up," she whispered, "but it's cold down here. Would you like to go upstairs? My mattresses are there."

He opened his mouth as though to say something but burst into a fit of coughing instead.

Aliwyn stood and retrieved a bowl of pottage she had set aside. Matthew pushed to sitting, still coughing into his elbow, and took the bowl from her. She watched him gulp down the pottage with her heart thrumming.

As he lowered the bowl, she said, "I've decided to come with you."

"Heh. I'm delirious, right?"

"No, you're not delirious. Get some sleep. We'll talk in the morning."

Hopefully, by tomorrow, she would feel more ready.

"What made you change your mind?" he asked.

She was too embarrassed to look him in the eye. "What you said...the reasons...they made sense."

"Good." Matthew wiped his mouth. "I forgot to tell you that Marie's been asking about you."

"Oh." Aliwyn felt a tug in her chest. "I miss her, too."

"So, tomorrow you carry one chicken? But don't those things...defecate constantly?"

She smirked. "We'll talk later, Matthew."

She led the way upstairs, and he followed with his blankets crumpled under his bulging biceps. The second floor was dimmer. Smoke hung in the air, and heat from the hearth rose and swirled with the cold drafts. Rain washed over the sloping straw roof with rumbles of distant thunder. Matthew couldn't straighten without bumping his head. Only one mattress, the one Aelfric once slept on, was long enough to fit him. He tossed his blankets on top of it and sat down.

Aliwyn sat on an adjacent mattress, clutching her hands, and Matthew lay his belt and sword parallel to his mattress. She never thought she'd invite a Norman soldier up here. The upper floor was a private place she had once shared with Miriam and Aelfric. By this time of the year, they would've pushed all three mattresses into one and huddled together to keep warm.

Matthew kicked the blankets over himself and didn't seem to mind that the mattress covers were threadbare, or that his blankets were made of old flour bags stitched together. She was grateful for that. He settled his head on the pillow stuffed with chicken feathers, and the rainstorm filled the silence.

If Aelfric had been there, he would've played uplifting music and dared them to sing. She studied the shifting shadows cast by the railing as if they would bring him back.

"Matthew," she said. "Did you find Aelfric's recorder before you buried him?"

Matthew grew still as he frowned at the roof. "No. I tried to look for it, but it wasn't in his pockets."

Aliwyn squeezed her eyes shut. Aelfric's recorder had been his most prized possession, something he'd loved to play. When his first recorder from his childhood had cracked, Miriam had whittled him another one. His melodies had livened the dark winter nights in their mill the way sunlight scintillated over fresh snow.

"How come you couldn't find it?" She raised her voice. "He *always* carried it with him."

"I don't know. It probably fell out of his pockets during the battle and got trampled into the mud."

Aliwyn shuddered and hugged her knees. Imagining Aelfric's last struggle made her stomach roil, and she never wanted to know the details of his death. She wished he could've died peacefully in his sleep. Maybe that's what she would tell herself from now on, for her sanity's sake.

"Aliwyn," Matthew said. He sat up and rested one arm over his knee. "When we have some time, I'll help you set up a gravestone for Aelfric. Somewhere nice, overlooking some water."

She blinked until she could see clearly again. Matthew's eyes were moist, but he held her gaze and didn't hide his pain. For the first time, Aliwyn grasped how much his best friend had meant to him. He was also aching over the memories that only two people could make, but now only one could carry on.

"Someplace overlooking the water would be fine," she whispered.

The corner of Matthew's lips jerked upwards. He lay down again, blinking at the roof.

"Good night, Matthew."

She hurried down the stairs as tears again welled in her eyes. What if she never came back? By the time the rebellion ended, her mill could be a pile of rubble.

Packing the rest of her smoked eels and Miriam's apron and shoes made her throat ache. She came across Aelfric's old stockings and hugged and smelled them until all his scents seemed to disappear. He'd probably be rolling with embarrassment if he'd caught her smelling his stockings like that, and his bright laughter echoed in her mind.

Five years ago, Aelfric had kept her company in the dark corner of a church when she had been too sick to walk. He had brought her food and improvised uplifting songs on his recorder. She'd always remember the melodies he'd played, for they had rekindled hope in her that words could not.

If only she could talk to Aelfric one more time. She wanted to know for certain he'd only loved her as a sister, and nothing more. Aliwyn chewed on her lips until they tasted raw. Only Heaven knew how she would move on from this heartache.

Maybe sewing would settle her anxiety. Aliwyn tiptoed up the stairs with a glove that needed needlework and was dismayed to hear Matthew's muffled coughing. She found him awake and scowling at the sloping roof.

"Is something bothering you?" she asked.

His chest rose and fell. A moment passed before he said hoarsely, "I'm sorry he's gone."

Aliwyn sat on the mattress closest to the rail. Matthew glanced at her, and her throat tightened even more. She forced a smile.

"Aelfric would be glad you came. My villagers haven't visited me here for a long time. They only use the millstone next door."

Matthew shifted under his blankets. "Maybe I should tell you something."

"What?"

"The people in your village donated some of the food I brought here."

"What?" Aliwyn stared at him. "You entered my village?"

"I sure did." Matthew gave a sly grin and pushed himself to a sitting position. "I scared your bailiff into letting me cross the bridge to your side, although I promised I wouldn't be crossing on the way back." He cracked his knuckles. "Heh, that's how I reached your mill without a long detour. Before I crossed, some households opened their doors and gave me food. They send their regards. Did you see the cheese and carrots in the bag?"

Aliwyn's lip quivered. "Which households?"

"I don't know their names, but they seemed worried about you, enough to disobey Sir Verdun and open the bridge gates. But just once."

Aliwyn pressed her forearms against her belly. After all the mistakes she had made, she had been sure her villagers resented her for being a wretched embarrassment of an apprentice. Where did their sympathy come from?

"But they don't like me," she whispered.

"Why? What's not to like about you?"

She hardened her jaw, but Matthew's forlorn gaze no longer held judgment, only concern. Finally, his expression relaxed into a smirk.

"I'm a lot harder to like. But you see, those people still talked to me for your sake."

Aliwyn couldn't resist a grin. Had she exaggerated how rancid things had become between herself and her former patients? No one had yelled at her or called her names, but the insults in her head had been loud and real.

Before the previous rebellion had reduced the village of her birth to ashes, she had been a happy girl with many friends. That girl remained within her, somewhere, but she couldn't go see the villagers of Brocklesby tomorrow to thank them. What if the ongoing conflict destroyed Brocklesby next? An image of her village razed and burned flashed in her mind, and tears welled in her eyes.

"Why are you upset?" Matthew threw up a hand. "Aren't you happy about free food?"

His bluntness was amusing. He acted like Aelfric when he was younger, and Aliwyn smiled despite her tears. Now Matthew looked even more confused. When he scratched his head and looked away, Aliwyn chuckled.

One day, if she returned to Brocklesby, she would enter the manor gates and speak to her fellow villagers with a smile. She hoped for another chance to practice medicine amongst them.

Matthew slid back under the covers and scowled at the sword he'd laid beside his pillow. "Since we can't take Brocklesby Bridge, we'll have to walk east for the next bridge then head north. That route crosses open plains, but there's still the risk of an ambush. Stay close to me tomorrow, all right?"

"I will."

"Have you ever stabbed someone with that fishing spear of yours?"

"No..."

"Well, you may have to one day. Bring it with you."

May that day never come. Aliwyn fumbled with the wooden sewing kit at the head of her mattress, retrieved a threaded needle, and began mending Aelfric's glove. Every stitch brought back the image of another person in her village. By the time she'd finished sewing, Matthew's eyes had closed. The worry had lifted from his face, and she struggled to find consolation in his peaceful expression. He could've sounded more confident about their trip tomorrow, but he was familiar with the conflict in a way that she wasn't.

The roof continued to leak. Downstairs, each dull stain on the dining table begged to tell its story one more time. The memories of her loved ones stirred in her bones, and Aliwyn couldn't soothe the ache in her chest.

Farewell to all those across the bridge. And thank you.

Something told her she wasn't coming back.

CHAPTER 8

For a long time, Aliwyn lay on her mattress and watched Matthew's stubbly face. Footfalls sounded from outside, probably from the Vasfians changing shifts.

She couldn't erase from her mind the horrid sight of Toby dangling with an arrow in his stomach. Matthew had gotten what he wanted, and perhaps so had Evelyn, Marie, and their allies. Even Aelfric would've wanted revenge, but these thoughts brought her no comfort. The loved ones she had lost would never return, nor would those who had died in the revolt.

The rain stopped, and an uneasy sleep finally overtook her.

Without warning, her chickens clucked and protested inside their coop on the other side of the mill's wall. Aliwyn rubbed her eyes and sat up. She had always wanted a door between the watermill and the coop, but Aelfric had said that making such a door risked the watermill's collapse.

The anxious clucking continued, and her pulse quickened. Matthew was snoring, and she didn't want to bother him. Vasfian voices echoed from her chicken's home. What were they doing, stealing eggs? Aliwyn crumpled her blanket and glanced at Matthew again. He didn't speak a word of Vasfian and would probably pick a fight. She picked up her spear and tiptoed downstairs to the watermill's entrance.

She had to set aside her spear to lift the plank barring the entryway, and it was still in her arms when Matthew shouted, "Where are you going?"

"My chickens—"

Fists pounded on the door. Aliwyn gasped as it flew open, knocking the plank out of her hands. An icy wind swept into the watermill.

"Where is Ransley Boltan's son?" a Vasfian man demanded. He stood in the rainy darkness, his dripping face drawn into a toothy snarl. He wielded a wooden club with metal blades protruding from it, and behind him stood several armed warriors all crowding around the entrance.

Matthew ran to Aliwyn's side and pulled her behind him. She sucked in her breath; he had already drawn his sword.

"What's going on?" he shouted.

The warrior responded in his own language. "We just changed shifts standing guard at the bridge, and that scoundrel is gone!"

The news sank in, and Aliwyn's mouth hung open. Her unspoken wish that Toby would escape had come true. Matthew kept his weapon raised. "Aliwyn, what's he saying?"

Aliwyn dared to step forward and stand beside him. When Matthew's glare shifted to her, she pleaded with her eyes for him to wait until she could translate.

"He's not in here," she answered the Vasfian warrior. "I didn't open this door all night."

"We'll believe you after we search!" The man at the forefront raised his club to force his way into the room. In a flash, Matthew struck the club with his blade.

"Matthew, stop!" Aliwyn cried. "They only want to look around!"

The two men nonetheless stood with their teeth bared and weapons grinding in a deadlock. Those gathered behind the warrior surged and forced Matthew to stagger backward. Aliwyn grabbed his arm and pulled him aside as a dozen Vasfian men and women pushed into the watermill, each with a dagger at their waist and a crossbow strapped across their back. Raindrops clung to their pale goatskin coats and glistened in the ember's glow.

"I don't want them here either, but you can't fight so many of them," Aliwyn stammered.

The intruders pulled over a large basket, then another, scattering what little she had left of her parsnips and apples all over the dirt. Aliwyn's chin trembled, but she gripped Matthew's arm and prevented him from advancing.

"What are they looking for?" he demanded.

"Toby."

His arm stiffened beneath her hand, and she avoided his fuming glare.

"What?" he shouted. "You said he was dead!"

"I said they shot him, but—"

Aliwyn cringed at the sound of shattering pottery from her storage room. Baskets rolled onto the floor between the scurrying boots, and several apples bounced across the floor to lie at her feet. She clawed at her scalp, and something within her snapped.

"Stop it!" she shouted. "Toby isn't here! How do you know he didn't fall off the bridge?"

The Vasfians didn't pay her any attention. Matthew snarled and lunged for a man about to ascend the stairs, and Aliwyn yanked him back. He nearly sent her flying with his force, but she clung on tight. How many people would perish in her mill tonight?

"Matthew! You can't fight so many!"

A pair of hands clapped twice at the entrance of the watermill. The Vasfian warriors in the room halted and turned to look at the doorway, where Reiya stood with her eyebrows knit and her braid dripping over one shoulder. Like the others, she wore a reverse goatskin coat that was tied around her waist.

"I told you to search, not destroy." She pointed outside. "Everyone out. I found more footprints leading into the woods. Go find Galiden—he'll show you."

The Vasfian chief stepped inside as the first of her clansmen hurried out the door. They ducked to avoid her bitter regard, and the only sound was of their departing boots squishing in the mud. Reiya turned to look at Matthew and Aliwyn, who both watched the retreat in bewilderment.

"We've met before," she said in English as she nodded at Matthew. "Toby has escaped. I'm sure those uneven footprints are his."

"What?" Matthew cried. "How did he manage—"

"That's what we all want to know. Reinforcements and hunting dogs are on their way. Regardless, we could use someone with a sword right now." Reiya turned and walked toward the open door. "Matthew, come with us."

Aliwyn tensed when he sliced his arm through the air.

"How could you all let him escape?" he shouted. "And how dare you barge in here and throw things around!"

Reiya cocked her head, her eyes glinting in the light of her warriors' torches.

"Matthew, just go," Aliwyn said. "I'm not that important."

He glared at her, an artery pulsing across his forehead.

"Are you coming or not, Matthew Marcotte?" Reiya set one foot forward and gripped the studded club at her hip. "I extended my alliance to you in honor of Aelfric and your father. Don't test my patience."

"Go, Matthew," Aliwyn whispered. Even if he disliked redheads, and even if Toby's escape frustrated him, now wasn't the time to start a brawl.

Matthew marched up the stairs, grabbed his damp clothes from the railing, and threw everything back on. He descended with his swollen right hand gripping the sword he held pointing at the ground. Aliwyn watched him with her arms folded, and their gazes met as he passed her. She caught a hint of fear, but she didn't know how to respond.

As Matthew neared the exit, he paused and looked back. "Bolt the door."

"My clansmen won't enter again." Reiya's face faded into the darkness. "I apologize for the mess."

Matthew held Aliwyn's gaze for a moment longer before he turned and followed the Vasfian chief into the night. She stared in a daze at the back of his departing shoulders and arms. His forlorn expression haunted her as she closed the door.

She pushed open the storage room door with a white-knuckled fist. Matthew was too sick to fight, and what if he never came back? What if bodies covered the clearing before her home again? Her mouth was dry as she swept the new shards of pottery into a pile with her bandaged feet. She squatted to pick up the smallest clay fragments, and the first scuffling sounds echoed from her kitchen.

A sneeze rang out, followed by the muffled sound of a man groaning. More scuffling sounds. She toppled sideways out of her squatting position. Pushing herself up, Aliwyn dashed behind the storage room's open door. There, her heart pounding, she peered through the gap between the door and the doorframe.

She had blocked the kitchen's rubbish hole with a rock, but no rock she could carry thwarted a determined intruder. The rock jerked inward again, and her throat swelled until she couldn't breathe. The brutality and yelling of the previous night came crashing back. What if Toby's men had returned to save him? What if the man breaking in was his uncle, Edward?

She could either wait in the storage chamber where she would be cornered, or she could run for the main door and escape. Aliwyn charged out of the storage room for the mill's exit.

An arm with a dark sleeve shot through her rubbish hole. Her vision went white, and she stumbled and slammed her cheek against the door. Aliwyn grabbed the plank and flung it aside.

"Wait!" came Toby's voice behind her.

She spun around. Once again, a man with dirty blond hair lay sputtering on the kitchen's stone slab. His cape was gone, and his drenched black surcoat jerked with each cough. Pain contorted his face as he clutched where the arrow had struck. Aliwyn strangled the scream clawing up her throat.

Help him, or run? When Toby looked up at her, she squirmed against the door but felt her legs rooted to the ground. She had to do something. What kind of healer would she be if she left his wound unchecked? Yet, the thought of pulling him onto a mattress clamped a vise around her throat. It won't be long before Matthew and the Vasfians returned and found her and a bloody rebel. They wouldn't forgive her.

Toby had just pushed to his knees when the door behind Aliwyn flew open with a swirl of damp air. She lost her balance. Stumbling back, she fell onto a Vasfian woman who stood with her hand on the door handle.

Aliwyn's shoulder landed by the redhead's boots, but the Vasfian regained her balance.

"It's Toby!" the woman screamed.

She raised her crossbow from her hip, her eyes fixed ahead, and Aliwyn's chest clenched. The next arrow would pierce Toby's face. She sprang to her feet and purposely rammed her skull into the underside of the warrior's chin. The impact made Aliwyn stagger, and the woman's crossbow snapped upward and fired into the straw roof with a loud thwack.

"You traitor!" The woman reached for her club, but Aliwyn shoved her opponent aside and ran into the night.

Her teeth chattered with each strike of her pounding feet. Straight ahead stood the evergreens flanking her mill. To her left, across the clearing, a line of torches flickered in the now rainless night.

"It's him!" the Vasfian warriors cried, their voices multiplying in her ears.

They dashed toward the mill with their crossbows raised. Aliwyn had bolted halfway to the forest when the first of many arrows flew in her direction. She shrieked as more arrows sang past her ears.

"Stop!" she shouted.

"The watermill woman hid him!" came the furious shouting. "Shoot them both!"

"I didn't hide him!"

But the slew of arrows continued, and what felt like a whip glanced off her left shoulder. She gripped the explosive pain and kept running, her heart shooting to her throat when the shadows of other Vasfians rose from the forest. Aliwyn skidded and swerved for the back of her mill.

She had no plan, only the rapids and the cliff flashing in her mind between the bounding torchlights and the warriors she imagined gaining on her. But diving into the ravine was crazy. The blackness of death devoured Aliwyn's thoughts, and she ran without direction.

The oak tree in her backyard loomed ahead. As she scampered past the trunk, her toe struck the roots. She yelped and flew face-down onto matted leaves. Another arrow landed beside her shins, then one close to her back. Her body throbbed, and she couldn't tell if they'd shot her again.

To crawl through the downpour of arrows was futile. Aliwyn covered her head with her arms and squeezed her eyes shut.

A pair of boots stomped to a stop beside her elbow. "Get up!"

Through her fingers, Aliwyn peered up at the silhouette of a man with a large wooden board held in one arm. The reek of blood and raw fish blew onto her. Arrows pelted the board from the other side, and Toby's bruised face swung into view as he knelt. He hooked his free arm around hers and pulled her to her feet with surprising strength.

The world spun as the blood drained from her head. Another arrow tip penetrated Toby's shield with a loud thwack, and Aliwyn jolted.

This was no shield. It was Aelfric's sled.

"Go inside!" Toby shouted.

The uproar in the clearing rose over her like a suffocating fog. Toby pushed her toward her chicken coop, but she teetered in the dark. When he grabbed her arm again and pulled her toward the cliff, fear finally pierced her trance.

"Let go of me!" she cried.

A club came crashing toward her head. Toby blocked the blow with the sled as he pulled her away, but the force of the impact made him topple backward.

"Run!" He fended off another strike with the cracking sled.

But there was nowhere to run. Aliwyn had barely regained her balance when two tall Vasfian warriors charged toward her, one raising a torch and the other a club. Firelight danced on their snarling faces.

"Traitor! How dare you rescue him!"

"No!" Aliwyn crossed her arms before her face.

Her left shoulder erupted in pain. Bracing it with her other hand, she shuffled back from the attackers until her heels slid over the edge of the cliff. The club swung down toward her head again, and at the last moment, she ducked and collided with Toby as he lunged for her. He parried the crushing blow with the sled and used it to shove away the warrior.

Matthew seemed to scream out her name amid the shouting and groaning. As Aliwyn looked up, Toby pulled her to his chest and wrapped his arms around her head and upper back. She was too startled to resist.

A heartbeat later, he jumped with her over the edge of the cliff.

CHAPTER 9

A DOG'S BARK JOLTED Aliwyn awake, and a warm tongue slathered across the bridge of her nose. She grimaced at the musty breath. When sharp teeth nipped at her ear, Aliwyn clamped her jaw shut on a mouthful of stagnant mud. She spat it out. Her eyes blinked open to the bared teeth and pink gums of the dog.

It was daybreak. The river's current had washed her ashore so that she lay on her stomach on the bank among the weeds and cold mud. She pressed with both arms to get up, but her left arm and shoulder gave out with throbs. The black dog snarled at her and shuffled side to side as if it were about to pounce. Aliwyn kept a blank face. With her good right arm, she pushed herself up to sitting.

The dog looked aside, and its ears shifted. It ran away with scattered barking.

Aliwyn exhaled with relief as the canine disappeared among the bushes along the shore's edge. Her muddy clothes clung to her body, and she picked off the matted hair from her cheeks. A breeze stirred the red and yellow leaves of trees nearby, chilling her until goose bumps skittered over her forearms. She shivered despite the unseasonably warm weather.

What had happened last night emerged through the haze in her mind—her fall over the edge of the cliff, the downpour of arrows, and how the Vasfians had mistakenly thought she had hidden Toby. What a disaster to have the Mehi tribe involved. They were even more irrational and ferocious than she had feared. What was she going to do? They'd shoot her if she dared to return home and explain herself.

Jaw clenched, Aliwyn squinted in the tender morning light. No one appeared between the trees. She ignored the trembling of her body and stood.

How had Toby escaped the bridge? Why had he bothered to shield her with Aelfric's sled? These questions begged for answers, but as she stared at the muddy shoreline, the warmth of a hearth and dry blankets called out to her. She needed to find shelter. Aliwyn turned in a circle and oriented herself in the sunrise's direction. Southeast of Brocklesby was Little Limber, a hamlet with a chapel where she could eat and get changed. It was only an hour away.

Maybe the priest would help her find Matthew Marcotte and clear her name with those wretched redheads. After all, she had left her mill with a gaping rubbish hole and the stone pushed inward. Toby had been on his hands and knees, on her kitchen's stone slab, when the Vasfian woman had thrown open the mill's door. All this supported the truth—Toby had crawled in without her help.

And Aliwyn bashing into the Vasfian woman who almost shot Toby? Well, that was Aliwyn standing in a panic to escape from a dangerous rebel. She could explain away everything she had done last night.

But unless Aliwyn found Matthew first, she didn't dare return to her mill.

She focused on setting one foot in front of the other, but the dog who had growled at her earlier barked in the distance as if it had found someone. Maybe that someone was Toby.

She searched the woods with a racing heart. Last night, the torrent had swallowed her into its freezing blackness and tossed both her and Toby like puppets through the rapids, but her body had struck nothing.

Aliwyn rubbed her hands to warm them and studied her forearms. Not a scratch or a bruise. Toby must've cushioned her with his body, and maybe he had been seriously injured. Memories of their scuffle with the Vasfians last night made her chest tighten. It wasn't right to forget about him.

But if she found him wounded, was she willing to bring him to Little Limber? If she wasn't, she shouldn't look for him at all.

Find Matthew, or find Toby?

Aliwyn was still deliberating over what to do when something moved in the corner of her eye. A ragged figure a stone's throw away sauntered from the shoreline and into the shadows of the pine trees. A hood hid the figure's face from the side and multiple layers of beige, loose clothing hung over his body. Only a gray beard protruded from his chin. A gnarly hand swung by his side, missing its little finger, and Aliwyn froze with her knees locking. Only lepers dressed like this, and they often lost fingers. Their appearance was so mutilated by disease that the villages ostracized them.

Somewhere behind the trees, a woman's voice ordered the barking dog to hush. The hooded man Aliwyn had been watching turned his head, his colorless eyes meeting hers. Wart-like masses covered his face. Aliwyn gasped and staggered backward, fumbling for the dagger around her belt.

"Hey Garett!" the same woman cried, "I've got another Boltan dastard! Come give him a thrashin'!"

Aliwyn stiffened. The woman could only be talking about Toby, and he was in danger. She seized the decision to find him first.

"You, there!" The hooded man stepped toward her.

Aliwyn sprinted through the bushes toward the woman's voice. Her legs almost buckled with the burst of speed on uneven ground.

"Hey, wait!" the leprous man shouted after her. "I'm not going to hurt you!"

Why should she believe that? She skirted past the pine tree trunks with glances back at the man who followed but fell behind. A stretch of bushes appeared ahead on a downward slope. Beyond the bushes, the land extended onto a flat, open beach. As the trees parted before her, the backside of the dog and another leper, a woman this time, came into view.

Wavy dark hair trailed down from a hood that otherwise hid her face. The woman and the black dog crouched on either side of a soldier, who lay face up and motionless. The canine bit repeatedly into his black surcoat with a golden griffin. Chills raced down Aliwyn's back as she ran close enough to see his face. His eyes were closed, lips parted.

"Toby!" she screamed.

Both the dog and the leprous woman looked up. The beast spun around and barked.

"Leave him alone!" Aliwyn charged as the branches whipped her legs.

The woman shot to her feet and raised a long dagger. "Who the bloody maggots are you?"

The dog pounced for Aliwyn as she stepped onto the beach. She veered to the side and dodged the canine's gaping mouth. Groping for her missing dagger, she approached Toby from another angle, but the dog drove her back again.

The woman commanded the dog to sit. The beast obeyed, but the leper stood by Toby's head and widened her stance.

"I found him first!" She spread apart her arms, her sleeves hanging like shaggy wings. "I get all the goods!"

Aliwyn grimaced at the woman's disfigured face, with its collapsed nose and one sagging eye. The leper chuckled and threw back her hood, revealing multiple nodules that bulged beneath the skin of her face. With a three-fingered hand, the woman clenched Toby's leather belt. The dagger in her other hand was clean.

She had been cutting Toby's possessions and not his body, but why wasn't he moving? Aliwyn panted, and her fingers poked into the empty sheath of her dagger. Her weapon was gone.

"You can't just rob him!" Aliwyn spread her arms apart. She glanced at the belt dangling from the leper's hand.

"And why not? This is the least I can do!" The woman looked back and stomped Toby's shoulder with her heel. "They've murdered dozens! Sir Marcotte's household, their children—"

Aliwyn found her chance. With the leper still ranting, she charged and butted into the woman with her shoulder. Her adversary stumbled backward, and Aliwyn yanked the stolen belt from her grasp.

The leper landed on her bottom beside Toby. "Churling maggots!"

Aliwyn had barely found her footing when the dog charged at her.

"Get back!" She whipped the beast across the nose with the metal clasp of Toby's belt. The dog yelped and scurried aside.

From behind her, a male voice ordered the canine to sit. The leprous man had finally caught up to her.

Aliwyn's head spun as her eyes darted between the beast and the newcomer. She clenched the belt, ready to strike either of them, but the dog only sat per the man's orders and whined.

"Garett, you flea-bitten swine!" accused the older woman. "You were watching this whole time!"

"Not true, Ida," the man said, panting. "I'm getting slow. Just got here. And didn't you tell me that when two women argue, I'd better keep out?" He took a step toward Aliwyn. "Aliwyn, it seems that you know this man?"

Aliwyn's chest heaved as she knelt by Toby.

"How do you know my name?" She stared at Garett as her fingers crept over Toby's clammy neck for a pulse.

"Well, Miriam was a good friend of mine," the man said. "I know you're her apprentice. I met you a few years ago."

Aliwyn hardly heard his words. Toby's skin was frigid under her shaking hand, and she couldn't find a heartbeat. She dared to look down. His eyes were closed, but he didn't appear as ghastly as she had imagined. Much of the blood had been washed from his face, and his blond hair swept over his forehead in layered wisps. Gently sloping eyebrows framed his sunken eyes in a peaceful expression. Was he gone already? Her stomach gave a lurching twist.

"Stop poking around," Ida spat out in disgust. "You're not even feeling where the pulse should be. That dastard was walking around until I clubbed him in the head. I'm goin' to cut off his fingers before he gets hanged."

"No!" Aliwyn shouted.

"That's the law," Garett said. "All of Boltan's followers will be hung for murder and treason. We must turn this soldier in."

"Hanging? N-no inquest?"

"Well, there should be an inquest. But certainly, the men investigating his case will sentence him to death. I was seeking alms yesterday when I heard the Boltans ambushed the Marcotte family, and only a few of their children escaped to tell the story. The Boltans are rebellious murderers, Aliwyn. They will be executed."

Ida stood and raised her dagger at Aliwyn. "You're wasting our time! Step aside!"

"He's not one of the Boltans' soldiers!" Aliwyn blurted out. She stiffened like a pole at her incredible lie.

"What?" Garett asked. "Then why has he got the complete uniform? The griffin surcoat?"

Aliwyn stared at him. What felt like an iron fist gripped her throat, and Toby's belt slipped from her fingers.

"We...He stole some clothing and dressed up like one. That's all." Her voice shook. "It was really cold, and we didn't have much to wear. Then the Vasfian clan attacked us, and we fell into the water..."

Garett shook his head. "Why didn't you tell us this earlier?"

"I..."

"Because it's a lie!" Ida shouted.

"No, please! We stripped these clothes off a dead Boltan soldier! The Vasfians have been killing them!"

"All right, all right," Garett held up his open hands. Only his moving beard was visible as he talked. "It's true, many of Boltan's soldiers have washed up here, all dead. Look, before I caught up to you, I let my cat go home to signal that we needed a cart. The driver will take you and your friend to where we live so you can warm up."

"This is ridiculous!" Ida flung her hand by Garett's head, almost slapping him. "You're going to believe her? This witchy hermit never leaves her watermill and suddenly she's got a lover?"

Garett hesitated. "Aliwyn does have a good friend, a young man who once worked at the watermill. He left several years ago and I don't recall his name. Is this him, Aliwyn?"

Aliwyn's face contorted as Aelfric's death pierced her once more.

"Well?" Ida demanded. "Answer the question!"

"Yes!" Aliwyn shouted. "Yes, this is him!"

She fell into a heap, hugged her knees, and buried her face. What had she done? She was imprisoned by this lie and would have to keep lying, scandalously intertwining Aelfric's identity with that of Ransley Boltan's son, of all people. But she couldn't stomach the thought of Ida torturing Toby before having him hanged.

Guilt boiled within her as Ida and Garett continued to bicker. The old man was one of Miriam's many friends, and Aliwyn had taken advantage of his trust. What kind of person was she?

From behind came the sound of wagon wheels rolling over gravel. She raised her head only to see Ida's menacing snarl within a finger's distance of her face.

"My son served in the Marcotte manor and the Boltans killed him!" Her voice rang in Aliwyn's ears. "If you're lying to us about who this man is, I'll get you both cut up and hanged. Do you hear me?"

Aliwyn frowned at the woman, her teeth chattering.

"Enough, Ida," Garett said. "The cart's almost here. I'll help you gather up the firewood."

They walked a few steps away, but Ida glanced back with a suspicious sneer. Aliwyn sat with her right arm holding her knees to her chest. She flinched when something frigid touched her left hand, which had been resting on the ground beside Toby.

"Ah, he's awake," said the leprous man. "Remind me, what is his name again?"

Aliwyn gazed at the pale fingers resting by her hand. Her eyes trailed over Toby's tattered sleeve, rising to look at his face, and her pulse quickened. Toby's hazel eyes were moist with worry. He must've heard all the lies she had spoken on his behalf. His bloodied lips parted, but no words came.

Aliwyn's vision blurred. She regretted yelling Toby's name when she had first found him, but it was too late to change anything.

"His name is Toby." She watched the rapid rise and fall of the young man's chest.

"Hmm...I thought it was something totally different." Garett cocked his head. "Well, that's memory at my age."

Aliwyn pleaded silently with Aelfric to forgive her for this monstrous lie, but she couldn't take it back. Toby's gashed hand quivered by her own. He must be freezing, and her urge to grasp his fingers and comfort him alarmed her.

Toby struggled to sit, and Ida and Garett were still close enough to see everything she did. If she was supposed to be Toby's friend, she had better act like it. She braced Toby's arm and pulled him up, her arms quaking so violently she couldn't withdraw them afterward. Toby's warm whisper came into her ear. "Get out of here!"

He spoke Vasfian with an accent similar to Aelfric's, but nothing could intensify her state of shock. She clutched Toby's arm. He was shivering also, and the intensity of his gaze matched the terror roiling within her.

"Where can I go?" she whispered in Vasfian.

"Little Limber. Run!"

If she ran, the lepers' dog would catch her, and she would leave Toby behind with his injured ankle. Ida would probably club him to death when she confirmed his identity. The thought petrified Aliwyn, and she couldn't let go of him.

"Aliwyn!" came a shout from behind.

The familiar voice made her turn around. A donkey and cart rolled to a stop a short distance behind her.

"Aliwyn! What are you doing here?"

The man who spoke sat on top of a wooden cart drawn by a donkey. He wore a linen hat that rested above his protruding ears. Climbing down, he limped toward her, and Aliwyn almost screamed.

Red eyebrows and red eyelashes. It was Kato.

His eyes widened like round shields when he saw who she clung onto.

CHAPTER 10

Aliwyn waited for Kato to tell the truth and expose her lies, but he was frozen in place. The beach seemed to rotate about her as she came to the verge of fainting. Toby didn't pull back his arm, and his presence kept her from falling.

The redhead stared at the scene before him as Garett explained Toby was not one of the Boltans' soldiers despite his griffin coat-of-arm surcoat.

"They both worked at the watermill," said the leper.

Aliwyn's eyes pleaded with Kato for help.

"Kato!" Ida shouted. "What's wrong with you? Did you piss in your trousers?"

"What? N-no!"

"Then why you got that look on your face?"

"I...uh...nothing. I'll take them in my cart right away."

"Take Garett with you," Ida said. "I want to strip the corpses here—"

"Garett can stay here and strip with you. Oh, frags—I mean, he can strip *the bodies* with you. I'll take Aliwyn and...and this man on my own. No problem."

Aliwyn didn't dare believe Kato's words or that Ida would accept his stammering reply. Yet the leprous woman turned away, mumbling to herself as she kicked driftwood into a pile. Aliwyn's chest heaved with relief.

"Kato, give this young lady and her friend a change of clothes and some food," Garett said.

The old man helped Ida load two large bags onto the wagon, and more conversation took place that Aliwyn couldn't follow. She prayed in silent gratitude but couldn't stop shivering.

With the lepers watching, she helped Toby rise to his feet and climb onto the wagon bed. Toward the rear were two large sacks holding what the lepers had collected from the dead soldiers. Both bags were filled to the top with bloody clothes, boots, and other looted items, and they reeked of blood and body odor. Her mouth sour, Aliwyn averted her eyes and lowered Toby to a sitting position. His arm slipped from her hold and left a cold patch on her chest. She sat beside him and didn't dare touch him again. Kato stepped onto the driver's seat, and the resentment in his scowl made her neck prickle.

The redhead set the cart in motion.

Once they were out of earshot, he turned around to face the other two. "What's going on, Aliwyn? How did you get him off the bridge?"

"I didn't...He escaped."

She braced her injured shoulder as the wagon rolled and swayed over rough ground. Pine branches whipped past. The small cart forced them to sit close together, and her shivering intensified as the wheels sped up over the muddy banks and made a turn into the shadow of the woods. The wind carried the smell of moist evergreens. Toby sat across from her, and Kato sat elevated on a bundle of firewood toward the front. Their positions formed a triangle in the cart.

"All right, forget it. Doesn't matter how Toby got here," Kato muttered. "The fact is, this man helped kill Matthew's whole family *and* pollute the Vasfian hot springs. Many people want him dead."

Aliwyn watched his back with chills racking her chest. She knew little about Kato. He could bring them both into the closest town to be killed, and he would be right in doing so.

"Hold it! Did you check Toby for weapons?" Kato asked.

"No—"

"Why, Aliwyn? You know who Toby is! Why did you lie to Garett?"

They had just turned out of the lepers' line of sight. Toby had remained motionless under the linen blanket, but now a bloody boot slid out from underneath the covering. Kato spun around. He pulled out a knife as he jerked on the donkey's reins with his other hand. The wagon came to a jolting stop, and Aliwyn's shoulder crashed against the railing of the cart.

She was too frightened to scream, but Toby cried out in pain across from her.

"Stay where you are!" Kato ordered in a hushed voice. He stood with his back facing Aliwyn and his blade pointed at Toby.

The wagon's sudden halt had flung Toby onto his side and cast off his blanket. His bloodshot eyes widened upon seeing Kato's weapon approaching his head, and Aliwyn stopped breathing.

"I'll go," Toby stammered. "Just let me off."

Kato didn't lower his dagger. "That's called setting you free. I'm not that stupid."

"Then do what you want…"

"Show me your hands, both of them."

A thousand pins lodged in Aliwyn's throat. Toby extended his forearms along the wooden floorboards. Both hands were empty. A wide gash ran across his right palm like a red stream. He squeezed his eyes shut, and Kato lunged down with his dagger in hand.

"Kato!" Aliwyn cried.

She grabbed his arm, but Kato shook her back. "I'm just checking for weapons."

With his blade pressed against Toby's neck, Kato pulled open the laces of Toby's gambeson. He patted down the man's tunic and searched through the gambeson's inner pockets. Nothing. With his eyes closed, Toby didn't move.

"Aliwyn, get the twine from my belt pouch and tie his wrists behind his back," Kato ordered.

Aliwyn pulled out the rope with shaking hands. God forbid should Toby struggle now. With his dagger still pushed against Toby's neck, Kato pulled the soldier forward from the wagon's railing so she could gather Toby's hands behind his back. His arms were limp and heavy, the sleeves damp. As she tied Toby's wrists together, the blood from his gashed hand smeared onto her own. The ache in her throat grew unbearable.

Kato checked her knot. As he wrapped more rope around Toby's wrists and forearms, he turned and glared at her. "I need to turn him in, but then word will spread about who he is, and Ida will hunt you down. She knows where you live."

With Toby bound, Kato sat back on the pile of firewood, took off his linen cap, and rubbed his carrot-red hair. "I don't know what to do with you two."

"Can you bring me to Little Limber's church?" Aliwyn whispered.

"And give this man a free ride to the sanctuary?" Kato shook his head. "Don't forget, he's a rebel and he's Ransley Boltan's son. His father led the attack on Evelyn's family."

Aliwyn licked her lips. How dare she even ask for a ride to Little Limber? Kato had every right to throw both her and Toby off his cart and leave them to fend for themselves. She searched the surrounding trees with an impulse to pull Toby off and run. But with his ankle injury, he couldn't run.

Did he have any life-threatening wounds? Toby remained on his side with his eyes closed. Kato had flipped the surcoat over the soldier's mouth and chin in his search for weapons. Underneath the surcoat, Toby wore a thickly padded, half-sleeved gambeson over his long-sleeved tunic. The gambeson was opened on either side. She scrutinized his black tunic for tears and hemorrhaging, but only one bloody hole remained of the Vasfian arrow, and the arrowhead itself was gone. This padded jacket must've protected Toby both from the arrow and the vicious dog, and Aliwyn's shoulders slumped with relief.

Kato faced the other two with his eyes always on Toby.

"Walk on, Mils." His hand drooped as he reached behind and took the reins.

The donkey trotted forward, and Aliwyn asked, "Where are we going?"

"The lepers' cabin." Kato massaged his neck. "I have to bring back those two bags there for Garett and Ida. Then I need to feed Mils, and then...I don't know. I need to think."

"Who's there at the leper's cabin?"

"No one. The lepers all leave to beg or do their chores during the day."

The cabin might be the best place to go for a while. Aliwyn crawled back into her original position in the cart and knelt beside the stack of firewood at Kato's feet, where she was within arm's reach of the injured soldier. Sunlight and shadows skirted over them as the cart rolled under bare tree branches. The wagon wheels ground steadily over fallen leaves.

"There's a little chapel connected to the lepers' cabin. Usually no one goes in there, except for Garett's cats." Kato sounded tired. "Problem is, eventually someone is going to recognize Toby. I can pretend not to know him, but Aliwyn, you'll be in danger. There are a lot of lepers; you won't be able to get away."

Aliwyn nodded but kept silent. She needed to escape to a sanctuary, and the leper cabin would only be a brief stop.

The wagon rolled over smoother ground, but Toby's breaths still shook. The acrid scent of blood wafting from his body pulled her from her inner turmoil. She reached to pull the surcoat off his face, but Kato called out, "What are you doing?"

"I'm pulling this down and putting the blanket back on him."

Kato neither spoke nor relaxed his scowl. She dared to do what she said she would. As she straightened the black surcoat back over Toby, he opened his eyes and gazed out the opposite side of the wagon, which was built with widely spaced wooden planks. Blood smeared onto Aliwyn's hand when she brushed past Toby's arm. She grimaced and wiped her hand on one of the loot sacks. The gambeson didn't protect his forearms, and he had lost both gloves. The blood soaking his tattered tunic sleeves wasn't obvious because the cloth was black.

She chewed at her inner cheeks. He had protected her from suffering the same injuries.

Toby's face wrinkled with grief as he stared out the opposite side of the wagon, behind Aliwyn. Finally, when Kato glanced in the same direction, Aliwyn turned around and looked as well.

She could only stand the sight for a heartbeat. Dead men lay scattered all along the riverbank, and Aliwyn spun back around.

"Don't look, don't look," Kato said, averting his own eyes.

She wrapped her arms around her head, but nothing could erase the scene from her mind. The worst of the last rebellion was repeating itself. Struggling not to cry, she drove her fists into both her eyes and held them there. Across from her, Toby sneezed. Aliwyn uncovered her eyes. Toby had turned toward the floorboards as he coughed and sniffled, and his face was red down to his neck.

He must've known many of those dead soldiers. Maybe they had been his friends. The fight in him was extinguished.

Her eyes throbbed. From stopping Edward's attempt on her life to protecting her from Vasfian arrows, Toby differed from his fellow soldiers. He shouldn't face the same fate as his men. The sanctuaries in churches across England welcomed all criminals and offered them time to renounce their illicit ways. Toby's troops had left him to die. His life as a rebel was over.

When he kept coughing into the floorboards, Aliwyn rubbed his upper back. His gambeson had been partially pulled off, and touching the bones of his shoulder blades startled her. His pain became her own, and a shock flashed down her spine.

The only person Toby had asked for upon entering her mill had been Miriam, not Matthew's cousin, Marie. Toby had likely arrived at Miriam's mill to seek her help in crossing the bridge. All the pounding outside her watermill's door, all the shouting and hostility that night—maybe it wouldn't have happened if Edward had been absent. She spread her hand over the faint warmth of his back as the pieces fell into place.

A life for a life. If she sought peace at a sanctuary, she would take this former English rebel with her. After all, if all the Norman knights were condemned for robbing, torturing, and murdering the English in the last decade, not one would be left standing.

Aliwyn pulled the gray linen blanket back over Toby, and the belt Ida had tossed onto the cart came into view. Attached to the belt were his empty sword's sheath, a flattened costrel, and another hand-sized bag. Next to Aliwyn, Kato held onto the reins but faced his passengers with a dull gaze. The donkey walked on its own.

"Did you both tumble through those rapids?" Kato asked. "He's in far worse shape than you are."

"He was holding me. He protected me."

"Really?" Kato held the reins with his teeth as he pulled off his coat and tossed it to Aliwyn. "This is for you," he mumbled before grabbing the reins again. "Sorry, should've given it to you earlier."

Aliwyn reached for the garment but didn't put it on. She wanted to drive Kato's cart, not take his ragged coat. The sun shone over them as they left the forest behind, and the rickety cart trundled over a smooth dirt road. Ahead in the grassy clearing, a large rectangular building with a sloping, thatched roof appeared. Chickens pecked around a fire pit built a safe distance from the main entrance. Two trees with trembling orange foliage stood in the clearing, but no one was there otherwise.

Kato called on his donkey to stop. "The lepers should be all gone. They only return in the early afternoon."

The cart lurched to a halt and Kato stood, pushing on his thighs for support. "Aw, haggards!"

"What?" Aliwyn whispered.

Kato stumbled off the cart's edge. Chickens scattered on either side of him as he limped a few steps toward the fire pit. Then he turned back to the passengers on his cart, his red eyebrows knit with worry.

"Move quick," he whispered. "I think someone's here!"

CHAPTER 11

Moving quickly was impossible with Toby hobbling along. Although Kato was also limping, he braced Toby's arm and pulled him toward what looked like a tiny shack attached to the end of the main building. The shack was little more than several dozen planks nailed together to form a shelter with a crooked door.

"This is the lepers' chapel," Kato said as they arrived before it. "Door's partly fallen off its hinges. Aliwyn, can you open it?"

She removed the wooden plank barring the door shut, lifted the door, and swung it open. As Kato hurried inside with Toby, she searched the clearing again but saw no one.

"Kato," she whispered, "who did you see?"

Aliwyn was about to go inside the chapel when a striped, gray cat darted by her legs. She gasped and jumped aside.

"It's all right," Kato said from within. "Just Garett's cat. C'mon in."

Aliwyn stepped into the windowless room, and the cool shadows enveloped her. The small chapel was long enough for a man to lie down in. At the opposite end of the room, the dim light revealed a few rocks and a small wooden cross standing upon the stones. A scattering of straw covered the dirt floor.

Kato lowered Toby to sit in the far corner of the chapel. He pulled out loops of twine from his belt pouch and bound the soldier's ankles. Toby kept his gaze on the ground, and his shaking breaths filled the silence.

"Who did you see outside, Kato?" Aliwyn repeated, her heart racing.

"Not a person, but I saw a horse's saddle by the building, so I thought we had visitors. It wasn't there this morning." He scratched the side of his head. "Or maybe it has been there all along. Sorry if I scared you."

Kato had no reason to live with the lepers, especially when he could contract the disease himself. But it wasn't the time to ask questions.

Kato crossed his arms as he studied Toby. "Let's go talk outside, Aliwyn. I have an idea."

She staggered after him but glanced behind. Toby slid against the wall with his wrists bound behind him and couldn't straighten himself. He fell onto his side with a shuddering gasp, and Aliwyn's chest seized. His belt slipped from her arms and tumbled onto the ground, but she didn't notice.

From outside the chapel's door, Kato watched her approach with his brows drawn. Perhaps he regretted saving her and Toby and getting pulled into this mess. She didn't blame him, but she still needed his help. And his cart.

"What's your idea?" She stopped beside him.

"I don't want to stay in this leper cabin, so I'm going to pack up and leave with you. We'll take Toby on my cart and turn him over to the Norman authorities at Barton-Upon-Humber. The big Saint Peter's Church there always has Norman knights guarding it." Kato rubbed his neck again. "Toby'll get arrested, and you'll find shelter in the church so Ida can't catch you. Stay there forty days and she'll get over her howling fit. Sound good?"

Aliwyn stiffened. During the last rebellion, the Normans had mutilated and hung the English rebels they didn't bother to ransom. She never wanted to see such atrocities again.

"Kato, the sanctuary at Saint Peter's Church exists for everyone, regardless of his or her crimes." She faced his deepening frown and dared to continue. "If Toby enters the sanctuary, it doesn't mean he's set free."

She didn't mention that the forty days often gave the outlaws time to negotiate a less violent punishment, such as exile.

Kato shook his head. "I can't do this to Evelyn. I must turn him in. I only lied to save you."

"I understand, Kato." Aliwyn kept a steady voice. "Thank you for what you've done for me. What you suggested sounds...fine."

It didn't sound fine. She would have to secretly move Toby into Saint Peter's once they arrived at Barton-Upon-Humber. It was a well-populated portside town with a lively marketplace to disappear into, but her plan would work best if Kato didn't linger around the church.

"Where will you go, after we turn Toby in?" she asked. "Will Reiya let you stay with her tribe?"

"No," the redhead muttered. "I'm not part of her tribe or any other tribe. Otherwise, I wouldn't be here. I used to wander around the port towns."

He didn't seem keen on giving details. What if the Vasfians had ostracized Kato for some crime? At least he had no obligation to bring her back to the warriors who blamed her for Toby's escape.

Kato cleared his throat. "I plan to find Norman once we get to Barton, but don't worry about me. I'll go pack some things and feed my donkey, and we'll get going. Watch Toby in the meantime, all right?"

Toby coughed in the background. The thought of having to watch him in this pitiful state made Aliwyn's stomach clench. If she gave him food and water, Kato probably wouldn't approve. She'd have to wait until the redhead was out of sight. Glancing at Kato, Aliwyn unfurled the large coat he had given her and put it on.

He began to leave, then walked a few steps backward, unlatched a water pouch from his belt, and handed it to Aliwyn.

"You can share this with Toby." He kept his gaze lowered.

She caught a hint of pity in his gaze, and she smiled at his hazel eyes and thin face. He was nowhere near as ruthless as Matthew. "Thank you for the water, Kato. Why are you doing so much for me?"

"In the past, many strangers have helped me. I thought I'd help you, too."

Kato walked away with an uneven gait, and Aliwyn stared at her dirty toes. She had just lied to him, too. Once they arrived at Saint Peter's Church, he would realize that she had never agreed to have Toby arrested.

She turned back to Toby and approached him. Her feet came across his fallen belt. A thin wooden rod with holes protruded from the belt's drawstring satchel.

A recorder?

She bent and pulled it out for a better look. Although she had always loved the sound of recorders, she couldn't play a complete song without feeling faint. Growing up, she had let Aelfric keep the only recorder they had, accepting that she would never do the instrument justice.

Aliwyn rotated the smooth body of the recorder between her fingers, and two carved crucifixes came into view. Her mouth fell open; this was Aelfric's recorder. She turned the recorder around and around with her fingers until chills rained down her back. There was no mistake. Miriam had whittled the object herself and engraving these familiar crosses had been her final addition. Aliwyn squinted at the delicate knife marks and shook her head.

Why would Toby have Aelfric's recorder, whereas Matthew couldn't find it despite searching the battle site?

"Where did you get this?" Her cry filled the small space.

Toby had been watching her with half-closed eyes. "He left it behind with a friend of mine."

"What? Why would he do that?"

"Aelfric lived in my manor for a month." The soldier stifled a cough. "He was my servant. We were friends, or so I thought."

Aliwyn bristled. "Friends? How is that possible?"

"My men found him washed up along the banks of my manor's moat. He was injured with a festering eye. He said bandits had attacked him. I took him in and treated his wounds, and he became my servant."

"I...I can't believe this. You're lying. You stole this from him!"

"Aliwyn, I'm not lying." Toby tried to settle his head on a stone on the ground. "Before he betrayed me, Aelfric had left his recorder with another soldier. Aelfric said that he didn't...didn't deserve anything with a crucifix on it."

Aliwyn's eyes rolled in the dimness, her face burning. She stuffed Aelfric's recorder into her front tunic pocket, whirled around, and marched for the entrance. Toby and Aelfric once talked and smiled together? Maybe once shared a swig of ale? This was too strange, too strange. And she never expected Aelfric to be a traitor, someone who had backstabbed the person who rescued him.

Kato had returned and was standing by the opening. He watched Aliwyn with his lips pressed into a thin line. Several loops of rope hung from his bent arm, and his other hand gripped a dagger.

"I came back 'cause I heard yelling."

Aliwyn eyed his dagger and swallowed. "S-sorry. Toby wasn't trying to escape."

Kato sheathed his weapon. "So, I didn't mean to eavesdrop, but Toby is telling the truth."

"What?" Aliwyn walked up to him, frowning. "How would you know?"

"'Cause...I was there when Toby took Aelfric into his manor." He shuffled his feet. "For several weeks, Aelfric pretended to be helpful, but he was actually spying on the Boltans to help Evelyn. Evelyn told me all this afterward."

Aliwyn stared into space. Aelfric had earned the Boltans' trust. So that's how he had come back to the mill wearing a new black tunic she didn't recognize. That's how he knew the Boltans had captured Matthew.

"Are you still going to give Toby water?" Kato asked.

"I'll do it," she whispered.

With Kato following, Aliwyn shuffled toward where Toby lay. Her eyes were blurring. She had wondered who had tended to Aelfric's eye, as the eye socket was a difficult place to debride and clean. Had Toby not treated it, she might not have seen Aelfric for that last time back at their mill, alive and strong.

From fabricating their relationship as siblings to spying on the Boltan household, her childhood love was not the man she had believed he was. And she had to stop thinking of him as her beloved. Aelfric had never loved her back in the romantic sense.

Aliwyn couldn't look Toby in the eye as she knelt before him. His mercy for a wounded fellow Englishman had been met with a horrible outcome. She was ashamed without knowing why, and sorrow over the events surrounding Aelfric's last days made her chest ache.

Kato pulled Toby to a sitting position, and she poured water between the soldier's injured lips. His hair was a matted mess, and his forlorn gaze locked onto hers.

Unable to focus, Aliwyn squeezed the pouch. Water gushed over Toby's nose and made him break out in a violent cough. She jerked back and corked the pouch. Stuttering an apology, she wiped his wet chin with her sleeve and rubbed his chest to stop the coughing.

Hang in there, Toby. I'm getting you out of here.

Kato knelt and pulled out a handkerchief from his pocket. He was about to wrap it around Toby's mouth when he stuffed it back into a different pocket. Old bloodstains covered the handkerchief, and Aliwyn gasped.

"Oh no, Kato, your poisoning. I never gave you more antidote!"

The redhead found a clean handkerchief and wrapped it around Toby's mouth. "Well, I left before you could come back from your garden. The lepers keep dried medicine plants in bags."

"Can I see them?" Aliwyn asked. "I'll prepare the antidote."

"Yea, but I'll have to unlock the cabin and dig up the right bag. It's a mess in there."

"Th-that's all right. I'll come with you. We can watch the chapel from the cabin's door."

Kato knit his brows. "Y'know what? You're right. Let's close the chapel. Us crowdin' around here will just draw attention."

He extended a hand to help her stand. His glove was gone, and she gulped at the sight of the freckles sprinkling his hand. But Kato had only treated her with kindness since they'd met. Aliwyn chewed on her lip and began to understand Aelfric's impatience with her fear. Under different circumstances, had Aliwyn not lost her sister or heard about redheads making child sacrifices and slaking their altars with blood, she would be Kato's friend.

She forced herself to take his hand.

With a smile, Kato pulled her up and adjusted the coat around her shoulders.

"There's probably something dry you can wear in the cabin. And we should fix up your shoulder. Let's go."

Aliwyn glanced at Toby several times as she walked to the shack's exit. It pained her to see him. His chest heaved with aborted coughs as he hung his head, but as she stepped into the sunlight, he looked up and said something in a muffled voice.

Aliwyn couldn't understand, but Kato said, "Aliwyn, Toby's asking if you found Emma."

Her eyes grew misty at the mention of the girl's name. "N-no. I didn't."

"Norman told me about a certain Emma falling into the river." Kato frowned. "But I didn't see her by the shoreline, and Ida and Garett would've said something if they had found a child."

The chapel's door squealed on its remaining hinge as Kato closed it. Toby's face flushed above the cloth gag, his eyes downcast in the fading light. Maybe he was crying; she couldn't tell. His grimace seared into her memory and intensified the ache between her ribs. If only she could've given him better news about Emma. Kato shoved the crooked door into its doorframe with a thud, and Toby was out of sight.

The redhead barred the door shut with the wooden plank and scowled at his boots. "All right, follow me."

"We should look for Emma." Aliwyn dragged her feet after Kato as they left the chapel.

"We'll look for her on the way to Barton-Upon-Humber."

Lost in thought, Aliwyn almost collided with him when he turned around and told her to wait. She had followed Kato back to the sunny clearing. Within arm's reach was his donkey, still hitched to the cart. The beast had a pleasant face and dark, charming eyes; she smiled at the way it looked at her and flicked its ears. Any distraction from her problems was welcome.

"This is Mils." Kato smirked as he undid the straps tethering the donkey. "He belongs to Norman, but I think of him as my donkey now."

He finished untethering Mils and beckoned Aliwyn to follow as he led the donkey toward the mud-and-straw cabin. A water bucket, a pile of hay, and parsnips awaited Mils a short distance from the cabin's entrance.

As she walked behind Kato, a few chickens pecking in their path clucked and scurried ahead. One darted past the leather saddle resting on the ground, the one which had prompted Kato to take precautions earlier. Aliwyn's hands quivered upon seeing chickens that resembled her own, and she longed to cuddle one in her arms. She followed Kato so closely that her cheek almost touched his bony shoulders.

He stopped beside the saddle and looked around the yard for the owner, but no one else appeared.

"Aliwyn." He sounded serious as they began walking again. "What exactly happened before you fell into the river with Toby?"

She told Kato the whole story, beginning with Matthew's arrival and ending with how Toby had grabbed her and jumped with her into the ravine. Kato remained silent, but his frown deepened when he heard how the Vasfians had mistakenly assumed she and Toby worked together. Finally, Aliwyn mentioned Toby seemed to know Miriam, her mentor.

"He even asked me if I was Miriam's relative," she added softly.

"Did you answer him?"

"No…"

They stopped at the main door of the cabin. Kato released his donkey, who ambled further to drink from the bucket by the door.

He rummaged through his pockets. "Well, if Toby thinks you're Miriam's family, that's probably why he's been protectin' you this whole time."

Aliwyn said nothing, but she agreed. Kato unlocked the padlock hanging from the cabin's door and swung it open.

Inside, a dozen straw mattresses circled a central hearth. A large table with bags stuffed underneath stood to the right of the beds, and sacks lined the perimeter of the spacious room. Rushes and dried lavender covered the dirt floor and sunlight filtered through small square holes in the walls.

Aliwyn held her breath as she entered. The room was stuffy with a disturbing mix of scents—smoke, lavender, and an occasional waft of pungent goat smell, but there were no goats in sight.

Kato hobbled to the table, but Aliwyn stood in the doorframe and hesitated to follow. The stained stockings scattered around the mattresses made her itchy all over.

"Kato," she called out. "Why are you here at all? Didn't you leave with Matthew and Evelyn?"

Kato's shoulders slumped, and he turned around. "I did leave with them, but he forced me to stay here."

"Who forced you?" Aliwyn asked. "Was...was it Matthew?"

Kato shuffled the straws scattered before at his feet. "Yea. I was asleep on a cart, and so were Evelyn, Marie, and Norman. Matthew pulled me off and shoved me against the door. That door." He glanced at the cabin door behind Aliwyn. "All the bishop's soldiers saw. No one cared. Then they all left."

Aliwyn clenched her fists. Even if Matthew wanted nothing to do with Kato, abandoning the redhead at a leper colony was downright cruel. So much for thinking they had found common ground last night. Matthew was a Norman soldier, and they had a reputation for arrogance.

Kato turned back to the table and pulled out a bag from underneath.

"Most Norman men I've met are like that, though," he said. "Anyway, Matthew's not all bad. He returned to your mill to get you, right? You said so."

Aliwyn looked away. Matthew's visit had done little good for her, or him. Hopefully, he hadn't irritated the Vasfians further and gotten himself hurt. As Kato pulled open the drawstring bags, searching for herbs, she leaned against the cabin's doorframe and watched the chapel. In the clearing, insects flew in the sun, chickens scratched at the dirt, and sparrows hopped in the grass.

"Wait," Kato said from behind her. "Didn't you say Matthew stayed with you the whole night? So, he knows you didn't free Toby. Don't you think he'd convince Reiya that you're innocent?"

Aliwyn bit the inside of her cheek. Last night, Matthew's first reaction to Reiya's request for help was to blame her and her tribe for losing Toby. Diplomacy wasn't in his bones.

"I'm not sure the Vasfians will believe Matthew. Most of them don't even speak English or French." She lowered her voice. "And you know that Matthew doesn't like the Vasfians. He has probably left their tribe already."

Kato seemed to think this over as he looked through a few more bags. As his ginger brows knit into a single line, Aliwyn wanted to say something reassuring. "But your idea of going to Saint Peter's Church is good. If Ida or Reiya ever wanted to come after me, the church is a good place to hide."

Her throat was tight. She didn't deserve all this help, and she couldn't pay him back.

"Then we'll take it one day at a time," Kato said. "It's how we all have to live, anyway."

He handed her the bag of medicinal plants along with a piece of bread. Aliwyn shoved the bread into her mouth, but she refused his additional offerings of stained tunics and stockings. She'd rather be wet than wear anything the lepers wore.

As Aliwyn picked out satchels of dried herbs and jars of ointment, Kato returned to the large central table and unfurled a green square of cloth. He reached underneath into the various sacks for apples, walnuts, and biscuits and dropped them onto the cloth.

"So...I first met Toby before this revolt began," Kato said.

"What? Really?"

Kato pulled clean bandage strips from below the table. "I was on the streets with some other beggars. One of the girls with me was named Emma, and she had curly black hair."

Aliwyn almost choked on her food. "Emma? The same Emma as the one who fell—"

"Yea, I think so." Kato dipped his chin. "Norman described the girl Matthew knocked down, and it sounds like the Emma I knew. She was my friend, too."

Hoofbeats were approaching outside, but Aliwyn didn't notice as Kato continued the story.

"About a year ago, Emma got into big trouble when stealing from a shop. The shopkeeper beat her and was goin' to cut off her hands." Kato pulled together the corners of the square cloth and tied them together. "She was screaming and crying, but a young man and a pretty lady traveling with him came by. They were both riding horses. The man paid the merchant a good sum of money so that he would free Emma. Then the rider carried Emma away with him 'cause she was hurt. I don't know who that lady was, but guess who the man..."

Kato's voice faded as the sound of the horse hoofbeats grew louder. The horse was approaching the building from behind; Aliwyn couldn't see it from where she squatted by the opened door. She froze, and Kato's grave expression made her anxiety soar. As she hurried to shove her remaining bread into a belt pouch, Kato rushed to her side and pulled her up by the forearm. Quickly but quietly, he closed the cabin door behind her.

"The lepers are back?" Aliwyn whispered, her eyes wide.

"Can't be." Kato bolted the door shut with a wooden plank. "They don't come back this early and none of 'em have a horse."

He beckoned her to follow him toward the large table. Ducking, he retrieved a dagger enclosed in its sheath. Aliwyn caught her breath. Underneath the table was a basket filled with daggers and swords.

"Stay here for now, but take this," he whispered as he handed her the dagger. He then limped over the rushes on the ground. "I have no idea who's here."

Aliwyn gripped the leather sheath of the dagger, her heart racing. The horse's hooves had come to a halt right outside. Kato stopped at one of the small windows and stood on his toes to peer outside. When his worried expression didn't ease, Aliwyn ran to his side and strained to see through the window herself. But she was shorter and could barely see the figure who wore a hooded cape and was tethering a gray horse to the tree.

"Hello?" the stranger called out—it was a woman's voice. "Is anyone here?"

CHAPTER 12

Kato jerked back from the window, ran for the door, and yanked it open.

"Blue!" he shouted. Bright sunshine shone on his beaming face.

Why would anyone be named after a color? Aliwyn stepped for the door, scowling, when the hooded woman dashed through the entryway and wrapped her arms around Kato.

"Finally, I found you!" she cried.

As Kato laughed and returned her embrace, the hood hiding the woman's face slipped back. It revealed her strands of brown hair and dark eyelashes.

"Blue?" Aliwyn whispered. The newcomer was Evelyn.

Aliwyn stood unnoticed by the wall, watching Kato and Evelyn from the side. The brunette pulled back from Kato and smiled. Her face glowed in a soft and rosy peach, and her charming smile was radiant. Aliwyn's stomach flipped, and she looked away.

"Who brought you here?" Kato asked.

"Who brought me?" Evelyn raised an eyebrow. "I brought myself. I was here earlier but this place was empty, so I took my horse to find water."

"Oh, so that was your saddle outside?"

"Yes. Actually, both the saddle and the mare belong to His Excellency. The mare's name is Silver."

A dazed smirk remained on Kato's face, and Aliwyn rolled her eyes. Had Aelfric once stared at Evelyn the same way? As Aliwyn shivered in her damp clothes, the possibility of Evelyn finding Toby just a few arm lengths away sent prickly heat crawling up her chest. But what could she do to make Evelyn leave? Aliwyn picked at her nails, bristling for an opportunity.

"I can't believe you came here alone, Blue." Kato's smile faded. "The bishop—uh, I mean His Excellency—he doesn't bother sending guards around here 'cause we're so far from town. The lepers told me there have been many robberies nearby."

"Well, I got here just fine. Even if Matthew forced you to stay here, he can't stop me from coming to get you."

"Get me?"

"Yes. Come with me to Barton-Upon-Humber. We can live in Saint Peter's Church for a while. I don't care how angry Matthew will be." Evelyn reached up and adjusted Kato's linen cap. "I told His Excellency's soldiers I was coming to get you."

Just brilliant. Aliwyn gnashed her teeth. If Kato left with Evelyn, who would give her and Toby a ride?

"And the soldiers let you leave Saint Peter's?" Kato asked.

"Not really. But they couldn't stop me either. Most of the soldiers had already left for Myton. They hope to catch the Boltans there." Evelyn smirked. "I snuck out when Norman got into the communion wine and got drunk."

"Oh," Kato said, suppressing a chuckle before his worry returned. "Blue, I'm happy to see you. But coming here alone...that was dangerous."

"I care for the people I love. That doesn't change when things get dangerous." She took out a jar sealed with a cork and raised her hand for Kato's face. "Before I forget, I asked a priest at Saint Peter's to prepare an antidote for you."

She smiled, stroking the young man's cheek, and the two continued to murmur to each other with blushing faces and occasional giggles. A crumbling sadness stole over Aliwyn. So much for her eagerness to help Kato recover from his poisoning; she wasn't needed anymore. This couple was happy together—a happiness she had once hoped for but might never see.

It might as well be this way. Kato never owed her a cart ride or any other help. Once he and Evelyn left, Aliwyn would secretly free Toby and help him hobble to Little Limber, where no Norman knights patrolled. But the two of them wouldn't survive if the lepers or the Normans caught them walking in the woods. Aliwyn glanced at the wall Toby was bound behind and steadied herself. He hadn't abandoned her when the Vasfian arrows rained down last night, and she wouldn't abandon him now.

"Why don't you two leave right away?" Her voice boomed above the other two's.

"Aliwyn?" Evelyn whirled around, her straight brown hair swaying over her shoulders. "Oh my goodness! It's really you!"

Her smile was full of concern, but Aliwyn kept a stone face.

"Why are you wet?" Evelyn asked. "And...you poor thing. What happened? Is Matthew here?"

"No," Aliwyn muttered.

"But he said he was going to get you and take you to Barton's."

"He did come, and he stayed overnight," Aliwyn stammered. "But the Vasfians somehow became angry at me. Just angry at me, not your cousin Matthew. They started attacking me, and I fell into the river. Don't worry, Matthew didn't."

Aliwyn curled her toes as Evelyn's breaths grew shallow and rapid.

"Why would the Vasfian people become so angry with you?" Evelyn asked.

"I don't know. But I'm sure they didn't hurt Matthew."

Aliwyn's endless lies coiled around her neck like a slithering snake, and she struggled to breathe.

"But if Matthew's not with you, then I don't know where he is," Evelyn said. "He hadn't returned to his troops at Barton-Upon-Humber when I left. And his wounds...he's barely recovered since the Boltans captured him, but he insisted on going back for you."

Aliwyn swallowed several times. "M-maybe Matthew stayed out all night looking for me. He must be close to my mill. You two should go back and see."

"All *three* of us are leaving." Evelyn frowned. "We're not leaving you here."

"You should. I've caused enough problems."

"What problems?" Evelyn's face relaxed, and she smiled. "You're Aelfric's sister. I've wanted to meet you."

"But I'm not his sister! I don't know why he lied to you!"

The hatefulness in Aliwyn's voice startled her, but the other woman remained calm.

"I know you and Aelfric are not related by blood, but he told me you're his adopted little sister, and Miriam is your adoptive mum. That's not a lie, is it?" Evelyn asked. "He spoke about you often, always lovingly. He said you were a good listener, always eager to help, and made the best turnip stew in the world. He cared for you very much, Aliwyn."

And she cared about him too, liar or not. Aliwyn braced herself against a crashing wave of grief.

"He said all those things about me?" She couldn't look away from Evelyn's vivid blue eyes. Was this why Kato had nicknamed her "Blue"?

"Yes, my dear Aliwyn. I have no doubt he loved you."

As a sister. Aliwyn hung her head. She was too tired to argue she wasn't Aelfric's sibling. What was the point when she could never marry him now?

Evelyn continued, "When this is all over, His Excellency will give Matthew the land he inherited from his father. I'll go live with him, and you can come live with us."

"But I'm not Aelfric. You don't have to be so nice to me."

Evelyn approached Aliwyn and took the ragged girl's hand. Aliwyn fought her instinct to draw back.

"Kindness isn't bought," said Evelyn. "Otherwise, there would be no more kindness in the world. My mother taught me that life is most meaningful when we can help others."

Kato nodded, his hands on his hips. "Aelfric was a hero, the way he helped Blue's family."

"He was." Evelyn's eyes brightened with unshed tears. "I'll always remember what he did."

"And you know the orange box I have?" Kato asked. "When I was locked up in the Boltans' manor, a man told me it was the antidote I needed and slipped it into my belt pouch. I was too groggy to see who it was, but he sounded like Aelfric.”

Aliwyn struggled for words. Kato and Evelyn were kind people, but if Evelyn knew Aliwyn had covered for one of the men who had murdered her family, dragged Kato into the same lies, and had hidden the criminal next door, what would she think? Aliwyn squeezed her eyes shut. She had already betrayed Evelyn’s goodwill. She couldn’t accept any more of her kindness.

Evelyn gasped when Aliwyn jerked her hand free.

“I can take care of myself,” Aliwyn said. “You and Kato should leave for my watermill. I hope you find Matthew.”

“All right, so we’ll leave Aliwyn here.” Kato’s voice carried a nervous edge. “I’ll ready the cart for you and me, Blue. And pack some bread and goat cheese.”

“Goat cheese?” Evelyn grimaced. “That’ll give you terrible breath!”

“Aww, but I love it. Just eat it with me. Then you can’t tell that my breath smells.”

He chuckled and hobbled toward a stack of crates in the corner. A smirk remained on Evelyn’s face, but it wrinkled with unease as she turned back to Aliwyn.

“Perhaps you’re angry with me?” she asked.

“W-what?” Aliwyn took a step back.

“I want to apologize for abandoning you at the watermill,” Evelyn said. “A while back, my parents told His Excellency about Earl Ralph de Gael’s plans to rebel. His Excellency remains grateful to my family. When his knight met us at the watermill, he wanted us to follow him immediately.”

“Don’t say sorry.” Aliwyn shook her head. “I wasn’t angry. Please, just go. Go.”

“But Aliwyn, I can’t leave you here in...”

Her voice faded. A dog’s bark echoed in the distance, growing louder, and Aliwyn tensed. She looked back at the meadow to see a black canine speeding toward them alongside a hooded leper. She stiffened all over. It was hard to be certain, but the leper appeared to be Ida. If Ida even mentioned Toby’s name, Aliwyn’s lie would be exposed.

"Don't be afraid of them." Evelyn strode forward. "My parents built this place, and the lepers here know me."

"Hey, Kato!" The approaching leper yelled in a raspy voice. An oversized hood hid his face. "Stop flirting! We need that cart!"

Aliwyn almost collapsed with relief. The leper wasn't Ida but an old man. His canine halted by the cabin's door, tail wagging, and he hurried to follow.

"What's the rush?" Kato asked, scowling. He limped back to Evelyn's side with a bag of food in one hand.

"Hehe...actually, tell me first where you found these young ladies?"

The way the man spoke made Aliwyn's skin crawl, but Evelyn stepped up as he came to the door.

"I'm Evelyn Marcotte." She put her hands on her hips.

The leper leaned forward as if to examine Evelyn's features. Then he jerked back, pulling at his hood to hide more of his face.

"Beg your pardon, Lady Marcotte." His voice faded into a whimper. "Pardon my rudeness, please. My name's Osgar. My eyesight's going, y'see. Couldn't tell it was you."

"It's all right, Osgar. But why such a hurry for the cart?"

"Well, it's to help carry some injured Vasfian folk we found in the forest."

"The Vasfians?" Kato cried. "What happened to them?"

"I heard that some of Ransley Boltan's men were ridin' horses and ambushed them out of nowhere. Now, I don't speak a word of Vasfian, but a female ginger head told me that in English. She be payin' us handsomely for some help."

"Did any of Boltan's men get captured?" Evelyn asked.

"Ehh...I think some of 'em died. But their leader rode off."

Aliwyn and Kato exchanged glances; the female ginger head Osgar spoke of could only be Reiya. Her tribe had clashed with the Boltans after all, but the Vasfians didn't strike a decisive victory.

"Was my cousin Matthew with the Vasfian group?" Evelyn's voice quivered.

"Naw, not yer handsome cou—" Osgar scratched his chin. "Actually, my eyesight's so bad, I can't really say. There were many bloody men, though."

Evelyn tilted back her head, her wide eyes searching the sky. "Kato, let's go. I pray to God Matthew's all right."

"Yes, it's urgent. You should all go." Aliwyn's tongue stuck to her mouth when all eyes turned to her. She grabbed Kato's forearm. "But I need one last thing from Kato. He'll be back in a moment."

Aliwyn shied from Kato's wide-eyed stare as she pulled him out the door and toward the back of the cabin. The bag of provisions swung from his other hand.

"What?" he asked. "What is it?"

Chickens scattered left and right from their pounding feet. They circled to the garden behind the building, where a cat napped under the clothes rack and withering crops undulated in the breeze. Aliwyn stopped, panting, and let go of Kato. The afternoon sun beat down on his sweaty forehead, and his look of concern made her shake.

"I just want to tell you…I know where Little Limber is," she said. "They have a church, and I'll head that way. But please keep Toby a secret until tonight, so I can get there first and take shelter. Please."

How awful it was to deceive someone this compassionate. She was not heading to Little Limber alone, of course. By the time Kato returned from helping the Vasfians, she'd be long gone with Toby.

"Fine. I'll do my best. Take some food." Kato handed her the bag he had been carrying. For an instant, his expression softened with a smile. "You were nice to me despite how I look. It means a lot to me. Good luck."

Aliwyn's lips twitched, and she said nothing.

Evelyn appeared at the corner of the building, frowning. Aliwyn turned and sprinted through the muddy garden.

"Aliwyn!" Evelyn cried. "Where are you going?"

"Oh, just nature calling!" Kato yelled back. "She couldn't hold it anymore!"

Aliwyn couldn't resist a grin. His excuse quieted Evelyn down, and no one followed her. Aliwyn wedged the food bag under one arm and gripped the dagger in her other hand. Kato's clear, lively voice echoed in her mind.

Once everyone deserted the cabin, she would return for Toby.

Chapter 13

It was a tiring climb uphill, but Aliwyn soon reached a height where she could watch the activity around the cabin. Here, many trees had been cut for firewood and only saplings remained. Lepers came and went in the distance, carrying firewood and bags of stripped items. They huddled in circles and divided the clothing and weapons they had taken from the dead. Others hung up washed clothes and fed their chickens. No one entered the shack, but someone always remained in the vicinity.

As time passed, Aliwyn grew jittery with impatience. It looked like stripping the dead was more profitable than begging today. How long before Toby made a sound and someone discovered him? Her head spun with hunger, and she forced herself to eat the food Kato had given her.

Loneliness made the wait unbearably long. Not since Miriam had died five months earlier had Aliwyn felt so alone.

She shed the coat Kato had given her and dressed her shoulder wound, which was fortunately only skin deep. Her deceptive ways with Kato and his last words troubled her. After all, his appearance *did* bother her. Her family had raised her to scorn the pagan Vasfians, who had murdered their beloved priest and left his body in the river supplying their village. Her disdain had only grown since the Mehi tribe had almost killed her. She couldn't dissociate Kato's striking red hair from those feelings, no matter how helpful he had been.

Aliwyn's shoulders grew heavy as she rebandaged her feet. She struggled to dissolve her feelings of discomfort toward Kato, but they remained rooted within her.

Her head hummed with fatigue. With the leper cabin always in her peripheral view, she trekked through the forest in hopes of finding Emma, but there were no signs of her. Lepers continued to circle the cabin downhill, and her dread for Toby's survival choked her. He needed to enter a sanctuary so she could tend to his wounds properly. Once he found shelter, she'd talk to him about his time with Miriam and Aelfric, and she'd have forty days in the church to plot her way back home.

Hopefully, Little Limber's church wouldn't be crammed like the ones around York had been several winters ago.

When her eyes crossed from exhaustion, Aliwyn sat in a patch of sunshine by a stream and cupped the refreshing water into her mouth. The moment she leaned against a tree and closed her eyes, she was asleep.

THE DEAFENING DRUM OF horse hooves shook her back to awareness. Before she could move, men on horseback sped past her hiding spot on their way uphill. A horse's piercing neigh echoed like a trumpet as the clopping hooves faded.

Aliwyn rubbed her bleary eyes. She was still alone. The sun was setting, and the forest was damp and dark. Goodness, how long had she been sleeping? All her plans from earlier that day spilled back into her mind, and she scrambled to her feet.

A cold wind swept through the trees, carrying the pungent smell of smoke and rotten eggs. Down the hill, a column of smoke rose from the clearing, and her heart lodged in her throat. The cabin had caught fire while she slept. Orange flames licked at one end of the straw-thatched roof. No one appeared to throw buckets of water onto the building. The lepers' chickens were gone, and all their clothing had been pulled from the drying racks.

Aliwyn was all too familiar with sights like this from the previous rebellion. Looters must've set fire to the building and stolen everything—maybe they were the horse riders who had passed her earlier. And those robbers were nearby.

Chills raced down her back, but she fought her reflex to run and hide. Unless Toby had been discovered, he was still bound and gagged in the shack. The fire would soon burn him alive, and she had to get him out. Her legs shook, but she gripped the dagger Kato had given her and steadied herself. With one last glance at the woods around her, she sped downhill with her feet flying over the leaves.

Aliwyn darted out of the forest and shouted every name she could think of. No one responded, and torrents of black smoke stung her eyes as she neared the building. Tongues of bright fire crackled through the wall's mud-and-straw bricks. She covered her nose with her coat sleeve, cringing at the heinous smell as she dreaded finding someone injured or dead. But the grassy plain was empty.

She circled to the cabin door, which was open. Inside, soaring heat and smoke blurred her view of the straw mattresses. Sparks showered down from the roof, but no one appeared from within.

What looked like tiny black pebbles littered the doorway. A few hissed as they erupted into flames. The edge of the spreading fire danced over the scattered black substance, and Aliwyn held her breath. These must be the Boltans' strange fire pellets. She had never seen anything quite like them.

How long before the shack caught on fire?

Covered in a cold sweat, she sheathed her weapon and ran for the shack's crooked door. She eyed the deserted clearing one more time before throwing off the wooden plank barring it shut. Grabbing the door, she lifted it and swung it aside.

Toby knelt at the entryway with his back turned to her. Ropes bound his hands and feet, and fresh blood stained the twine around his wrists. He strained to turn and look at her, his bloodshot eyes flashing.

Aliwyn frowned at the blood around his wrists and tugged off the gag cloth. "What are you doing?"

"It's just you?" he croaked.

"Just me."

Aliwyn knelt behind him. The injuries around his wrists were only superficial ones because of the rope, which was shredding. Toby had been rubbing the twine against the nails of the door to break free.

"I'm letting you go." She pulled out the dagger Kato had given her.

At the sound of her blade being drawn, Toby fell onto his side and rolled onto his back. Aliwyn flinched when she saw his face—streaked with dirt and blood from the many reopened cuts. His sunken eyes bore into hers as he bared his teeth.

"I said I'm letting you go!" she shouted.

Toby's head fell back, his chest heaving. His hands were still tied behind him. Rancid smoke hung in the cramped space, and heat rose from the other side of the wall. Toby's reaction made Aliwyn squirm, but she had already come this far to free him. She crawled to where he lay with his knees bent and sawed at the ropes, holding his bloody ankle to protect it from her blade.

The sound of their panting echoed in the dark. Aliwyn could hardly hold her knife steady.

"Dear Heavens," Toby murmured. "What was he thinking?"

"Who?"

"Ed. He used the compound to start this fire."

The compound. He must mean those black, stinky rocks in his family's wagons and within the leper's doorway. Toby had told Matthew that the rocks were used to start fires. Many questions crowded into her mind, but it wasn't the time to talk. The rope shredded, and Aliwyn tore the remnants from around Toby's ankles. As he struggled to sit, she hooked her arm around his elbow and pulled him up. Blood surrounded the black arrow hole in his padded jacket. Though the gambeson had saved him, the arrow had taken its toll.

As soon as he stood, the soldier pulled away and hobbled for the exit. His wrists were still bound behind him, and Aliwyn bit her lip as she hurried to follow. Not even a glance of appreciation? As she caught up to him by the entrance, Toby stopped and turned back to the burning building.

Smoke with the stench of rotten eggs billowed out in a wide column. The orange evening sun blazed on his worried and sweaty face. He lowered his head, panting, as Aliwyn circled behind him. She began cutting at the ropes around his wrists.

"Why did you come back?" he asked softly.

"I...Why did you save me from the Vasfians?"

"On that bridge, I prayed I wouldn't die. I swore to do as much good as I could if I survived." He pulled his wrists apart as the twine wore thin. "And there were other reasons, but never mind them."

The rope snapped. With his hands freed, Toby spun around and wrenched the dagger from Aliwyn. "But I never knew you were Aelfric's sister. Adopted or not." He snarled and pointed the glinting blade at her face.

Aliwyn gasped. Toby had overheard her conversations with Evelyn and Kato. She stumbled backward and fell, but he advanced on her. The blazing firelight cast shadows below his furrowed brows.

"I don't want anyone calling Aelfric a hero! Saving him was the biggest mistake of my life. He's the reason I lost my soldiers, my friends! After all I did for him..."

Aliwyn tried to stand, but terror melted her limbs like wax. She stared at the weapon he had stolen from her. The more her senses screamed danger, the more paralyzed she became.

"I wanted revenge. I wanted to hurt the people he loved as much as he hurt me." His voice cracking, Toby moved the blade ever closer.

Aliwyn's eyes blurred until she could barely see, and sobs racked her body.

Suddenly, he withdrew his arm. "Get away from me!"

She pushed to her feet and sprinted with her ragged coat flying, too terrified to check if he was following. Toby's words consumed her, and his voice echoed in her head like the chant of a thousand demons. Aliwyn gagged as the hot breath of the fire rose through her hair with its monstrous stench.

If only she had heeded Kato's warning that Toby was still Ransley Boltan's son. He was entrenched in a past that made him hate her.

Tears formed cool streaks on her burning face as her hand fell over her empty dagger sheath. She had lied to her allies and sacrificed the freedom to go home for someone who wanted her dead. Her legs aching with exhaustion, Aliwyn staggered toward the forest with her heart slamming against her ribs. She was a wretched fool. If Toby attacked her now, she wouldn't even care.

She tripped over something and landed with a pain she ignored. As she struggled to stand again, galloping horse hooves sounded behind her. The clearing transformed into a whirl of lights and smoke, and Aliwyn squeezed her eyes shut. The bandits were back, and she had nowhere to hide.

CHAPTER 14

"ALIWYN!"

The rider jumped off and ran toward her. Aliwyn squinted in disbelief as she sat in a heap on the ground. It was Evelyn, her brows drawn in a pained frown. She pulled Aliwyn up by the forearms. "What happened here? Where were you?"

Aliwyn was too choked to speak. She didn't know where to begin.

They hurried across the grassy plain with smoke blowing overhead. Silver was tied to a tree at the edge of the clearing. Evelyn had returned first with her mare, and Kato and the others would surely follow.

"We were staying with the injured Vasfian people until their clansmen could fetch them. There were too many people for Kato's cart to carry." Evelyn ran even as Aliwyn fell behind. "Garett was worried about you. He and Osgar came back, but then the cabin went up in flames."

"I didn't see either of them here," Aliwyn stammered.

Evelyn glared at her. "They're probably dead. In that cabin."

Aliwyn covered her mouth with her hand. She slowed to a shuffle as her knees wobbled. Evelyn had risked everything by coming back alone to investigate the flames, but the only person she could save hadn't deserved it. They were within moments of reaching the gray horse when Aliwyn collapsed onto the ground.

Evelyn spun around and pulled on her arms. "Get up! Whoever burned the building is still around!"

"No! Leave me here!" Aliwyn pushed off Evelyn's hands. "Didn't Ida tell you what I did?"

"Tell me what?"

Aliwyn tensed at the sight of Evelyn's sword strapped to her belt, but the truth needed to come out. She looked up at Evelyn and cried, "I hid Toby in that cabin, but then I freed him. He's still here!"

To Aliwyn's vexation, Evelyn only reached down again to pull her up. "Aliwyn! Have you lost your mind?"

As if answering her question, the horse tethered a few arm lengths behind Evelyn whinnied and reared up on its hind legs. A man dressed in a black tunic held onto the horse's saddle. It was Toby, and Aliwyn shrieked.

Evelyn spun around with a sweep of brown hair. She pulled out her sword and charged. "Don't touch my horse!"

Toby had been struggling to pull himself onto the saddle with his injured ankle. As Evelyn dashed forward, he looked up with rounded eyes and backed off, pulling out the dagger he had stolen from Aliwyn. But it was too late, and Evelyn slashed his left shoulder. Toby cried out and doubled over.

Aliwyn stood with fire coursing through her veins, but she couldn't move.

No blood seeped from where Toby had been struck. His gambeson shredded over his shoulder, but its padding had again protected him. Evelyn circled to his side and swiped at his legs. Toby bared his teeth and parried her rapid swings with his dagger. Beside them, Silver rose on her hind legs with a sharp neigh and tore at her tether.

The ring of their clashing blades tore through Aliwyn's heart. Toby blocked Evelyn's blows without striking back, but she was at a dangerous disadvantage because of Toby's gambeson. Aliwyn widened her stance, her muscles twitching for a chance to tackle Toby to the ground.

Evelyn yelled in frustration. Her strikes came faster, but Toby blocked them all.

"Evelyn!" he shouted. "Please give me the horse!"

"Never!"

Evelyn ducked and slashed. This time, no metallic clang rang out. Her blade cut across the bloodstained hole of Toby's gambeson. He cried out and clenched his side. Aliwyn stopped breathing. Toby stumbled backward, and his nape peeked from his collar. If Evelyn struck him there, he'd be dead.

But Evelyn stood with her sword pointing at the grass and a manic look in her eyes. Toby straightened, his face stricken and flushed, and only then did she attack again. He parried her blow with a flash of his blade.

No blood spilled forth. Aliwyn's legs almost buckled with relief, but something was amiss. Why did Evelyn hesitate? And the way Toby had pleaded for the horse—did they know each other from before?

Neither seemed willing to kill the other. Aliwyn had been too horrified to leave, but she added nothing by staying. Now was her chance; she should steal the mare they were fighting over and escape to Little Limber.

Aliwyn tiptoed toward Silver and extended a hand for the reins, but she never reached them.

Toby blocked another strike from Evelyn's blade and shoved her. She gasped and toppled backward. In her moment of weakness, Toby grabbed her arm and turned her sideways. He gave a sweeping kick behind both her knees and buckled her legs. Aliwyn's throat seized as he threw Evelyn down. Her sword accidentally smacked against Silver as she fell.

The beast reared once again on its hind legs, and its shadow rose over Evelyn as she pushed to her knees. Aliwyn dove for Evelyn and pushed her away from the thrashing hooves.

"Aliwyn!" Both Toby and Evelyn shouted.

The thunderous hooves stomped within a hair of Aliwyn's body as she rolled to dodge them. Too frightened to scream, she didn't see Toby pull on Silver's mouthpiece and move the horse aside. She made the mistake of trying to stand, and the horse kicked her in the upper back.

Aliwyn slammed onto the ground and shrieked into a mouthful of grass. The shock of landing rattled through her ribcage. Horse hooves stomped past her, and in the dying commotion, Evelyn called out her name.

Aliwyn tried to get up but couldn't. Hands rolled her onto her side and brushed aside the hair sticking to her face. Aliwyn's eyes focused on a piece of rope hanging from the trunk of the tree. The horse was gone, and so was Toby. Evelyn's face hovered over Aliwyn. Pushing to her feet, Evelyn backed away with her fists clenched.

"Why, Aliwyn?" Her voice broke.

Between the sharp pain in her ribs and the devastation of having betrayed Evelyn, Aliwyn didn't know which hurt more. She lay on her side, shaking as panicked voices echoed from across the clearing. Toby sped away on the galloping horse, past the smoke of the burning cabin and into the darkness. Numerous ragged lepers had crowded into the clearing before their burning home, and their wails and screams filled the air. No one seemed to notice as Boltan's son vanished into the woods.

The jostling of a creaky wagon grew louder, but Aliwyn was too numbed to move. Finally, Kato's voice rang out in the distance.

"Blue! Aliwyn! Are you all right?"

"What in tarnation happened?" It was Ida's voice. "Why is the cabin on fire? Why were you fighting with Toby?"

"Because Toby is Ransley Boltan's son!" Evelyn shouted.

"What? Churling maggots—Aliwyn said he was a friend!"

Horrible consequences lay ahead of her, and Aliwyn's limbs jolted with panic. She rolled and pushed to her knees, only to face a dagger slicing for her head.

"You pock-faced liar!" Ida cried.

Aliwyn dove to the side and dodged the leper's blow. She staggered to her feet and Ida lunged after her again, but this time, Kato grabbed the woman's arms and pried them back. He wrestled her away as she screeched and kicked.

Mils and the wagon stood behind the struggling pair as if inviting Aliwyn to get on. She sidestepped Kato and Ida and dashed for the cart.

"Ride for Little Limber!" Kato shouted in Vasfian.

Aliwyn clambered on board the wagon and shook the reins, but Mils took one step forward and stopped. Evelyn stood before the wagon with her sword raised. Aliwyn panted as pins and needles sank into her scalp. The noblewoman blocked the wagon's escape. Although she glared at Aliwyn, her words were directed at Kato.

"Kato, you knew all along, didn't you? Why are you still protecting her?"

Aliwyn stared as Evelyn drew back her arm as though to strike. Yet, even as her eyes flashed and her chest heaved, her arm and the sword remained frozen in midair.

Kato shouted, "If you would just let her explain—"

Before he could finish, Ida kicked him in his wounded thigh, and he crumpled onto the ground. Aliwyn's shaking hands dropped the reins as Kato moaned and curled up in agony. A heartbeat later, Ida leaped toward Aliwyn with her dagger. Her hood flew back to reveal piercing, colorless eyes on an outraged face.

"You! You're why the cabin is on fire!"

Aliwyn searched the cart bed for anything to strike with. The donkey's whipstick protruded from a stack of hay. She snatched it and spun around as Ida's gnarly hands came within reach of the wagon's rail.

With a fierce cry, Aliwyn cracked the whip across the leper's face. Ida yelped and tumbled onto the ground, beside where Kato had dragged himself on his stomach. He grabbed the leper's boot and blew two sharp whistles through his teeth.

The donkey responded to his command by bolting forward. Evelyn gasped and jumped out of the way. The beast brayed, charging over the grassy plain and tossing Aliwyn back onto the hay in the wagon bed. She shrieked and scrambled to grab onto the reins again. Before she could reach them, Ida's voice rang out over the clearing.

"Kill her! She hid Boltan's son and freed him!"

Aliwyn gripped the wooden side of the cart and sat up. When she looked back, Kato was still on the ground. Her heart sank as Evelyn ran away from everyone and left him behind. Kato had saved her one last time, even as it severed him from Evelyn. Aliwyn had caused a disaster everywhere she went, and sobs rose in her chest. *Kato, Evelyn, I'm so sorry, so sorry...*

A dozen lepers chased the wagon or gathered ahead with projectiles in their hands. Ida continued to rally the others, screaming at the top of her lungs that Aliwyn was a traitor.

Stones, pottery, and pieces of burning debris rained down on the wagon. Aliwyn tried to dodge as the donkey brayed and screamed. Its nasal cries pierced through the uproar of the people swarming behind the wagon.

Although they couldn't keep up, their attacks made Mils quicken until the wagon jostled and jumped. Aliwyn covered her head with her arms as she was bruised from all sides.

"Slow down! Slow down!" she yelled, bouncing over the scattered hay. The reins were also dancing beyond her fingertips.

Mils sped on as the ground sloped upward at the forest's edge. Aliwyn opened her eyes when the path grew increasingly rocky, and she struggled to raise her head from the rattling floorboards. To her horror, many smoldering torches had landed among the pottery shards and rocks. Smoke rose from the hay that had caught on fire.

Aliwyn crawled and swept her arms over the wagon floor to clear everything out. Yet, as she shoved the burning hay overboard, smoke appeared from the edges of the wagon bed. The first flames flashed in the shadows. Aliwyn tore off her oversized coat and tried to smother the fire, but the flames burned her hands, charred the fabric, and continued to spread.

She had to jump and save herself, now.

But Mils' braying had become desperate screams. Kato's beloved donkey couldn't escape the burning cart and would die if she didn't think of something. As the cart's wheels crashed down from another boulder, the rebound of the wagon bed gave Aliwyn momentum to lunge for the reins and grab them.

"Mils! Water this way!"

She had napped close to a stream, and she reckoned it was to their left. Mils veered sharply in the correct direction and Aliwyn's chest swelled with hope. She had never driven a cart in her life, but this was a good start.

As she scrambled to her knees, the glistening water came into view through the bushes and trees and Mils dashed for it. The wind stung Aliwyn's wet eyes and chilled her open mouth. As the donkey neared the water, a horse's neigh rang from the trees to the right.

The robbers who had looted the leper cabin had ridden along this river on their way uphill.

It was too late for Aliwyn to hide. Men on black horses charged out from the evening shadows several arm lengths away, and the hooves of those powerful beasts drummed over the forest floor. Among them was a single silver horse. She couldn't look for long. Mils veered to the left as he nearly collided with the horses. The wagon flipped onto its side and Aliwyn flew out. Too stunned to scream, she hit the ground and rolled over the rocks, underbrush, and leaves like a rag doll.

Her forehead struck a tree, and Aliwyn screamed. Her body slid back from the tree trunk, and she rolled onto her back. She wanted to grab her skull to stop the throbbing, but she couldn't move. The pink and orange hues of the sunset sky swerved into view as her vision blackened from the edges. Pain trickled in from all her limbs, but the worst ache tightened as a band around her head.

The branches overhead whirled and stopped and whirled again.

Men yelled and footsteps tore through the rustling leaves. Her strength dwindling, Aliwyn turned her head away from the tree. Numerous men surrounded her with their swords in hand. One of them had blond hair, but her eyes were too blurry to focus on his face.

She still knew who he was. Her heart pulsed in her throat, but that too faded as she sank into darkness.

CHAPTER 15

"Get off your horse!"

Aliwyn stirred at the man's voice, which was only a whisper but charged with anger. Her head pulsed as she moved. She longed to fall back asleep, but whoever spoke next shook her to her senses.

"Ed, I'll get off after I leave her outside the town walls."

It was Toby. Aliwyn wanted to scream, but her dry mouth was sealed shut. When she tried to move her arms, she found herself wrapped in blankets.

A voice she recognized as Edward's spoke next. "Leave her outside the town walls? No one's allowed near the gate anymore!"

"Oh, she's awake!" came another hushed voice. It belonged to a child.

Aliwyn forced her eyes open. She sat sideways on a horse's saddle with both her feet hanging off to one side. A girl with curly black hair held an oil lamp below. The child looked up at her and grinned.

Aliwyn sucked in her breath as Toby and Edward continued to talk. The girl smiling at her was Emma. Matthew had driven her over the cliff. Yet there she was, standing beside the horse. What was happening?

Edward spoke again. "That cretin of a bishop sent knights to stop anyone from leaving or entering Myton."

"What?" Every time Toby spoke, his chest vibrated against her left ear. "Did he also seal the—"

"No, he didn't, and so we'll go that way now. But this wench! Why did you bring her?"

"She pulled me out of the building *you* burned!"

"Get yourself out of this mess!" Edward hissed. "You're on your own."

The bearded man Aliwyn recognized as Edward walked into her field of view. He glared at her before joining the other men who were running into the darkness of the forest. They were all dressed in plain tunics and carried sacks over their shoulders. No more horses? Was Toby the only one left riding a horse? The young man's heart thumped under her ear as her cheek rested against his chest. She remembered losing consciousness, but at some point, that had transitioned into sleeping and snuggling against something warm. And that something warm had been Toby.

Aliwyn's temples throbbed. So much for thinking Toby's life as a rebel had ended. He had sped right back to his uncle and his troops. Her mind spun into a frenzy, but her body wouldn't move.

The oil lamp flickered on Emma's scowling face as the last of the men dashed past them. "Toby, what's wrong with you bringing another girl to—"

"Go follow Ed, now!"

"Well, make me," the girl retorted.

"You—"

How long had Toby been carrying her? Aliwyn's anxiety boiled to its peak, and she pulled out her arms from underneath the blankets.

"Toby! Why is she so scared of you?" Emma cried.

Aliwyn screamed and thrashed until Toby's hold loosened. She fell into the chilly night air.

"Aliwyn!"

She landed hard on her hands and knees, making her bruises throb, and her headache returned like a thunderclap. She slumped onto her side. The ground sapped her of warmth, and icy shivers tingled up her spine. Dogs barked nearby.

"Oh no!" The child's voice came beside her ear. "Quick, get up!"

"Emma, go run after Edward!" Toby whispered.

"No," came the same stubborn response. Emma's nails dug into Aliwyn's arm as the child tried to pull her up. Such thin fingers. Aliwyn trembled; she shouldn't have kicked and shrieked. The girl's pull was relentless, and Aliwyn sat up again in the strong winds.

A dozen torches wove through the tree trunks. Footsteps rustled the leaves less than a stone's throw away, and barking dogs scampered over the ground within an arm's length of where she sat. Behind her, the horse Toby rode nickered anxiously. Its hooves shuffled close to where Emma and Aliwyn huddled on the ground.

"*Qui est là?* Who's there?" boomed a man's voice. His English carried a heavy French accent.

Emma clung onto Aliwyn's arm as the hounds growled and circled them.

"We're pilgrims, sir," Toby said.

"Why do you disobey the curfew? Get off your horse."

Toby hoisted his leg over the horse's saddle and tried to slide off carefully. His injured ankle buckled, and he fell with a thud onto one knee. Other soldiers crowded around them. Some carried torches that cast eerie, dancing shadows over Toby's gray tunic. His griffin surcoat was gone, and he wore a sackcloth cap over his blond hair. Nearly twenty armed Norman soldiers surrounded them. When the same voice demanded that he hold up his hands, he obeyed as he scowled at his feet.

"Young lady, what happened to you?"

Emma yelped, and Aliwyn's gaze flew up to the figure before them. To her astonishment, Emma crawled toward her and buried her face in Aliwyn's chest. Wind howled over them both, and Aliwyn wrapped her arms around the girl. The man towering over them had a chiseled jaw under his conical helmet, and his mail clinked with each breath. His surcoat was blue underneath a yellow cross. A thrill raced through Aliwyn—he was one of Bishop Geoffrey's soldiers.

More Norman soldiers in blue and yellow surcoats surrounded Toby, trapping him within a circle of long swords and elongated, teardrop-shaped shields. He finally stammered, "She fell—"

"Silence. I was not speaking to you," the soldier said. He turned back to Aliwyn.

"Young lady, what's your name and where are you from?"

"Aliwyn," she whispered, "from Brocklesby."

"Aliwyn of Brocklesby. Was this man hurting you and the child?"

"No," Emma pulled her face away from Aliwyn. "He didn't hurt us. We're traveling together."

The soldier shook his head. "I cannot take answers from a child. No one is to be wandering outside Myton after sunset. Why did you disobey His Excellency's orders?"

Aliwyn stared at him. This twist of fate was startling—she could now watch her enemy crushed before her eyes. Toby needed to be arrested; if he survived this, he would rejoin the robbers who had looted and burned the leper cabin. What else would they destroy? But as Emma whimpered and quivered under Aliwyn's hands, her grief over losing her only sister stabbed through her. Her heart felt too big for her chest, and the incriminating words wouldn't come.

"I didn't know there was a curfew," Aliwyn said. "I know it's late, but we were just trying to enter town."

"What business do you have in Myton?"

"I was robbed recently. I needed more food for the winter." Everything Aliwyn said was true, although she concealed many details. The tranquility of her voice stunned her.

"And who is this man with you?"

Aliwyn held her breath. She bought time by touching her scalp where it hurt the most. Someone had wrapped a strip of cloth around her forehead, and it could only have been Toby. She frowned as her heart tapped in her throat.

"He's our escort," she said. "I fell off a donkey cart earlier and hit my head. He was there and wanted to help us get into town."

She glanced at Toby. He knelt with his hands held in the air and his eyes closed, but his lips moved as though reciting a prayer.

At her answer, the soldier grunted. He squinted at Aliwyn's face. She kept a cool demeanor, reminding herself that everything she said was true. Placing her hands in the girl's messy curls, Aliwyn stroked Emma's hair with a glimmer of joy. She thanked Heaven that the child was alive and well.

"Hmm, I've seen you before," the man said. "You're that girl living shut up in Brocklesby's mill. I used to grind my grain there. My name is Sir Jacques Verdun. So, you've finally ventured out into the world?"

He smiled, and Aliwyn struggled to match his expression. Here was the Norman scamp who had robbed her mill, smiling down at her like he was a saint. Heat rose to her face. She said nothing, afraid her first words would be ones she'd regret.

"Wait." Jacques raised one eyebrow. "Didn't a squire named Matthew Marcotte come to fetch you yesterday?"

Aliwyn took a deep breath. "Oh yes, I saw Matthew. But I didn't leave with him."

Jacques barked a laugh. "I'm not surprised! A surly and loud fool, wasn't he? If you see Matthew again, tell him I've reported him for desertion."

Aliwyn stared at the knight's clean-shaven face. She didn't know how the military worked, but desertion sounded like a crime, and Matthew had crossed the Brocklesby Bridge against Jacques's orders. What kind of trouble had Matthew gotten himself into by returning alone to her mill?

"He didn't...Matthew never came back to you?"

"No." Jacques grinned. "I don't mind—Matthew was a pain to have around." With this, his smirk vanished. He turned to Toby, whose arms shook as he struggled to keep them lifted.

"Look up. What's your name?"

The torches cast moving shadows over Toby's discolored and swollen face. "Phineas."

He glanced at Aliwyn, and the apprehension in his eyes forced her back to the present. Worries over Matthew's fate nonetheless haunted the back of her mind.

Jacques's icy gaze remained on his suspect. As he drilled Toby with questions, the troop's dogs scurried deeper into the forest, one after another, as though after an unfamiliar scent. Aliwyn hugged the child, her mind racing for an excuse to save Emma and herself should Toby be recognized as Ransley Boltan's son.

Finally, when the dogs barked again, one of Jacques's men came to his side.

"Sir, we found footprints in the mud over there. Many footprints." He pointed in the direction where Edward had gone.

A frown flickered over Toby's eyebrows.

"Toward the cliffs?" Jacques and the other soldiers looked over in the same direction. During this moment of distraction, Toby's left hand descended for the sword strapped to his belt.

Aliwyn reached out and closed her hand over his. "Don't!" she mouthed silently, her scowl deep. A struggle against so many would be hopeless.

Toby glared back but didn't pull away. From above, it appeared as though they were holding hands, and the soldiers surrounding them with their glinting swords didn't react.

"Vincent, Francis, awaken the others and light the watchtower," Jacques said. "The rest of us must track the footprints."

"Sir, maybe we should wait for reinforcements?"

"No. Our orders were to pursue suspicious activity, not to wait until the trail is cold."

As his men began to leave, Jacques fixed his gaze back on the three before him. "You may go." Aliwyn couldn't believe her ears as he continued. "I cannot let you enter Myton despite the danger out here. But do you know where the next town is?"

"Yes," Toby answered.

What happened next was a blur. Jacques handed Aliwyn one of his long, staff-like torches; he gave her some instructions that she didn't register. Rallying together his troops, he left as suddenly as he had come. Their footsteps were soon inaudible.

Aliwyn squeezed the torch, her arm shaking. She was still on her knees. The ache of her body that frenzy had kept at bay gnawed its way back into her awareness. Emma twirled about with muffled, joyful squeals, but Aliwyn couldn't move. She had been desperate to avoid another round of bloodshed, but had she made the right choice? The torch's fire added to the scorching heat of her face.

Emma squatted again and threw her arms around Toby's neck. Giggling, she whispered in his ear, "I can't believe he didn't recognize you! That knight didn't recognize you!"

"By a miracle of God." Toby's brows were knit. "Jacques has hardly seen me in years."

In the near darkness, his eyes then flicked to Aliwyn. She stared back at his beaten face with a tightened jaw. In the end, at the most crucial moment, the knight assigned to hunt for Toby hadn't even recognized him, but Aliwyn grudgingly understood why. With all the bruises on his face, the beginning of a beard, and a cap to cover his hair, Toby looked vastly different from when he had first entered her watermill. And no one would've expected to find him with a girl and a skinny peasant woman.

The torch was slipping from her fingers when Toby caught her hand. He loosened the flaming object from her grasp. His warmth lingered on her skin and made Aliwyn tremble; she didn't dare look at his face.

"Aliwyn, this is goodbye," Toby whispered. "Take the horse."

"What do you mean, 'goodbye'?" Emma demanded. She picked up her extinguished oil lamp.

Toby ignored her and stood, shuffling to keep his balance with his wounded ankle. The blankets keeping Aliwyn warm felt like iron weighing down her shoulders.

"Why did you take me with you after the cart crash?" she whispered.

"The lepers would've killed you. I realized...I shouldn't have blamed you for what someone else had done."

Aliwyn blinked back her tears. Toby didn't want to hold her accountable for what *Aelfric* had done. Toby turned to leave, but Emma drove her shoulder against his stomach with all her might.

"Why can't she come with us?" she asked between grunts. "Didn't she just help save us? And—"

"No, Emma." For the first time, Toby's whisper was harsh. "You don't know who she is."

Aliwyn kept her head lowered while their footsteps departed. As they carried the torch away, darkness enveloped her save for the moonlight from above. She sat with her legs folded beneath her and her hands clenching her kneecaps. A knife of despair sliced through her heart.

Had Sir Jacques Verdun dragged Toby away with Emma shrieking as she watched, would Aliwyn have felt any better? The answer was no. Aliwyn stared at the silent, spindly tree trunks overshadowing her. There had been no good choice, but her trail of lies would one day snap back like a venomous adder and sink its fangs into her neck.

Heaven forbid Jacques should discover her deception. She could only flee to a sanctuary now and hope the forty days would reduce her lies to an inconsequential matter. Shouldn't the Normans be more concerned about traitors like Lord Yeaton?

Aliwyn used to snub her nose at the sanctuary seekers squatting in the corner during Sunday mass. How could anyone sensible possibly spoil his or her life to a point of no return?

Now she knew.

Silver whinnied and stirred. As her back hooves brushed against her, Aliwyn came to her senses and pushed to her feet.

"Shhh, Silver." She took the horse's reins and stroked her forehead.

The smell of putrid eggs wafted to her nose. It was the telltale sign of yet another fire.

Dread twisted her stomach. For a moment, she couldn't move. Not again—how could this happen again? She searched for the smoke rising from the burning pellets, but around her were only evergreens cast in the moonlight, fading into the infinite night sky. The horse snorted and tore at the reins until Aliwyn stumbled.

"No, Silver!"

The beast rose on its hind legs with a piercing cry and forced Aliwyn to let go. Her shoulders shook as the horse galloped away. Without the mare, it would take all night for her to walk to the next town. Her temples throbbed, and she leaned against a nearby tree with her vision going in and out of focus. Hitting her head had come with consequences. She didn't know how long she stood there, afraid that she would collapse should she move. Finally, the shouts of frightened men and the overwhelming stench of the fire compelled her to open her eyes.

The treetops nearby were ablaze.

An alarming heat blew onto her face. Aliwyn staggered back as yelling in French—undoubtedly Jacques's Norman soldiers—echoed through the crackling flames. Edward must've started the fire to help himself escape.

When a flock of birds flapped past overhead, Aliwyn gathered her resolve and turned to run.

Shrubs whipped past and sticks snapped under her feet. Up ahead, still shrouded in darkness, Silver's feverish neighs rang out through the tree trunks. Aliwyn's breath rasped in her throat, and she kept going. The bright light from the fire behind her faded. She stepped into an open clearing, and ahead of her stood a vertical cliff.

She clenched her fists until they hurt. How could she come so far only to face this impasse? The looming cliff stretched as far as she could see on either side. To her distant right, beyond her line of sight, Silver's galloping hooves echoed forth as she also sought to escape the advancing flames. Aliwyn staggered toward the sound. She yanked off the bandage Toby had wrapped around her scalp laceration and threw it down.

She reached into her front tunic pocket. Both Aelfric's and Toby's recorders were inside, and to her relief, the first one she pulled out was Aelfric's.

Her eyes blurred. The memories of Miriam and Aelfric's smiling faces rekindled her stamina, and a melody both she and Aelfric had loved played in her mind. Aliwyn ran in bursts parallel to the encroaching line of fire. The orange, dusty sky over the flames both amazed and horrified her. Birds and swarms of bats flew as black specks in and out of the smoke.

Aliwyn was determined to move until the flames burned her alive.

Suffocating fumes made her cough. She covered her nose with the blanket Toby had given her. Finally, when Silver galloped back toward her in the distance, sobs rose in her chest—the horse must've turned back because it couldn't find a way out.

Aliwyn shuffled onward as she squeezed Aelfric's recorder. The fire etched her shadow across the ground and scorched her nape. When Silver galloped within several arm lengths of her, a swarm of bats fluttered out from somewhere along the rocky cliff.

Aliwyn's heart leapt, and she quickened her pace. Was there a cave she could dive into? As the horse sped past, she found a thin crack high in the wall from which the remaining bats took flight. The crevice extended down to the ground where it became obscured by bushes. The blazing flames seemed to illuminate an opening behind the tangle of bare twigs.

With the fire nearly engulfing her, Aliwyn coaxed her legs back into a run. She reached the area of dense shrubs and pushed her way toward the bare wall. A dirt passage running parallel to the cliff appeared, well hidden behind the rows of shrubs. This passageway led to a black opening in the wall, the one she had spotted from afar in the fire's light. It was the width of a narrow door but only half as tall.

Did the opening lead to a way out, or to a deadly beast or a vertical drop? There was no time to hesitate. Aliwyn ducked and eased herself into the opening.

A light flickered in the darkness but soon vanished. Aliwyn chewed on her cheeks; her vision must be adjusting. Her panting echoed in the small space. After a few steps, her instincts urged her to turn back. Her pulse drummed under her palm as she pressed against the frigid walls, and her other hand squeezed Aelfric's recorder. The darkness made her fears soar. She closed her eyes and forced herself to move forward. There were only flames awaiting her outside.

Her open hand slid across short blades protruding from the dirt. Aliwyn jerked back, her eyes blinking open. Although she saw nothing, her fresh wound stung sharply. She pressed her fingers against her blanket.

The metallic ring of swords echoed around her. Lights flashed, illuminating the men who had pulled the shades off their lanterns. Aliwyn winced in the brightness before something struck her across the chest.

She screamed until she smacked against the wall and snapped her head backward. More hands grabbed her, pinning her arms to the wall, and a salty hand slapped over her mouth. A dagger's tip flew for her stomach, but it halted just as it touched her clothes.

"You!"

Aliwyn stiffened at her attacker's voice. Her eyes remained open, but only lights and shadows swirled before her.

"Why did you follow me?"

It was Toby. He sounded furious, but the weapon he had intended to stab her with remained still against her abdomen.

"Kill her!" Edward's voice shouted.

Men on either side of her held her arms against the wall while Toby stood in front. Aliwyn squeezed her eyes shut, wishing she would die instantly or lose consciousness. All the same, her senses sharpened to the jagged wall pressed against her back.

"Geoffrey's dogs will sniff out her corpse and find this whole passage," Toby said.

"Then burn her outside!"

Aliwyn felt Toby's hand sliding along her waist for weapons. When he pulled something out, she opened her eyes, terrified. But it was only her metal tweezer, used to harvest plants. Toby slipped it back into her pocket.

"Ed, the men ahead are awaiting your orders. I said I would command the rear, so let me take care of this."

"Take care of this?" Edward cried. "She should've died in the watermill!"

"Sirs, we must hurry," another voice interjected. "The tunnel is filling up with smoke."

"Then go on with the cargo." Toby pointed his dagger at a few men. "You three—close up the opening."

Several soldiers rushed to stack stones at the tunnel's entrance. Rows of metal blades lined the walls just inside the opening to injure those who, like Aliwyn, didn't know any better. Blood trickled from the cut on her scalp as Edward cursed under his breath and trudged off.

Toby pushed his dagger back into its sheath along his belt. He lifted his hand from her mouth, and she gasped for air.

"Take her to the boat." His voice was emotionless.

Aliwyn was peeled off the wall. Two men on either side gripped her upper arms, almost dragging her as they marched deeper into the tunnel. Something slipped from her hand. Aelfric's recorder bounced on her foot and out of sight.

"No!" she screamed.

Another hand clapped over her mouth, and the men holding onto her pressed forward. Her hatred surged for Toby, his men, and all their cruelty in raiding the lepers' house and setting the forest ablaze. She latched onto her rage as a source of strength.

Aliwyn didn't see Toby, and neither did she want to see him. Staring at her ghostly shadow, cast by the light of a swaying lamp, Aliwyn swore she would escape or die trying.

CHAPTER 16

Aliwyn emerged from the other end of the tunnel, and her sore feet stumbled onto the sand. The men on either side of her pulled her onto a small beach encircled by an evergreen forest. Moonlight outlined the shadow of a single ship along the shoreline—the kind she recognized as a hulk. The lengthy vessel allowed a dozen men to row on either side, and its flat bottom was easily beached. A wide plank extended from the deck of the ship onto the shore. There, a few soldiers holding lamps illuminated the others who stood in a line and passed bags onboard.

Aliwyn teetered onward with waves of cold sweat. She had been on a boat with Aelfric before and was so seasick she could hardly stand. Now the men were dragging her onboard another ship? Her eyes skimmed the moonlit beach, but there was no steed or donkey to ride off on, and the woods were too distant for her to dash into.

Her captors gripped her upper arms as they neared the other men.

"Where's Toby?" asked the man to her right.

"Don't know," the other man grumbled. "But I'm telling you, he's lost his mind since Odrianna died. What are we doing with this girl?"

Aliwyn squirmed within their hold. Who was Odrianna? But she couldn't ask, and other footsteps arrived. The men holding her halted and straightened themselves to attention.

"Toby, we were just awaiting your orders," said one of them.

Aliwyn turned away but caught Toby's troubled expression as he limped toward them. He braced his left side with his injured hand, and shackles dangled from his other hand.

"Did Edward and the others search the ship for stowaways?" He was panting.

"Yes, they did."

Toby's scowl remained, and he handed the shackles to one soldier. "Zelrin, put these on her."

Zelrin was the soldier clenching Aliwyn's right arm. He moved to obey Toby's orders, and Aliwyn felt frigid metal rings close around her wrists behind her. The blanket that had been loosening from around her shoulders drifted to the ground. An icy wind sliced through her tunic, and Aliwyn swelled with bitterness. When Zelrin knelt to shackle her ankles, she glared at his dark woolen cap and wanted to kick his head, but any struggle now would get her killed.

Toby's boots hobbled away. "Wait here until I signal, then bring her."

The last bags had been carried on board, and he joined the dozens of men boarding the ship. The boat's long hull loomed like the shadow of a sleeping beast, and its many long oars protruded like legs from either side.

"I'm telling you. Stupid decision," muttered the man on her left.

"Stop it, Blakke. How would you react if your fiancée died?"

"I wouldn't replace her with a fleabag." Blakke squeezed Aliwyn's thin arm. "But being a baseborn, I guess he doesn't have good taste!"

How could Toby's men be so rude? And 'fleabag' could only refer to her. Aliwyn clawed at the icy shackles binding her wrists together.

Her captors pushed her forward. She staggered up the wooden plank with the iron links between her ankles grating the floorboards. As she stepped onto the deck, the soldiers whispered in a language she didn't understand, but every word sounded as though they were talking about her. She hardened her jaw.

"I'll take her from here," came Toby's voice.

The two men on either side let her go. Her stomach lurched when Toby draped a blanket over her head and shoulders as though to hide her. He pressed his hand between her shoulders and guided her toward the ship's rear, but Aliwyn resisted him instinctively.

"Stay below deck until I talk to Ed," he whispered in her ear.

Once again, he spoke in fluent Vasfian. How did he know their language? Bitterness kept her mouth shut. When Toby tried to move her again, she wouldn't budge.

"Do you want to live or not?" His tone grew harsher. "I'm trying to stop my uncle from killing you. He's the captain of this ship!"

Aliwyn's breath burned in her throat. Men pounded past, making the deck quake beneath her, and Toby halted to let them pass. Her eyes slid left and right. The railing of the ship came up to her chest. If she dashed for it, someone would slash her before she got a leg overboard. She was trapped.

Tendrils of heat climbed up her neck. She resisted Toby's push, wanting to whirl around and smack his face with her shackles.

But that didn't happen. Toby stopped pushing her when his uncle addressed the crew behind them. His bass voice resonated over the background murmuring and pierced her with fear again. Defiance now was foolish.

"These are the only crates left?" Edward demanded.

"Yes sir," a soldier said.

"What happened? You know we're paid by weight!"

"The Vasfians stole our crates. We'll have to explain—"

"The Danes take no explanations!"

The Danes. The crates had to be filled with those flammable pellets and other weapons. Aliwyn strained to hear the conversation. Six years ago, Denmark had joined the English natives in their failed revolt against King William. Now that another rebellion stormed the country, it seemed as though the Danes were back on the rebels' side. They would land with their longships to burn and pillage everything in sight. How many were coming?

Aliwyn wanted to know more, but Edward shouted other orders in what she guessed was Danish. The men who ran past her turned a crank to pull up the ship's anchor, and as the weight lifted, the vessel shifted with the river's current. Aliwyn shuffled to regain her balance, and Toby took this opportunity to move her again.

This time she didn't resist. He no longer braced his lower left side, and the bloody patch on his gray tunic startled her. For whatever reason, he had taken off his protective vest.

They hurried toward a set of stairs leading below deck. The faces of several men brightened as they recognized Toby.

"By Thor's hammer! You're back!"

"Who's that girl?"

Toby didn't slow down. "Let's get the boat moving."

He led Aliwyn down a staircase and into the blackness of the ship's hold below the deck. Her shackles thudded with each step, and she strained to see in the darkness. Toby's hand maneuvered her forward along the ship's side, and the harrowing sense of blindness made her chest seize.

"Sit down and keep quiet."

Toby pressed her down. Aliwyn's legs buckled, and she fell hard onto the floor. Her back hit the wooden sideboards along with her hands bound behind her back. The place reeked of rat urine, and her feet slid on the slimy floorboards. Her throat swelled until she couldn't breathe.

The ship's hull ground against the sand and pebbles of the riverbed. Oars splashed outside, moving the boat in jerks, and each stroke dashed her hopes of escaping back onto the shore. Sobs finally burst from her mouth.

Toby held onto her arm, and she couldn't even pull away.

His voice softened. "I gave you a chance to find sanctuary back outside Myton. But now that you've discovered the tunnel, I can't let you leave."

Aliwyn gritted her teeth. Of course she'd tell Bishop Geoffrey's men everything she had seen and heard if she got away. She hoped someone had already alerted them to a Danish invasion. The grinding of the boat along the river bottom grew louder and jarred her from her thoughts. From up on deck, a call came for more rowers because the ship was running aground.

A ruckus of creaking floorboards and pounding feet sounded overhead, and Toby's hand lifted from her arm. She couldn't see; her eyes were adjusting to the moonlight from the staircase's opening. Had he just drawn a weapon?

She was on the verge of screaming when Toby placed something against her bound hands.

"Here," he said hoarsely.

Her fingers glided over the object's smooth surface, and she grasped it in disbelief. He had just returned Aelfric's recorder.

As the creaking of the floorboards died down, Toby sighed.

"Aliwyn, Ed joined my father's army recently as a reinforcement. He doesn't know about your brother. But you must not mention his name." Aliwyn caught the metallic scent of blood as he stood. "I'll be back."

He left her side with uneven footsteps. Aliwyn stroked the recorder with her thumb and released a breath of relief. She was surrounded by the enemy and yet shown mercy. Even after Aelfric's betrayal, Toby hadn't learned to kill his enemies at the outset. Edward wouldn't make the same mistake.

Toby pulled another tunic over his head to conceal the bloodied one he already wore. He walked up the stairs, his shoulders cast in silver by the square of moonlight that came through the opening. When the ship scraped free of the sand and swayed, he fell with a thud. A few cheers rang out from the deck as the boat gained speed.

Aliwyn wrung her hands behind her. She could pretend to care about him and gain his trust the way Aelfric had. It could be her only chance for survival until she escaped.

Toby pushed to his feet near the staircase. "Emma, I told you to stay on deck."

The child scuffled forth from the shadows close to where Toby stood. She lowered her chin with a sour frown and carried an unlit oil lamp.

"Why did you put Aliwyn in shackles? She saved us from those soldiers outside Myton. And she tried to protect me—"

"Go upstairs," Toby ordered as he approached her.

Emma jerked back. "No! What if you hurt her when I leave?"

Aliwyn's opened mouth quivered as Emma dodged Toby's grasp. They had just met, but the child already cared about her. Aliwyn wanted to dismiss Emma, but the boat rocked incessantly with the current, and she closed her mouth to contain her bouts of nausea.

Coughing rang out from the darkness, and Aliwyn flinched. A shadow floated from the hay mattress like that of a large animal. Aliwyn's cracked lips parted. "Toby!"

Her face flooded with warmth. She shouldn't call for his help.

Toby approached, and Emma hurried after him. He left behind the last rays of the moonlight and pulled out his sword, silently. The coughing came again.

"Who's there?" Toby shouted.

For a moment, only the splashing of the oars filled the silence. Then, a deeper male voice called out in the blackness, "Tobias?"

Toby inhaled sharply. His sword sang as he pushed it back into its sheath. "Father!"

Boltan the elder was on board. Aliwyn's heart raced until her head swooned.

"I thought you were on a separate boat!" Toby sounded overjoyed.

"Ransley got hurt earlier today, so he came on our ship instead." Emma squatted and struck flint and metal together to light her oil lamp.

A light flickered on, illuminating the spacious hold of the ship. Fishing nets hung like spiderwebs from the ceiling, and dozens of hammocks wavered in between wooden posts. Several spears glinted from their positions on the wall. Everything glowed in shades of brown, and countless wooden boxes lined the perimeter of the boat's hold. Probably all filled with fire pellets.

Aliwyn bristled and writhed. This was it. Here was Ransley Boltan's hideout, stocked to the brim with weaponry, on a ship bound to meet the Danes. And she couldn't do anything about it.

Or could she? After everything she had seen and heard, she'd never forgive herself if she remained a passive passenger. Aliwyn shuddered as she gathered resolve. She couldn't fight these men, but maybe she could destroy their precious vessel. There had to be a way. Was there anything in the hold she could steal and use?

Toby limped past her, where a bearded man lay on top of a hay mattress. He seemed unwell under his beige blanket.

"Father, your arm..."

"My head is bothering me the most." Boltan the elder gestured to his right temple. "I got hit rather hard on the side there."

Toby pushed a clump of hay behind his father's head to elevate it. "It's very swollen. I'll dress it right away. Who attacked you?"

"We ran into the Vasfians just downstream of Brocklesby...and that old ruffian, Rochefort. I had no choice but to attack first." Ransley sighed. "I'm sorry to tell you that I lost one chest. The enemy must have it now."

Toby's back stiffened, and Aliwyn glowered at him. What was so important about Ransley's single lost chest? After all, they had already lost plenty of fire pellets. Unless the chest contained something else.

"Some setbacks are unavoidable." Toby hung his head. "I pray the loss won't hamper our efforts. At least you were spared, Father."

"Indeed. It's so good to see you, son. Ed said you were as good as dead."

"The Lord has been merciful to me."

Toby knelt beside the bed, and his father raised an arm with a tattered sleeve to embrace him.

Aliwyn wanted to burst. Where had she heard the name Rochefort before? Was it Norman's last name? Whoever Rochefort was, he had failed to cut down Ransley Boltan, and now the old scoundrel was back to conspire with his son and his men.

Toby used his sleeve and water from his costrel to clean his father's wounds, and Emma knelt by his side to assist him. The rising and falling of the ship intensified Aliwyn's motion sickness, and she pulled at the shackles around her wrists in vain. A long time passed, and she lost her balance against the wall and slumped onto her left side.

Emma called out her name, but Aliwyn squeezed her eyes shut. The girl patted her upper arm as boots stormed downstairs.

Aliwyn peeled apart her eyelids when Edward's voice boomed in the hull. The man strode forward but didn't see Aliwyn in the dimness.

"I gathered all the medicine I could after I saw Ransley like this. You'll need to look through the stash and pick out—" Edward paused before shouting, "What? What is this wench doing here?"

"Why can't she stay?" Emma held onto Aliwyn's arm.

"Who are you talking about?" Ransley Boltan asked.

Aliwyn cringed when Edward's feet approached as though to kick her face, but the blow never came. Toby and Emma's boots already stood close by, blocking his way.

"Her name is Aliwyn," Toby said. "She…"

"Let me see her," Ransley said.

Toby knelt and unlocked the shackles binding Aliwyn's wrists behind her back. She tensed at the tugs of his hands. He relocked them before her instead, arranged the blanket back around her shoulders, and lifted her into a sitting position.

The blood drained from her face. Toby's father sat a few arm lengths away with the sleeve of one arm shredded and drenched with blood. She had never seen him before. With light brown hair and a strong jaw, he appeared like any man in his fifties, but she gawked as though he would spew snakes from his mouth. The knight gazed at her through wrinkled, hooded eyelids.

"A peasant?" Blood crusted his beard.

This gruesome murderer was speaking to *her*. Aliwyn spun to her side and tried to crawl away, but shackles still bound her wrists and ankles. The metal links clattered on the floorboards until Toby pulled her back into sitting. His bandaged right hand dampened her skin.

"You know better," he warned in Vasfian.

"She's seen everything—this ship and the tunnel!" Edward shouted, pacing in between the hammocks. "What if she escapes?"

Ransley nodded at his brother before turning to Toby with a solemn face. "Son, what happened? Why did you bring a woman on board?"

Toby said nothing as he seemed to stare past Aliwyn. He held onto her forearms without squeezing them, and she wanted to flatten herself against the wall and vanish.

"I suppose Odrianna's death left you desperate to fill a void," Ransley said.

Toby's hold loosened. He released Aliwyn and lowered his gaze, his brows knit and drawn. The redness rimming his eyes glistened in the dim lighting, and she held her breath.

"Tobias has continuously jeopardized our mission," Edward charged. "He allowed this woman to track us here, whereas I eliminated all witnesses and left not a trace. When I raided the outskirts of the town, I burned my trails so no dogs could track—"

"But Aliwyn saved Toby's life," Emma cut in. "She pulled him from a burning building. Isn't that what you told me, Toby?"

Ransley chuckled, and Aliwyn gathered her knees to her chest. Edward rolled back his upper lip with a murderous glint in his eyes. Ransley's chuckle didn't help the strained dynamic between Toby and his uncle. If Edward's ways ever prevailed over Toby's, she was dead.

"The currents are strong today." Edward eyed his nephew. "Come help us row as soon as you can."

Ransley nodded. "Go on, Toby. I'm not going anywhere."

Edward marched away as the boat continued to toss with the waves. No one else seemed to care, but every rapid tilt made Aliwyn's stomach heave. She covered her mouth, lunged to the side, and retched. The chains of her shackles rattled onto the floorboards.

"Aliwyn!" Toby's hand landed on her back.

She was grateful nothing came out. The relief ended when she saw her empty hands hovering over the floorboards. Aelfric's instrument was gone.

"Oh look, a flute!" Emma crawled after the rolling stick as her curly black hair flopped about her ears. She slapped her hand over the instrument. "Got it!"

Aliwyn wiped her sweaty palms on her sleeves. She wanted the recorder back, but the joy on Emma's face stopped her from speaking. Toby gripped Aliwyn's shoulders and eased her back up against the wall.

"Emma," he called over his shoulder, "get her a crate or something to lean on. And a bucket."

"Of course!"

The child pushed to her feet and ran to do his bidding. Toby released Aliwyn and sat to her right. The smell of smoke wafted from his clothes, and the warmth of his side made her want to scream. Emma returned while pushing a crate about her waist's height along the floorboards, and on top of the crate was an empty bucket. Toby told Aliwyn to lean against the crate on her left, and she scooted against it with her face burning. She hugged the bucket Emma passed to her and curled her back to Toby.

Ransley Boltan watched, smirking and rubbing his swollen temple. What felt like spiders crawled along Aliwyn's spine. This had to be a bad dream. She was going to wake up the next instant staring at her mill's leaky roof.

"Aliwyn looks awful," Emma said. "Toby, let's take her upstairs for fresh air."

"Just a moment." Ransley folded his legs under his blanket. "Tobias, you didn't tell me how you met her?"

"I found her in the watermill," Toby answered. "The watermill where Miriam once took care of me."

Ransley raised his eyebrows. "You went back? Did you see Miriam?"

"No, but I've since learned that Aliwyn is Miriam's daughter. Adopted."

"I see."

Aliwyn stared at Ransley Boltan. Why would he, of all people, know Miriam? Or maybe he had been one of Miriam's many patients. There were few as skilled in wound care as Miriam. The world was terribly small.

"Where is Miriam now?" Ransley asked.

Aliwyn clutched her bucket, her shackles dead weight around her wrists. "Miriam passed away."

Water splashed along the hull's sides, and voices from upstairs echoed in the dank air. Ransley's expression sank. Miriam's legacy wasn't forgotten, and Aliwyn's head spun. Everything was unreal. Had anyone tortured or killed her, she would've understood it to be her fate, but both Toby and his father had shown her mercy.

Ransley passed a hand over his face. "I heard Miriam had two apprentices. When did she adopt children?"

What a creepy man. Had he sent his merchants to spy on Miriam all these years? "Miriam never adopted, and I'm not her adopted daughter. Someone spread false rumors. I'm Miriam's *apprentice*, and her other apprentice is dead."

There. She finally dispelled the hideous lie that nearly killed her, and she glared at Toby. His rounded eyes seemed to bore into her flesh. Shifting his back against the wall, he raked a hand through his hair and grabbed a fistful.

"May Miriam rest in peace," Ransley said. "Her medical knowledge and skills were unparalleled. I'm pleased to meet one of her apprentices."

But Ransley hadn't heard of the blunders this apprentice had made in Brocklesby. Aliwyn's stomach twisted at the way his eyes roved over her, as though assessing her worth. Miriam's legacy had helped win her acceptance amongst murderers, of all places, and she had better not make another mistake.

"So that means Aliwyn's staying?" Emma grinned and twirled Aelfric's recorder. "I can give her lots and lots of ginger, so she won't throw up! And she can help me with all my stupid...I mean, all my chores."

Ransley observed his son. "I sense that even if I don't want her to stay, you won't listen to me. She may be an asset to our crew, but you must watch her carefully."

"I will." Toby shuffled in his seat beside Aliwyn.

Ransley smiled. "And one woman on board is enough."

"I agree."

Emma giggled. "I've seen the ladies following him around. It's not Toby's fault he's handsome!"

"Thank you, Emma." Toby's voice had an oddly high lilt, and Aliwyn rolled her eyes away.

They would not hurt her, at least not yet, and she tried to relax her tense muscles. She would need to take full advantage of her reputation as Miriam's apprentice and earn her place on board. Once the men let their guards down, she could explore the vessel for a weapon and the easiest component to destroy.

Her mind raced ahead. What if she crippled the Boltans' ship and swam to shore? She could report the dangerous cargo to the closest manor and redeem herself with the Norman authorities and the Vasfians.

Redemption.

Her chest seized at the possibility of clearing her name and returning to her watermill in Brocklesby. She would earn another chance to connect with her fellow villagers. Hope came as a tingling warmth that radiated down her shoulders.

Aliwyn resolved to win the faith of the crew, and above all, Toby's trust. He still held the key to her shackles.

CHAPTER 17

A CHILLY WIND GUSTED down the staircase and carried the voices of men counting their rhythmic strokes. Toby led the way upstairs with his left hand around Aliwyn's forearm. She grasped the handle of the empty bucket with her wrists shackled before her. Her dirty feet dragged the metal links between her ankles, and behind her, Emma followed so closely that she almost kicked Aliwyn's heels.

"We need more manpower on starboard, sir!" one man hollered as Toby stepped on deck.

"I'm coming. Just a moment."

A square sail billowed from the towering mast at the center of the ship. Four pillars on either end of the vessel supported raised wooden platforms, and lamps affixed to each post flickered from within their wire cages. The flames illuminated the two dozen soldiers who sat rowing in two lines along the length of the vessel. They stared at Aliwyn, and she drew up her blanket around her face.

What she saw next made her heart leap in horror. Glowing orange smoke poured into the sky from the hamlet of Myton. The fire she had escaped was burning out of control.

Toby and Emma had also frozen at the sight of the skyline. It flashed as bright as sunrise in the night, as though the earth had split open and unleashed a ravenous fire. Flames leapt from beyond the cliffs and advanced to the plains on either side, engulfing forest, farmland, and the homes of countless peasants. The putrid smell of the pellets made bile rise in Aliwyn's throat. She clenched her jaw, ever aware of Toby's hold on her arm. Hatred for him and his men roiled within.

These were the homes of mothers, fathers, grandparents, and children. The destruction of six years ago was repeating itself, and these lawless rebels may burn Brocklesby next. Set her watermill ablaze next.

"This is really bad!" Emma's shrill voice pierced above the background of voices and water. "How are they goin' to put that out?"

Toby led the two of them toward the ship's rear as he squinted at the sky. He had looked at the burning lepers' cabin with the same dejected expression, and a tinge of sadness softened the edge of her fury. This raging blaze had nearly killed him also, and he wasn't the one who had started it.

"Toby, who burned up Myton?" Emma teetered with the ship's rocking.

"Someone who should've known better."

Aliwyn glanced at the frown darkening his face. It wasn't the time to ask questions.

She kept her eyes on her clanking shackles as they walked. The three of them ducked under the back platform. Sacks of plunder crowded around them, and Aliwyn wrinkled her nose at the fetor of blood and sweat. Toby tossed aside a few of the dirty bags and guided Aliwyn forward.

"Stay here." He released her arm. "It's close to the ship's midline, and you won't feel the waves as much."

Aliwyn's knees buckled and hit the floor. She swallowed the twinge of pain from her bruises as Toby knelt beside her. He pulled open a nearby bag.

"You'll find food and medicine in these. Take what you need."

Aliwyn nodded and kept a blank face. She had already spotted one bag she wanted—the bag of daggers she had seen in the leper cabin. It sagged against the farthest platform post, mingling with everything else stolen. A blade would be useful, but how to get one? Her heart drummed in her ears. The rowers sat watching her like hawks tracking prey, and her wrists and ankles were still shackled.

Emma ran off without a word and scampered toward the vessel's side. There, by the railings, a copper cauldron hung by its handle over a large, open sandbox. The pot had three legs underneath for stability as it stood over a hearth in the box, but the porridge inside lapped close to the edges with each rock of the ship.

"I forgot to put out the fire!" Emma pulled her sleeves over her hands and grabbed the pot's handle.

"Emma! Wait!" Toby hobbled after her.

The girl couldn't steady the heavy object, and hot porridge splashed out. She shrieked and released the cauldron just as Toby caught it from her. The scalding contents splashed onto his legs and boots, and the oarsmen nearby grimaced. Aliwyn seized the chance to scoot toward the bag of weapons, but Toby didn't yell and create a scene as she had hoped. His back turned, he set the pot back on the hearth and wrapped chains through its side handles to brace it against the ship's movements.

Emma clutched her hands. "I'm sorry, Toby. I know I'm supposed to put out the fire when we sail, but I forgot." She picked up a shovel strung to the sandbox and mixed sand into the low flames to extinguish them.

"You're also supposed to secure the cauldron before we set sail." Toby's voice was firm but not angry.

"Yes, I know..."

Aliwyn slid toward the bag of weapons, her hairline wet and her limbs twitching. This rebel leader was remarkably patient.

Her side brushed against the bag. With wrists shackled together, her hands fumbled with the drawstrings to loosen them. It wasn't easy, and the guilt of stealing from someone who had been merciful to her and a young child gripped her throat. But she had heard enough to know the ship was delivering pellets to the Danes. They would burn and pillage more villages, and she had to stop that at all costs.

As her fingers crept into the sack, heavy footsteps vibrated the floorboards. A large hand locked around her arm, pulling it backward and twisting her around. Tearing pain shot from her elbow to her shoulder. Her bucket went flying, and Aliwyn screamed.

"Ed! Stop it!" Toby shouted.

"She was going through our loot!"

"Because I told her she could!"

As Toby limped back toward the platform, Edward yanked off the blanket once covering Aliwyn. He pulled her by the arm toward one of the four posts elevating the platform they were under. Aliwyn gritted her teeth. She was determined not to scream again, and the chains binding her ankles did a wild dance along the floorboards. The burly man dragged her toward a post with chains already wrapped around its base.

"If she stays, she's a prisoner. You can't leave her untied!" Edward reached for the chains, but Toby intercepted his arm.

"You're responsible for your hired hands," Toby said. "And I'm responsible for Aliwyn."

Edward threw down Aliwyn's arm, and she tumbled onto the splintering planks. The men continued to argue, but she couldn't comprehend their words. Her blurry eyes focused on Emma's thin figure and the girl's petrified, wide eyes.

Edward's insult pierced through Aliwyn's daze. "You baseborn son! You've lost your mind, keeping this filthy wretch!"

"And you, burning all of Myton!" Toby snapped back. "Have you gone mad?"

A blow hit flesh, followed by a cry of pain.

"If I hadn't, Geoffrey's men would've found our tunnel!" Edward yelled.

Aliwyn forced herself to sit up, her mind screaming danger. Toby had doubled over, clutching his stomach where he'd been punched, but his face warped with fury as he bared his teeth. An instant later, he launched back at his opponent.

"Stop!" Aliwyn shouted.

She didn't know whether her cry or the relentless jolting of the ship in the currents made Toby hesitate. When neither he nor Edward moved, Aliwyn looked up at the cowering child.

"Go downstairs, sweetheart." Her voice hovered above the commotion.

The girl turned around as though her legs had been cut free and scampered down the ship between the two rows of men. Relief washed out the strain of Aliwyn's muscles, and she slumped back against the post.

"Portside, stop rowing and throw out the anchor!" Toby hollered as Emma disappeared down the steps. His arm rose above Aliwyn's head as he held the post for balance.

Half the men dropped their oars and scrambled to follow Toby's commands. Edward stomped over to the steering oar just outside the raised platform. He had abandoned it earlier to grab onto Aliwyn, and he rowed with vigorous strokes to direct the boat back on track. The ship jerked to its left as though skipping over obstacles on its right, and Aliwyn hugged the post. As the horizon of water and sky rotated, her stomach heaved toward her mouth. Unfazed, the oarsmen shouted in Danish and coordinated their strokes.

"Ed!" Toby called out. "Where are the flags bearing Norwich's coat of arms?"

"We're not going there! We're going straight for Ravenser's Point!"

His answer made Toby's mouth fall open, and Aliwyn's heart fluttered as she leaned against the platform's post. Toby limped forward, his hand sliding over the thick post until only the back of his tall frame was visible. The anchor splashed into the water, and the ship dipped sharply to the left. Toby toppled over, and his weight vibrated the floorboards under Aliwyn's thighs.

She held her breath. Toby lay on his side, facing her, with his arm around his torso. He was gasping. Her arm shot out for him, but she pulled it back with a tightening of her jaw. She had seen this same pained yet fierce expression when he had threatened her outside the leper cabin. The ship crested a wave as it spun, and none of the sailors came to Toby's aid. Whether it was because they didn't see him fall or they didn't care, Aliwyn didn't know. A gust blew across the deck, and the boat's movements became smooth again. Wind filled the massive square sail above her as dawn spilled a soft light over the deck.

The sailcloth displayed the same yellow and blue strips as Bishop Geoffrey's army, and Aliwyn pressed her lips together. The Boltans had disguised their ship as one of Bishop Geoffrey's. She'd need to flag the ship as suspicious if His Excellency was to identify it amongst the many he owned.

Cheers and nervous chuckling came from the men as the ship glided out of danger, but Aliwyn kept her scowl on the deceiving colors of the sail. Ropes extended from each corner of the sailcloth, and the mast groaned under the wind's strength. She could cut through those ropes if she had a knife, releasing the sail that would flail about and draw attention. Aliwyn's hand curled into a fist against the post. She liked that plan. It would sabotage the ship and distinguish it from an ordinary merchant ship.

But to snatch a knife, she'd need to wait until fewer men were watching, maybe after sunset. It would be a long wait.

Toby pushed himself to a sitting position. "Well done, everyone."

Edward clapped his hands once. "Keep rowing, half speed. First shift gets a break."

About a quarter of the men tossed aside their oars. As they conversed in a foreign language, Toby sat cross-legged and hunched forward with his right hand pressed against his arrow wound. Spilled porridge covered his stockings and shoes, and the muscles of his face twitched with agony. Aliwyn tried not to stare.

"Thank you for thinking of Emma." Toby picked off barley from his shins.

"You're...welcome."

His faint smile pulled at the scabs over his lips. He seemed to suspect nothing of her, and a knot tied in Aliwyn's throat.

"What are you going to do with me?" she asked. "Where is this ship going?"

"We're sailing for the North Sea, eventually to dock in Denmark."

"Denmark?"

"Yes. It's where I intend to live after all this ends."

Aliwyn shook her head. "And what about me? Do I go too?"

Toby's hazel eyes remained calm as she chuckled at her useless question. She had no choice. "But I have nothing there! I don't even speak Danish!"

He went back to staring at the floorboards, and Aliwyn remained motionless with her eyes wide. It came as no surprise, but hearing that the ship sailed for another country still tore through her like a jagged knife. She would never return to her watermill, her chickens, her garden, and everything she had cherished and known.

Bitterness against all the men on board pressed onto her shoulders like a stone mantle. Yet, the alternative to being held captive was to be killed. She had to tread carefully.

Toby reached for the closest bag of stolen goods and rummaged through it. "It's impossible for you to return home after what has happened between us. I hope you realize that."

Aliwyn kept a stone face. Going home was not impossible. She could redeem herself if she turned in this ship and thwarted the rebels' fiery plans. Toby was the one who didn't realize she still had a chance.

"Maybe when peace returns to England, you can go back." He glanced at her. "It's too soon to talk about that now."

The calls of water birds echoed from overhead, and a crisp autumn breeze pulled at the bloody hair matted against her temple. Aliwyn's face itched as she pinched the skin on her hands. Part of her still believed she would awaken from this outrageous dream.

Time rolled on nonetheless. She struggled to keep her eyes open. Closer to the mast, the men spoke cheerfully in Danish, and one man knelt to wipe up the spilled porridge. Another soldier carried a bucket as he walked about, giving out ladles of water. Others stretched with their arms in the air or massaged the back of a comrade. One bearded man took out a gloved puppet; it held a tiny stick and began beating the soldiers nearby. Loud laughter rang out, but Aliwyn couldn't watch. These were looting, murdering, barbaric men—doing everything that normal people would do.

"Here's a piece of ginger." Toby broke into her thoughts.

He handed her what looked like a shriveled nugget. The ginger juice stung her lips as she bit into it, but she forced herself to chew and swallow it all. To her frustration, the ginger burned her throat, and she coughed until her ribs ached.

Toby handed her his costrel, and she grudgingly drank from it. The way the soldiers watched her made hair rise on the back of her neck. She was nothing worth staring at.

When Toby lifted his good hand to touch her, Aliwyn yelped and almost smacked his face with the water pouch. Water sprinkled over his eyes and made him blink. He looked apologetic as he lowered his arm.

"Aliwyn, as long as you live at peace with us, I won't hurt you. And once we get to Denmark, I can help you find a place to live and work."

She pinched the top edges of his water bag. Did he expect her to follow him like a coward all the way to Denmark and settle down with his help? Because of him and his family, Aelfric was dead. She couldn't overlook that. The fact they were both connected to Miriam didn't erase anything.

"Do you have a manor in Denmark?" She kept her tone neutral.

"My grandparents gave me a piece of land there, but I've never lived on it before." He flicked off another grain of barley, his voice was pleasant. "I was a merchant when not on military duty, and I traveled often. I learned many languages that way."

Act friendly. Act interested. "Where did you travel?"

"Very far, southeast of England. There are luxurious ports by the sea, full of traders with spices, dyes, perfumes..."

"Oh, that must've been interesting."

"It was." There was an unexpected pause. "It was nice while it lasted."

The change in his voice made her nervous. When she looked at him again, Toby hunched over and gazed at the floorboards. His past was not as simple as she had assumed. At some point, this young merchant had deteriorated into a murderous rogue.

Aliwyn picked at the hem of her tunic. "What happened?"

"How did Miriam die?" Toby asked at the same time.

The two of them stared at each other, as if unsure of who should answer first. Toby opened his mouth. Although Aliwyn wanted to hear his response, footfalls quaked the floorboards underneath her. She scooted backward as several men stomped to where she and Toby were.

"All right, we've given you two enough time alone!" one of them hollered. He threw up his hands with a broad smile. "Tobias Phineas Boltan, you're back from the dead!"

"It's really you!" another exclaimed.

The four soldiers crowded around Toby, each landing with a quaking thud on the boat's deck. Aliwyn shuffled to get out of the way, but her movement made all the men turn to her.

"I'm Axlan," said the first man who had spoken. He had gray hair and thick, arching eyebrows. "So, you must be Odrianna?"

Another man punched him on the shoulder. "Idiot! Would Toby marry that?"

His words felt like sharp stabs. Aliwyn couldn't quell her shame as they leaned forward and squinted at her face.

"Cilebi, leave her alone," Toby said. "And Axlan, you must not have heard about Odri. She passed away."

"What?" Axlan's high arching eyebrows shot up even higher. "What happened? I'm so sorry! I'm so, so—"

"It wasn't your fault." Toby smiled, but sadness lingered in his gaze.

"This girl—isn't she from the watermill?" Another soldier jabbed a finger at Aliwyn. "You brought her to be our thrall?"

"No. She saved my life. I won't order her to do anything."

Aliwyn swallowed until her mouth ran dry. The gathering fell silent until one man cleared his throat with what she sensed was contempt. Her pulse quickened. Peering up at their sweaty and bearded faces, she whispered, "My name is Aliwyn."

"I'm Cilebi," said the man who had punched Axlan. "And this is Axlan, Svein, and Blakke."

Aliwyn tried not to stare at Cilebi's shiny, bald head. What a strange contrast to his voluminous beard. He had an accent and stank of ale and sweat, much like the other men clustered around her. She'd have to earn her place amongst these disgusting brutes.

"Nice to meet you all," she said. "I'm happy to help on this ship."

"So, what can you do? Sing? Dance?"

Aliwyn steeled herself against the mockery in his voice. "I can sing. But I also spear eels."

Her answer only brought lopsided grins all around.

"For real? How 'bout emptying them privy buckets?"

There was scattered chuckling. Aliwyn pressed her lips into a stale grin.

"Spearing eels takes great aim and skill." Toby glared at the other soldiers until their smiles fell flat. Turning back to Aliwyn, he continued. "On this ship, we use nets to catch fish instead. They're hanging from the sides of the ship."

Aliwyn lowered her scowl to the floorboards. Even if Toby was defending her, he was the reason she was stuck on this vessel. The floorboards vibrated again, this time with lighter footsteps, and a teenage boy with a woolen hat approached the gathering. He carried a basin of water with a few rags hanging off its edge.

In the morning light, her eyes fell back on Toby as he smiled at the newcomer. The stubble of his beard was growing. Despite his darkening bruises, his smile was full and sincere. In a moment so bizarre that it shook Aliwyn wide awake, Miriam's smile appeared on Toby's face. She sucked in her breath and looked away. All this sleep deprivation was making her crazy.

"Always the thoughtful one, Zelrin," Toby said as the newcomer set down the container of water.

Zelrin didn't smile. "We should all talk later. You need to sleep."

He was one of the two men who had pulled her out of the hidden tunnel. Probably fourteen or fifteen, he had a squared face and sand-colored hair sticking out from underneath his cap.

"I agree." The bald soldier, Cilebi, stood again. "You look rather beaten up, Toby. But you're craftier than Loki, escaping that bridge."

"How did you get off?" another man asked.

Now that the attention had shifted elsewhere, fatigue swathed Aliwyn like a heavy blanket. Gone was the flighty energy once sustaining her. She fought to stay awake as Toby told his story.

His gambeson of thirty-two layered linens had reduced the impact from the Vasfian arrow, which had struck his left hip bone instead of his abdominal muscles. The rain had distracted the Vasfian guards and made it difficult to keep lighting near the bridge. Every time the redheads changed shifts in the darkness, Toby used his eating knife to cut at the suspension bridge's ropes. Finally, he could pull out his ankle. He looped his cape around a plank and hoisted himself up onto the bridge. Then he had crawled back onto land.

"Very smart," Cilebi smirked. "I've heard my share of survival tales, but by Odin's hammer, this is a bloody good one!"

The other sailors nodded with admiration, but Toby's face remained stark. "The Vasfians used low draw-weight crossbows, and I played dead. I had hours to plan my escape. Thank Heavens you all found me, or else the lepers would've finished me off."

"Ya weren't hard to find. That gray horse you was ridin' made so much noise!"

Aliwyn didn't hear the rest of their dialogue. She dozed with her head against the back platform's post until something wet touched her hand. Aliwyn jerked back to attention. Zelrin squatted before her and offered a damp rag. "Want one?"

Aliwyn was too shy to look into his gray eyes as she accepted the cloth from his hand. The other men had gathered around the cauldron and were serving themselves porridge. Watching them wolf down their food stirred her hunger, but she was afraid of throwing up. Her fingertips throbbed as she held onto the wet cloth. She had forgotten that she had cut them in the cave, and she dropped the rag.

Toby stopped wiping his face with his cloth and fingered his belt pouches. He took out the metal tin, nudged open the lid with his bandaged thumb, and offered it to her.

"Here, try this on your hands."

The layer of green ointment inside the box smelled of honey and mint. Aliwyn wanted to thank him, but the words wouldn't come. His kindness was dumbfounding. She couldn't relax her frown as she dipped her injured fingers into the paste.

She wiped her face with the rag. When Toby struggled to press the lid back on the ointment tin, a thought made her freeze. Toby's tin was identical to Kato's orange one. Maybe Toby, and not Aelfric, had filled a tin with antidote and saved the redhead's life with that critical first dose. Maybe that's how Toby had known the formula offhand while hanging upside down. Aliwyn squinted at her dirty rag, her mind fogging with exhaustion. The longer she stayed stuck with Toby, the less he made sense to her.

Zelrin sat cross-legged before them. He suppressed a yawn as he pulled off the cork of his costrel.

"I can take your next shift, sir," he said between sips. "That'll give you more time to sleep."

"No need. Just wake me up when it's my shift, and stop calling me 'sir'. It's too formal."

"Well, you're a full-fledged knight now. And you were knighted a year younger than the other squires. It's out of respect." Zelrin grinned as he patted the cowlick in his hair. "But fine. If you prefer ol' Toby, I can do that, too."

He stood to leave.

"Wait, Zelrin," Toby said. "Your brother—"

"Lukas didn't make it." Zelrin halted. Aliwyn crumpled her cleaning cloth and glanced at Toby and Zelrin. Grief marked both their faces.

"I'm sorry," Toby said. "I saw him get shot in the leg, but I had hoped…"

"The Vasfians also beat him. We did get him back, but…" Zelrin's eyes glistened. "The next day, his leg had swelled up, and it had these black bubbles around the wounds. He was sweaty and confused before he passed. I swear those sardin' Vasfians put something on their arrowheads. Something deadly."

Chills erupted over Aliwyn's scalp. Lukas' death sounded horrifying, and an arrow had wounded her as well. What if there was indeed some toxin coating those arrowheads? She struggled to breathe.

"Is there anyone injured on board?" Toby asked. "I can help."

"Too late. Everyone who got shot died or was washed away," Edward called from his position at the oar.

His bass voice swept away Aliwyn's drowsiness. The dull ache in her shoulder, the one grazed by an arrow, intensified. Toby had been shot as well. If anything happened to him, no one would stop Edward or someone else from killing her. Her heart racing, she waited for Toby to mention his injuries, but he only frowned at his uncle.

"Zelrin, come take over," Edward ordered, panting.

"Yes, sir."

The youngster began to leave but then turned back to Toby. "Pardon my rudeness, sir. I wanted to welcome you back, too." He gave a half grin. "You're proof good things still happen."

As Zelrin left and Edward marched in their direction, Aliwyn scooted backward, but the sacks behind her blocked her way. The older man sat before them and rested his elbows on his knees. He no longer looked angry, but neither did he appear to be in good spirits.

"Look at the herbs for treating your father. As I said, we're not stopping until Ravenser's Point."

"But that's several days away," Toby said. "My father needs proper treatment right now."

"He decided to make no more stops. We have too many hounds on our heels. Whatever medication we have is what you have to work with."

A scowl settled over Toby's tired expression. "I need to talk to him. And you too, downstairs."

"Hmph," Edward smirked. "Stop trying to sound serious; you're not regaining any of my respect." His eyes slid to Aliwyn. "As she's a mere woman, I'll let you keep her for entertainment...whatever this flimsy wench can offer you. But the other men will show no mercy if they find her wandering about."

"I'll meet you downstairs," Toby said coldly.

Aliwyn remained rigid as Edward pushed himself up. His threats buzzed in her mind as he left, but she was too tired to be afraid. She glared at Toby as he reached into the bags. Men ate and talked under the crimson morning sun, and a few of the others lay down or stretched out along the middle of the ship. One scarred mercenary tried to mend a stocking, the needle pinched in his meaty fingers, but others kept bumping into him. She cringed when Axlan began singing off-key.

Sunset couldn't come fast enough.

"Believe it or not, my uncle wasn't always like that," Toby murmured as he took out a block of cheese. "His wife was with child in Dover when William burned it, even though the town had surrendered. She died, and he was never the same."

Aliwyn didn't care. Almost every peasant in Brocklesby had lost family members because of the Norman invasion, but they didn't go on to burn villages and forests and raid leper cabins.

"Toby," she said. "Why didn't you mention your own wounds?"

Silence. Her jaw tensed with aggravation as Toby pulled out plums from a nearby bag. He spread the lower half of his tunic over his lap like an apron and set the plums on top.

"Morale is already very low," he responded in Vasfian. "I'll tend to myself later. I...don't know why my cuts are so itchy, and they won't stop bleeding."

"They won't stop bleeding?" Her eyes rounded. "Then you *must* tell someone!"

"Not so loud. Our best surgeon is dead, and I'm the only replacement."

"Then let me look at it!" She regretted her outburst.

"I have no idea what you're both sayin' but let me know if I can help!" Zelrin hollered from his post at the steering oar.

"No, but thanks for the offer!" Toby called back.

Other soldiers onboard also looked in their direction, but no one seemed to understand Vasfian. Aliwyn almost jumped when Toby withdrew a plain eating knife to slice the cheese resting on his knee.

"Stop making a scene." As casual as he sounded, he glared at her until she averted her eyes.

Aliwyn's dull headache intensified as she watched Toby use the knife. She drew on the last of her strength to stay awake, fighting not to think of her fate if Toby should die. Or perhaps he would get rid of her for being annoying. Just seeing him cut food with a sharp utensil made her shake.

"Hold out your hands," Toby said.

Aliwyn dropped the rag she had been squeezing. Her wrists were reddening around the shackles, and she extended her skinny fingers. When Toby placed four tiny plums and thick slices of cheese onto her hands, she almost dropped them. He had given her a more substantial meal than she had eaten in days, and Aliwyn shuffled in her seat.

"You may look at my wounds after I talk to Ed," he said. "And if it matters to you, the food I just gave you wasn't stolen."

Aliwyn took several deep breaths. So striking was the contrast between the Toby she was getting to know and his reputation as Ransley Boltan's son, who had led his soldiers to commit one crime after another. But it had been Toby's choice to rejoin his men as soon as she had freed him. She balanced the plums as one question burned in her mind.

"Why did you stop being a merchant?" she whispered in Vasfian. "Why turn against the law and—" She stopped herself with a lurch of her stomach.

"Never mind," she stammered. "Forget I said anything."

Aliwyn forced a bite of cheese into her mouth. The dose of ginger had quelled her nausea, and the more she chewed the fatty food, the hungrier she became, but she couldn't enjoy her meal. Toby's silence made her heart race. Her bold questioning would be her death sentence. As she tore into the plums, Edward spoke to the men on her right. He walked toward the stairs and waved for his nephew to follow.

Toby pushed on his knees to stand up. "After Odri died, I thought joining my father would take my mind off things. And there were other reasons." His voice carried no menace, and Aliwyn glanced at him.

"I'm sorry to hear about your fiancée," she said.

"Headin' off, Toby?" Zelrin called out.

"I'm meeting Ed downstairs. Keep an eye on her."

Toby stayed for a moment longer, resting his left hand against the platform post. Aliwyn finished eating the last plum and collected the pit in her hand.

"Glad to see you like plums," he said. "I used to own two dozen plum trees. They're my favorite fruit."

He braced his arms around his stomach and smiled at her juice-stained face before he left. No one else had noticed his injuries because his tunic was black, and Aliwyn chewed on her lips. This ship didn't allow anyone to recover properly. Had her plans prevailed, Toby would be resting in a sanctuary by now, with his wounds dressed and his stomach full. But he was one stubborn dolt.

Not that she was any less stubborn.

Aliwyn placed the other slices of cheese back into the bag. Dirty rags floated within the water basin, and she clutched the slimy plum pits. Maybe she'd seem more useful if she cleaned. Aliwyn reached for the basin and stood, the chains between her wrist and ankles clinking.

"Hey!" Zelrin shouted. "Where are you going?"

"I wanted to put this—"

"No. You stay there!" The harshness in his voice stunned her. Hands jittery, she dropped the slimy pits into the water basin. Another soldier walked past and grabbed the basin from her.

"Disgusting," he muttered as the pits sloshed in the water. "You get down and stay down."

Aliwyn lay on her side and curled her knees to her chest. Bitterness swelled inside like a billowing thundercloud. She found the blanket Edward had pulled off earlier and pulled it up to her nose. It reeked of armpits, but she endured it. Toby's presence no longer shielded her on deck, and he might not survive the injuries he kept hidden from his crew. She had better finish her business and escape.

Her eyes wandered again to the ship's rigging system. She had already tried to steal a blade and failed, and she had been foolish to try during the daytime. Nightfall couldn't arrive fast enough to bring her another opportunity.

The voices echoing from underneath the floorboards caught her attention. One belonged to Emma, and the other to a man. Aliwyn shook off her grogginess. She could eavesdrop on Toby and Edward's conversation. Gathering information on the Boltans' plans on behalf of the Norman authorities was just as crucial as sabotaging the ship.

Aliwyn raised her head and scanned the deck for any cracks between the wooden boards. There was one the width of her little finger. She pushed herself along on her side, planted her ear over the gap, and nestled between the bags with her back facing the crew. Her heart drummed against her ribs, but she remained still.

Over the stench of soggy wood and mold, Aliwyn caught a whiff of goat cheese—the food Kato loved. She glanced at the bulging sacks, all stolen from the lepers' cabin, and her eyes watered. What had happened to everyone she had left behind? She wouldn't let them down.

Like Aelfric, she had become a spy among the Boltans' men.

CHAPTER 18

"But I heard Loki!" Emma's words rang out from below.

"Never light anything bigger than a lamp down here," boomed Edward's voice. "This torch is unacceptable!"

Aliwyn struggled to hear the conversation over the creaking floorboards. Emma explained she had lit the torch to scare off Loki, and Aliwyn nibbled on her lip. Loki was but a mythical Norse god whose stories some families told their children for entertainment. Emma took those stories too seriously. But why did she believe someone lurked in the hull?

The girl's footsteps tapped up the stairs. She was coming, and Aliwyn fought the urge to get up and greet her. Edward and Toby spoke in lowered voices, which made eavesdropping difficult. Aliwyn licked her lips as she focused on their dialogue.

"It's too late for Norwich. She held out for months, but Bishop Geoffrey captured it," said the deeper voice, which was Edward's.

"What?" Toby sounded stunned. "How do you know?"

"Lady de Gael sent me a messenger. Geoffrey permitted her escape, but Norwich is now in that blasted bishop's hands. So, you understand why it's useless for us to sail there."

Silence. Aliwyn held her breath. Ralph de Gael was one of the earls leading the rebellion, and Lady de Gael must be his wife. Evelyn had mentioned Ralph's name outside the lepers' cabin.

Toby continued anxiously, "What happened to Lord de Gael? Wasn't he with his wife?"

"Before Norwich fell, he'd sailed for Denmark to seek reinforcements. I also wrote to the Danish prince about your potash compound, Toby. He has expressed much interest in purchasing everything on this ship." Edward sounded pleased. "That's why we're meeting two hundred longships at Ravenser's Point."

Aliwyn had never heard of Ravenser's Point, but two hundred longships were sailing to England to purchase the Boltans' cargo? Horror exploded in her chest.

Ransley spoke next. "The goal is to terrorize the Normans with sweeping fires they cannot control or escape. The Danish longships have the speed to land in strategic locations simultaneously and trigger the catastrophe we need."

Just as she had feared, the Danes would spread fire with an efficiency never before seen in England. Setting Myton and the surrounding woods ablaze had been but a small taste of the destruction to come, the result of Edward's actions alone. What would two hundred longships accomplish, each starting its own fire?

Sure, the combined rebel and Danish forces would devastate the Norman's food supply, burn up their decadent manors, and maybe terrorize the king into submission. But they would also destroy the farms and homes of thousands of English peasants just before winter set in. Famine would ensue, like the famine that had killed Aliwyn's family after months of agonizing hunger.

She gnashed her teeth. Even one more village burnt was too many, and she worried for Brocklesby. The Boltans didn't care or understand. They were too filthy rich to be bothered by the peasants' suffering every time the powerful struggled for more power.

Meanwhile, Emma pattered around on deck. Ignoring the child's footsteps was impossible, but Aliwyn squeezed her blanket and strained to listen as Toby spoke again. His voice was as resonant as it was indignant.

"I made the compound to scatter the bishop's troops, to stop their siege on Norwich Castle and rescue Lady de Gael. And even then, I had planned to use only a fraction of the cargo."

After a pause, Edward asked in a low tone, "What are you implying?"

"The compound is not for sale, especially not to a foreign country!"

Edward chuckled, but it was throaty and brooding. "I can't believe this. You finally accomplished something worthwhile, I found a market to sell it, and then you tell me this spineless garbage!"

Ransley's voice was low and contemplative. "Danish reinforcement is still the key to winning this revolt, Tobias. With Norwich defeated, our lives depend on..." Much to Aliwyn's frustration, his words became obscured by the grating of a heavy object dragged across the deck. She cringed as the sound intensified.

"Hey, runt! Let your friend sleep!" Zelrin called in a hushed voice.

The noise stopped, and Emma answered, "But I wanted to give her something to eat."

"Like rat-flavored biscuits from that bag?"

Aliwyn struggled to lift herself from the gravity of all she had just heard. She rolled over and opened her eyes. Emma glared at Zelrin as she dropped the large sack she had been pulling. With her other hand, she threw down a miniature gambeson.

"Don't do that to your armor!" Zelrin scolded.

"But it's so hot and stuffy. I hate wearing it all the time."

"That thing saved your life. Put it back on!"

Aliwyn sat up, stretching out her sore back. "Emma, what's wrong?"

Emma's scowl melted into an expression of misery, and she shuffled toward Aliwyn. Aliwyn held out her hand to greet the child.

The padded jacket Emma had discarded featured row upon row of stitches. It must've protected her from the rocks when Matthew had knocked her over the cliff into the tossing rapids.

"I heard Loki downstairs, and no one believes me," the girl grumbled, plopping beside Aliwyn. "Toby's papa was sleeping, so I know it wasn't him movin' around."

Aliwyn placed her hand on Emma's shoulder. "I believe you, Emma. Please tell me when you hear it again."

What if Emma had heard a person? Toby had been worried that the ship had stowaways; who knew how long the vessel had been beached and vulnerable to intruders?

"What exactly did you hear?" Aliwyn tapped her ear. "If you tell me, it'll be our secret."

"Some footsteps," the girl whispered back. "And I heard a box move!"

Aliwyn kept a blank face. If she ever got these rotten shackles off, she could inspect what lay below the deck. She didn't believe someone was hiding there, but she might find another cache of weapons.

Zelrin stood, crossing his arms. "Emma's been acting up since she saw Odri die. Afraid of the dark, having bad dreams, hearing things..."

Aliwyn rubbed Emma's shoulders as Zelrin's words sank in. "You saw Odrianna die? I'm sorry. That must've been terrible."

"Yea, she was Toby's traveling partner, too," Zelrin said. "He still blames himself every day 'cause he couldn't save her. And he sure quit the merchant life afterward. At least for now."

Emma turned to Aliwyn, sadness marring her otherwise rosy face. "Can you tell Toby to stop everyone from burning and stealing?"

Aliwyn stared at the girl, speechless.

"She can't do that." Zelrin threw up his hand.

"Why?" Emma asked. "Odri died because robbers attacked us. And now we're doing the same things—stealing and burning stuff. We're just as bad."

"Watch what you say," Zelrin snapped. "Don't forget, those robbers were *Norman* knights on a drunken rampage. And you aren't old enough to remember what happened six winters ago." He nodded at the man who'd replaced him at the steering oar. "We're givin' William the Turd and all his followers the sardin' scat they deserve."

Aliwyn lowered her eyes. The king's razing of northern England and the subsequent famine had killed her own family. She had obeyed the foreign ruler, hoping her submission would bring order and security to her life, but she could understand why others would choose differently. Zelrin's words echoed in her mind, and memories of her dead relatives resurfaced. If they were alive, would they want revenge too?

Perhaps they would, but nothing justified the rebels' strategy of igniting a dangerous substance to destroy villages like her own. Angst boiled like a cauldron within her. The Danes couldn't care less about how the English peasants suffered.

Zelrin cleared his throat. "So Aliwyn, sorry about earlier."

Her eyes widened, and Zelrin continued. "All these seadogs on board are the mercenaries Sir Edward hired. They're Danes, in case you didn't notice them yappin' in Danish—"

"Except Axlan," Emma cut in. "Axlan is an aristocrat who got lost in a snowstorm once, and Toby saved him."

"Axlan is an *ex*-English aristocrat," Zelrin said. "And he wasn't lost, more like runnin' for his life from the Normans who stole his land."

Aliwyn twitched. William's loyal subjects entered England after the conquest and became many of the bishops, earls, barons, and knights who held power today. The territories they overtook, of course, had once belonged to the English nobility.

Zelrin chided Emma into crawling back to her gambeson and putting it on. As he knelt to help her tie the laces, he looked back at Aliwyn and said, "Anyway, as I was sayin', Sir Edward pays the other folks to fight, so they listen to him. He's letting them kill you for the smallest reason, like movin' around on your own. That's why I told you to stay put. You can't even get water 'cause they be afraid you'll poison it."

Emma scratched her chin. "What if she has to use the privy pot?"

"We'll figure it out when the time comes." The boy rolled his eyes. "The cesspit is downstairs in the far back, in case you didn't smell it already."

Aliwyn's eyes skimmed the rear of the ship. Pretending to use the privy might give her unsupervised time, but she must use the opportunity wisely.

Zelrin stood to scrape the last of the porridge out of the cauldron and passed Emma a bowlful.

"That's all that's left for you both to share. You've got to make 'em barley taste bad, Emma. Then those sweaty seadogs won't eat so much." He smirked and sat down.

Emma handed the bowl to Aliwyn. "Here. I already had some earlier."

Aliwyn received the pottage but didn't trust herself to keep food down. The oatmeal fragrance made her chest tighten with longing. It was the smell of home.

"Give me your drinking bag," Zelrin said. "I have to fill it for you."

She unbuckled her water pouch strap and handed it over in the brightening sunlight. He seemed to be Toby's close friend, and she had to earn his trust, too. Zelrin wore a drab tunic like the other men, and the front of his stained, beige gambeson was undone. Although the youngest male on board, his perpetual frown and thick eyebrows made him appear older.

Zelrin approached the water barrels chained along the boat's edge, and Emma retrieved Aelfric's recorder from her pocket.

"Do you know how to play, Aliwyn?" She folded her thin fingers over the finger holes. "Toby taught me, but I'm not very good."

"I can make loud noises on it." Aliwyn smiled. "Does that count?"

Emma grinned and handed Aliwyn the recorder. "Try it."

Aliwyn accepted the slender instrument and stroked its smooth surface with her thumb. This was Aelfric's recorder, his most treasured possession. Did she have the right to play it?

A shadow appeared over her head as Zelrin returned.

"Where did you get that?" he cried. He threw her full water bag, and it flopped beside her like a dead fish.

Terror seized Aliwyn. The crucifix engraved on the recorder made it readily recognizable. Zelrin had likely seen the instrument before—in Aelfric's hands.

"Why are you yelling?" Emma asked. "This is Aliwyn's recorder."

"No, it's not." Zelrin's glare was hateful. "This belonged to that demon, Aelfric."

"What? This belonged to him?"

Aliwyn stopped breathing. She had made a disastrous mistake in displaying the recorder. Zelrin must've been with Toby when Aelfric had betrayed the Boltan's household.

"Where did you get that?" Zelrin shouted again.

"T-Toby gave it to me."

"Why the flip would he keep it? Give it to me." Zelrin's arm shot out to grab the instrument.

"No!"

Aliwyn threw herself to one side. A wave of stars washed over her vision as she scrambled to her feet. The shackles around her ankles clanged loudly as she circled to Zelrin's right. Her hand protected the recorder against her stomach, but another hand grabbed her arm from behind, and Aliwyn shrieked. Thick fingers wrenched the recorder from her grasp. She spun around, shivering with sweat when the wind cut through her tunic.

Edward's scowl sent her heart hammering in her throat. He had grabbed her, and his fierce grip remained on her forearm. Slowly, he twisted her arm.

"Causing trouble already?" His voice was calm, sinister.

"Let her go!" Emma lunged forward, but Zelrin pulled her back by both shoulders.

Aliwyn doubled over but was determined not to scream. Everyone was watching.

"She's not causing anything," Zelrin stammered. "It's me. I was—"

"Who's this Aelfric?"

Edward had never heard about Aelfric. As Toby had said, his uncle arrived only after Aelfric's betrayal.

"Someone I have a grudge against," Zelrin said. "I'm overreacting, sir. I'm sorry about the yelling."

"Hmm. I understand your brother has just passed away, Zelrin. But even if you are upset, fighting over a toy is unacceptable."

"Yes, sir."

The older man eyed the recorder with distaste. "Deal with this as you'd like." He released Aliwyn and handed the instrument to Zelrin.

Aliwyn's mouth opened in a silent scream. For the last time, she saw the crucifix that Miriam had lovingly carved onto its surface. Zelrin hurled the recorder over the side of the ship with a powerful swing of his arm. The instrument spun in the air and disappeared.

Aliwyn covered her face with her hands, squeezing her eyes shut until the muscles of her face ached. Her temples pulsed from the pressure of rising sobs.

"All this over some stupid stick?" One soldier muttered.

Emma held onto her sleeve. "Aww, Aliwyn. Don't be so sad."

Zelrin marched past her, and Aliwyn could no longer hold her breath. She inhaled sharply and folded her arms around her stomach, trembling now that the raised platform no longer sheltered her from the wind. The other men on board lost interest and went back to their tasks.

"Sit back down where you were," Edward ordered.

"Wait, Ed. She can help me downstairs."

Aliwyn looked up. Toby was leaning against the side of the stairwell, where he'd stopped halfway up the steps. Had he just seen everything? His expression of sympathy made her chest swell. The irony of the situation was overwhelming. She couldn't stop staring at him; he seemed to care about her loss.

Edward grunted. "You make sure your father gets back on his feet, Toby."

"Can I come down and help too?" Emma ran toward Toby as he limped upstairs.

"I'll get you later. I need some time alone to talk with Aliwyn."

Emma scowled, but then a sly grin stretched her lips. "Ohhh, time alone. I get it."

The thought of being isolated with Toby and his father made Aliwyn's stomach twist. "Oh, no. Emma, please come down with us."

Toby watched Aliwyn as though waiting for her to descend with him, and she avoided his gaze. Shuffling toward the steps, she turned to ensure Emma was following. The child stared back. She took hesitant steps with a bowl of unfinished porridge, and Aliwyn tightened her jaw. Sooner or later, Emma would see the stern and frustrated side of Aliwyn that she had tried to conceal.

Aliwyn trudged down the stairs, and the chain between her ankles clattered one step after another. Toby followed her.

"Emma," he said, "bring that bag of biscuits with you."

"Aw...it wasn't my fault the rats got into it. Why do I have to pick out their poo?"

"Not too loud. I can help you with that later."

ALIWYN DESCENDED TO THE foot of the stairs with a stone crushing her chest. An oil lamp flickered in the ship's keep, casting shadows from the fishing nets suspended from the ceiling. Hammocks hung in between the multiple pillars of the underdeck, adding to the crowdedness of the crates, chests, and sacks. She wanted to mourn the recorder in solitude, but she had nowhere to hide.

A bag of biscuits thumped on each step as Emma pulled it down, and Toby spoke softly to her in the stairwell. Aliwyn's eyes adjusted to the dimness. Ransley appeared on his straw mattress several arm lengths away. At least he was asleep, and she didn't have to deal with him watching her and his son with that irritating smirk.

When Toby spoke behind her, Aliwyn spun around.

"Aliwyn, I apologize on Zelrin's behalf," he said. "It's been very difficult for him. Lukas was the only family he had left."

Toby sounded sincere, but she didn't respond. When he offered her the costrel Zelrin had slammed on the floor, she jerked it out of his hand and strapped it back onto her belt. Nothing would've felt better than punching Zelrin in the face.

"That Aelfric, he got so many people killed." Emma approached with the porridge. "He pretended to be Toby's friend but was a big fake, and he stole—"

"No need to say more, Emma," Toby said.

"Fine. Then let's just say I'm glad we threw away his recorder. But Toby, how come Aelfric's recorder looks so much like yours?"

Aliwyn stared at her dirty feet as Emma's question burned in her mind. She peered up at Toby, who walked to a wall with spears affixed to it.

He reached for a purple cloak that hung from a spear tip. "I don't understand why our recorders were made so similar. Aelfric had seen my recorder, but he said nothing. He also never showed me his recorder, but before he turned against me, he gave it to Zel. And Zel showed it to me because it looks like mine."

Emma stuck out her lower lip. "You shouldn't have kept Aelfric's stuff, Toby. That dirty rascal. I hope he burns in the big fire pit."

Aliwyn kept her eyes downcast. Had Aelfric been trying to tell Toby that the two of them had Miriam in common? Why had that been an important message to convey? Aelfric was a level-headed person, but he made mistakes, too. Aliwyn pinched her fingers as she imagined Aelfric on military duty. It was a side of him she had never seen. Knowing that he'd helped rescue Matthew was enough, and she never wanted to know how he did it. It tore at her heart to hear how much others hated her best friend.

Toby stepped before her and unfurled the woolen purple cloak he'd retrieved. Golden flowers blossomed along a vine embroidered around the hood.

"Try it on." His face was blank. "It should be the right length for you."

Aliwyn scowled at him. If he'd peeled off that cloak from a murdered Norman, she was clamoring back up the steps. "Where did you get that?"

"Toby," Emma whispered, "this cloak belonged to Odrianna, didn't it?"

The child's question cracked over Aliwyn's head like a whip, and she sucked in her breath. Toby was offering his dead fiancée's clothes? What was the meaning of this? He blinked several times as his eyes darted between Aliwyn and Emma.

"This did belong to Odri." His lips twitched. "But it's all I have that fits Aliwyn right now. And Odri...she wouldn't mind if I lent it to someone who could use it."

Aliwyn's skin crawled under the rough linen covering her body. Toby held up the cloak as though he were a statue, and she glanced at his downcast eyes with a stirring of sympathy. To refuse his offering would be heartless.

Nonetheless, the filth covering her hands and wrists made her hesitate. "I'm too dirty to wear this."

"Not to worry," Toby said. "Unless it's pouring rain, it's difficult to stay clean on this ship."

"How many days are we sailing for?"

"Probably four days till the first stop. It depends on the wind."

Emma yawned, still balancing the bowl in her hands. "Aliwyn, can you put the cloak on already? I want to give you this food."

Aliwyn shifted her body to fit into the cloak. Her injured shoulder twinged, but she kept silent as Toby lowered the purple cloth over her shoulders. Its fine wool graced the base of her neck, and its perfect length flowed over her old clothes. She quivered as Toby tied the laces holding the cloak in place. He said something about giving her stockings and shoes, but she shook her head without registering his message. Her mind caved into an exhausted spiral.

Four days until the first stop. Assuming that stop was Ravenser's Point, four days were all she had to sabotage the ship and jump. She still had no knife and no strategy to cut the sail's ropes without being seen. The harder she pressed herself for a plan, the muddier her thoughts became.

Someone overhead cleared his throat. Aliwyn stiffened when she saw Zelrin leaning over the opening of the stairwell. Axlan knelt beside him with a grin on his bearded face.

Zelrin tapped the stairwell's opening with a gloved finger. "Sir, can I help with anything?"

"Not for now, Zel. But thank you."

"I think that more people should be downstairs with you, in case something—"

Axlan grinned and nudged his shoulder. "C'mon, boy. Give Toby some time alone with his ladies. Now's not the time to get jealous."

Zelrin shot him an icy glare. He backed away from the staircase, and soon both men disappeared.

Emma took Aliwyn's wrist and placed the bowl of food in her hand. The girl leaned against Toby's stomach, sleepy but smiling as Toby stroked her hair with his good hand. Kato had told of two people on horseback who had found Emma on the streets and saved her. One of the two passersby must've been Toby. Aliwyn tried to imagine that she, too, had entered a welcoming family. The peace she felt was fleeting and bittersweet, like the wings of a doomed butterfly fluttering past her cheek before the first frost. She could never belong with Toby. His life as an outlaw was far from over.

Images of the leper's cabin and Myton in flames resurfaced in her mind. To have this destruction sweep through England was unthinkable. Toby could clothe her in expensive cloaks if he wanted, but she was the same inside. Still a woman ripped from her home, desperate to go back. Still a woman loyal to King William and the peace he'd maintained for a few blissful years. She refused to go to Denmark and abandon a country steeped with memories of her loved ones. Four days would be enough time for her to sabotage the ship and escape.

But right now, she needed to play on Toby's kindness.

"Toby," she said. "What did you need help with?"

"It's something I can try on my own. You should get some sleep now."

"And your father, how is he doing?"

Toby looked away. "His head still hurts, but I don't know what else I can do. I'm letting him rest." He reached up and tousled Emma's curly hair. "And you should get some rest too, Emma."

"Well, I was tryin' to until you and Ed stomped down here."

Toby let go of the child, and she skipped away in between the cluttered crates. As Aliwyn sipped on her porridge, the girl stopped before a large bed of hay covered by two linen sheets. Two folded blankets rested at the foot of the mattress. Emma jumped onto the pallet with a sweep of her arms.

"Oh, you made my bed bigger! A lot bigger!"

"Shhh, Emma. The extra space is for Aliwyn." Turning to Aliwyn, Toby added, "The mercenaries sleep in hammocks, but Zel, Emma, and I are not used to it. So, we will sleep on the floor."

Aliwyn scowled at the blankets and hay. She had trouble sleeping with only Mathew in her watermill, let alone on a ship full of ruffians. But it must've been difficult for Toby to put together everything with one hand, and she muttered her appreciation.

"I'm supposed to look at your injuries," she added.

He took her emptied bowl. "It's all right, Aliwyn. When I took a closer look, I saw tiny thorns stuck in the cut. That's likely why it was so itchy and keeps bleeding."

Aliwyn relaxed her shoulders as this news sank in. So, the arrows had probably not been poisoned. "Were you able to take the thorns out?"

"I'm working on it."

There was the sound of hay being shuffled, and Emma called in a sleepy voice, "Aliwyn, are you coming?"

She hesitated. Toby slid his injured hand behind his side, but the bloody strips of cloth were hard to miss.

"I'll be there soon, sweetheart," Aliwyn called out to Emma.

"Aww, no one's ever called me sweetheart before. I like it." The girl rolled in the blanket, chuckling as she wrapped herself in it. Aliwyn smiled. She turned back to Toby as he arched back to drain the last drop from her bowl. He lowered the bowl with a sheepish grin and wiped his mouth.

"You didn't eat?" Aliwyn scowled at him.

"I was too slow."

She studied his shy smile. This young man with probably a voracious appetite had left the food for everyone else. On an impulse, she reached for his bandaged right hand and tugged the bowl away. She set it on the ground and said, "I have a pair of tweezers. I can use them to take out the thorns."

Aliwyn fumbled for the tool in her pocket and came across Toby's recorder, which she brushed aside. She found the tweezers in another pocket, but her fingers still grasped Toby's hand. It was hot and swollen, and he had not pulled away.

Warmth flooded Aliwyn's cheeks, and her heart skipped a double rhythm. This was all part of the big show, all part of the ploy to survive. Toby was falling perfectly into her trap. She ignored the vise closing around her throat and released him.

"I'll free your wrists so you can work," Toby said. He retrieved a key from his pocket, and she raised her handcuffs with her face still burning.

The way he cupped her hands as he unlocked the metal rings made her twitch. He set the clinking shackles on a barrel nearby, and Aliwyn shuffled to the foot of the stairs, where a square of golden sunlight illuminated the steps. Toby followed. Nearby, Emma appeared to be asleep already.

The two adults sat on one of the lower steps, and Toby unwrapped the bandages. When he extended his hand on the wooden planks, the pressure in Aliwyn's throat intensified. She had not worked with wounds in months.

The gash on his hand was deep and raw, and jagged edges ran from the base of his thumb to under his ring finger. Aliwyn scrutinized it for thorns in the tangential lighting, trying to swallow the despair bobbing up her throat. What looked like countless silver hairs gleamed in the sunlight, all embedded into his flesh. She twirled the tweezers between her fingers, and Toby asked, "Do you see the thorns?"

"Yes..."

"Go ahead, Aliwyn."

She stalled for time. What if she made his hand into a bloodier disaster? "I was thinking about Lukas' horrible black blisters before he died. Why did he get that?"

"I've seen that happen when wounds are soiled. But I don't have a good explanation."

"What if it happens to you?"

"There are some things you can't control. We shouldn't worry about them."

His voice was reassuring, but Aliwyn's discomfort deepened. She was taking advantage of Odrianna's recent death. After losing Aelfric, she understood what the insatiable hunger for companionship felt like. Toby had lost his judgment. The vacuum in his heart blinded him, and he seemed to accept her sympathy without suspicion.

"Toby." She struggled to look at his face. "It's been a while since I've worked on an injury like this."

"Then...that's fine. May I borrow your tweezers?"

Aliwyn handed him the tool and pulled her knees to her chest.

"I'm sorry," she whispered.

"What are you sorry for? I'm glad you have tweezers, 'cause otherwise, I'd have to use my fingernails." He grinned as he studied his fingertips. "And I don't have any."

She mustered a smile back as he lowered his head to begin his task.

Toby worked on his wound with swift, rhythmic movements. She glanced at him from the corner of her eye. The boat's swaying didn't hamper his progress. He had probably worked with many wounds in the past. Toby's grimace deepened as he smeared the bloody tweezers on his old bandages, and goosebumps formed along Aliwyn's neck. So much pain, and he endured it.

"You're good with your left hand." She tried to distract them both.

"I learned to use it well. When I was a child, someone broke my right arm."

"Oh, you've mentioned that before. What happened?"

"I was twelve or so. My father sent me to train as a page with other boys at Sir Devereux's manor. We were a bunch of boys learning to fight together." He drew a deep breath before continuing with the tweezers. "It was chaos, but that's how boys train for knighthood."

She nodded. With Toby focused on something else, her eyes traced over the balanced features of his face.

"One of the older boys beat me up one day, and he snapped my arm."

Aliwyn gasped. "How awful! I hope he got punished for it."

"He...you probably think differently of him now."

"What? Think of whom?"

Toby was silent for a long time. "Matthew."

Aliwyn's fingers curled over her kneecaps at the unsettling story. "You knew him even back then?"

"Yes, and our families knew each other. This was shortly after William had become king and the country was still in shock. The few knights who still had energy to train boys took on more than normal. Anyway, Matthew and I ended up in the same manor. He was a popular boy."

"Oh, really?"

"You sound unconvinced." Toby chuckled. "Matthew was from the wealthiest family, so everyone...almost everyone was on good terms with him."

"But he must have been punished, right? For what he did?"

"No. The other boys didn't like me either. They lied...said I broke my arm by accident. At least Matthew was transferred to Lord Seville's manor afterward, and I didn't see him anymore."

His voice faltered. Toby set down the tweezers and used another cloth to cover the oozing blood. Aliwyn stared at the top of his head and the tousled blond hair. The story's unfairness bore into her mind like a parasite.

"Why did the others dislike you?"

Toby didn't answer. Aliwyn ducked to scrutinize his wound, and she gasped. Blood had seeped out onto the wood below his hand and was spreading as a black patch onto the bandage. Aliwyn grabbed the hem of her cloak, wrapped the cloth over his gash, and raised his hand above his chest.

Toby opened his mouth in a silent scream, but she maintained pressure to control the bleeding. Her lips trembled as he reeled in agony.

"I'm sorry," she said.

He kept his head bowed, neither moving nor speaking. His breath shook between jerking gasps. He raised his left elbow onto a higher step, set it down, and rested his temple on the bend of his left arm.

"You're doing the right thing," he whispered. "I didn't dare press that hard."

The blood coating his fingers gleamed in the sunlight, and Aliwyn waited with her body covered in a cold sweat. Thankfully, no blood soaked through her violet sleeves. It was such a lovely cloak that she was ruining, but nothing else had been at hand.

"Wait, did you get all the needles out?" she asked.

He shook his head, his bloodshot eyes squinting back at her. Was pressing on his wound the right thing to do, after all? She had pushed even deeper whatever thorns were left. Aliwyn fought a wave of frustration.

"I'll get them out, Toby."

She lowered his hand again and peeled back her sleeve. In the sunlight, the gash of his hand flashed red along with the tips of several dozen thorns. Aliwyn gripped the fingers of his wounded hand and turned it so she could see them better. Picking up the tweezers, she bit her lip and pinched the first needle.

A tug, and Toby flinched. She wiped the blood and the dislodged needle onto his old bandages and plucked another one. And another. Toby's bloodstained thumb quivered, and her throat swelled. But this had to be done. She adjusted her grip on his fingers and pinned them down again.

"Do you have a soporific sponge?" she asked. She should've asked earlier.

"I..." He gritted his teeth. "One left. Saving it."

The soporific sponges were infused with opium, henbane, and other herbs. Patients would inhale vapors from dampened sponges and lose consciousness before a painful procedure. Had Toby used the sponge, he wouldn't have suffered this much. Who would one day use that last sponge, and for what injury? Aliwyn didn't want to think about it.

"You're very skilled," Toby whispered.

She plucked two needles at a time. "Only with my right hand."

Aliwyn didn't speak again until all the needles were gone. She wrapped Toby's hand with her coat sleeve again, lifted it above the level of his heart, and applied pressure. His eyes were half-closed, his breathing still uneven.

"I pulled them all out," she said.

"Thank you." Toby smiled. "Miriam trained you well."

The tense muscles of her face relaxed, and she beamed. She hadn't forgotten her training, after all. Who would've guessed she'd be on a rebel ship when she performed her first medical procedure without panicking or freezing?

"If direct pressure doesn't stop the bleeding," she said, "I'll have to heat the tweezers and..."

"Cauterize it. I know. I was afraid it was coming to that." His hazel eyes rolled back before he blinked into attention. "Doing the right thing...can be so painful."

"Why don't you lie down beside Emma? I'll take care of your hand."

"But I don't want to sleep when my father is...and I have to talk to Ed again."

"About what?" she whispered.

"Where this ship is going."

Aliwyn swallowed. From what she had heard during her eavesdropping, Toby seemed opposed to delivering the pellets to the Danes, but Edward was the ship's captain. Toby couldn't possibly redirect the ship when it was his will against that of his father and uncle's, could he? With time, Toby's eyes rolled back again and closed with the rocking of the ship. His arm grew heavy and limp in her hold. Even while lying sideways on the rigid steps, he slumbered with his head resting on his left arm.

Aliwyn watched him with her chest heaving. She had pulled out those needles because it was the ethical thing to do, not because she had intended to soothe him to sleep. But Toby had begun to trust her, enough for him to lay defenseless with one hand resting within hers. He had left her wrists unshackled, and she could wander the hull and find a weapon.

She couldn't waste this opportunity. Aliwyn waited for Toby to pass into a deeper sleep before she moved.

Footsteps tapped on the creaking floorboards overhead, and the rhythmic splashing of the oars echoed from around the ship. The morning sunshine highlighted the angles of Toby's face. She loosened her grip on his hand but kept her sleeve over his injury.

Waiting made her squirm. She counted to pass the time, but her tired mind soon wandered. Wind stirred through Toby's golden blond hair. The way his tunic settled over his lean but muscular frame made her face glow. Mauve bruises covered his forehead, and his eyelashes cast long shadows over already sunken eyes, but he still had a handsome face. Aliwyn's eyes rounded, and her senses sharpened with dread. She severed the attraction budding within. A drifting mind was dangerous.

When Toby's breathing grew long and even, Aliwyn looked up to check the opening of the staircase. There was a patch of blue sky and wispy clouds with no one in sight, but the background of low voices warned her that soldiers were just beyond the edge. She had little unsupervised time.

Aliwyn hardened her jaw as she lowered Toby's hand onto the wooden steps. She waited in case he woke, but he didn't.

Pushing to her feet, Aliwyn shook out a stiff leg. The chain between her ankles clinked, and her hair stood on end. She separated her ankles as far as possible and began a slow waddle toward where Ransley slept, trying not to scoff at how ridiculous she looked. Nothing was funny here. Waddling kept the chains between her ankles stretched out and quiet. Her heart hammering, she kept Toby in her peripheral vision. If anyone asked, she desperately needed the privy.

Emma soon came into her field of view. Aliwyn ignored the girl's darling face and focused on the dense collection of crates, barrels, spears, chests, and linen bags surrounding her.

To her dismay, the crates were nailed shut at all four corners, and the first sacks she searched through revealed nothing useful. She lacked the time to rummage through everything. About a dozen chests were secured with rope netting along the perimeter. A few black chests painted with gold stripes caught her eye, but those were also padlocked. Maybe the one chest Toby and his father had fretted over losing resembled those painted chests.

Frowning, Aliwyn waddled further into the ship's hold. No weapons except the spears were affixed against the wall, but they were far too big for her to conceal. When her foot landed on hard objects, she nearly screamed.

Aliwyn spun to her left. She had stumbled into the straw mattress where Ransley was sleeping, and she had stepped on his adorned belt and belt pouches. Aelfric would have acted with absolute stealth in this situation. Aliwyn dared to look at Ransley's pale face. He was still asleep. Slowly, Aliwyn lifted her bandaged foot and looked down. She discovered the answer to her search—there were several blade handles protruding from the holsters of Ransley's belt.

They were perfect, and Aliwyn squealed inside. She bent down and fingered the various handles, assessing which one would be the easiest to hide and to use. The smell of pine sap that Toby had used to dress his father's wounds drifted about her as she pulled out a dagger the length of her hand. Seeing her reflection on the clear, cold metal threw her into a spiral of excitement and yet dread. The blade seemed sharp—sharp enough to saw the rope upstairs.

Where could she hide her new weapon? She grabbed a bundle of bandaging cloth and began to wrap it, but there was no safe way to carry the knife and keep it hidden. Hiding it anywhere on her body would not do, should she be searched. Finally, with her pulse drumming in her ears, Aliwyn waddled to two of the largest chests and knelt. She pulled off the bandages from the knife and slipped the naked blade underneath one chest. The knife slid and disappeared into the narrow space, but the handle remained within reach. She had a few days to retrieve it.

Another object caught her eye just before she stood. An acorn-shaped ceramic object the size of her hand was wedged between two crates, as though it had accidentally fallen. There seemed to be a small dome protruding from the top, but it was too dark to be sure. She had seen nothing like it before. Was it a container for ale? Medicine? It was best to leave the object there; she had the knife she wanted.

Aliwyn stood again, returned to the stairs, and stared at Toby. He slept on. The guilt of stealing when he'd shown her compassion made her shake. When the chilly wind blew from above, Aliwyn waddled to where Emma rested and retrieved a spare blanket. She lowered the blanket over Toby and knelt to examine his hand. The gash brimmed with blood but wasn't hemorrhaging like before.

Aliwyn used the bandages she had just unwrapped from her stolen knife to dress his hand. Brushing past his rough fingers with her own made her jittery from the inside out. How ironic it was to dress his wound just moments after her theft.

Aliwyn exerted pressure around Toby's hand, hoping to stop the bleeding completely. He grimaced in his sleep. Once he was awake, she would have to address the wound on his side in the same manner. She squirmed at the thought of pulling off Toby's tunic, examining his chest and back for other injuries, and leaning close to this bare torso to clean his wound. But it had to be done, not only because her life depended on his survival, but because she wanted to help.

A tan line graced the skin of Toby's left ring finger—all that remained of a missing ring. Wealthy couples often exchanged engagement rings, but Toby could no longer wear his. Aliwyn tied and tucked in the loose ends of the bandage strip, her eyes growing misty. Not long ago, she had also lost someone she had hoped to marry.

Toby had opposed the aggression of the other soldiers as they'd demanded the bridge's key. He had protected her or spared her when he barely knew her. Hanging from the bridge, he'd made a pact with Heaven to do as much good as he could if he survived. It was a bold venture, but because of his mission, his conduct had already fallen short.

But she held onto a thread of hope. She was willing to wait two days before retrieving the stolen dagger. Perhaps Toby would redirect the ship so the Danes would never set eyes on the flammable substance. If he aborted this mission and surrendered to the Normans, maybe they'd spare him. The Normans and Vasfians would decide between themselves what to do with the Boltans, and she'd go home.

Aliwyn lay the way Toby did on the steps, on her side and across from him. Her palm maintained pressure on his right hand. Every bruise and cut on his face spoke of what he'd suffered, and a strangling bramble wrapped around her throat.

What a ridiculous fantasy she had just conjured up. The Normans wouldn't spare Toby even if he surrendered because Matthew Marcotte wanted this rebel dangling from the gallows. This was the fate awaiting Toby if she reported this vessel.

Her frigid fingers quivered over the warmth of Toby's hand. He wasn't what she had expected. She didn't want him to die, but she could no longer take him to a sanctuary. How could his life be spared once the Normans captured this ship? The royal writ dictated justice. Reconciliation sounded like a dream.

And even after the rebellion ended, many would continue to hate the Normans. Aliwyn closed her eyes, exhausted at the thought, drained by the endless cycles of bloodshed. Ending the rebellion wouldn't end the rancor within people's hearts, and her chest tightened with despair.

A prayer ran through her foggy mind for peace. Peace for all of England. Peace between Matthew's family and all those who had wronged them, including Toby. Peace so that all her grief, regret, and resentment would ease. She wanted to stop hurting. Her hopes were impossible by human means, but Aliwyn had faith.

Maybe she had been placed here on this ship to save as many people as possible. For a moment, she forgot where she was and what she planned to do.

Her breathing grew even, and sleep overtook her before she knew it.

When Zelrin and Axlan peered down the staircase again, they found Aliwyn and Toby asleep on the stairs. Her hand rested over his as they slept.

Edward's shadow stretched over his head as Zelrin muttered about moving the couple off the steps. Both Zelrin and Axlan turned around with a start.

"Sir—" the youngster began.

Edward held up an open hand and silenced him. His brows knit, he stepped into the stairwell.

"You left her unsupervised!"

At Edward's seething voice, Aliwyn jolted back into awareness. The shadow of a large man stomped downstairs with his boots thundering in the narrow space, and she pulled back and pressed herself against the wall.

Then she regretted it. On the opposite side, Toby had barely moved. His upturned right hand lay on the step, and his half-opened eyes blinked at her listlessly.

Aliwyn curled her fingers around the cooling patch his hand had left behind. How long had she been sleeping? She should've shaken Toby awake to tend to him, to give him food and water. Her squeamishness in dressing a half-naked man shouldn't have been an excuse to delay it.

"What's wrong with you?" Edward squatted, grabbed Toby's shoulders, and hauled him to sitting. Toby winced when Edward pushed him against the wall.

Aliwyn pulled on Edward's thick biceps. "Don't be so rough! The Vasfians shot him in the lower abdomen. I can dress—"

"What?" Axlan hollered from upstairs. "They shot you?"

Edward flung off Aliwyn's hand and adjusted his grip on Toby's upper arms.

"Why didn't you say anything?" he whispered through his teeth. "I would've cleaned it for you."

Unease crept into his voice, and he glanced down the hull toward where Ransley slept. Aliwyn didn't hear Ransley or Emma stir in their beds, but Toby's eyes widened with fear behind Edward's broad back. Aliwyn's stomach dropped. She couldn't reach him with Edward in between them. Overhead, the mercenaries clustered around the stairwell with hushed and worried voices, and their darkened bodies blocked the sunlight.

"Axlan," Edward said. "Help me walk Tobias upstairs. Blakke, heat up a few daggers."

Axlan's footfalls thudded down the stairs, and the two older men lifted Toby to standing. His knees knocked, and Aliwyn caught a whiff of soured blood wafting from his body. His wound was beginning to fester. She steeled herself against a flurry of emotions and staggered to her feet. Edward could easily make Toby worse, and she had to stay close during whatever he planned to do.

The two men took one step up the stairs with Toby sagging by his outstretched arms in between them.

"The Vasfian arrow embedded thorns into Toby's wound," she said after them. "You must use tweezers—"

What felt like a brick hit her face, throwing her back against the stairwell.

"Ali!" Toby called with a broken gasp.

Aliwyn shuffled to regain balance with flashes of light blinding her vision. Her cheek numbed and reheated in searing pain, but she refocused on Edward's menacing face and clenched her hands.

"Why didn't you say anything earlier?" Edward hissed. "You want him to die, don't you? I'll slit your throat if he leaves you unsupervised again."

Edward turned back the stairwell and pulled Toby onto another step. "Zelrin, shackle her to the mast."

Aliwyn tasted blood on her lip where Edward had struck her, but she scrambled after Toby's dragging feet. What about the last soporific sponge that would keep Toby from feeling the pain? Did she dare mention it to Edward?

She halted when Zelrin pattered down the stairwell. He paused to murmur something to Toby before gliding past the three men and skidding to a stop across from her with his back to the wall. His lips were clamped in a thin slash, his breathing ragged. She didn't know he could be this silent.

When he reached for her arm, she didn't jerk away.

"You know those black bubbles that killed my brother—" He began.

"That's not happening to Toby," she said.

How was she so sure?

Zelrin held onto her wrist with an unsteady hand, and Aliwyn struggled to calm the tossing of her chest. What could she still do for Toby if she was chained to the mast?

She and Zelrin ran up the stairs.

CHAPTER 19

October 1

EMMA YELPED AND DROPPED her needle. A red drop beaded on her thumb; it was the third time that day that she had pricked herself. Aliwyn sighed and set down the surcoat she had been sewing. She shifted to her hands and knees to search for the lost needle, and the shackles around her wrist clattered onto the planks. Toby's screams from hours ago, when Edward had cauterized his wound, still echoed in her head, but Aliwyn wanted to behave with some semblance of normalcy before a child.

"Emma, I told you to slow down."

"But I don't want to do this anymore. It's so boring!"

Aliwyn found the needle beside the pile of golden griffin surcoats yet to be repaired. Returning the needle to Emma, Aliwyn sat back against the mast and scanned the deck.

Thankfully, Edward Boltan hadn't been around to hear Emma complain. Zelrin, Axlan, and several other mercenaries sat around the cauldron's sandbox. Their greasy necks glistened in the afternoon sun as they prodded the dying embers. Other men sharpened their knives with a stone or wiped the oars stacked along the vessel's sides. The wooden hull creaked with the waves. Aliwyn shifted her weight over the floorboards that baked her thighs with the stench of sweat and ale. The sickening smell turned her empty, growling stomach. She had gotten over her seasickness but kept an empty bucket nearby just in case.

No one rowed. Small shutters blocked the oar holes, and round shields rested against the railings. After hours on board, Aliwyn understood rowing was only necessary for sharp turns and unfavorable winds. The ship's speed relied on wind power, and the wind was strong right now.

Everyone acted as though Toby's ordeal had never happened.

Edward had probably gone downstairs to see his brother, but finding him absent didn't quell Aliwyn's simmering angst. He had forced Aliwyn and Emma to empty privy buckets, scrub the deck, and wash and sew the griffin surcoats. She was so tired she could close her eyes and start dreaming.

The powerful gusts had also prevented the crew from starting a fire. Gnawing on biscuits and smashed, dried cod wasn't enough. Without fire to boil a cauldron of much-desired pottage, they had instead been guzzling ale and singing off-key about imaginary food.

"Emma, just be patient. We'll be done soon." Aliwyn reached into the inner pocket of her purple coat, the one Toby had given her, and pulled out a clean rag. "Take this for your finger, sweetheart."

Emma had already stuck her bleeding thumb into her mouth. She sat in the shade offered by the mast—a place Aliwyn had relinquished so the child wouldn't get sunburned. With her cheeks sucked in, Emma resembled a fish wearing a hood.

Aliwyn grinned. "Don't do that! Your thumb is dirty."

Emma pulled out her thumb and smirked. "But I got you to smile! You didn't smile the whole afternoon, you know?"

"Emma...thank you for your concern."

Tugging on the hood of her tunic, Aliwyn ducked her head. She had blunted her emotions for everyone and everything.

Earlier that day, Edward and others had pulled Toby on deck, stripped off his tunics, and pinned down his limbs. The only relief came with seeing he had no black bubbles forming under his skin. She had shouted about administering a soporific sponge, but no one listened. Without mercy, the crew flushed and scrubbed out Toby's wound and its embedded needles, then Edward cauterized it with hot blades. When Toby screamed, they pressed a sack of barley over his face. Emma had been downstairs, at the opposite end of the ship, and had thankfully slept through the noise.

Aliwyn had watched everything, chained to the mast and feeling like her heart was being mashed into a pulp. After the mercenaries had carried Toby onto a blanket to sleep, she had buried her face in her hands. The truth had come crawling like icy fingers down her neck. Edward remained the ship's captain, sailing it wherever he pleased and abusing the crew whenever he wanted. Toby couldn't gain the upper hand, and she couldn't afford to care about him anymore.

He still conspired against His Grace, and she still intended to sabotage his household's vessel and escape. Toby would suffer the consequences of treason even if he surrendered, and any closeness she indulged in now would only shatter her later. These unforgiving facts made her ribs spasm with pain.

But Emma's lingering smile came into focus, bringing Aliwyn back to the present, and her throat swelled.

"Why don't we have a break?" Aliwyn whispered. "I'll brush your hair. You told me you'd love that."

"We can have a break?" The girl looked around with a mischievous jerk of her eyebrows. "Ohhh, Ed went downstairs!"

"That's right. We'll hear him when he comes back up. Then we'll start sewing again."

Emma grinned and took out a comb from the inner pocket of her gambeson. She passed it to Aliwyn and spun around on her seat. Aliwyn worked her fingers through the knots in Emma's black hair before reaching in with the comb. Her back was sore and her left shoulder burned, but as Emma's warm curls flowed through her fingers, Aliwyn smiled.

"Sorry my hair's so messy," Emma said. "Toby usually combs it, but he's been busy. And Zel just pulls my hair out, so he's not allowed to touch it. *Ever*."

Aliwyn chuckled, but Toby's name made her face fall flat.

He was curled on his side and asleep under the shade of the front platform, or the forecastle as the soldiers called it. A line of washed tunics and capes flapped on a twine running from one platform's edge to the other.

The sight of his bruised face made Aliwyn's chest ache. No one deserved what he had suffered, but she could only blame him for dragging her onto this floating prison.

"Having fun pricking yourselves?"

Aliwyn growled at the familiar voice. Zelrin stood nearby, watching them with his arms crossed. Now that Toby's condition had stabilized, she wasn't about to show him any more sympathy. She tried to scoot away, but Edward had bound her wrists to the ship's mast with a short chain.

"Yes, Zel. It's so much fun." Emma narrowed her eyes. "Why don't you try sewing?"

"Why don't you try lighting that sardin' fire?" Zelrin pointed at the hearth. "So much cinder blown on my face." He took off his woolen cap and wiped greasy ash from his cheek. "But...Sir Edward went down to fetch something he said for sure will light it up."

"Oh, really?" Emma straightened. "What's he getting?"

Aliwyn held her breath, waiting for an answer. But Zelrin only pulled his cap back on as his gray eyes shifted from Emma to Aliwyn. Their frowns locked, but not for long. This wastrel had thrown Aelfric's recorder overboard. Her nostrils flaring, Aliwyn slammed the comb down with a loud clatter and looked away.

"Sardin' barnacles, missy," he muttered. "You still mad at me for that flute? You're worse than my baby sister used to be, y'know? That thing was a stick with holes. Toby can buy you another one, easy."

Aliwyn clenched her kneecaps. She hated being called 'missy'. With a sprinkling of chills, she gloated over his watery death should she burn and sink the ship. No. She would not sink to that level of evil.

Slow, deliberate thumps echoed up the stairwell. Everyone knew who it was, and Aliwyn grabbed her needle again. Emma went back to her stitching while Zelrin uncrossed his arms and rolled back his shoulders. The heads of Edward and Ransley Boltan appeared from the dark hole. Their thick woolen capes swayed after them and ushered forth the scent of smoke and ale. Aliwyn's lower lip, swollen and crusted from where Edward had slapped her, throbbed with renewed vigor.

Hopefully, they would ignore her and keep walking.

She was about to resume sewing when something in Edward's hand stole her attention. He was carrying the ceramic acorn at his side. She had seen it earlier that day, wedged between two crates when she had stooped to steal Ransley's knife. So, was this the miracle item he was using to start the fire? She didn't have time to wonder.

Ransley's hoarse voice made her neck prickle. "Someone stole my dagger. It was part of a prized set from my father."

Edward stomped his boot beside Aliwyn's knee. "Thief! Get up!"

Aliwyn's heart shot into her throat, but as calmly as she could, she set down her needle and looked up.

"Why are you blaming Aliwyn?" Emma asked.

"Emma, go downstairs," Ransley ordered.

The child pushed off everything she had been sewing, crawled over, and wrapped herself around Aliwyn's arm. Aliwyn tried to stay collected when she saw the child's drawn eyebrows and down-turned lips.

"Emma, it'll be all right. Listen to Ransley and go downstairs."

She tugged her arm free and was glad when Emma finally shuffled down the stairs. Not a moment too soon.

Edward reached down and grabbed Aliwyn's shackled wrist. He unlocked it with the swift turn of a key and pulled her to standing. A chilling breeze blew over her stiff hamstrings. The surcoat she had worked on tumbled to the floor, and the open beak of its ugly, embroidered griffin seemed to mock her. Aliwyn steadied herself on her shoeless feet and faced a wall of frowning men, gathering in a semi-circle. Axlan and Cilebi were amongst them.

"I found this under Ransley's belt, where his weapons were." Edward held up Aliwyn's tweezer with a piercing glare.

She stared at the object. Last night, back in the tunnel leading to this ship, Toby had pulled that tweezer from her belt pouch while searching her for weapons. Edward had only seen it for an instant, but he remembered that it was hers.

"I don't know why that was there," she stammered. "I didn't steal anything."

Edward ignored her. He wrenched her arms behind her back and ordered his men to search her. Aliwyn clamped her mouth shut to avoid screaming. One man moved forward and patted down her sides. Terror tightened her throat and numbed her legs, but Aliwyn kept silent and blinked at her feet.

She carried no dagger, even if she had stolen one. Hands fumbled at the violet coat Toby had given her, and she bristled as they touched places they shouldn't touch. Her belongings clattered onto the floorboards—a jar of ointment, two coins, and a small drawstring pouch of pretty pebbles she had been collecting. Finally, Edward pulled off her coat in a crumpled heap. No dagger appeared.

"I didn't steal anything," she said, matching his icy frown.

"Well, looks like she's innocent."

Zelrin spoke from behind her ear. He was the one bending back her left arm and hurting her shoulder. She wanted to spin around and slap him.

Axlan scratched his beard with a dirty finger. "I have to say, we've watched her all day, and she's been tied to the mast. There be no chance she did somethin' foul."

Cilebi snickered. "Look at her. You expect *her* to stage a steal?"

Aliwyn's breath scorched in her nostrils. Holding Toby's hand that morning had solidified her reputation as his helpless plaything. So be it. The less these men expected of her, the more she could do. After what felt like an eternity, the many hands touching her withdrew and left her face burning.

The soldiers scattered, but Zelrin remained beside her. Edward ordered her to sit as he closed the shackles back around her itchy wrist. She resisted spitting in his face.

"I'll keep looking for it, Rans," Edward said. "Go back down."

His voice was suddenly gentle, unrecognizable. Aliwyn glared at him.

As Edward stood, he asked Zelrin to show his belongings. Aliwyn curled her toes. Even if Edward could sound decent, she would always see him as putrid to the bone. The youngster shuffled his feet a few times before he emptied the inner pocket of his gambeson and his belt pouches. Out came plum pits, yellow snail shells, and carved miniatures of birds. He displayed his leather sling and a few egg-shaped slingstones. No dagger.

Edward placed a hand on Ransley's shoulder. "You said the sunlight makes your headache worse. Please go downstairs."

A stained linen bandage still wrapped around Ransley's forehead, and his face sagged along every wrinkle. "Then let Odrianna go. You just saw she didn't take my dagger."

Aliwyn clenched her jaw. She was neither innocent nor Toby's dead fiancée. How eerie it was to be mistaken for Toby's former lover.

As Ransley descended the stairs, Edward said, "I'll take care of her."

That was a threat, not a reassurance. Aliwyn's scalp tingled as Edward marched toward his mercenaries and ordered them to remove their belts for inspection.

A voice within screamed that she had better escape tonight or get attacked in her sleep. This body search was just the beginning. She couldn't wait another day for Toby to reconsider his mission. All he had done since this morning was sleep.

Aliwyn lifted her eyes. Lines radiated from the mast's peak and supported the structure upright against the strain of the sail. Many other ropes tethered the square sail to the ship's rear and kept the sailcloth from flapping. The rigging was balanced to keep the mast standing and the sails full.

Which lines should she cut to throw everything into mayhem?

EMMA'S VOICE ECHOED UP the stairwell. The girl ran to hug her, and tears smarted Aliwyn's eyes. This was no place for any child. She wrapped her good arm around the child's delicate shoulders and yearned to take her home, but she couldn't expect Emma to sever her ties with Toby and Zelrin.

Zelrin scooped up the violet cloak and dusted it off. He dropped Aliwyn's drawstring pouch and other belongings back into her inner coat pocket.

"Hurry and put it on." He shook it out before her.

With her muscles still stiff, she let Zelrin throw the cloak back over her shoulders.

"I should've noticed you had bandages around your shoulder," he said. "Didn't mean to hurt you."

Aliwyn frowned at the floorboards. Even if they were concerned, she had to distance herself. Today would be the last day she saw either of them.

The grumbling and cursing from the sandbox turned into excited chatter. Aliwyn looked up, her eyes throbbing with fatigue as the rush of the body search fell away. Men crowded around Edward as he stood before the sandbox. Two mercenaries held wooden planks on either side of the embers to shield them from the wind, and Edward shook the clay acorn over the edge of the fireplace. Black pellets poured from a coin-sized hole at the acorn's tip.

Instinct told Aliwyn that his actions would cause problems, but she kept her mouth shut. If she spoke again, she could lose her head.

"Ugh! That stuff smells like rotten eggs!" One raspy voice called from the crowd.

Edward chuckled. He set the presumably empty clay acorn on the corner of the sandbox. "Just fan it a bit. The smell shouldn't last long."

Gesturing for his men to make space, he picked up a metal rod and pushed the black pellets beneath the cauldron. Smoke rose from between the two wooden boards. The mercenaries around Edward erupted in cheers.

"Jumping magpies! The fire's starting!" Emma hopped to her feet.

Edward straightened with a proud smile. His toothy grin below a sharp nose made Aliwyn grimace.

"Add more tinder," he said. "And get some firewood in there."

Two mercenaries hurried away for supplies, and others huddled shoulder to shoulder as though to block the wind. Emma ran for the sandbox, but Zelrin caught her by the forearm.

"Zel! I want to see!"

"You can see from here." He scowled back. "Toby told me not to touch those thundercrashers."

Emma cocked her head. "Say what? Thundercrashers?"

"That's the ball thing Sir Edward was holdin'. It's got some fancy name from the East."

"Oh, it's not a stink-proof container for carrying the rocks?"

To Aliwyn's vexation, Zelrin glanced at her and fell silent. She turned back to the scene unfolding around the sandbox, her pulse escalating. So the clay acorn was another object Toby had procured from the East, probably thanks to his former life as a merchant. She needed to observe what it did and report it to the Normans.

Beyond the hearth, under the front platform of the ship, a blanket flew off the body lying underneath. Aliwyn gave a start.

"Something's burning!" Toby shouted.

He pushed himself to sit, and Edward muttered, "Calm down. I just started the fire."

Toby stared at him with wide but puffy eyes. With his hair flattened from sleeping, he looked so much like his scraggly father, and Aliwyn wrinkled her nose. Toby's gaze swept the deck until they met with hers.

Memories from the stairwell came surging against her will. Holding Toby's hand had been a total loss of control on her part, and her face scorched with shame. How could she have done that after years of desiring to be with Aelfric?

"My friend!" Axlan waved at Toby. "You must sell this potash compound to all the households in the country! By golly, folks'll never have trouble startin' their fires again! And you'd be stinkin' rich!"

Chuckles and lighthearted commentary followed from those sitting by the hearth, but Toby's frown didn't waver. Aliwyn stuck her needle into the surcoat and crumpled the fabric with her hands.

"Put out the fire," Toby ordered. "You must not use the potash compound on board."

"I told them they can," Edward said. "I let you sleep the whole bloody day while I ran everything and cared for your father. Now keep your mouth shut."

He and Toby glared at each other, and the merry faces around the sandbox fell flat. The disgruntled muttering that followed sent goosebumps skittering down Aliwyn's neck. If the crew turned against Toby, what would happen to her?

As per Edward's instructions, one mercenary pushed leaves and small sticks into the growing smoke. Edward prodded the fire, ignoring Toby as he sat, alone, on a sheet behind the line of laundry. Zelrin sighed. He put his arm behind Emma's shoulders and began guiding her toward Toby.

"Aliwyn, we'll be back," Emma said softly.

They left, and Aliwyn caught Toby watching her through the many bodies on deck. She was sweaty, sticky, and sore, all because he had dragged her onto this ship, and he couldn't control anything thanks to his despicable uncle. It was a good thing she was leaving that night. He'd never grow a backbone.

As she glowered at him, what looked like remorse, even shame, flickered over Toby's eyebrows. Aliwyn narrowed her eyes. His expression lasted for only an instant. He pushed to his feet, his stark frown erasing all traces of their silent exchange as he passed the platform's pillar.

"Ed!" He hobbled into the sunlight. "I told you! I couldn't mimic the exact formula from the East. What we have is too dangerous to use on board!"

He could still muster a commanding voice, and chills poured over Aliwyn's smoldering resentment. She hadn't expected to influence him.

But the mercenaries disregarded Toby's warning, and one picked up the clay acorn and brought it over to the fire. He inverted it, presumably to add more pellets. A cloud of black powder poured out instead, as fine as flour. Toby's eyes widened at the clay object— probably the first time he had seen it through the wall of bodies. He screamed.

Zelrin and Emma were passing the periphery of the hearth gathering when a blinding light flashed. A cloud of fire billowed through the black dust, engulfing the hand holding the acorn and rising like an ephemeral mushroom. The flame extinguished quickly, but a column of smoke in its wake enveloped the men nearby. Aliwyn couldn't hear herself shriek amongst the cries and coughing on deck. As wind dispersed the smoke, men fell and rolled as fire licked up their sleeves and collars.

The acorn tumbled onto the floorboards, spinning like mad and spewing fire out of its gaping hole. Toby bolted toward Zelrin and Emma as they cowered from the sudden commotion. He pulled them down and covered them with his body.

An instant later, the clay object spun into the ship's railing and shattered in a boom reminiscent of thunder.

Aliwyn's face was numb. She stumbled to her feet only to slam back behind the mast as clay shards ricocheted off the railings and clanged off the hearth's cauldron. Sparks showered onto the wooden floorboards. Aliwyn grabbed her vomit bucket and ran for the rainwater barrels, but the shackles chaining her to the mast jerked her back and kept her from reaching them.

"Toby!" She tossed him the empty bucket instead.

Toby let go of Zelrin and Emma, who looked stricken but unharmed as men rushed by. He grabbed Aliwyn's bucket, and several mercenaries threw their upper bodies into the barrels along the vessel's railing. Others lay rolling on the ground, covering their eyes and moaning. With shaking arms, Aliwyn unfurled golden griffin surcoats to extinguish any remaining sparks on deck. The rotten egg smell made her stomach heave. She leaned against the mast and covered her mouth.

Toby doused the men with rapid throws of the bucket. Glistening water cascaded over the floorboards, washing aside shattered clay and blackened debris. He pulled a few men to sitting. Moving aside their charred collars, he ordered others to fetch damp linens.

Aliwyn's heart hammered as the deafening noise from the incident echoed in her mind. She had probably just seen burning pellets, in powder form, set ablaze by a spark. And it had come from a container that could burst.

What felt like a fist tightened around her throat. Just when she thought Toby's cargo couldn't get more dangerous.

Where was Edward? How could he have been so careless? She finally saw him standing by the railing, beside the stacked oars. Toby grabbed him by the shoulders.

"Edward!" he shouted. "Where did you get that?"

The older man blinked several times. "Your father found it. He told me to crack one and use it to start the fire."

"He said what?"

"Why are you talking about me?" Ransley's voice rang out from the stairwell, and Aliwyn tensed. His head was close to her feet from where he stood on the steps.

"And what was that ruckus?" Ransley shouted.

"Father!" Toby cried. "We agreed not to open those chests!"

"What chests?"

Aliwyn's pulse tapped in her throat. How could this mastermind murderer have become so forgetful?

"You don't remember?" Toby let out what sounded like a chuckle mixed with a sob.

"Remember what?" Ransley ran a hand through his thinning hair. "Oh, the chests. I didn't open any chests. I found a receptacle of the compound on the ground. Ed said he was having trouble with his fire, so I told him to open one and use it."

"It's not a simple receptacle!" Toby limped toward his father, shaking his head. "And you found it on the floor? Then the chests downstairs have been compromised."

"Compromised?" Edward asked. "By whom? When?"

"Probably when the Vasfians attacked me," Ransley muttered. "They stole one chest from us, Ed. I think I told you."

Toby stopped by the stairwell as though contemplating his father's words and searched the deck. When he met with Aliwyn's glare, he ducked his head. He swept together the wet, broken shards with his boots like some guilty child after breaking his family's water jar.

But his grim expression made no difference. He should never have brought these demonic objects into England, let alone persist in bringing them to the Danes. Was he so convinced that freeing England was worth the cost of certain havoc?

Aliwyn had just witnessed one clay acorn, or thundercrasher, explode. And it had been cracked and partly emptied. What could a whole chest of intact thundercrashers do? A ship full of them?

Her vision went white. They would destroy bridges and crumble churches where the neediest sought shelter. Reduce watermills like the one she lived in to rubble. The flying shards would throw Norman knights off their horses and kill their foot soldiers, and most of the foot soldiers serving the Normans were Englishmen like Aelfric.

Aliwyn gasped for air.

She must report this deadly, fist-sized weapon to the Norman authorities so they could confiscate it. And once they came, Toby would have to deal with the consequences of his decisions.

Emma wove between the stricken mercenaries scattered on deck, and the worry on her face brought Aliwyn back into the moment. Blinking back tears, Aliwyn opened her arms, and the girl ran into them. Aliwyn squeezed the child against her chest.

Edward cleared his throat. "Brave men of the Fortuna. I did only what I thought was in everyone's best interest. I was not properly informed of the risks, so I cannot take responsibility. You have until the beginning of night watch to recover; all duties are suspended. Much feasting, celebration, and riches await you at our destination."

The mercenaries muttered amongst themselves and returned to tending to their burned and blinded. Zelrin and others threw their buckets overboard to fetch more water. The late afternoon sun outlined their bodies in glowing silhouettes, and seabirds soared in the distance.

Edward marched up to Toby, his teeth bared. "You realize that if you weren't so tightlipped about what your little clay eggs could do, I wouldn't have made this mistake?"

"The mistake was mine," Ransley called from the stairs.

Toby didn't budge. "Ed, you joined me and my father only recently. If you want to talk, we can talk downstairs, and also examine those chests."

Ransley descended the steps. "Toby, I'm so nauseous. I apologize for the error."

Aliwyn stroked Emma's hair and tried to calm herself.

Toby scanned the mess on deck with his shoulders slumped. Some mercenaries curled up on the floor while others stood staring at the sandbox, now covered in black soot. He had done nothing to reroute this ship. Why pretend to be ashamed?

One mercenary yelped while wiping his eyes, and Toby left the stairwell to see him. He knelt and coaxed the injured man into uncovering his eyes, but Aliwyn looked away. She would not let Toby and his family get away with their plans.

"Toby! We talk now!" Edward shouted from downstairs. "These men can take care of themselves!"

Toby pushed to his feet again with tension wrinkling his face.

"Aliwyn, Emma." He approached them. "Are you all right? I should've come to see you earlier."

CHAPTER 20

EMMA RAN TO EMBRACE Toby. She avoided squeezing the cauterized wound on his left torso, but he still winced.

"Toby! Are you feeling better?"

He kissed her forehead. "Thank God nothing happened to you. I'm less tired now."

Without Emma to hold, Aliwyn crossed her arms. The shackle around her wrist chilled her through her tunic's sleeves. A glance over the choppy gray waters revealed no neighboring ships, and her heart sank into the pit of her stomach. It would've been too convenient had another vessel come to investigate. All day, the mercenaries had climbed up to the crow's nest to report nearby ships and steer away from them.

"Aliwyn, I'm sorry I was out for so long," Toby said. "And for what just happened..."

She squinted at the distant, sandy beaches with a rim of pine trees behind them, followed by golden farm hills that rose and fell into the reddening sky. Toby had not spoken to her since they had fallen asleep on the stairwell. After a day of toiling on deck, wallowing in resentment, and plotting her escape, the memory of holding his hand felt surreal.

"Zel!" Toby called out. "Please come here."

Zelrin had taken off his gambeson and tunic. He wiped his torso with a wet rag as he hurried over. A fleshly scar ran down the right side of his lean body, maybe an old sword slash. Had it come from a Norman's sword? Aliwyn didn't want to know.

As Zelrin drew close, Toby said, "Make sure Aliwyn and Emma are safe while I'm downstairs."

"No problem for Emma. But are you sure about this lady?" He flicked a finger at Aliwyn. "I think she wants my head axed off and roasted."

"Oh, Zel!" Emma put her hands on her hips. "Aliwyn's not that mean!"

Aliwyn swallowed with a tug of shame. She had just fantasized about watching the young man drown. When Toby switched to the Vasfian language, she looked up. His brows were drawn with concern.

"Aliwyn, I know you don't like Zelrin, but I trust him more than any other man on deck."

She turned away from his puffy and purplish face. The three companies of mercenaries on board had been cursing and teasing each other all day. They were bound not by loyalty, but by the promise of payment. Of course, Toby didn't trust them.

"I don't care if you trust Zel, because I don't," she muttered back in Vasfian.

Zelrin threw up his hands. "Stop speakin' your secret language, will you? Fine, I'll watch her. And you, Emma, help me sweep up. These two are needin' to talk."

The two youngsters began picking up the golden griffin surcoats Aliwyn had laid out to smother the embers. When Toby put his hand on her good shoulder, she stared at her curling toes. The way he caressed her shoulder only made her rigid.

What did he hope to accomplish between them? She knew too much about his plans. Thanks to Ransley and Edward's blunders, she had also seen what those diabolical thundercrashers could do. She would never forgive herself if she didn't cut the rigging tonight.

Toby again apologized for sleeping for so long. He reminded her to get stockings and shoes from bags under the front platform, but she ignored him. She refused to wear stolen items and had wrapped her legs and feet in linen strips instead.

Toby sighed. "Please, Aliwyn. Can you help the injured men here?"

She glanced at him. His cracked lips were bleeding again. It was a pitiful sight, but she almost scoffed. Help the very men bringing unimaginably dangerous goods to the Danes? They wanted England engulfed in flames and carnage and were better off blind.

"I don't know what to do when eyes are injured like this," Toby said. "Washing isn't enough, is it? And I don't recognize every medicinal plant."

He took out a key from his belt pouch and asked to see her shackled wrist. She stared at the key, her mouth dry. Freedom? She raised her left hand, grimacing at the rash developing underneath the metal ring.

Toby took her hand. He shook his head, scowling, and inserted the key into the shackle's lock mechanism. "About your shackles...I'll speak to Edward."

Aliwyn crushed any gratitude as he unclasped the metal ring from around her wrist. She wanted to squirm out of her skin, but Emma, Zelrin, and several mercenaries stared at her from behind Toby's back, and she finally faked a smile.

Toby didn't see it. He reached for an orange tin from his belt pouch as he held onto her hand. "I'll dress it for you, Aliwyn."

With careful sweeps of his finger, he spread a cooling ointment over her wrist's rash. Aliwyn remembered doing something similar for Matthew Marcotte in her watermill, and she hung her head.

Jacques Verdun, the Norman knight who had stopped her, Toby, and Emma outside Myton, said that Matthew had never returned to the Norman army. What had happened to him? God forbid he should be sent, as a Norman squire, to the front lines against the Danes. She tensed. The thundercrashers. One could shatter in his face and blind him.

Toby's hand quivered as he covered her wrist with a folded handkerchief. "Aliwyn, the herbs are at the ship's stern."

All stolen from the leper's cabin. Aliwyn sucked in her upper lip and stared at the wispy, golden clouds drifting on the horizon. Toby's right hand was still bandaged, and he struggled to tie the handkerchief around her wrist. The scent of pine sap from his wound wafted to her nose. It was the scent of her watermill when Miriam had been alive and tending to the sick.

The moaning of men on deck amplified in her ears. Her mind flashed back to the clearing outside her home, covered with the Boltans' wounded and dying soldiers. A prickling sensation crawled up her spine. Pain was pain, regardless of who felt it. Miriam never asked any of her patients for their criminal history. She treated everyone.

Toby finished tying the knot on the handkerchief, and Aliwyn followed his gaze toward the mercenaries under the front platform. Some circled the sacks of herbs, while others pulled out pinches of shriveled leaves and sniffed them with puzzled frowns. Her focus shifted back to Toby and his bloodshot eyes, and she shivered. She didn't understand him, but she knew how it felt to watch companions suffer.

"I won't force you to do anything," Toby whispered.

He turned to leave, but she said softly, "I'll do what I can here, Toby."

He exhaled, and his expression brightened as he faced her again. "Thank you. I'll come help as soon as I can."

He held her gaze for a moment longer before turning to leave for the staircase. She disregarded the appreciation in that look. He could care for strangers who killed and stole, but joining his father in murdering Matthew's household was somehow acceptable. Toby was a walking contradiction.

But she was no different. She had just agreed to care for injured mercenaries despite her determination to sabotage their ship. Aliwyn frowned after Toby's back as he descended into the darkness. People were complicated. One day, maybe, she'd find them easier to decipher.

Patting the bandage on her wrist, she watched her feet as she walked around the puddles and clay shards. Halfway to the platform, her forehead bumped into Zelrin's nose.

"Watch it!" He jerked back, scowling. "I didn't want Ed to grab you again."

She blinked several times at his gray eyes and overgrown bangs. He seemed to take Toby's orders to watch her seriously.

"Toby asked me to look through the herbs." She backed away from him. "Are there linen squares to make poultices? A mortar and pestle?"

Zel pointed at the ship's stern with his broomstick. "Just go look. Everything's under the aftcastle."

Aliwyn sidestepped him and glanced behind her. Zelrin faced the stairwell with his broomstick upright like a spear. He was of similar height and build as Kato, whom she had last seen in the foreground of a similarly painted sunset, and her feet staggered to a stop.

She had never thanked Kato, who had defended her against the lepers in a way that she'd neither asked for nor deserved. What if the lepers had killed him after she'd sped away on his donkey cart? Her eyes stung with tears. Kato deserved better. She hoped to see him again, alive and well, so she could thank him.

When Zelrin turned around, positioning his broomstick to sweep the debris on deck, Aliwyn saw Kato turning in her mind's eye. Her vision clouded again.

Zelrin jutted his chin. "Why you starin' at me?"

"N-no reason."

Aliwyn sniffled and searched for the bucket she had passed to Toby earlier. She needed the object for her plans later that night. Any hopes to see Matthew, Kato, Evelyn, and others again involved her fleeing this ship.

She found the bucket and picked it up, her fingers digging into its damp wooden contour. A group of huddled mercenaries looked up as she approached. She mustered a smile. A few men smiled back, and goosebumps prickled the back of her arms.

If they thought she was harmless, they were wrong.

Aliwyn brushed aside the row of damp laundry and ducked under the aftcastle. She squatted and opened the drawstring bags, but her eyes darted to the rigging to her right. Most lines wrapped around wooden pins driven into the rail, while other ropes ended in a pulley attached to the rail. She could reach and cut several ropes if she leaned against the railing.

Aliwyn plotted a way to get herself into that position after dark.

"Aliwyn! Zel said you wanted linen squares? I know where they are!"

Emma's shout sent Aliwyn's heart shooting to her throat. The girl dove through the laundry and landed beside her with a broad grin.

Aliwyn touched the girl's shoulder with an unsteady hand. "Th-that's great, Emma."

Emma carried the folded golden griffin surcoats they hadn't finished mending. They were damp and dirty from drying the floorboards, but when Emma stuffed them into an empty bag, Aliwyn didn't object. Why would she care?

"Can I help you make pulled...tricks?" Emma asked.

Pulling tricks was what Aliwyn intended to do, and blood rushed to her face. "It's called a poultice. It's a linen square with mashed medicine inside and tied into a pouch."

Her ribs hardened into slabs of stone. She would also betray Emma's trust that night, but cutting the rigging wouldn't put the girl in danger. It would just slow the ship down and mark it as suspicious while Aliwyn rushed to the closest manor. When the Normans arrested the rebels, surely they wouldn't punish the children. After all, a Norman priest had transported Aliwyn and many other English children to safety years ago.

Emma pawed through the sacks with a smile. "Aliwyn, can you brush the other half of my hair later? And make a braid for me tomorrow morning? Please."

"I can do that," Aliwyn lied.

Behind Emma lay the linen sheet Toby had been sleeping on, still wrinkled around the shape of his body. Her pulse racing, Aliwyn took out one satchel of herbs followed by another. She scowled at a large pulley with ropes looped around it and swept away her guilt. Wouldn't any good person want to report a hoard of criminals plotting their next crime?

Tonight, she would cut the rigging.

CHAPTER 21

Two candles, locked in metal cages on support pillars, illuminated the hull full of flammables. The last man on watch snored when the candles burned to half-length. Aliwyn had been dozing on and off in the dank hull of the ship. Not a moment passed without a creak, a snore, or footsteps. It was a miracle anyone slept at all, yet sleep the mercenaries did. Many had fallen asleep drunk, sprawled out on hammocks strung between the crates and the bags. With helmets tucked under their arms, the men stank of ale and sweat.

To control the drinking, the Boltans had moved the barrels of ale and mead to the rear and secured them behind netting. Also behind the netting were stacks of chests—probably each packed with thundercrashers. They were forbidden for the rest of the journey.

Aliwyn lay pressed against a pillar supporting the staircase, her eyes skirting in the darkness as she prepared to retrieve her stolen dagger. Edward had shackled both her wrists and ankles. Toby couldn't argue against his uncle, and Ransley had only wanted the argument to end. At least she had bandages to wrap around her itchy wrists.

Emma and Toby slept beside her, and Ransley rested on a hammock nearby. Edward, Zelrin, and Axlan were on duty on deck.

The light flickered over Emma's delicate features, and the scent of lavender drifted from the flower satchel under her pillow. Her peaceful face bound Aliwyn in guilt stronger than any metal ring, but now, with the last guard asleep, she had to move.

Aliwyn sat up with her wrists pressed together and the loose chain clenched in her fist to silence it. Her eyes widened upon seeing Toby's upturned face. For some reason, he slept with his body perpendicular to both her and Emma, and his head was close to where hers had been.

She must've been asleep when he had shifted to this position. What a bizarre thing for him to do. Scowling, she scooted back from him and stood.

Her head spun as she shook off her tiredness. Two dozen men spilled out of their hammocks into the shadows, and every man slept with a dagger strapped to his belt. A dim glow outlined the privy door at the rear of the ship.

Space was tight. Aliwyn spread apart her ankles until the chain between them was taut and silent. She waddled toward the two massive chests the Boltans had not pushed to the rear. Although she had tried to pray for her success in cutting the rigging that night, her mind couldn't compose a sentence.

Aliwyn passed one snoring mercenary, then another. When she reached the chest with her dagger underneath, she almost collapsed in a heap. Her breath shuddering, she slid her fingers beneath the chest and felt for the weapon until she found it. In a smooth motion she had rehearsed a hundred times in her mind, she pulled it out, wrapped it in bandages, and slipped it into a deep inner pocket of her coat.

Aliwyn looked around with pins and needles dancing on her scalp. Probably not a single person on board believed she could do what she had just done, to their loss.

Now she had to wait on her mattress until it was Toby's shift on deck; he had negotiated with his family to undo her shackles while he was on duty. As she forced her legs to stand again, a hand-sized shadow darted between crates to her left. It was just a rat. The ship was full of them, just like the fields back in Brocklesby manor. Aliwyn refocused on waddling back to her mattress. The chain tapped lightly on the floorboards but was inaudible over the splashing of water.

A heavy object ground over the floorboards, and she froze. When the noise came again from the darkness, she ducked on reflex. The metal chains between her wrists came within a hair of striking the floorboards. She spun toward the stern of the ship, where the candlelight failed to illuminate the ship's far edges. The noise had come from underneath the netting.

Emma had complained that Loki was in the hull and moving boxes around. Could something be lurking in the darkness? Or did ships routinely make this sound because of shifting contents?

She was on all fours between the hammocks of two odorous men whose thick arms dangled close to her back. Her tremulous legs were slow to move. Not trusting herself to stand again, she crawled back toward her mattress.

She had retrieved her dagger. Part of her squealed silently with excitement while the other fidgeted with renewed fear. Heaven forbid she should get caught with the blade on her body, and she still had to go upstairs and saw the rigging.

Aliwyn flinched when another rat with a wretched long tail brushed past her hand. She wrinkled her nose and quickened her crawl. Too fast. Her knee landed on the chain in between her wrists. She couldn't lift her hand and keep crawling, and Aliwyn gasped. She had a flash that her life was over before she lost balance and fell on her face.

Her nose struck something warm, with a slight give. Both she and a man yelped. She had just landed on Toby, who lay parallel to the direction of her crawl. He writhed underneath her, and Aliwyn whimpered and scrambled to get up. An instant later, she was back on all fours, and her hands slid over linen sheets.

Toby's round eyes and gaping mouth appeared just below her. Aliwyn gulped. She was pressing the chain between her wrists squarely over his neck, and he was wheezing.

Aliwyn shrieked and withdrew her hands. Toby gripped her upper arms as she fell like a log onto her left side. Her limbs melted with terror. Now he would yell and rally the entire crew to punish her.

"Aliwyn?" he asked in a hushed voice. "Are you all right? What happened?"

Hands and shackles covering her face, she couldn't believe her ears when Toby repeated his question. He rubbed her elbow.

"I'm so sorry," she stammered. "I saw a rat. I was coming back from the privy, and I trip—"

"Haw, Toby!" a voice shouted. "You could've at least waited till we docked!"

Aliwyn looked between her fingers. Several men were awake. Two sat on their swaying hammocks while others rolled around to see the action, or the lack thereof. Amongst those smiling was Toby's father, Ransley. He seemed to wink at his son as he rested on his hammock. Aliwyn's face burned. Squeezing her eyes shut, she pressed the shackles over her eyelids.

"I-It's not what you all think," Toby said. "Go back to sleep. Nothing is happening here. Aliwyn tripped on her way back from the privy, that's all."

The men chuckled and muttered amongst themselves. When the mirth died down, Toby laughed. It was the first time she had heard him laugh for so long, and it was a pleasant sound without a hint that something was amiss. Aliwyn's sweaty hands clenched the chains, but she also opened her eyes and forced a chuckle.

Just a harmless accident. No one suspected her.

Both she and Toby lay on their sides, facing each other, and his hand rested on her arm. The sympathy in his gaze made her want to scram like the rat that had crossed her path. Thankfully, both she and Toby had wiped themselves with ash and water before nightfall. She had hung capes by their drawstrings to dry along the back platform, and the clothing had formed a makeshift curtain behind which she could clean herself privately. Toby had redressed his wounds and changed into the clothes she had washed. He smelled like pine sap. So much better than that steaming pigsty of mercenaries.

It made this face-to-face moment slightly less awkward. Slightly.

"Did I hurt you?" she whispered.

"No. But I told you, if you need the privy, just tell me and I'll unlock you."

"I...didn't want to wake you up."

He had bought her privy excuse. But something was wrong, as a hard object prodded beneath her left breast. Aliwyn stiffened. The dagger's handle was sliding out of her right pocket.

She didn't dare look down. Toby would probably see the weapon if she lowered her arms. Aliwyn held back a scream, though she couldn't hide her wide eyes and pressed lips. He studied her face with concern.

Finally, as though to dispel the tension, Toby smiled.

"I'm sorry about the rats on board," he said. "Zel calls this ship a rat brothel, but her real name is *Lady Fortuna*. She's a merchant ship that once sailed between the ports of Norwich and Flanders. Unfortunately, both ports have a rodent problem. The critters boarded and hid in the ship's bilge."

Aliwyn tried to smile back. She was lucky. Her fall had seemed accidental, but Toby could've questioned her intentions and come to a different conclusion—especially with how she had pressed the chain over his neck. When he looked down at her shackled wrists, she curled her toes. Hidden just behind them was the dagger's handle.

"Did you get to use the privy?" he asked. "I can free you now."

"I went," she lied. She needed to distract him. "Wh-what's a ship's bilge?"

"It's the level below the ship's hold, so one level below where we are now. Water collects there if it rains. It smells terrible. No one goes there except to bail out the water, but the rats don't mind, I suppose."

Sweat broke at her hairline. He was still scowling at her shackles and the bandages covering her wrists.

"H-have you thought about bringing a cat on board?" Aliwyn asked. "To help you catch the rats here?"

He finally shifted his gaze to her eyes. "I wanted to bring *two* cats, but Edward is not fond of cats. So I didn't bring them."

Aliwyn gave a disarming smile, sliding her wrists down along her chest. She only breathed again when the dagger moved and seemed to stay in her pocket. Toby said something about Edward believing cats at sea were bad luck. Aliwyn nodded, but she wanted to roll her eyes instead. Could Toby do anything without having his uncle or father's approval?

"Holding festivities without me?" came a voice from upstairs. "I heard laughter."

Aliwyn looked up to see Edward standing by the stairwell opening, his face hovering over the scene with a smirk. Beside him was Zelrin, who held a lantern and seemed far less amused.

Toby repeated Aliwyn's excuse for the fall, and Edward grunted. "Since you're awake, come take over the helm. Axlan's getting tired, too."

A fine tremor ran down her back. This was the moment she had been waiting for—when Ed finally retired for the night, Toby started his shift, and she got rid of these aggravating shackles. Toby looked at the candles secured to either side of the stairwell; how far they burned seemed to keep the timing of their shifts. "I'll be there in a moment. How are the winds?"

Edward grinned. "Excellent. We've already cleared the River Witham. Hug the coastline and sail north."

Aliwyn narrowed her eyes. The River Witham emptied into the North Sea. She would like to have jumped while they were still sailing in the river, where the water was calmer, but no matter. Even if she had never swum in the ocean, she had a plan to keep afloat and wasn't quitting her mission tonight.

"Who will be on duty with me?" Toby asked.

Zelrin jutted his chin. "Me."

"Zel, you've been awake since—"

"I'm not tired."

"He has a bad case of insomnia." Edward nodded at Zelrin. "So I told him, might as well work."

Edward descended the steps as Zelrin's lantern cast shadows over his hawk-like face. Aliwyn's heart raced. The second half of her plans would begin now. When Toby sat up and began putting on his gambeson, she sat also and smiled.

"Toby, can I come with you? I'll bring my blankets and sleep under the platform like you did."

Toby smiled as he pulled on his leather shoes. "I planned to take both you and Emma with me upstairs." His expression grew solemn as he switched to Vasfian. "Aliwyn, I heard about how the men searched you for my father's dagger. I'm sorry I wasn't there. These men have an appetite, not just for food. I also couldn't stop my uncle from hurting you in the stairwell." He paused, and Aliwyn caught his apologetic gaze before she averted her eyes. She hadn't blamed him for what happened, but her swollen lip was a sore reminder of Edward's domination.

"From now on," Toby said, "I'll keep you and Emma close to me."

So that's why he had slept beside her and Emma—to form a fence between them and the mercenaries with his body. Aliwyn gathered her blankets and watched Toby shake Emma's shoulders and whisper in the child's ear. A lump settled in her stomach. He still tried to protect her on this ship, as he had promised, but she couldn't return his kindness.

As Emma yawned and sat up, Toby rose and limped to his father's hammock. Ransley had fallen back asleep. For a moment, Toby stood by the hammock and didn't move. With his eyes downcast in the candle's flicker, he pulled his father's blankets higher on his chest.

Aliwyn shuddered. Thorns of guilt ensnared her just as her goal was within reach. Had Aelfric felt the same way? She stopped her thoughts short. In the days following Miriam's death, she had shut off all her emotions, and she would have to do the same now.

Emma had blankets trailing over her arms onto the floor, but Aliwyn didn't offer to gather them up. She ascended the stairs behind Toby and was greeted by the raw scent of the sea blowing across the deck. The nearly full moon was bright in a sky broken by clouds, drifting like ghostly ships across a black sea. A gust of wind chilled Aliwyn. She pulled her cloak's hood over her head and followed Toby, Emma, and Zelrin toward the steering oar, where Axlan stood on duty.

He turned around with a smile. "Good to see you, Toby." Looking at Aliwyn, he added, "Miss, thank you again for your help earlier today. Blakke told me his eyes feel much better."

Aliwyn tried for a smile. She had given each man a poultice to reduce the swelling around their eyes—a job she did without heart. For better or for worse, the fire had blinded none of the mercenaries, and their pain had come from their scorched eyelids.

As Toby took the oar from Axlan's hand, Zelrin helped Aliwyn and Emma spread the linen and woolen blankets into makeshift mattresses. Aliwyn sat on her blankets with her knees to her chest. Toby, Zelrin, and Emma were all within arm's reach. Too close. Aliwyn took a shaking breath, but she refused to back out now.

Her eyes traced a pair of ropes that tethered one lower corner of the square sail to under the back platform. The billowing sail pulled both these ropes taut. If this pair was cut, she reasoned, a quarter of the sail would flap up like a loose bed sheet. The ship would be marked, and it would slow down.

Footsteps echoed up the stairs. Edward's face and hair were wet as if he had cleaned himself. Appearing content, he carried a large sheepskin bag folded in half. Aliwyn's eyes widened as he approached the back platform and bid Toby goodnight.

When Edward brushed aside the curtain of cloaks, she blurted out, "You're sleeping there tonight?"

"Why not? My noble Danish forefathers slept on the deck of their longships for every raid." He tugged on a cape she had hung to dry along the platform. "I do appreciate the draperies for added atmosphere."

The "Danish forefathers" he spoke of were Norsemen, horrid monsters who looted villages, carried off peasants as thralls, burned churches to the ground, and repeated these atrocities across England. There was nothing noble about them.

Edward disappeared behind the capes. Those capes were meant to conceal her while she sawed the rigging. Even her vomit bucket, which she had planned to flip upside down and use as a flotation aid, was under that platform.

Aliwyn gritted her teeth. So much for thinking she was clever. Edward was ruining her plans—by going to sleep!

The dagger was still in her pocket. What was she going to do now? What if Edward slept on the deck every night?

Her nerves on fire, Aliwyn stood and shuffled about on her blanket. What if she just jumped and let the ship continue? But without a flotation aid, she would drown. Heat spread from her neck to her forehead as she faced Toby, Zelrin, and Emma's puzzled stares. She covered her mouth and struggled to bottle in her emotions.

"Aliwyn," Toby said, "can you come closer?"

She glowered at him. "Why?"

He kept his wary gaze past her, toward an unseen Edward whose footsteps sounded under the back platform. Licking his lips, Toby reached between the laces of his gambeson and pulled out a key. His eyes darted to her shackled wrists, and then she understood. Toby was keeping his promise to free her, at least while he was on duty.

Aliwyn approached him with her head lowered and her jaw clenched.

"Ed agreed to free you for now, but let's keep it discreet." Toby took her hand and unlocked one of the metal clasps. He pushed the key into her fingers. "Here. You unlock the rest."

Aliwyn's hands shook as she sat to undo the rings around her ankles. Silvery moonlight illuminated the keyholes. Next to her, Zelrin was wrapping Emma in blankets, and she whispered, "Zel, what did you do? Aliwyn's angry again."

"I just breathe and she gets mad, all right? She's bloody difficult."

Aliwyn tore off the shackles around her feet and shoved the mess of chains and metal clasps against the railing. The grating of metal across the floorboards made her neck prickle.

She hugged her knees until the dagger's tip, still tucked in her pocket, prodded into her side. Against her will, Aliwyn smelled pine sap again. Toby's gambeson with the bloodstained hole was just beside her head. She rubbed her ankles, which she had bandaged along with the rest of her lower legs to compensate for the lack of stockings. Toby had freed her, and no one suspected her of anything. Chills washed up and down her chest. The urge to dash for the railing now and throw herself overboard gripped her, but that would be reckless.

Aliwyn hastily wiped her eyes. Aelfric must've had some of his plans ruined when he was spying in Toby's household. She needed to wait for another opportunity.

Next to her, Emma grinned and pointed at the sky. "Zel, did you see the stars? There are so many."

As Zelrin looked up, Aliwyn wanted to pull Emma into her arms and sob. She couldn't put into words why.

Edward's mention of Norsemen raids helped her see what the crew thought of her—a helpless maiden who had been carried off like blacksmithing tools or expensive beeswax candles. She had never heard of kidnapped women returning home, let alone sabotaging their captors' ships. But like a trickle of water determined to find a lake, Aliwyn's hopes refused to dry up. She would devise another plan.

The thought of blowing up a hundred thundercrashers and burning down the ship flashed through her mind. Placing just one thundercrasher close to kindling seemed enough to ignite it. But setting the ship ablaze would also kill everyone, including herself, two children, and Toby. How could she have such a wicked idea?

Aliwyn wrung her hands, wishing she could throw her heart in a cage and walk away with nothing but a cold, calculating mind.

Toby's legs shifted nearby. "Aliwyn, may I have the key again?"

She pulled the key out of the tangle of chains by the railing. Without looking at him, she held it up for him to take. Toby accepted the key.

"Something's upsetting you." His voice hovered over her head.

Why yes, a million things, starting with you! She almost laughed. "I'll be fine. I'm just nauseous again."

"It's not nausea."

Her pulse quickened with erratic beats. The longer they stayed stuck together, the harder it would be to keep secrets. What would Toby do to her if he ever discovered she had overheard his plans to meet the Danes?

Both Zelrin and Emma watched her for a response. Keeping silent would not do.

"I'm..." Aliwyn scrambled for an excuse. "I was thinking about the incident on deck earlier today. It was terrifying."

The moonlight cast shadows over Toby's solemn frown. He dipped the oar deeper into the water, and the ship tilted to one side before straightening again.

"I understand," he said quietly. "That object is called a thundercrasher. My father and I did everything to keep them out of the wrong hands. But as you've heard, Father lost one chest when the Vasfians ambushed him."

If he was willing to tell her all this, what other information could she extract from him?

She faked a smile. "The Vasfians and Normans will never know what those acorn-like things are, even if they find them."

Toby looked Aliwyn, Zelrin, and Emma one by one in the eyes. "Here's something you won't hear the Normans publicizing. One of the three earls leading this revolt is Roger de Breteuil. He's the son of William's cousin. And he's Norman, of course."

"What?" Zelrin and Emma exclaimed in unison.

Aliwyn was too startled to speak. One of the rebellious earls was...a Norman?

"Zel and Emma, I've been telling you to stop thinking of all Normans as evil," Toby said. "Regardless of what you've heard, this rebellion is not about the English driving out the Normans. It's about the oppressed inhabitants of England overthrowing a tyrant king, who happens to be Norman."

Aliwyn repeated his words in her mind, and her stomach twisted. Prior rebellions had all been about the English driving out the Normans, but this time, the Normans rebelled against their own king?

"What's a tyrant, Toby?" Emma asked.

"Someone who cares about nothing but himself. His wants. His power. His reputation. My worst fear is that someone with insatiable greed gets ahold of our cargo. Norman, English, Danish, Vasfian...it doesn't matter."

Water trickled along the oars as he paused. Toby glanced at Zelrin, who had taken off his woolen hat. The youngster grabbed a fistful of hair and stared at his boots.

"Why would King William's own family want to overthrow him?" Aliwyn whispered.

"William didn't want Earl Ralph to marry Earl Roger's sister. Who does William think he is, dictating whom his earls can marry? And that's hardly scratching the surface."

Indignation bolstered Toby's voice, and Aliwyn glanced at him. She had triggered a topic Toby was passionate about—the reasons he had risked everything for this uprising.

"William gave himself absolute power over every acre of English land," Toby said. "He can take away anyone's home if he wants to because he owns everything. He created royal forests where only he and the aristocrats could hunt. Any poor farmer caught poaching to feed his family is blinded. And perhaps worse, William appointed his yes-men and relatives to the highest positions in government and the church. These officials feel invincible. They control hundreds of manors and extort the local peasants."

Aliwyn felt compelled to say something. "I once lived under a Norman baron. His taxes were fair. He fed us during droughts and floods. I haven't had trouble with Normans in my watermill."

"You were fortunate." After a pause, Toby narrowed his eyes. "So you've already forgotten about the Norman knight who robbed your watermill?"

She had indeed forgotten, and blood rushed to her face. Her selective memory was appalling.

"I couldn't intervene. I was hanging behind the mill." Toby shook his head. "The knight who robbed you was Jacques Verdun. He also stopped us outside Myton. Thank God we got away. He's notorious for raiding peasant homes during times of unrest, and he's only one of many abusive Norman knights."

Aliwyn pinched her thumbnail until it hurt. Matthew had been working with Jacques. Had Matthew joined in when Jacques ordered her baskets emptied and her chickens stolen? She didn't want to know.

Toby recalled how thousands of English thegns, or aristocrats, had been slain or exiled since the Norman invasion. How William collected heavy geld taxes from the English to pay for the hundreds of castles he built around England while he sent the rest to enrich Normandy. Finally, Toby brought up the Harrying of the North six years ago, when William had led troops to burn everything—oxen, housing, food, farm equipment—north of York in the dead of winter. He mutilated peasants and starved thousands to death, leaving homes with rotting bodies and no one to bury them. The land lay in waste to this day. Aliwyn grimaced, and her feet scuffled on the floorboards.

Toby continued quietly, "Aliwyn, I apologize if I brought back frightful memories, but I wanted you to understand why I'm here. Zel and Emma were both orphaned because of the Harrying. Perhaps you were as well."

His words brought a surge of rage and sorrow. He knew how to salt the one wound she could never recover from. There was no forgiving what William had done to the poor people of northern England, but she had chosen to submit to him. Never again did she want to witness so much bloodshed.

Aelfric had also chosen to live in peace, probably because of the Marcottes. This household of knights had shown him kindness, taught him French and fighting skills, and given him a new life. But had Aelfric not bonded with Matthew Marcotte in particular, perhaps he would've become a rebel instead. Maybe he'd be on Toby's ship, still alive.

Zelrin's voice pulled her out of her memories but not out of the heaviness in her heart.

"So you're sayin' even if we win this bloody thing, we'll still have a skin-headed Norman lordin' over us? A relative of William the Turd *himself*?"

A steely glint shone in his eyes, and the way he cracked his knuckles made Aliwyn nervous.

"When this rebellion is won, God willing, I'll serve as Lord Yeaton's knight," Toby said. "Lord Yeaton is a baron under Earl Ralph de Gael. Neither man is Norman. But even if they were, I would still serve them. Zelrin, I'm not here because I hate all the Normans." The wind fluttered the edge of Toby's hood as he scowled at the silvery waters ahead. "As for England, she will be divided amongst the three earls—a Breton, an Englishman, and a Norman."

Aliwyn's throat seized. Divide England into three? Her three brothers used to pummel each other to the ground over one loaf of fresh bread. How could three men with incredible military be expected to share England peacefully? Just as she feared Toby might convince her to side with the rebellion, he had thrown in that piece of absurdity.

"But you should hate the Normans." Zelrin raised his voice. "They gave you and your household four months to disappear so they could steal your land!"

"That was *William's* decree," Toby said. "As for the other Normans, it's complicated. The man who trained me for knighthood was a Norman, although he's passed already. My father survived as an English knight for years because he had a fragile friendship with...certain Norman households."

He was still talking, but Aliwyn stopped listening. For all of Toby's insight into why he was fighting, why couldn't he see that this division would lead to civil war?

Her tongue flooded with a metallic taste. The anguish over hearing Toby's words had elicited a fresh wave of nausea. She slapped a hand over her mouth and searched for her vomit bucket, but it was under the back platform where Edward was sleeping.

Zelrin scrambled to get up. "Don't go throwin' up on me, missy!"

"Zel," Toby said, "go grab Aliwyn a bucket from downstairs."

The youngster shot up and ran for the stairs. Aliwyn whimpered, her hand still over her mouth, and Toby and Emma backed away.

No one stopped Aliwyn when she stumbled to her feet and hurried for the opposite railing.

"Aliwyn," Toby said. "Please don't vomit into the fishing nets. They're hanging along the sides."

The nausea had subsided by the time she rammed into the ship's left railing, which came up to her chest. Below her, nets hung along the ship's hull like flattened hammocks. The black, glistening waters sloshing against the vessel at once terrified and tempted her, but Aliwyn wasn't about to jump. She had sworn to stall the ship before she escaped. A cold mist dampened her face with the raw scent of sea and salt, and her pulse throbbed behind her eyes.

She would need to be patient. There would be another chance to wreck this prison.

Zelrin's footsteps vibrated up the stairs. "Take your bucket," he muttered.

She turned and glared at him. With his head lowered, the youngster swung the bucket by its handle as he walked, but he stumbled into the rope ladder extending toward the crow's nest. Zelrin spun around with a growl and swung the bucket. The object struck the rope soundlessly and bounced. He bared his teeth and struck again with the bucket, this time hitting the mast with a thunk. Aliwyn's heels backed against the railing.

Toby and Emma called in hushed voices for Zelrin to stop. When he didn't, Toby abandoned his steering oar, hobbled over, and gripped Zelrin by his forearms. "Zel! What's gotten into you?"

CHAPTER 22

"YOU LIED TO ME!" Zelrin cried, the wind carrying away his voice. "And my brother died for that lie. And Myton burned up for that lie. I...I still have friends there."

His shoulders slumped. As the bucket handle slipped from his fingers, Toby caught it and set it down by the mast. Straightening again, he pulled back his hood and placed his hands on Zelrin's shoulders. The moonlight outlined their profiles in silver, and gusts of wind tousled their hair.

"Zelrin, how did I lie to you?" His brows drawn, Toby studied the teen's face.

"You never told me William's bloodline would still rule a chunk of England, even if we overthrew William himself. How is that worth fighting for?" Zelrin's voice grew foggy. "I swore I'd follow you. I didn't ask many questions. But this...suddenly the rebellion feels blasted stupid."

Zelrin had lost heart, just like that? Emma's tearful face in watching all this nailed Aliwyn to the railing. The girl begged with her eyes for Aliwyn to intervene, but Aliwyn only wanted to cripple the ship and escape. Her heart hammering, she couldn't move.

"Zel." Toby lowered his eyes. "I never meant to lie to you. I honestly didn't know how to tell you the whole truth. Earl Waltheof is the only English earl remaining. He cannot possibly oust William by himself. Pitting William against his own household is the best strategy that remains."

"No, it's not!" Zelrin shot back. "England isn't free until all the bloody Normans are gone! That's what this rebellion *should* be about!"

Toby frowned. When the ship tilted to one side with a nagging creak, he released the youngster and limped back to grip the steering oar. He dipped the oar into the water and straightened the vessel.

"We cannot get rid of the Normans," he said. "No more than England could get rid of the Danes who invaded a few decades ago. And we are both descendants of those Danes."

Zelrin turned away and crossed his arms, and Aliwyn tensed all over. Toby had readily admitted that even he was not of pure English descent. His statement resonated with what he had said earlier—that this rebellion was not about the English overthrowing the Normans, but about the inhabitants of England ousting a tyrant. And the inhabitants of England, after centuries of conquests, immigration, and intermarriage, were people of various origins who eventually called themselves *English*. It was easy to forget this and heap hatred on the latest invaders, the Normans.

Aliwyn swallowed several times. Being reminded of these subtleties, and how complicated war was, tore at the boundaries of her understanding. What did being English mean? Maybe even she was descended from some Norseman raider who settled in England generations ago.

When Zelrin remained sullen and silent, Toby continued. "The Normans have trade routes and alliances across Europe. Many children have been born to Anglo-Norman families in England, and even Earl Waltheof married William's niece. If all the Normans are driven out, this web of families, alliances, and trade routes...they would rip apart. England would become unstable. Scotland and Wales would pounce on us like a pack of wolves."

Zelrin shuffled as though kicking invisible rocks. "I can't think like that, all right? I lost almost everyone I loved to Normans. They killed our chickens and stole our cow. They burned my house and neighbor's house and cut down folks as they ran with their babies. I hate them *all*. And a sardin' Norman almost killed me." Grimacing, he gestured along his side, where Aliwyn had seen the fleshly scar.

"And Toby saved you." Emma hugged her knees. "How can you yell at him like this?"

"To shove some sense into him," Zelrin said through his teeth. "Toby's got his grandpa's land waiting for him in Denmark. He has us. If England's lost to those skin-headed Normans for good, why are we still fighting? Why not leave this rat island of a ship to Ed and his seadogs?" He pointed at the open waters. "We can get on another boat for Denmark, and Ransley will come with us."

Aliwyn's mouth fell open, as did Toby's.

"That's absurd," he said. "I'm a knight. My father's a knight. We have responsibilities. We swore our allegiance to Lord Yeaton and Earl—"

The ship quaked with shuddering creaks. A moment later, it ground to a halt, and Aliwyn stumbled forward. Never had the floor rocked like this. Spinning around, her eyes widened on a wall of blackness instead of wispy clouds drifting across the moonlit sky. The outline of a jagged cliff stood a stone's throw away. This ledge stood twice as tall as the ship's crow nest, and below it, a sandy beach stretched into the sparkling waters like the foot of a giant. She gasped. One side of the vessel had slid onto a sandbank.

Toby and Zelrin shouted and ran for the lines controlling the angle of the sail to the wind. Edward flung aside the capes of the back platform.

"Toby! What have you done?"

Edward stomped to Emma's side and gathered the girl into his arms. To Aliwyn's amazement, he hurried with her toward the stairwell.

"All hands on deck!" he called.

His words snapped Aliwyn to her senses. Things were finally working in her favor. The first mercenaries pounded up the stairs with their pointed helmets, and she raced for the back platform that Edward had just abandoned. Shouting erupted on deck. The floorboards quaked beneath her feet as she ducked behind the makeshift curtains, and darkness engulfed her.

Voices and footsteps echoed downstairs as men slid cargo toward the ship's buoyant side. The vessel jerked forward with a broken creak of the mast. Aliwyn stumbled against the platform's post and gritted her teeth. The wind still propelled the ship; it might be only moments before it freed the vessel from the sandbank, and everything returned to normal.

Not if she could help it.

Moonlight filtered through a square of sky formed by the elevated platform and the railing. Mist blew upward and salted her eyes. She stared at her prize—several rigging lines wrapped around their respective metal rings, silvery with moisture and stretched taut from the relentless wind.

The capes hiding her from view flapped, and she tossed a few bags to weigh them down.

Pulling out her dagger, Aliwyn unwound the bandages concealing its blade and darted for her target—a line that held the lower corner of the sail in place. She pressed the blade against the twine and sawed with vibrations humming up her fingers. Shreds flew as fine, icy sprays blew up her sleeves. The ship shuddered with low, aching groans, and its right side rolled with the waves while its left ground against the sand.

A violent rock threw Aliwyn down, but she ignored the pain as fire erupted over her chest. She lunged for the railing only to stumble over a bag. A sack of griffin surcoats was at her feet—probably Edward's pillow. Hatred for the man seized her by the throat. She ripped out two fistfuls of surcoats and threw them overboard. Grabbing onto the rail again, Aliwyn sawed at whatever rope she could reach. The ship rocked and her knife got bumped to another rope, but she kept cutting. Frenzy drove her onward with a single thought—don't stop.

"Aliwyn! Where are you?"

Toby's cry, raw with despair, pierced through the commotion on the other side of the curtain. Aliwyn's working arm grew heavy, but the fraying rope before her compelled her to continue. She couldn't allow Toby's mission to succeed.

Floorboards quaked under her feet. Someone was approaching. Aliwyn spun around and hid her dagger behind her back just as a hand yanked aside one of the capes serving as a curtain. A bearded mercenary stepped in. She blocked the fraying ropes so he couldn't see them, and their rounded eyes met in the ghostly moonlight. A moment later, the man swerved and ran away, leaving the corner of one cape dangling off the clothesline.

The triangular opening exposed Aliwyn to the scene on deck. Men rowed vigorously, and Edward waved and barked orders from the steering oar. He was close enough to grab her. Aliwyn shook until she almost dropped her weapon, but the naked blade prodded her back and sent her a flash of strength. Now or never. Aliwyn spun back to the fated rope and resumed her sabotage.

Before she could cut through, the rope snapped and whipped back. She yelped. Searing pain shot up her hand as she fell on her back. She scrambled to prop herself up, but the sound of snapping wood made her cringe. Her mouth fell open. Not only had she cut one rope, but the heightened strain on the neighboring line had snapped its belaying pin off the rail. Now two ropes were gone.

Aliwyn's surge of pride didn't last. She had dropped her dagger overboard. Her fingers dug into the crevices of the slimy floorboards. She had wanted to cut more. Were two broken lines enough to cripple the ship?

The wind carried screams from on deck. What sounded like a whip whizzed through the air, followed by a loud crack, and Aliwyn winced. She imagined the freed ropes whacking the platform's railing and everything within its reach. Forcing herself to move, she scooted on her elbows to the curtain and lifted one cape of the clothesline so she could see. A lower corner of the sail flapped in the wind, just as she had planned. Powerful gusts twisted the sail toward the fully rigged side, and both severed ropes flew like the tail of a deranged beast.

The oarsmen who had taken their positions to row scattered under the beating whips like flies from a manure pile. Some fell and rolled on deck. If she was supposed to be enjoying this, she wasn't. She couldn't find Toby. He had a hurt ankle; what if he had slipped?

Aliwyn inhaled in shuddering gasps. She needed to stop caring. She had better jump before someone discovered what she had done.

With aching back and shoulders, she pushed to her hands and knees. She couldn't believe she had succeeded or the chaos that had ensued. The crooked sail billowed and strained the mast; what if it toppled over and smashed the crew? She had wanted to slow the ship, escape, and warn the Norman authorities, not crush people.

When dogs barked in the distance, terror swelled in her throat.

She hadn't expected those on land to arrive so quickly. If she jumped off, who would be waiting for her on the shore?

"Aliwyn!" Toby shouted.

The relief in his voice warned her that she had been discovered. Toby ran up the last steps of the stairwell. Maybe he had been tending to Emma and his father, and guilt flooded her. Aliwyn scrambled to her feet and ran for the side facing the shoreline. The sand was just below. Her hands clenched the edge of the railing, and she stuck her head out beyond the platform. A howling gust carried the scent of smoke. She was about to step on sacks of loot and clamber overboard when lights caught her eye—dots of orange firelight.

She froze at the sight. Dozens of torches flickered in a row, halfway up the dark cliff. The bird-like whistles the Vasfians used to communicate echoed in the night.

Aliwyn staggered back from the railing. The ship had beached on Vasfian territory, and her heart sank to the sour pit of her stomach.

All the Vasfian tribes worked together. Maybe the local tribe had heard about a skinny peasant woman with short brown hair who had helped Toby Boltan escape. Aliwyn was a wanted woman, and she was about to get caught. If she jumped now, the Vasfian dogs would pounce on her.

The first of many arrows whizzed through the air and ricocheted off the platform just over her head. Aliwyn shrieked and doubled back. Not all the Vasfian tribes had treaties with the Normans or cared that this ship's sail bore the colors of Bishop Geoffrey. They didn't want a vessel landing in the dead of night.

The severed lines seemed to have whipped themselves over the rails and into the water. Although they had stopped wreaking havoc on deck, arrows now struck the deck or blew onto the square sail. Men pulled out their slings. Others lunged to grab their shields as arrows fell around them.

Aliwyn pressed herself against the post. How would they survive this?

"Zel! Grab Aliwyn and go downstairs!" Toby's voice cut through the commotion.

"No!" Zelrin shouted back. "I stay here and fight!"

Aliwyn searched the deck until she saw Zelrin facing the shore with a shield strapped over one arm. He stood without a helmet amongst the armored mercenaries. Swinging his sling in an elaborate arc, he let out a fierce cry and launched a stone back at the row of torches lining the cliff. His rock was only the first. As other men found their footing, they stood beside him, behind their wavering row of round shields, and fired back.

Aliwyn couldn't breathe. Two torches on the cliff tumbled and fell into the blackness below, and the downpour of arrows stopped. A chorus of cheers erupted onboard. With Zelrin's taunts resonating above the others, the men coordinated fetching stones and firing more rounds.

Moments later, the Vasfians started throwing rocks themselves.

The stones fell with more precision than the wind-blown arrows. They smashed into the rowers below, who had taken their positions and couldn't defend themselves. Toby rallied a few men to raise the wooden board they had used as a gangplank, but it was hefty and difficult to maneuver. When the board jerked to one side, rocks struck one mercenary who was suddenly exposed. He yelped and fell.

Aliwyn swept her eyes over the deck in the eerie moonlight, at the myriad of bodies, strewn shields, and flying rocks. She wanted to bash her head into the wooden post she clung to. Half the oars were useless because one side of the ship was beached. They needed the wind to get themselves out, but she had destroyed two lines so the sail no longer functioned properly.

Maybe she had successfully sabotaged Toby's mission, but now everyone would die. What had she done?

The floorboards beneath her vibrated. One man crawled under the platform, close enough for her to kick him, but he didn't notice her. He fell, covered his conical helmet with bloody hands, and sobbed. Aliwyn wanted to kick him. *Get out there and fight, you coward! How dare you crawl over here and cry!* But she had no right to think that way.

As tears rose in her eyes, Toby ran out from behind the board he had helped raise as a shield. He lifted a fallen mercenary and dragged him toward the shelter of the back platform. The rocks clattering all around didn't deter him. Lowering the man to safety, Toby hobbled out to get someone else. No one else was doing this. Toby had no helmet and he couldn't even walk properly, but that didn't stop him from pulling back the wounded.

If the crucible of chaos exposed a person's true nature, Toby displayed only selflessness. And Zelrin, at his young age, fought with a ferocity that made shivers rain down her back. He was not just fighting for himself; he was defending them all.

After all that she had seen, were Toby and Zelrin still her enemies?

The mercenary still lay curled before her, shaking with muffled sobs. Aliwyn struggled to remain standing. Was this man pining for his wife and children? Maybe she could help him up, but shame paralyzed her.

Zelrin screamed. She had subconsciously focused on his bright voice. Now, halfway across the ship, he was face down on the floor. As men stomped around him, fetching rocks and dodging projectiles, she couldn't see Zelrin move in the shadows. He was the smallest of the team, and the others would stomp him to a pulp. No air came from her lungs when she tried to call for help. When Toby didn't appear to help Zelrin, her gaze fell on the circular shield discarded by the man at her feet. She pulled it up and bolted.

Aliwyn left the shelter of the back platform, and part of her screamed to turn back. The memories of being shot at outside her watermill flashed before her eyes—scenes of the past melded with the shifting shadows before her in a bewildering mirage. The shield's strap bit into her arm, and the wood struck her knees as she darted between the mercenaries like a frantic hen after her chick. Rocks struck the other side with deafening thunks in her ear. Toby was nowhere to be seen. Fear for his safety almost buckled her knees, but Zelrin was still writhing on the floor. She sucked in her breath and kept running. The least she could do was shield them both.

The floorboards beneath her rose like the belly of an inhaling beast. Aliwyn's eyes rounded at the feeling of weightlessness before she landed again with a twinge of her ankle. Everyone on deck froze to readjust their balance. The shouting resumed with renewed frenzy, now punctuated with cheers.

Aliwyn didn't understand the cheering. She ran as soon as her footing allowed and shouted Zelrin's name. With men dashing by his side, the youngster raised his head from the floor. The lower half of his face was bloody, and the whites of his eyes flashed in the moonlight. Aliwyn almost ground to a halt at the ghastly sight. A mercenary rammed into her shoulder, but she kept going.

Zelrin fell again with his back curled to her. By the time she ducked beside him, she couldn't feel her legs. The rocks banging against her shield made her quake. She squeezed her eyes shut and gasped for air that didn't satisfy. With a jerking arm, she felt for the youngster beside her. How bad were his injuries?

Her arm struck emptiness. Aliwyn swerved around but couldn't see him in the darkness. Had Zelrin gotten up and left? She hardened her jaw. Even when she tried to be helpful, she wasn't.

When another mercenary cursed and stumbled into her, Aliwyn tried to scurry out of the way. The ship rose again, and her body floated before falling. Her knees and shield landed with a groaning shudder of the ship.

Could it be? The waves were lifting the rear of the vessel. The ship began rotating into the sea with its stern turning outward, and the momentum pulled Aliwyn to one side. Overhead, the sail she had scorned day and night billowed unevenly with the wind, but the half that was full and undamaged was on the side of the waters. The oarsmen continued to row on that same side.

Finally, their efforts were spinning the ship free.

As the ship swung out, fewer rocks made the distance to strike the deck. Or maybe the Vasfians were already satisfied to see the trespassers leaving. A flicker of hope flashed in the darkness of her mind. But as the ship turned, its momentum increased.

Precious freshwater spilled from barrels chained along the rail. The heavy cauldron, once immobile on its sandbox, crashed onto the floorboards with a rattling of loose chains. It bashed into a mercenary, changed course for the ship's stern, and continued its rickety roll over scattered firewood toward where she lay. Aliwyn wanted to get up, but her limbs wouldn't react. She shrieked when arms wrapped around her from behind.

"Aliwyn!" Toby's voice was hoarse in her ear.

With a burst of gratitude, she reached up and squeezed his forearms. The round shield slipped from her wrist as Toby dragged her out of harm's way. He steadied Aliwyn on her feet and guided her toward the railing as the cauldron crashed into the ship's stern.

Aliwyn exhaled with relief. Zelrin was already slumped against that same railing.

"Hold on to this," Toby said.

He smelled of sweat and blood as he sat her down, grabbed her hand, and closed her fingers around a rough rope once securing shields to the railing.

"Thanks for protecting Zel," he panted, getting up again. "I couldn't move fast enough."

Aliwyn mustered a smile at his grimy face. Toby hadn't seen what she'd done just before helping Zelrin. She hoped he'd never find out.

Toby limped away, picked up an oar, and disappeared behind the men gathered to row. The loud straining and intense gaze of this row of men, now facing her, made her stomach twist. Their ship was back in the water, so why weren't they relieved?

The vessel continued to spin, and its mast groaned in stutters with the whistling wind. Arrows scattered on deck skirted past Aliwyn's legs in a jerky dance, and the rotational forces pressed her back against the railing. She shivered all over. Maybe there was such a thing as turning too much, too fast. When the men frowned up at the mast towering beside them, she followed their eyes. *Please, please don't have the mast topple over now.*

Zelrin coughed beside her, and she caught a metallic scent drifting from his body. When he lifted his head to look at her, his blood-streaked face moist below the eyes, her vision clouded. The ship's movement slid her toward the stern. She fought it and hooked one arm around Zelrin's. Her other arm wrapped around the railing's rope. Zelrin tilted his head back, his chest heaving.

"Something bad is goin' to happen," he croaked.

Aliwyn was too afraid to acknowledge she thought the same.

Edward shouted orders to the men, who changed the direction of their rowing several times as frigid water sprayed up the side of the ship. The crew cursed, and oars flailed at random. Despite their efforts, the vessel continued to turn with its stern swinging outward from shore. Aliwyn braced Zelrin's arm as the dark hills in the distance swung from one side of the ship to another. The sail's horizontal support beam twisted around the mast in a way she had never seen it do. Finally, the vessel turned a half-circle, so that the bow and stern switched places. A gust plastered the sail against the mast, and the yelling on board intensified. Overhead, a loud crack pierced the night.

"The yard!" someone cried.

The yard was the horizontal beam suspending the sail on the mast, and it had just cracked in two. Groaning echoed over the deck. A man laughed bitterly. Edward, undaunted, continued to shout orders. The mercenaries fell silent and obeyed his commands. The ship began to turn in the right direction, but the wind only fluttered the sides of the limp sail. Half of it inflated only to deflate again. In the powdery moonlight, it hung like a wrinkled rag.

Aliwyn couldn't breathe. Edward was going to pummel Toby for beaching the ship, but beaching the vessel had not been the most devastating incident. The ship had been jerking forward, on its way to sailing again, when Aliwyn had cut the rigging. Perhaps the ship's rear rotating outward had been the only way to free it, but it had turned too much.

Aliwyn withdrew her arm from Zelrin and covered her head with her hands. It had taken a near-fatal accident for her to admit to the truth—that if Zelrin and Toby died because of her actions, she would never forgive herself. Was she still willing to jump and bring the Normans to torture these two rebels? Would she be content to watch Emma scream as her loved ones were dragged away? Aliwyn imagined Toby's and Zelrin's corpses dangling and rotting outside the manor gates as an example for all to see. She shuddered and clawed at her scalp.

She couldn't do it—she couldn't turn in this ship.

Then what about the cargo? Who was going to confiscate it? She couldn't jump overboard and seek sanctuary until she was sure the cargo wouldn't reach its target.

Zelrin slammed back against the railing. Torn from her thoughts, Aliwyn stared as he grabbed his head with both hands and bared his teeth in misery. "Make it stop!"

"Make what stop?"

"My head's spinning. It won't stop!"

"You all right, Zel?" someone hollered from the row of oarsmen.

He wasn't. Aliwyn struggled to rise above her inner storm when Zelrin turned to her in a panic. "What's wrong with me?"

Blood trailed from his nose. He looked alert, so why was he dizzy? Aliwyn turned to him and tugged off his woolen hat. She checked his ears; blood wasn't coming out. She parted his messy hair in sections and looked for injuries.

"Where did the rock hit you?"

"On the face. But I was fine till I looked up just now. Everything's spinning!"

The rawness in his voice sent shivers down Aliwyn's back. Tightening her jaw, she scooted closer to Zelrin. "Shhh, Zel. Hold still."

She spread her fingers over his head. His scalp felt boggy, probably bruised in many places. Zelrin squirmed and whimpered. He could be recklessly brave against an external threat but was still terrified when his body failed. His jerking breaths made her chest squeeze.

But the dizziness had started when he'd looked up, not when the rock had struck him. She was examining him the wrong way. Aliwyn brushed back his bangs. "Zel, look at me."

He obeyed. In the moonlight, his gray pupils always beat back and forth to the same corner of his eyes, and Aliwyn froze. This was vertigo. She had seen Miriam treat this before by moving the patient into certain positions. But what positions again?

"Is it real bad?" Zelrin whispered. "Did I crack my skull?"

Aliwyn shook her head. Fire burned in her throat as she struggled to remember the treatment. "Hold on. I've seen this before."

She tried not to squeeze his head as the rowing mercenaries stared. The memory of Miriam's smile and movements to treat this condition glimmered in the recesses of her mind.

Before she could act, Edward shouted for Toby to check on Ransley downstairs. Toby rose from behind several oarsmen. He started for the stairwell but skidded to a stop, mouth hanging open, when he saw Aliwyn and Zelrin. She was kneeling and holding the teen's head.

"Toby, go help someone else!" Zelrin cried. "Aliwyn's got me!"

Toby's gaze locked with Aliwyn's, and his frown faded. Her eyes blurred as he turned to hobble down the stairs. Both Toby and Zelrin had faith in her—too much faith.

"Zel," she said. "I'm going to lie you down on one side. After a bit, I'll get you up and make you lie on the other side. All right?"

One corner of his mouth jerked upward. "How's that goin' to help? B-but I'll do it."

The two of them were close to the back platform, and Aliwyn settled the youngster on his side. Nearby, at the steering oar, Edward greeted his crew in English, but the rest of his speech followed in Danish. Goosebumps prickled Aliwyn's neck as the rowers watched their captain and rowed with full vigor. Had Edward announced they were stopping somewhere to fix the ship? If only she could understand that gibberish.

But wait, Zelrin was of Danish descent. Toby had said so.

"Zel," she said. "What is Edward saying, do you know?"

Zelrin had squeezed his eyes shut. No one had cleaned his bloody face, and Aliwyn dipped her chin. She shouldn't question him when he was so miserable.

After a moment, she rubbed his shoulder. "I'll move you to the other side now."

She pulled him up. He was ridiculously heavy for how slender he looked.

She laid him on his other side, trying not to drop him in a heap. The wrinkles over his eyelids faded.

"You still mad at me for the recorder?" he whispered.

Aliwyn stiffened. Of course she was still upset, even if she and Zelrin had nearly died, even if holding onto that grudge now felt silly and meaningless. Aliwyn nibbled on her lip to hold herself together.

Zelrin kept his eyes closed. "'Cause if somethin' happens to me, I guess I should say...I'm sorry for upsettin' you."

His face went in and out of focus. "You'll be fine," Aliwyn said softly. She hoped so.

"Then why is the spinnin' getting worse?"

"Sometimes it gets worse before it gets better. Count to a hundred, then get up slowly."

She kept her hand on his shoulder, which was thickly padded by his gambeson. Sniffling, she wanted to erase the heartbreaking image of Zelrin hurling Aelfric's recorder overboard, but she couldn't.

Zelrin cracked his eyes and raised an eyebrow. "Uh, don't get too close. I want to throw up."

His words caught her off guard. She smiled, but it didn't last long. Two lines of oarsmen watched her with their oars rising and falling to the rhythmic sloshing of the waters. The ship seemed to be back on course, but the irritation of having to row darkened each man's face. Fear flashed in Aliwyn's heart. She hadn't planned to stay on the ship after sabotaging it. What if they figured out she had cut the rigging?

Zelrin cleared his throat. "I counted to a hundred. Can I get up now?"

Aliwyn tried to focus on her patient. She pulled on Zelrin's arm and helped him up. "Do you feel better?"

Zelrin picked up his woolen hat and pulled it back over his head. "I'm not as bad as before. But I'm still dizzy."

"Sometimes you need to repeat the whole thing four times."

"Four times? Fine, I'll do it again." The way he eagerly lay down again made her chin quiver.

Aliwyn placed her hand on Zelrin's shoulder again to ground herself. She still had a few days to deal with the cargo, but the crew surely wanted a reason for the failed rigging *now*. She'd have to talk her way out. Aliwyn closed her eyes and gathered her resolve. Blood smeared the base of her thumb, where the severed rigging had whipped it, and she pulled on her sleeve to conceal it.

Zelrin sat up and smirked. "Stop lookin' so scared, will you? I'm the one with a problem here."

Aliwyn gave a thin smile. When Zelrin lay down on his other side, she turned to the stairwell. What were Toby, Ransley, and Emma still doing downstairs? Toward the stern, Edward handed the steering oar to another man and walked for the staircase himself. His brows furrowed with concern, he studied Zelrin for a moment before descending the steps, and chills sprinkled over Aliwyn's scalp. She acknowledged one speck of good in that man; he seemed to care for Zelrin and Emma's safety. Aliwyn scowled at Zelrin's shoulder, feeling its warmth as it rose and fell with his breathing.

"Hey, look who's here," he said.

Emma stood by the mast with her arms hugging her belly.

"Ed wants a grown-up talk," she muttered. "He made me go upstairs."

Her eyes rounded on Zelrin's figure, partly hidden behind Aliwyn's bent knees. "Zel! What happened to you?"

"I'm fine. Just taking a break." Zelrin wagged a finger for the girl to come closer.

Aliwyn scooted out of the way as Emma plopped down by Zelrin's head.

"What is it, Zel?"

The teen's eyes slid from side to side as he whispered, "Let's not tell anyone Toby was distracted when he was steering, all right? Let's make up an excuse."

"But Toby doesn't like lying," Emma said. "He was telling his papa and uncle the truth downstairs."

"Sardin' scat! He *needs* to lie sometimes! Well, good thing Ed's here. He'll think of some good excuse."

Emma glanced at Aliwyn, her brows furrowed, and Aliwyn blinked. If the girl didn't like liars, she didn't know what Aliwyn was capable of.

"What are we going to do now, Zel?" Emma asked. "The ship's broken."

"Sir Ed told his seadogs we need to stop somewhere, cut a tree, and replace the sail's crossbeam."

Aliwyn turned toward him. Zelrin had understood Edward's speech in Danish, after all.

"But won't that take long?" Emma asked. "Toby said we need to be—"

"I don't know. I just know this ship is a real pain to row. She's not a longship, more like a pig floating down a river."

Emma giggled, but Aliwyn tightened her jaw. Zelrin had stopped Emma right before she'd revealed Toby's plans. It could take a week to fix the ship. The thought made her freeze. The Danes wouldn't wait that long to meet someone; their style was to plunder, burn, and abandon the ravaged village before reinforcements came.

Maybe she had indeed ruined the Boltans' plans by slowing the ship. Perhaps the Danes would leave Ravenser's Point empty-handed, wondering what happened to their promised delivery. The possibility sent excitement shooting up her spine, but she shook her head as she gazed into nothingness. It was too good to be true. She had to wait and see what would happen.

"You all right, Aliwyn?" Emma asked.

"I...don't know."

"That was scary, wasn't it? I was scared, too."

Emma snuggled against Aliwyn's side. She urged Aliwyn to drink from her water pouch and took out a hard biscuit for her to eat. On Aliwyn's other side, Zelrin grumbled that he had lost count before he restarted counting to a hundred. Aliwyn raised her costrel and took a sip. The cool water washed down her throat and soothed her nerves.

Emma's shoulder was warm, and her long hair tickled Aliwyn's chin. Flickers of gratitude melted her heart. She hugged Emma's shoulders and chewed on the stale biscuit until it tasted sweet. As the girl began braiding her lavender-scented hair, Aliwyn's eyes wandered up to the vast dome of a thousand stars. It made her feel so small. She wanted to believe the Heavens were still in control, but the heaviness in her chest remained.

Patience was not something she had much of.

Zelrin finished counting, got up, and lay down on his other side. The steps of the stairwell creaked as Edward, Ransley, and Toby ascended. All the mercenaries looked up in attention.

CHAPTER 23

Edward and Ransley addressed the mercenaries in Danish while Toby stood behind them. The wind lifted their capes and tousled the hair that escaped from their hoods. Edward and Ransley made elaborate gestures during their speeches, but Toby stood staring at his feet like a dirty scarecrow. Aliwyn clenched her hands. Was he going to be that passive for the rest of the trip?

"Ha, I knew it," Zel said in a hushed voice. "Sir Ed just blamed a wave for pushing the ship to shore."

"You can understand all that?" Emma asked.

"Sure. I'm half Danish so I understand, but I can't speak it much. Same with Toby. So, from now on, we all blame our friend the Big Wave. All right?"

"All right," Emma whispered, eyeing Aliwyn with a scowl. A lie to help someone was still a lie.

Several men wandered up to Toby, covering their swollen foreheads and nursing bloodied arms, and he flinched. Aliwyn's pulse drummed in her ears; he had to be blaming himself for the whole accident. With his head bowed, Toby led the men toward the ship's bow, but he paused and searched until he found Aliwyn and the two youngsters. His face appeared flushed even in the moonlight.

"Toby," Aliwyn called out. "We're all right. I'll stay with Zel and Emma."

His expression remained bleak. Turning away, he limped toward the front platform as others followed with the floorboards creaking below them. Toby stumbled over his injured ankle and fell to the back of the procession. Aliwyn watched him with a growing ache in her chest. He cared about his crew and would risk his life for them, but it seemed as though he didn't want to take charge.

Her eyes refocused on Ransley and Edward, who were peering over the opposite railing. Edward had hauled up the broken rigging dangling from the side of the ship, the rope coiled loosely in his hands. Both men examined it with their backs turned.

Aliwyn's chest heaved as she caught a glimpse of the twine's ragged edge—the strands frayed and uneven, as though it had unraveled under immense tension while she sawed through it. It was far from a clean cut. If questioned, she'd insist the rope had snapped from being strained beyond its limit.

A few steps away, Cilebi set down his oar and stood. So here was the coward who had collapsed at her feet during the Vasfian attack. She hadn't recognized him then, but his bulbous nose and thick beard were unmistakable now. He ambled toward Edward and Ransley, and chills raced down her back.

Cilebi tapped on Edward's shoulder and murmured something, jerking his head in Aliwyn's direction. He had seen her from under the platform when the rigging failed. Aliwyn matched his stare and rehearsed her alibi. Either she sold everyone her lies and excuses, or she'd lose her life.

Beside her, Zelrin lay on his side and taught Emma how to count in Danish. Aliwyn pretended to listen and kept a blank face, but Ransley soon turned around and stepped toward her. She backed against the railing, her linen-wrapped feet scuffling on the floor. Ransley looked as tired as he had during the day, but he was smiling.

"Hello, my dear. I wanted to apologize for the scare."

He paused, as though expecting a response. When Aliwyn only gawked, Ransley gazed up at the broken crossbeam. "There has been a trend to build vessels that rely solely on wind power. I advised Toby to buy a cargo ship that still had oars. I'm glad he listened to me."

Say something. Anything.

"Is this ship a hulk?" she stammered.

"Ah, very good. You've heard of hulks? It's a cargo ship but still has oars, like a Scandinavian longship. Edward admired it enough to purchase it from Toby." He held his arms behind his back. "I want to show you something. Please follow me."

Aliwyn stood with her knees knocking. Behind her, Emma poured water on a handkerchief to wipe Zelrin's face. They didn't look at her, as though a walk with Toby's father was nothing unexpected. Sweat beaded at Aliwyn's hairline as she shuffled after Ransley, and the arrows and rocks littered on deck threatened to cut her feet. They passed the steering oar and arrived before the back platform, where the capes which had concealed her sabotage still swayed on a clothesline. Aliwyn offered to take them down with a faltering voice.

"No need to hurry," Ransley said. "You've worked all day. After I show you the canoe, you should go to sleep."

What canoe was he talking about? "Th-thank you, sir."

"Please call me Ransley."

Disbelief choked her. This soft-spoken man had almost killed Matthew Marcotte's entire family. Behind his courteous façade was a cavern of vipers.

Ransley was about to lift aside one cloak when Edward called his name from behind, and Aliwyn spun around. Walking beside Edward was Cilebi. As the two men approached, both glowering at Aliwyn, she stumbled back until a bolt of courage nailed her to the floorboards. She had been preparing to face their questions.

"Rans, are you chaining her to the aft castle?" Edward asked.

"No, I want to show her the canoe."

Edward shook his head. "Don't let your guard down around this woman. Cilebi just informed me she was under the aft castle when the rigging failed."

Cilebi glared at Aliwyn. "What were you doing under there?"

Stars washed before her vision, but Aliwyn held her chin high. "I just wanted to get out of the way. Men were running up the stairs, so I hid under the back platform. And I stayed there because arrows were falling."

Straight gaze. Steady voice. She was becoming a master at deception. Turning to Cilebi, she continued smoothly, "During the battle, a man crawled to my feet, sobbing. Was it you?"

Cilebi's eyes widened, and she repressed a gloating grin as he ducked his head. Stupid man; she had seen him, too. Both Edward and Ransley now turned to Cilebi.

"What were you doing under the aft castle?" Ransley cocked his head.

Cilebi squirmed like a man who had just split his trousers. From the corner of her eye, Aliwyn caught Zelrin and Emma scurrying toward the front platform, where Toby was bandaging someone's arm. Whatever the youngsters said made him shoot to his feet. Was he coming to question her, too? She couldn't see his expression in the dimness, and Aliwyn's hands shook. She had imagined lying to many faces, but not to his.

"Regardless of what Cilebi was doing, there have been too many coincidences with this wench," Edward declared. "I found her tweezer right where your dagger should've been. And now the rigging...two lines snapped exactly where she was hiding."

Ransley stroked his beard. "I saw the broken line and the cracked pin. Both were black with rot underneath the surface. Could it be that when we trimmed the sails, the wind was simply too strong?"

Aliwyn struggled between saying something or keeping her mouth shut. The floorboards quaked below her. Toby approached the small gathering with his teeth bared and his fists swinging. She did a double take and stumbled back; with his brows furrowed into a single line, he looked downright vicious.

"Edward, leave her alone!"

"What did I do? I'm asking questions."

"I'm sick and tired of you blaming her for everything!"

"Why shouldn't I suspect her?" Edward raised his voice. "Look at everything that's gone wrong! She's been a curse since the moment she embarked!"

"A curse?" Toby shouted. He pointed at the staircase. "You said the same about cats on board, and look at the rat problem we have now!"

In the ensuing silence, the oarsmen grumbled amongst themselves.

"Aliwyn saved my life more than once," Toby continued. "She cared for our wounded and jeopardized herself to protect Zelrin. For which of these things are you calling her a curse? And does it look like she can tear apart ropes with her bare hands?" Toby thrust a finger at the many lines that still extended from the mast. "Our ropes were fraying, but you wanted to save money. Why not blame yourself for not replacing them?"

"Tobias!" Ransley scolded.

Toby straightened, the muscles of his jawline tensing. "I've said what I needed to say."

Aliwyn braced her arms around her torso. She couldn't bring herself to look at anyone. No one had ever defended her like Toby had, but he didn't know the truth. She covered her mouth, but a sob escaped. Then another.

Toby's voice softened. "From now on, I don't want Aliwyn tied down like some dog or cow. She's important to me. You treat her as you would treat me."

No one had ever called her important, and Aliwyn covered her face with both hands. Edward and Ransley spoke some more. Toby spoke also, but he no longer yelled. To her amazement, mercenaries with heavy Danish accents said she was a hard worker and didn't complain—that they appreciated clean clothes and the privy pot emptied often. Perhaps they spoke in English so she would understand.

Aliwyn's fingers felt like wet snakes on her face. Finally, a tug came on her coat sleeve, and she opened her eyes to see a blurry image of Emma and her doleful brown eyes. Zelrin stood beside the girl, his arms crossed.

Aliwyn dried her tears with her sleeve. The wind was icy on her wet skin, and she wanted to crawl under the covers of her straw mattress back home. Water splashed against the side of the ship as before, and most of the crew rowed. Others stood by the mast and pointed above them, perhaps discussing how best to lower the broken yard and its hefty sail. Edward manned the steering oar with his back turned. No one grabbed her wrist to shackle her again. Toby had made his point, and the crew had agreed with him. It was a freedom she didn't deserve.

Zelrin cleared his throat. "So, Aliwyn. The strange movements you had me do worked. My head stopped spinning."

"Good," Aliwyn whispered. Zelrin seemed stable on his two feet. There was a smirk on his face, and his gaze was sharp. She offered a silent prayer of thanks that she had calmed and treated a distressed patient all on her own.

Had other events not eclipsed this moment, she'd be beaming with pride. Miriam would've been so proud of her, too.

But someone's voice was missing. With his head lowered, Toby stood with his side turned to her while his father gripped his elbow. Although Ransley spoke in Danish, the tone could only mean discipline. When the older man finished, Toby glanced up at this father and murmured, "I understand. I'll speak to Ed when he's willing to listen."

Toby didn't register what a scare Zelrin had gone through, and Aliwyn didn't blame him. She wanted to tell him the broken rigging wasn't entirely his fault, but she couldn't risk turning the blame back on herself again. Her misery deepened into a raw ache within her chest. So much for believing she could cut off from him by jumping overboard.

"Toby." Ransley smiled and patted his son's shoulder. "I wanted to show Aliwyn the canoe behind this ship. Why don't you show her instead?"

Toby didn't look at him. "Good idea. Before something else happens."

"You're too serious, my son. And too hard on yourself."

Toby's chest rose and fell. "Father, wait for me at the forecastle. I'll change your bandages."

"I can do better. I'll go downstairs to clean up. And give me your glove—I'll wash it."

Toby pulled off his glove from the hand the Vasfians hadn't shot. It was covered in blood and grime, but Ransley took it without hesitation and departed.

Toby watched his father go. He lifted a cloak hanging from the back platform and glanced at the others. "About that canoe...please follow me."

Aliwyn released a quivering breath. She so wanted to lift that crushing guilt off his shoulders.

She followed Toby under the back platform. At her feet were the bags and sleep sack that she had trampled over earlier that night, and Aliwyn kept a blank face. No one could prove she had done anything wrong.

The scent of seaweed greeted her as she leaned against the rail, and the canoe bobbed in the sparkling waters behind the ship. It was covered by a black, tarred canvas to keep out the rain. A thick cord tethered it to the ship's stern, and Aliwyn had not noticed it before.

Toby gestured at the pulley and crank used to reel in the canoe. He picked up a length of a rope ladder folded at his feet. "The oars are under the canoe's covering. If something happens to *Lady Fortuna*, like a fire or a leak, climb down this ladder and escape. All of you."

Aliwyn gripped the rail. All the ways she had fantasized about the ship getting destroyed, Toby had already considered. His plan involved saving certain people, and she was one of them.

Zelrin shifted his weight. "I have a question."

"Yes?" Toby asked.

"Why you tellin' us this? You're going to be on the canoe yourself, right?"

"I...can't promise."

"If you sink with this ship, I'll sink with you."

Emma tugged on Zelrin's sleeve. "Zel! What about me?"

"No, Zelrin," Toby said firmly. "You take Emma and Aliwyn and escape. You're not responsible for me. And remember what I told you and the friends who are no longer with us. If something happens to me, help my father flood the base. I need you to do that, please."

Aliwyn remembered the men who had died during the Vasfian attack outside her watermill. They had been Toby's friends, probably the foot soldiers who served under his leadership as a knight. What was this base he wanted to flood? Toby and Zelrin remained silent, their gazes lowered in a moment of mourning. She pinched her fingers and didn't dare ask.

Toby tossed the rope ladder down by his feet and passed his hand over his face. "That's all. All of you, get some sleep somewhere on deck. It's a disaster downstairs. I'll join you after my shift."

His eyes were swollen and red in the moonlight, and he didn't look at Aliwyn. Lowering his chin, he brushed past her, and her chest tightened.

"Wait," she said.

When he turned around, Aliwyn closed the distance between them with a smile and reached for his unbandaged hand. She had just grasped it when Emma squealed and clasped her hands together in delight. Her grin was too big for her face, and warmth stirred within Aliwyn as she smiled back.

Zelrin raised an eyebrow. "All right Emma, you heard what the man said. Your order now is to sleep...somewhere not here."

He held Emma by the shoulders and scooted her away with a waddling gait behind her. The girl snickered as she resisted him, and they both disappeared behind the curtain of capes.

To Aliwyn's dismay, Toby's hand remained heavy and stiff within hers. It matched his expression—not a hint of humor as he stared at his feet. His father was right. He was too serious and too hard on himself.

She stroked the back of his hand with her thumbs. "Thank you for standing up for me, Toby."

"It was the least I could do," he whispered. He switched to Vasfian. "I can't even begin to apologize for my inattentiveness, Aliwyn. I'm so sorry."

Aliwyn struggled for words. She couldn't tell him the truth. "It was...it was an accident."

"Some accidents one can't afford to have happen. I can't imagine what the Vasfians would've done to you if they had caught you tonight." He finally looked up, and unspoken terror shone in his eyes.

"Don't imagine. I'm right here, and so are you."

She smiled and traced her fingers over his wrist, feeling the tendons that promised strength in his forearms. He was warm, and his hand twitched beneath her coat's sleeve. Unable to resist, Aliwyn explored the rest of his hand—the straight fingers befitting a musician, but also the hard calluses recounting many hours with the sword.

Toby withdrew slightly and gave her fingers a squeeze. His frown lifted, and his eyes were calm and clear on his dirty face. With his other hand, he reached up and tucked her wind-blown tresses behind one ear, and Aliwyn beamed. The warmth of his caress flushed from her ear and bloomed over the rest of her body.

"Go find a place to sleep next to Zel and Emma," he said. "I'll be nearby. I still have a few men to bandage up."

Still holding her hand, Toby led her back toward the main deck. Aliwyn felt as though she were floating off the deck.

What on earth had just happened?

She was not fawning over his handsome features like she had the previous morning, when they had both fallen asleep in the stairwell. Toby was grimy enough for her to wrinkle her nose and avoid him had she not known him, and yet he was irresistible. Holding his hand sent her soaring into a sky of rosy clouds and spring mist that she didn't want to come down from. All this in the dead of night. Was she falling in love?

Whatever it was, the feeling was a dangerous development, and her elation came crashing down. Had she forgotten what Toby had done to Matthew's family, and what his goals were? Hadn't she for years loved another man named Aelfric, except that she'd never had the nerve to tell him? Even if Aelfric never reciprocated her love in *that* way, it was still ridiculous to fall for another person so soon.

Aliwyn's legs wobbled. She wallowed in this bewildering attraction like a fly in honey, stuck in something delicious while drowning at the same time.

When Toby brushed back the makeshift curtain, the sight of men rowing outside slapped her in the face. Axlan was sweeping nearby, and a mercenary wiped his bloody shield with a concentrated frown. Toby was still a rebel leader with a mission. Aliwyn's stomach flipped, and she jerked her hand free.

He spun around.

"Go ahead for the front platform," she stammered. "I'll stay and help Axlan clean up."

Toby was silent for a moment, and the cheer drained from his face.

"You're sure?" he asked. "You've worked all day. I was going to help you lie down with Zelrin and Emma."

She brushed off his concerns with some hasty replies. Finally, Toby left her standing with her back to the curtain of capes. He dragged his hurt ankle more than before.

Aliwyn stood for a long time, hugging herself by the elbows. Her mind cried out for sleep, but she was too tired to move. Finally, someone swept rocks past her feet.

"Young lady," Axlan said. "I'd appreciate it if you'd step aside."

She sidestepped out of his way. On deck, a full cleanup was in progress. Several men knelt to wipe up stains and spilled water. One tall man lifted the cauldron back onto the sandbox, while another stood by with a hammer, ready to nail the chains back into the rail. Some tied Vasfian arrows into bundles to be reused.

The deck was falling back into order, but the yard overhead remained snapped, and the sail hung like a wrinkled bed sheet. Maybe Aliwyn wasn't escaping for a sanctuary tonight, but she had sabotaged the ship and survived. Toby had even argued for her innocence, and she allowed herself a breath of relief. It remained to be seen what would happen to the rebels' plans. For now, she needed to sleep.

The night was still bright with a nearly full moon and drifting clouds. She shuffled toward the forecastle, where Zelrin and Emma had settled between the platform's post and the closest oarsman.

As she passed the stairwell, she caught sight of Toby embracing his father halfway down the steps. Ransley, the man who had led the massacre of Matthew's family, was still Toby's beloved father. No one was a villain in his own story. She turned back to her bandaged feet and kept walking, wanting to forget the sight.

Emma was already asleep, tucked in between several blankets folded in half. Beside her head, Zelrin sat against the railing and wiped his face with a rag. Resting against his shoulder was a lute protruding from an opened sack. With a sour tang in her mouth, Aliwyn stared at the instrument, its polished wood and wiry strings. Which poor bard had he stolen that from?

Zelrin had prepared a basin with rags hanging over the edge, just like the morning she had first met him. She ignored the basin and slumped beside him. Now that the sail was broken, she might have to sleep on this ship for many, many more nights. She had to remain on board until she was certain the cargo wouldn't reach the Danes, but the deck was nothing like home. Her composure threatened to crumble as she ached for her sunbathed mill and her chickens.

Zelrin snapped his fingers before her face. "You there? We're short on clean blankets after the privy pot sloshed around. I only found these, and I gave 'em to Emma. Will you be warm enough with linens?"

"Yes." She didn't look at him.

"And why you still not wearin' stockings and shoes? There are plenty—"

"I don't wear stolen things."

Silence.

Her spine rigid, Aliwyn grabbed a rag and wiped her face and neck. She turned her back to Zelrin and dabbed the red patches on her hands. Unwinding the linen strips from around her legs and feet, she wiped her skin clean. The dampness made her shiver. Aliwyn lay with her head to the rail and wrapped herself in linen sheets. Behind her, Zelrin carried away the basin and returned without a word.

Sleep wouldn't come. She was desperate for silence, but the splashing, voices, and footsteps on deck wouldn't stop. Revisiting the chaos from tonight made her heart race, and only Toby's words when he'd defended her before everyone lightened the heaviness inside. Had he meant what he'd said, that she was important to him?

Zelrin extended his legs before him, wagging his foot like the annoying boys at the back of her church every Sunday. The floorboards below him creaked incessantly. Aliwyn rolled around with a frown and almost slapped his knee, but she froze when she heard sniffling.

Zelrin scowled at her and fingered a row of sling stones he had arranged by size along his leg. Aliwyn saw the blood-stained tears on his trousers, probably from his fall, and her irritation lifted.

"Are you going to sleep, Zel?" Her voice hovered above the rhythmic creaks.

He didn't seem to hear her, and she tensed at what he said next.

"I need to set something straight with you, Aliwyn. This thing isn't stolen." He jerked a thumb at the lute still in a bag beside him. "This belonged to me and my brother, Lukas. We shared it. We were Toby's minstrels when he owned a manor in Fiskerton, and Ransley and Ed had manors, too. Doesn't look like it now, does it? The Fiskerton folks loved Toby to pieces. He always took care of them, but the Normans drove him out."

The bridge of his nose twitched, and Aliwyn's tongue lay thick in her mouth. Had the condemnation in her eyes been that obvious? Her assumptions about the instrument's owner were wrong, and it was jarring to imagine Toby presiding over a manor and not wandering with other outlaws. Yet, she didn't doubt the villagers of Fiskerton had treasured their benevolent young lord. She bit her lip and pushed to sitting.

"You think Toby and I want to be here?" Zelrin continued, his voice shaking. "Stop struttin' around like you're better than the rest of us."

His words punched her in the guts. She was no saint, and judging others wasn't going to change that. Aliwyn gathered her knees to her chest, and the linens fell to her waist. The wind dispersed whatever warmth she had gathered under her clothes. Zelrin averted his eyes and wagged his foot again.

She had marveled at his courage but had also reduced his identity to that of an outlaw—someone divided from her side of humanity. Yet, he was wounded and hurting like anyone else who had lost a loved one, and it didn't matter if he was Danish or English or Norman, rich or poor, a thief or a king. The sorrow of loss transcended all divisions.

An apology was not what Zelrin needed. She needed to see him differently, to treat him as a person. He would be the age of her younger brother had he lived, and Aliwyn struggled to speak through the knot in her throat.

"Zel, what are your favorite songs to play?"

His scowl faded. "Toby and I like the same ones. But they're mostly Danish songs, so you wouldn't know them."

"Can you play them tomorrow?"

He shifted against the railing. "I don't want to play without Lukas. We were always a duet, always." He looked up with a smirk that quickly turned sour. "We were twins. If you see me, it's like you see him."

He stretched out his gloved hand and studied it before setting it back on his thigh. His forehead wrinkled with grief, and a hollowness expanded within Aliwyn's chest.

Twin acts were popular, and Zelrin and his brother were probably talented musicians if they could make a living by entertaining their lord. But such a life was impossible if no lord resided in the manor, and the Normans had forced Toby off his property. Aliwyn pulled the linens back around her body, and her shoulders shook as the Boltans' plight drew closer to her. After all, none of them could go home.

Zelrin had grown still, his eyes moist as they stared into nothingness. Aliwyn wanted to rub his shoulder. It must've been devastating to watch an identical twin die.

"Zelrin," she said softly. "I hope you play again one day."

"I don't know. Why aren't you sleeping?" He wagged his foot again, although not as fast as before, and the floorboards creaked in cadence.

"Well, what about you? Aren't you tired?"

"I can't sleep. I've barely slept since Lukas died. Now I have these shaking fits that somethin' will happen to Emma or Toby whenever I shut my eyes."

"Zel, you know Toby is with others. He's not in danger. And if you hold Emma as you sleep, would that help?"

Zelrin hesitated. He ran his forearm over his eyes and sniffed. "Maybe."

He stopped wagging his foot and collected his sling stones, some for his pockets, some for a bag tied to the rail. Turning the lute on its side against the rail, he slipped under the covers beside Emma and lay with his head perpendicular to the instrument. He gathered the sleeping girl into his arms, and Aliwyn smiled. She tucked the loose edge of the woolen blanket behind Zelrin's back.

"She's lucky." He smirked up at Aliwyn. "Always sleeps like a little piglet."

"And she's safe with you. Just close your eyes."

He did, and Aliwyn's smile faded. She and Zelrin had their differences, but he had taken Toby's order to keep her safe seriously while she'd had fantasies of him drowning. It wasn't right. She still had a decision to make—to forgive him or not for throwing away Aelfric's recorder. Aliwyn scowled at her spindly fingers and could almost see the instrument materialize on her palm, but it wouldn't, no matter how long she slogged in resentment.

And she had to admit something; had she experienced Zelrin's side of the story, she would also despise Aelfric.

Aliwyn had to let go. She blew out her bitterness in a puff of air, and the burden within lightened for a moment before the sadness descended again.

She rubbed her eyes and watched Zelrin sleep. It seemed like forgiveness was a path to undertake, not a sappy decision to make once and forget about. Maybe one day this moment would bring her peace.

Aliwyn lay with her back to the teen, and his blanket warmed her back. Her groggy mind recalled how he had declared Toby's mission to be "blasted stupid." Zelrin might be on her side after all, but it was too early to tell.

The mercenaries roamed the deck, performing their duties and not roaring mad as she had expected. A few men sat along the railing, sipping from their costrels, and she scrutinized their movements. What did they still have up their sleeves?

CHAPTER 24

ALIWYN DRIFTED INTO A light sleep, but the scent of something burning jolted her awake. She scrambled to sit up. Her head spun from the exertion, but no danger jumped from the shadows. Zelrin and Emma slept beside her as before while a dozen men sat cross-legged and slurped from their bowls. Further down the ship and against the opposite rail, Toby stood by the hearth and wiped porridge from the side of the cauldron. He had taken off his gambeson in the heat, and it lay folded on top of a barrel.

Axlan was amongst the men sitting. He looked up from his bowl and chuckled. "She's not happy with you, Toby."

"Someone burned porridge?" Aliwyn asked, her pulse still racing.

"I did." Toby raised his eyebrows and rubbed his forehead. "I thought making pottage was like boiling water, but it wasn't. I promise not to cook again."

"It's oats flambé." Axlan kissed the tips of his fingers. "Today's special flavor. Maybe you'll like it, Aliwyn."

She mustered a smile through her exhaustion. Being the son of a knight, Toby had probably never cooked in his life, and it was sweet of him to try. Some oarsmen even licked their bowls and didn't seem to mind. Toby knelt to wash out his rag in a nearby bucket before returning to wipe the cauldron, and Aliwyn followed his every move with her face glowing. She delighted in his sheepish grin and the shifting of his slender, muscular frame covered by only a loose-collared tunic. He carried himself gracefully and with a sincere gaze.

But the crowd behind Toby made her remember where she was.

The crew had lowered the snapped crossbeam to deck level. They stood alongside the furled sailcloth and used rope to lash the two broken pieces parallel to each other. The overlapping segment made the crossbeam shorter, but it still extended toward the back platform. Other men carried coils of rope and gestured at the furled sail; they were going to replace the rigging.

Aliwyn stopped breathing. "Th-that's how they're fixing the ship?"

"It's a temporary fix." Toby hung his rag on the railing with a determined scowl. "It'll last us until we reach a barrier island off the Lincolnshire coast. Then we'll have to fell a tree and fashion a new yard."

"How far is the barrier island?"

"We should reach one tomorrow. Don't worry, Aliwyn. It'll only be a brief stop, and we'll all get off soon enough."

Aliwyn stared but saw nothing. She ducked her head and pressed a palm over half her face. Sobs mixed with anguished laughter bubbled up in her chest. Her best efforts to stall the ship had been for naught. Short of death, Toby and his crew wouldn't give up on their promised bounty.

Toby ladled pottage into a wooden bowl and carried it toward her. "Do you want some, Ali?"

Only Aelfric and Miriam used to call her "Ali." She gathered her knees to her chest and buried her face, her ribs shuddering. She couldn't give herself to a man with such destructive goals, and her mind reeled in a void for her next steps. The plan had been to escape or drown tonight, not to be stuck with a knight she was drawn to but couldn't be with.

"Ali, tell me what's wrong." Toby touched her shoulder. The fragrance from his bowl of porridge teased her hunger.

She was too tired to filter her words. "It smells like home. I want to go home."

Lying down, she turned her back and pulled the linen blankets over her face. The Heavens were mocking a foolish girl who knew nothing about sailing or ships. All along, the crew had known how to rig together a snapped crossbeam within hours.

One last solution prodded her like a knife. Set the cargo on fire. Sink the ship. Dead mercenaries couldn't win.

Gasping, Aliwyn pulled down her blanket. Not that thought again. Moving bodies spun in a whirl in the moonlight and darkness, and she wrung the rough linen in her hands. If sacrificing several dozen people on board, including herself, could save villages upon villages, would she do it? Her teeth chattered, and waves of prickly heat washed down her spine. No. She'd think of something else if only she could get some sleep.

The floorboards quivered as Toby sat beside her. Aliwyn covered her face again, but he stayed there. And stayed there. Aliwyn wanted to slither between the dirty planks and vanish.

"Toby," a man called out. "Is your uncle coming to eat?"

"He's avoiding me. Please save him some food." Toby sighed. "I'll take some down for my father now."

"How is he doing?"

"We're trying different medicines. He says his headache is getting better."

"Good!"

A breeze chilled her hairline as Toby's footsteps departed, and one foot was heavier as he descended the creaky stairs. Behind the safety of the blanket, Aliwyn let her tears flow. Toby's face and voice came and went in the darkness. How frightened he'd looked hanging up-side-down. His smile in the sunrise onboard this ship. His fury as he shouted for Edward to leave her alone. His laughter echoed in her mind, and she missed the warmth of his hand.

Here, chick chick chick!

Through her tears, Aliwyn grinned at the memory. Toby had been doomed on that bridge, but he had been thinking of Emma's future, and he didn't forgo the chance to help a poor peasant find her chickens.

If only they had met under different circumstances.

Aliwyn dreamed of waking up the next day and stealing a flint and metal striker stored by the hearth. She went downstairs, and no one stopped her. Standing over the wooden chests, still secured behind netting, she struck sparks that showered down like bronze rain. At that point in the dream, the cold chilled her awake. Goosebumps formed all over her neck, and she blew out her dread. Good thing none of that had happened. Her fingers numb, Aliwyn pulled the blanket off her face.

She caught her breath. Toby lay beside her with a sackcloth hat on his head, and he slept face-up in a long sheepskin sack that covered him up to the collar of his gambeson. It was the same kind of sleep sack Edward had slept in. A bag of grain propped up his head, and beside him was another bag, a spare pillow.

Aliwyn envied his gambeson. There must be nothing like wearing over thirty layers of linen to stay warm, but she didn't have a gambeson, and the night air had gotten cooler. Pins and needles shot from her toes. Aliwyn sniffled and curled tighter into a ball.

Her heart skipped a beat when Toby opened his eyes and turned to her with a smile.

"Ali, I found this hudfat in a bag downstairs. Are you willing to share it with me?"

So he wasn't sleeping after all. She felt tricked, but curiosity overtook her. "What is a hood fat?"

He chuckled. "Sorry, I don't know why I assumed you knew. A hudfat is this sleeping bag I'm in." He hesitated. "It's meant for two people. You can see the hired hands sleeping in them."

These brawny men, sleeping in pairs? Aliwyn pushed up on her stiff arms. The deck was littered with these hudfats with two men asleep in each of them like oversized children. Was this how the Norsemen once slept on the deck of longships?

"Are you willing to share one with me?" Toby's voice faltered.

The second bag of grain was ready to serve as Aliwyn's pillow, and her neck was indeed sore. Aliwyn's teeth clattered as a breeze scattered her hair. Desperate for warmth, she nodded.

Toby's eyes were half open as he grinned. Aliwyn crawled toward the hudfat. The linen blankets she'd used slipped off her back, but she was too tired to care. She stuck one foot into the sack. Her toes wiggled into soft, woolen tufts that embraced her in luxurious warmth, but they were warm because of Toby. He lay blinking at the sky, and Aliwyn sighed. Things could be worse. She slid herself into the sleep sack, turned her back to him, and pulled the bag of grain under her head.

Her muscles melted with relief at the heat, but Toby's smile as she had approached him haunted her. He could be insightful in some ways but be blind to other things, like her treachery. She wanted to slap him for wasting his charm and youth and an otherwise promising life on this mission. Why couldn't he see what a disaster he would cause? Why couldn't he be happy with that estate awaiting him in Denmark? Short of killing him and the crew, how could she stop him?

As her head buzzed with fatigue, a mercenary walked by, scooped up her discarded linens for himself, and left. Now she'd freeze if she abandoned the sleep sack. Aliwyn growled.

The hudfat tugged as Toby moved behind her, and he rubbed her back and shoulders. Aliwyn pinched the strands of her hair that fell onto her hand, unwilling to admit how soothing it was to feel someone's touch.

"Aliwyn, I know how homesick you are," he said. "Please, can you turn around? I want to tell you something."

His breathing was uneven. She remembered how he had defended her before his uncle and the whole ship, and how she had felt when she thanked him. She was going nowhere tonight and cutting him off wasn't right. Aliwyn sniffled. Hesitantly, she rolled onto her back.

Her grainy eyes pulsed as she strained to keep them open. She stared at the bright moon in the sky, quivering as the hudfat's cozy wool graced her neck. Toby was close enough to embrace her, and her stomach flipped. What had she been thinking, crawling into this thing? She crossed her wrists over her collarbones as though she were still shackled.

Toby gathered her hand with his own. His warm fingers folded tenderly over her scrapes and bruises, as though he were holding a dove with a broken wing. Without saying anything, he told her again she was important to him. He wouldn't give up on her, and Aliwyn nibbled at her lower lip. The firestorm within began settling in a blanket of ash.

She could tally up all the ways they had wronged each other and their loved ones. All the reasons they should hate each other. Or she could let that all go, if even for a moment. Her body tensed and ached. How draining it was to ride these waves of bitterness.

When Toby brought her hand to his lips, she gave a start and almost jerked away. He blew on her fingers to warm them. It was comforting, and her scalp tingled. She glanced at him, and the gentleness in his eyes made her look again. He smiled faintly.

"Ali, I mentioned it in passing, but I do want to bring you back to your watermill." The stubbles of his beard tickled her hand as he talked. "God willing, I'll live to see peace return to England. It will be a better place to live for people like you and me. Once it's safe to go back, I'll sail back to England with you."

Aliwyn's hand trembled within his.

"What if it's never safe to go back?" she whispered. "The Vasfians won't let me go home."

His brows furrowed. "When we go to Denmark, I'll build a watermill with a chicken coop attached. The coop will have a door that opens directly into your living quarters." He smirked. "Then you won't have to walk outside just to see your chickens."

How did he know she had always wanted such a door? She couldn't swallow the lump in her throat.

"That sounds good," she whispered. "But my chickens are all going to die."

Toby's face went blank. "What?"

"I mean...I mean the ones I had. They're all stuck in a tiny, cold room with no window or food or water, wondering what happened to me. They're all going to die."

A tear rolled from the corner of her eye. Most people thought of chickens as head-bobbing dolts whose only saving grace was laying eggs, but Aliwyn had held them since they were baby chicks. They were all affectionate with their distinct personalities.

Toby stroked her hand with his thumb. "Ali, can I tell you what I think happened? The Vasfians may despise you and me, but they have nothing against your hens. Hens lay eggs and are valuable. The tribe adopted them after you left. I'm sure of it."

Aliwyn held her breath, and his words echoed in her mind. They made sense, but she had been too much of a wreck to think this way. The weight on her chest lifted as she exhaled. She'd never forget her feathery friends, but they'd live on without her. It was one less thing to be miserable about.

She smiled at him, and Toby's smile back carried the warmth of the sun.

"We can arrange the furniture inside to match the way your watermill looked," he said. "You know, when I went back, everything inside...looked the same as when I had lived with Miriam, eight years ago."

His voice faltered, and the smile disappeared. Toby adjusted his head on his pillow and lowered his chin. As shadows crept over his moonlit face, Aliwyn's heart skipped. Recreating Miriam's watermill in Denmark would not be just for her, but also for himself.

The questions she had been afraid to ask churned within her. "Toby, why didn't you go back to visit Miriam?"

Toby let go of her hand and rolled onto his back. A breeze chilled her palm as his warmth departed, and the way he grimaced under the silvery light made her stiffen.

She turned toward him and lay on her side. "I didn't mean to make you feel guilty."

"But I should feel guilty. My deepest regret right now is not going back." The knob in his throat slid up and down. "Maybe you'd understand. Life gets busy. Something always seems more urgent. You think you'll have time to tell people you love them. But things...happen."

The ship squealed with a slow rock to one side, and men shuffled in the background. Toby's eyes brightened as he searched the sky through his tousled bangs, and Aliwyn bit her lip until it stung.

"I don't have a good excuse," he said. "I met Miriam a year after the Normans invaded, when I was twelve. I had eight years to come back. Maybe I would've met all three of you in the mill. Then we would've met...under different circumstances."

Aliwyn's gaze blurred with longing. Miriam had accepted her two apprentices five years ago, and had Toby returned for a visit within the last eight years, maybe everyone would've met at the watermill. If Aelfric and Toby had become friends back then, who knows where everyone would be by now?

"I think you said that Miriam never talked about me?" Toby asked.

"She never did…"

He shook his head. "I must've been too much of a burden. I came to Miriam like a mangled dog, and it wasn't just my broken arm. After all the bullying at school, I was done. I didn't want to do anything with my life. My father passed me to Miriam to cool off, but for weeks, I either stared at a wall or smashed her earthenware and yelled at her." His voice cracked. "I was unpleasant, to put it lightly. But every day, she'd tried to hug me. She never raised her voice. And she would hold my hand and take me on walks, point out the flowers and animals and tell me life was still beautiful. She told me she believed in me. But I didn't leave her acting like I was grateful. The gratefulness came later, as I got older."

Aliwyn smiled as her lips trembled. Miriam had been like that—someone who could piece shards of a broken life back together, shards others didn't want, and Aliwyn missed her dearly.

Toby had grown still, his gaze distant. "I was also too ashamed to see her again after I left. I'm sorry, Miriam…"

Aliwyn bumped his shoulder with her hand. "Toby, don't blame yourself. You were just a boy, and you were going through a hard time."

"But why did she never talk about me?"

"Miriam was a very private person. She didn't talk much about her past, even to me. Remember the way she treated you. She cared about you very much, so hold on to those good memories and don't overthink it."

Don't overthink it. She was sure good at giving advice she didn't follow. Aliwyn kept a steady gaze and ran her hand over Toby's padded shoulder. He gave a shaky smile back and said, "If we go back to England, can you show me where she is buried? I'd like to visit."

"Of course I can."

He turned back to the sky. "I feel like she's still with us. Like those stars up there. We don't always see them, but they're always there."

Aliwyn didn't have the habit of stargazing. Following Toby's eyes, she lifted her gaze. She had been missing out. The longer she looked, the more specks of light appeared and twinkled from the vast dome above, stunning and limitless. Shapes appeared as she connected the dots, and she smiled. She could make out a waterwheel, a pig, maybe a chicken. But her eyes could just as easily make burning trees and swords appear. Aliwyn took several deep breaths. The stars were unchangeable, but she determined what she wished to see out of them. Like the position of the stars, some situations were out of her control, but could she still see the good in them?

When she turned back to Toby, his eyes were closed.

Aliwyn snuggled against his shoulder. Talking to him just now, she had forgotten that he was a Boltan. Forgotten about what his family had done and planned to do. Toby was patient and considerate.

A thought thawed the iciness within, like the first crack of a frozen pond at springtime. Under different conditions, her enemies could have been her friends, and her friends could have been her enemies. No one was perfect enough to be always lovable. Sooner or later, even a compassionate, selfless person would make appalling mistakes, but it was still possible to love that person despite his decisions.

All the inner turmoil expressed in those around her shouldn't stop her from caring about them. Their brokenness wasn't a reason to shut herself in and never love again.

Heaven knew how many times Aliwyn had hurt those who loved her, especially her father. All those screeching fits she'd thrown whenever he'd tried to court another woman, because young Aliwyn couldn't stand the thought of her father replacing her deceased mother. Aliwyn's father had never remarried. After every outburst, he would welcome her back into his arms. He had loved her anyway, mistakes, flaws, tantrums, and all.

She studied Toby's face—the deeply set eyes and the straight nose. Her affection for him grew unbridled, and she pressed her face against his gambeson with her cheeks burning. The warmth of his embrace before they'd jumped into the ravine, and again when he'd carried her on horseback, made her limbs tingle with longing.

There had to be a way to destroy the cargo without taking everyone's life. There had to be a way to overcome evil without more evil. The noises of the ship fell away as she prayed for guidance, and her mind spun with fatigue.

Zelrin's snoring beside her ushered her back to awareness. Enough wind entered the sleep sack to chill her neck and chest, but Toby and the others slept peacefully in their gambesons, and she didn't want to bother them. She reached behind and patted Zelrin until he stopped snoring. Withdrawing her frigid arm, she finally sneezed into Toby's shoulder.

He flinched, and Aliwyn stiffened like an icicle. "S-sorry."

Toby sat up, and she stared at him. Would her sneeze send him away in disgust? But Toby barely opened his eyes. Taking off his gambeson, he spread half of it over the hudfat, on the side where she lay. He lay down again, under the other half of his gambeson, and pulled Aliwyn against him.

The burning warmth of his body made her gasp. She drew up her legs and accidentally kneed him on the thighs.

Toby jerked back, and the cold air rushed in between them.

"I apologize." His arm hovered in the air, his eyes wide. "I didn't mean to make you uncomfortable."

Aliwyn's eyes trailed down to her hand. It still rested against his torso, and her fingers graced over the shape of his chest—the defined, relaxed muscle under a layer of warm linen. Goodbye, puffy gambeson. A hundred butterflies took flight within her. She couldn't resist a smile, but Toby only watched her, his tired gaze laden with worry.

Her lips quivered. She had been a nobody in her village—a skinny girl who always smelled like fish. But Toby valued and cared for her as if she was his lady, and she was grateful. They had survived Vasfian attacks, surging rapids, murderous lepers, and a near shipwreck. She had seen more depth and honor in Toby over the past three days than in other men in the past three years. There was more of him to discover, understand, and perhaps love one day. Their story needed a leap of faith, and she was willing to take it.

Reaching for his neck, she drew him close again.

"It's all right, Toby. I want to be with you."

She curled up against him and reached into the soft hair of his nape. His arm slid up her back. Cradling her head with his hand, Toby enveloped her in his warmth. His chest rose against hers with a drumming of his heart, and Aliwyn closed her eyes and tried not to shake. To say she wanted to be with him was a bold statement, but it wasn't another lie.

Her fingers descended for the warmth of his sides. It was heinous to keep plotting behind his back. She'd had enough of the excuses, with the web of deceit she spun only to ensnare herself in a deeper tunnel of lies. She had to confront Toby's reality and probe him about his intentions for the cargo as though she didn't already know. If she cared about him, she wouldn't let him spiral down a destructive path she doubted he wanted to take. Perhaps, in his drive to please his father and uncle, he was drifting under a fog of denial. Until she challenged his motivations, all she did was hack at thorns without destroying their roots.

Aliwyn would whittle away at his goals with carefully chosen words. She would talk to him about throwing his cargo overboard and sailing straight to Denmark, where he still had a future. The Normans were unlikely to pursue and kill him if he exiled himself and never returned to England. But everything could go wrong thanks to her meddling. She could lose Toby. Shatter the fragile tolerance of the crew. Get herself killed. Tears filling her eyes, Aliwyn wrapped her arm around the firmness of Toby's back. He stroked her hair, and his fingers loosened the tangled strands as his palm warmed her ear. His soft touch smoothed the biting edge of her fears.

Toby adjusted the gambeson covering them both, and Aliwyn withdrew her arms to warm them against his chest. He pulled back and looked down at her.

She didn't expect to see sadness in his gaze. Her breath came in gasps, and she shivered despite the warmth shimmering through her body.

"What's wrong?" she whispered.

Tension wrinkled his forehead. "I'm sorry for how I treated you outside the leper cabin. And again, in the tunnel leading to this ship."

He looked away, his lips pressed into a thin line, and Aliwyn's throat swelled. She had not looked back to those moments when Toby had been at his worst. People could become unrecognizable during times of war. She had heard about it in Aelfric's last days and had witnessed it in herself.

Aliwyn opened her hand and stroked Toby's collarbone with her thumb. "I forgive you, Toby. Don't blame yourself anymore." She smiled when he looked at her again. "We can move on."

His hazel eyes and sweeping bangs seemed to glow in the moonlight. The way he smiled back made her wish she could freeze this moment between them, but sorrow lingered in his gaze. What was still bothering him? Maybe it would pass after the sun rose again.

"Get some rest now," Toby said. "Tomorrow, I have some things to show you downstairs."

Like what? She smiled, but before she could ask, Toby turned with a passing grimace to lie on his back. The wound on his left side must still hurt, and she rubbed his upper arm. She rested her arm over his chest and snuggled against his shoulder. Aliwyn saved her curiosity for tomorrow—they had already talked long enough. His body rose and fell under her arm, and she caught the scent of pine and burned porridge. The burned fragrance made her smile.

"Good night, Toby."

"Good night."

His breathing slowed as he fell asleep. What a blessing to fall asleep so quickly. Aliwyn wasn't so fortunate. Her mind wouldn't stop. She wouldn't see Matthew, his cousins, Kato, or her chickens again. *Farewell, everyone.* The brambles tangled around her heart unraveled. She missed what she had left behind, but hope for the future relieved the emptiness inside.

Only the memory of one person, Aelfric, made her breath hitch. She still considered him her best friend, but resentment now tainted the moments they had shared, from the slimy snail races on the Brocklesby Bridge railing, to building snow sculptures, to the evening music duets of "Kyrie Eleison" forever etched in her mind. Why did she blame him for not loving her back in a romantic sense? Such love couldn't be forced.

Aliwyn smiled wistfully. She would let the hurt go eventually—hopefully soon. She had been blessed to be loved as Aelfie's sister. One day, she'd see him in heaven, and they'd have plenty of time to talk.

But the promise of heaven felt distant, and her tears came and went. With time, Aliwyn could no longer remember the previous sentence in her thoughts.

Her heart still fluttered from all that had happened. Water splashed against the ship, and men muttered to each other.

Edward approached. She would recognize those heavy and spaced footsteps anywhere. Was he going to drag Toby away again like he had that morning? Her chest seizing, Aliwyn snapped out of her light sleep. She almost pulled Toby's head into her chest to protect him, but Edward strode past where she and Toby lay, and a few mercenaries greeted him in Danish. Axlan spoke in English and offered Edward the remaining porridge.

"I'm not eating his garbage," Edward muttered. "Make me a new batch."

"My pleasure, captain," Axlan said. "After I'm done with—"

"By Jove! Y-you're skinning rats?"

Axlan chuckled. "There were four dead in the traps downstairs. They're swarming out of the bilge like you wouldn't believe! And they're delicious. Want to try—"

"No. Take those rats away and leave me be. I'll make my own porridge."

Footsteps walked in all directions. Aliwyn spread her hand over Toby's chest. Instinct warned her trouble was coming, but he slept on.

After a moment, Axlan said, "Uh, Captain Edward, can I ask you what you said to the mercenaries earlier?"

Edward grunted. "Ah, yes. I forget you don't speak Danish." He paused, and someone poured water into the cauldron. "In short, I pledge to find someone to buy our cargo so everyone will get paid. People have mouths to feed at home...let me speak to Ransley now. He must know of alternative clients if we can't reach Ravenser's Point on time."

"Should you wait for Toby to—"

"He doesn't exist. Restart the fire, will you?"

Aliwyn clenched her jaw. Toby needed to hear this, and she almost got up and shook him awake. This selfish uncle of his was walking all over his nephew to serve himself and his pockets. Who else would he sell Toby's product to? One of the rebellious earls?

Edward's footsteps descended the steps, and Aliwyn drew back from Toby's shoulder enough to see his face. His tranquil expression told of deep, much-needed rest, and Aliwyn resisted stroking his hair to wake him up. He was a heavy sleeper in more ways than one, oblivious to the signs that his uncle was a tyrant. Edward was the same kind of selfish man Toby vowed to depose from the throne. It wouldn't be enough to convince Toby to get rid of his cargo; she would need to pit him against his blood—an uncle who was taller, bulkier, and had more influence. Toby had clashed with Edward tonight over Aliwyn's freedom and won. No one had shackled her since, but that was nothing compared to what Toby still had to face. And whose side would Ransley take?

Worrying for Toby's safety stole her sleep. The mercenaries on board also wanted payment and would turn against him. This was too much to ask of one person. Her heart sinking, Aliwyn pinched her fingers and rubbed her ankles together within the hudfat. A moment later, Toby shifted his head and yawned, and Aliwyn sighed. She was sorry for wiggling so much.

Toby turned to her, and his tired eyes opened but closed again.

"Bad dream?" he whispered.

"S-something like that."

"Would it help if I held you?"

Aliwyn struggled against a reflexive fear. No man had held her before in bed as she slept, but she had secretly longed for it all those nights alone on her mattress. Toby had been respectful and considerate of her since she had boarded.

"Maybe it would help," she answered softly.

She lifted herself, and Toby extended his arm underneath her. Eyes closing again, he felt for her back and hugged her shoulders, settling her cheek on his chest. His arm slid down to her waist and remained there. Aliwyn melted into his warmth as she lay on her side. She fit perfectly into the curve of his shoulder, as though she had always belonged. Toby didn't speak again, but his soothing embrace was enough.

Stop worrying, Ali. It changes nothing.

She rested her bent arm on his torso. He had drawn her to where he was most vulnerable because he trusted her. She wanted to trust him, too, and trust the Heavens they would survive whatever happened next. Aliwyn spent the last of her energy praying for Toby's safety and the safety of everyone he intended to harm. Then she decided to follow her advice—to stop overthinking, except for one last thought. She held a handsome knight without his armor. It was a reason to smile, and she did.

Her anxiety lifted as her body grew too heavy to move. The footsteps, squeaky floorboards, and splashing gave away to the sound of Toby breathing and the steady beat of his heart. Aliwyn fell asleep with his arm still around her side.

EPILOGUE

October 2

Vasfian warriors of the Ahitan tribe descended the cliff toward the shore of the North Sea. They collected arrows as they went, and many murmured about the mysterious ship that had slid onto their beach the night before. Despite the colors of the sail, that ship had not belonged to the Normans. Who were they trying to fool? The whole crew had been screaming in Danish.

Crumpled black clothing appeared on the beach in the distance, wet from the waves that lapped the shore. They hadn't been present yesterday afternoon. The golden embroidery on the cloth shimmered in the early sunlight. A Vasfian woman picked up the clothing and unfurled it. She grimaced; it was a surcoat typically worn by those dirt-headed outsiders, and it smelled like a serious case of indigestion.

Although the surcoat was torn and had partially sewn patches, the golden griffin embroidered across the front was unmistakable.

Her eyebrows shot up. Waving over her comrades, she shook out the surcoat for all to see.

"The spirit of Lenus is smiling upon us today!" she cried. "Send Reiya a message—the Boltans passed us a few hours ago!"

Would you kindly leave a review?

List of websites to leave reviews: Kyriewang.co
m/leavereviews

Reviews are the lifeblood of indie authors. They encourage us to keep writing and help our books get discovered. Your review is unique and so greatly appreciated!
Please consider writing one for *Healer's Blade* on <u>Amazon</u>, <u>Goodreads</u>, and/or <u>Bookbub</u>.
Thank you!

A teaser of *Traitor's Heart (Enemy's Keeper Book 2)* follows at the end of this book.

The Adventure Continues!

Traitor's Heart (Enemy's Keeper Book 2)
Available on Amazon (Kindle Unlimited)
For a list of all retailers, please scan below:

A healer forced to destroy. A warrior forced to betray. In the shadow of rebellion, every choice leaves a scar.

Aliwyn awakens to chaos as tragedy strikes the rebels' ship. As loyalties fracture and danger closes in, she must betray the knight who holds her heart or watch innocent lives burn in England's destruction.

Desperate to reclaim his honor, Matthew forges an uneasy alliance with the Vasfian chief, Reiya. His quest to save Aliwyn becomes a journey of devastating revelations as he uncovers Aelfric's secret double life. Each step toward redemption forces him to choose between duty to the crown and the people he's sworn to protect.

With a rebel-Danish alliance threatening to shatter England, Matthew and Aliwyn must navigate a treacherous web of deception and shifting alliances. Only one thing is certain: their choices will either save the kingdom...or destroy it.

<u>*Reader Reviews*</u>

"Kyrie Wang does a tremendous job expanding her world in this second installment in her Enemy's Keeper series. The stakes are higher. The characters are deeper. And the journey to the end will have you sitting at the edge of your seat...Definitely recommend this book if you're a lover of heroic, troubled knights, fearless warrior women, and heart-gripping romances." - ***Goodreads***

"<u>Traitor's Heart (Book 2)</u> has everything I loved about <u>Healer's Blade (Book 1)</u>, but even better! I love the descriptions and the medieval medicine. It's fast-paced, and every chapter leaves you on a cliffhanger." - ***Goodreads***

"My goodness, I felt this one sink DEEP. Kyrie took me from being mad at a character to absolutely rooting for him as the story unfolded. It was simply, unequivocally wonderful. The character transformations are among the best I've ever encountered. It's a wild ride, guys. Buckle up." - ***Goodreads***

Healer's Blade Audiobook

Relive the adventure with a 100% human-narrated audiobook!

It's free on Hoopla and streams at no extra cost for Spotify Premium members.

For a complete list of retailers, including Audible and more:

Books2read.com/HealersBlade

MEDICAL NOTES

How Toby Survived the Bridge

Kyriewang.com/Toby

This blog post discusses the medical science behind how Toby survived hanging on the bridge, upside down, without becoming incoherent. The post draws from forensic literature and my knowledge as a physician trained to perform autopsies. It's the most popular blog post I've written and has no gruesome graphics.

Kyriewang.com/crossbow

This related blog post explains how Toby survived the Vasfian arrow. It includes a re-enactment video, demonstrating how a crossbow arrow simply bounces off a gambeson.

Leprosy is not as contagious as historically believed. According to the Center of Disease Control (USA), "Prolonged, close contact with someone with untreated leprosy over many months is needed to catch the disease. You cannot get leprosy from a casual contact...like shaking hands or hugging." Therefore, none of my characters will develop leprosy from their brief contact with lepers. *Source:*

Lukas died of **gas gangrene**, which is commonly caused by the bacteria Clostridium perfringens. His symptoms, as described, are classic for this illness.

On the ship, Zelrin experienced an episode of vertigo. Today, this is known as **benign paroxysmal positional vertigo**. The maneuver Aliwyn performed to treat him is called the Semont Maneuver, which is not complicated and may have been discovered, albeit not recorded, centuries ago.

Author's Note

Thank you for reading book one of the *Enemy's Keeper* series! The interwoven stories in these books are dear to my heart and are a culmination of daydreaming over nine years and counting. I hope to publish four books in the series.

Before *Enemy's Keeper*, I wrote the prequel, *Seeker*, when I was around sixteen years old and published it in my early twenties. The story was a novella that followed Kato, Evelyn, Aelfric, and Matthew before they met Aliwyn. However, I only sold *Seeker* in a medical school talent show and it was never widely distributed. As of this writing, *Seeker* is not available for sale because the writing style and story content no longer reflect who I am almost two decades later. I also did not plan on writing a sequel to *Seeker*.

However, as I continued my training in medical school and residency, I needed a means of escape—and sometimes I could only escape in my head. Writing also helped me process the emotions and vignettes from my daily life. The sequel to *Seeker* took form in my head as the *Enemy's Keeper* series. I hope to convey my experiences that good and evil, and right or wrong, are not always clear-cut, and that individual decisions and actions matter even when cultural norms and overarching institutions seem to have the final say. Finally, writing the Enemy's Keeper series helped me process the sorrow of witnessing many autopsies as a medical resident.

While many details of daily life in AD 1075 England are historically accurate, I took several major creative liberties:

<u>The Vasfian Tribes</u>
Vasfians didn't exist. I created them based on peoples such as the Celtic Britons, who inhabited England before the Anglo-Saxons arrived. I thor-

oughly enjoyed incorporating elements of their culture, such as the Celtic god Lenus, into this story.

"Burning Pellets"

This is the name my characters use for gunpowder in the book. The specific term "gunpowder" cannot exist in their minds because no one in my book wields a gun.

No record of gunpowder existed in 11th century Europe. However, thermal weapons had been used since the time of the Greeks (the famous "Greek Fire"). In addition, 11th century China already produced gunpowder weapons, including fire arrows and firebombs, in large military complexes and waged war with their products. It was only a matter of time before gunpowder made it westward. The Silk Road connected China with Rome, amongst other destinations, and facilitated the shipment of goods across the Mediterranean Sea. Traders carried silk, teas, porcelain, dyes, and eventually gunpowder along these routes.

One of the earliest mentions of gunpowder in Europe is accredited to Roger Bacon, an English friar and philosopher, in his AD 1267 work the *Opus Majus*. By the 1320s, the first gun appeared in Europe fully formed and powered by *gun*powder, which was named for its importance in guns. What may have happened all those years when China mass-produced gunpowder for battles within their own country, while Europe had apparently never heard of the substance? This is where I speculate by writing fiction.

Maybe merchants carried China's gunpowder into Europe, in secret, before it was documented in writing in AD 1267. I hinted at this when Toby told Aliwyn that he used to travel far southeast to luxurious ports. I was specifically thinking of Italian ports along the Mediterranean Sea, where the Silk Road traversed.

The Normans had conquered sections of Italy decades before their famous invasion of England in AD 1066. By January AD 1072, three years before the events of my story, the Normans Robert Guiscard and Robert Bosso had invaded Palermo in southern Italy. This made it possible, and even probable, that inhabitants of Norman England had contact with merchants in conquered Italian territory. England would have had access to items that traveled along the Silk Road—such as gunpowder.

Sources

Andrade, Tonio. *The Gunpowder Age: China, Military Innovation, and the Rise of the West in World History*. 2016. Print.

Mark, Joshua J. "Silk Road." *World History Encyclopedia*, World History Encyclopedia, 13 Jan. 2022, https://www.worldhistory.org/Silk_Road/.

Theotokis, Georgios. "The Norman Invasion of Sicily, 1061–1072: Numbers and Military Tactics." *War in History*, vol. 17, no. 4, Sage Publications, Ltd., 2010, pp. 381–402, http://www.jstor.org/stable/26070819.

"Thundercrashers"

These are based on Chinese proto-bombs documented in the military text *Wujing Zongyao*, dated AD 1044. These proto-bombs were called "thunderclap bombs" (pilipao) and "burning heaven fierce fire unstoppable bomb," among other names.

Beaching the Hulk and Fixing the Yard

This was a fun but particularly difficult section to research! I relied on the knowledge of maritime historians, former navy sailors, shipwrights, and other enthusiastic helpers on Quora.

We discussed how to stage the ship accident, and about how sailors can repair a broken yard.

The idea of rotating the ship free and snapping the yard came from these discussions. I am indebted to the Quora community!

Other notes:

I referred to Aliwyn, Toby, and others as "English" rather than Anglo-Saxon because not every reader is familiar with the latter. While the link between Normans and Normandy, France is clear, it is less obvious that Anglo-Saxons lived in England. Thus, I chose the term "English" to describe the inhabitants of England to help facilitate the understanding of my story.

Got questions? You can ask on my blog page dedicated to reader questions (KyrieWang.com/EKQ)

I hope you have enjoyed the story and are looking forward to the next book, *The Traitor's Heart,* which is now available!

ABOUT THE AUTHOR

By day, Kyrie is a medical sleuth (also known as a pathologist, MD) in a small mining town in Quebec, Canada. By night, she scrawls story inspirations on various notebooks by her bed. These eventually become novels with medical intrigue sprinkled throughout!

She has been writing fiction since age nine and has always been fascinated by the tales of loyalty, redemption, and sacrifice from the Middle Ages. Few things excite her more than attending medieval fairs and cheering for jousting knights.

Her character-driven stories feature nuanced protagonists, rivetting adventure, forbidden romance, and ordinary people who discover extraordinary courage from within. When she's not writing, she enjoys Zumba dancing and cycling with her husband and daughter.